PATH OF THE BROKEN

THE BEING OF DREAMS BOOK 2

CATHERINE M WALKER

ALSO BY CATHERINE M WALKER

Shattering Dreams

Path Of The Broken

Elder Born - Coming Soon

NEWSLETTER

If you'd like updates of my progress, promotions and advance notice of when the next book comes out drop by my website and join my newsletter.

You'll receive a copy of the character chart that I created while I was writing the Shattering Dreams and a few other extras as well.

Visit my website to get started!

Catherine M Walker

ISBN 978-1-925776-04-1 (eBook)

ISBN 978-1-925776-05-8 (Paperback)

ISBN 978-1-925776-06-5 (Hardcover)

ISBN 978-1-925776-07-2 (Audiobook)

❀ Created with Vellum

To all those who have helped me along this journey.
Thank you.

WILD FIRE

a cacophony of noise hummed throughout the jungle, from insects, birds, animals small and large that called it home. The uninitiated could be forgiven for thinking the wilderness would be quiet, believing it was mostly uninhabited. Human settlements close to the tree line contented themselves with foraging on the edges. There were many legends involving the great forest and most, being superstitious, avoided venturing too far inside. Outsiders, explorers and merchants at various times had set off to exploit the riches contained among the trees. There were no roads or trails beyond the edge, so any who wanted to venture beyond the boundary were forced to use hunting knives to hack at bushes and vines to get farther. They either returned frustrated and empty-handed, or were simply never seen alive again. Only experienced huntsmen survived, with a series of basic huts scattered in the depths of the wilds only they knew how to navigate.

Alex had no notion how long he lay there stripped down to undergarments on the hard wooden cot in the hunter's cottage in his weakened state. His dark brown hair was plastered to his forehead as sweat beaded on his skin. Uncontrollable tremors wracked his lean, well-muscled body as he expended energy he was fast running out of in the effort of maintaining his mental barriers. He was drifting in and out of consciousness no matter how much he tried to prevent himself from doing so. It was too dangerous for him to slip into the darkness, yet that knowledge didn't keep it from happening. Another wave of sickness crashed over him, and moaning in despair he lost control of the barrier he'd been sustaining; it flickered, then collapsed.

As the power he'd been holding at bay hit him, Alex's eyes flared open, glowing. His body arched off the bed as thick bolts from the veil crossed the curtain between the worlds and appeared in the air all around him, repeatedly hammered into his flesh—energy hungry to get to him after being denied. Like a series of lightning strikes the power channelled through his body and mind. Every muscle in his body contracted, fire sang and raced through him. Incredible pain lanced with it as if his body and mind were being reforged in the fire. His mouth opened to scream yet no sound came out to disturb anyone, not even the animals. There were advantages to occupying an abandoned hunter's hut. Even if he'd screamed out loud, there was no one near enough to hear him. If he lost control, there was no one else to hurt.

Those with abilities to perceive the world around them in other ways were not so lucky. Alex's mental cry rang out, reverberating through the rank and file of the Tainted—Sundered, Kin and Elder. The veil churned though him at levels he couldn't contain. Between one breath and the next it stopped, as if someone had turned the power off at its source.

A groan escaped his lips as he rolled over onto his side, curling into the foetal position and relaxed. As if that was the cue the energy had been waiting for, the surrounding air crackled with multiple bolts launching into him. The whole cottage seemed alive, the power writhing across the roof, down the wooden walls, filling the hut top to bottom. Alex stiffened and screamed in pain, and fire erupted from him; he saw everything around him disintegrate as his world exploded.

WHERE ONCE A HUNTER'S hut had stood, there was a circular, blackened, dead patch of forest. In the unnatural silence, the only sound was a crackling noise from small flames dancing and flickering in the air around Alex's naked, unconscious form on the ground.

Alex stirred, his groans muffled among the trees. The cheery flames flicking in and out continued their dance above him. Alex twitched, then jerked upright. He landed on his feet, looking around wildly, and the flames, seeming to recognise his fright, leapt higher. He looked at them, wide-eyed. Then the flames went out as if they'd never been except for the mute testimony of the blackened forest.

Alex looked down at himself. His memory told him he should be gravely injured with bad burns, yet his skin was flawless, even if he was naked, which suggested that perhaps his fragmented memory was correct. He'd been trying to stop himself from reaching the veil. Obviously that hadn't worked so well. His powers had exploded out of his control, burning the hut to the ground along with the surrounding forest. Alex sank to his knees, hysterical laughter erupting from his lips. Despite what the healers had always recommended his whole life, he was rapidly coming to the conclusion that trying to cut himself off from the power of the veil wasn't a good idea.

Just as he settled, the current, almost lucid state he seemed to have achieved fled from him once more, and he lost control again. The veil surged into him from all around. His control faltered, filled to bursting point with energy that had to escape somewhere. The building power seemed to throb and burn as

3

it raced through him. Feeling his mind scatter like dust in the wind, he threw his head back and screamed in pain. Flame rose around him, roaring up into the sky, yet contained to the already burnt patch he'd been standing in.

The wildfire ceased, and Alex collapsed onto his knees, tension draining from his body. Power glowed from him as he looked up, eyes blank, and then he disappeared into the veil.

2

A BETRAYAL

*E*dward heard his nephew's mental cry ringing in his mind again and winced. No matter what the reason, it felt like a betrayal and hurt a lot more than he'd thought it would. He had gotten closer to the boy than he had ever imagined was possible. He sent his words out to the far-off mind even though he was aware Alex would not hear them.

Forgive me, Alex.

Edward closed his eyes before sighing and turning to look at the three people who had been at his side through what seemed like an eternity.

"Kat, I know we've done the right thing, but the betrayal of their trust still hurts. He may never recover from this. Not all who go through transition alone do." Edward looked towards Kat, his eyes almost begging her—although he couldn't work out for what.

"Alex is stronger than anyone knows, Edward. In case you've forgotten, that was the idea: push him to early transition so that some of our less sociable brethren do not learn about him until it's too late." Kat looked at him, calm as always; growing up on the streets like she did as a child thief meant it took quite a lot to shake her. "They would have killed him if they'd known his potential. They would have assessed that he would grow and, at full power, threaten their power base. He will pull through this."

"We've discussed this ad nauseam, Edward. We had to push him, all of them, to transition. Their survival depends on it. We could not continue to hide their existence much longer. We already failed." Cal was practical, always.

Joanna's lips thinned, eyes narrowing. "Besides, abandoning him to learn for himself will make him stronger."

Ed saw the mad gleam in her eyes; there was no reasoning with her when she was inflicted with a psychotic break. He cursed himself again for being too late all those years ago when she'd been attacked. They'd spent a great deal of time in the intervening years monitoring Joanna and not just because she was the former queen and Alex's mother. He'd been horrified the night he'd heard her mind voice scream from her tomb, where she'd been buried alive. It hadn't been hard to keep track of her with the three of them, although sometimes they left her to her own devices. Unfortunately one of those times it had been long enough that she'd made Kyle her thrall. That was a circumstance he hadn't been able to convince her to change.

"Expediency is one thing, yet it doesn't mean it wasn't a betrayal. Still, they all would have transitioned, eventually. My lady, now that Kyle is aware of your existence, it won't be long before he passes on what he knows to Alex. I fear Alex will not react well." Edward did not bother to hide his concern.

The mad light in her eyes faded, and a satisfied smile spread on her lips.

"No, I was lucky enough to be there when Kyle showed up in Simon's lair. He is mine now, which is just as well. To give himself to another is technically treason."

Simon tried to suppress his annoyance, knowing that Edward would not take it lightly. As far as Ed was concerned,

Joanna was under his protection. "Now Joanna, if you hadn't been there, all I would have done is called for Ed, Kat or Cal. I may be the Skull Lord, but I'm really not all that bad. I try to keep that den of thieves in line." A pained look crossed Simon's face. Somewhere in her crazed mind she seemed to think if she came to his place it put her closer to Alex but didn't break Edward's injunction not to go to the palace. It had been most unfortunate that Joanna had decided to pop in at that time to check on Alex as she did periodically over the years—right at the precise moment when Kyle had shown up in his lair. "Still, I've met Alex, and I fear Ed is correct. He will not take this news well."

"Kyle won't tell Alex anything." She closed her eyes and a flicker of pain crossed her face, tears tracking down her cheeks as her mood swung to the opposite end of the spectrum, as it often did. "Do you think me speaking with Alex drew attention to him? I was meant to stay away, it wasn't safe, but he was in so much pain all these years. I had to help."

Ed shook his head. It was hard to keep track of her mercurial moods when Joanna was like this. She fluctuated from murderous, to psychotic, to filled with guilt and pain. He walked across the room to Joanna and gathered her in his arms. He had known that she had been keeping track of Alex's progress, speaking with him. He had stood watch when she had done so; the contact seemed to soothe her guilt.

"No, Joanna, I think your interactions helped him stay sane." Edward smiled as she tilted her head up and he kissed her obligingly.

"Joanna, can you help Kyle become strong again? It is not good for him to be bound to you for too long. The longer he stays bound to you, the harder it will be for him to be independent again." Kat's face remained impassive with a flicker of what Ed suspected was concern in her eyes. It didn't surprise him. Joanna taking Kyle was a concern for them all. Edward cursed again the fact that he'd been away when she'd bound him as her own. That had been a nasty shock. Still, Kat had many virtues, but compassion, kinship or concern for others were generally not among them—yet the situation with Kyle got under her skin.

"He's not ready to be on his own. Kyle is broken, hurt. I won't abandon him to suffer the madness alone." Joanna stiffened, her face closing down, obstinate, blue eyes flashing with anger.

"You didn't answer my question, Joanna."

"Kat, enough. He's mine. I'll decide what is best for him. I know his mind in a way you cannot understand." Joanna smiled possessively as she thought of Kyle; he was hers and they wouldn't take him from her. "Kyle is safe with me now. We'll secure Alex as soon as we can, once he's grown strong. What of Jess? Where is she?"

Cal frowned, his first sign of concern. "I don't know. She's disappeared, and it appears there is yet another player in this game."

Edward knew that while on the surface Cal was displaying concern, his friend was grateful that Jess was out of Joanna's reach. Even if he would rest easier knowing where she was, he recognised that she was better off out of this.

Edward looked up as Joanna stood up abruptly.

"I must check on Kyle. He needs me." Joanna smiled at them all and walked out of the room with a single-minded purpose.

SIMON WATCHED PATIENTLY as Joanna left the room to check on her thrall. He was almost grateful that she felt compelled to check on Kyle. Joanna was extremely unstable, and it was never easy to predict how she would respond. Sighing with relief as the door closed behind her, he looked back at Ed.

"You can't afford to check on Alex. Leave it to me." Simon smiled, hoping his sincerity was apparent.

"Simon, you've put yourself at risk enough. Leave it to us, we will sort it out." Ed's voice was firm.

"Ed, you know as well as I do you all need to keep an eye on the situation here. Alex has met me before, he'll trust me. I'll keep an eye on him. If any of you try, Joanna will likely follow, and if she takes Alex as well, then where will we be?" Simon glanced between Edward, Cal and Kat, smiling with relief to receive their consent all around.

THE BROKEN ONE

*R*yan shivered, wind whipping around him straight through his threadbare shirt, he tugged at the edge of his cloak, trying to pull it further around to protect himself more. He grimaced; he'd grown too much in the last year and the cloak no longer fit him the way it should.

Hunching his shoulders, he glowered up at the looming figure of Tyson walking ahead of him. To call Tyson 'father' wasn't something he could bring himself to do. Just because the man had shacked up with his mother didn't make him his father. Then his mother had died, leaving him alone in the world except for Tyson. Tyson was a merchant, or at least liked to call himself one. He dealt with many goods but was an expert in none, and had seen better days. While alive, Ryan's mother had controlled the finances. When she'd died, things had gone from bad to worse. Tyson's drinking and gambling habit had increased, old friends had drifted way. The people they mixed with became those his mother would never have approved of.

Ryan looked around the darkened alley. The lamps had all guttered out, probably on purpose. Thugs and thieves ran around this area; it was not a good neighbourhood. He was aware they did because he ran with them when he didn't have to help Tyson. Saying a silent apology to his mother, he scowled. His mother would not have approved of the company he was keeping.

There had been better days once. His mother and father had been respectable merchants. Not the richest, but enough that they had sent him to the central town hall three mornings a week to learn his letters from the scholars. That became less frequent with his father's death, and stopped altogether when Tyson came on the scene. By then they couldn't afford the luxury anymore.

Ryan shivered, but not due to the wind this time. His head jerked up and he looked around, trying to spot who or what the danger was. It was nearby, that much he sensed.

Tyson suddenly grabbed hold of him, shoving him into a side alley.

"Hush boy, there's an easy mark. I'd warrant we'll eat well this week," Tyson's rough voice whispered down at him.

Wrenching himself out of Tyson's grasp, Ryan breathed a sigh of relief. Carefully he eased himself off the rough stone wall and peered around Tyson's bulk to stare down the alley at the stranger that had caught Tyson's attention.

Dread descended on him, and Ryan swallowed and stepped back further into the darkness. The stranger glowed. Glowed in a way he knew most couldn't see. The dark cloaked figure who walked down the alley was no one's mark. He was dangerous, the glow told him that much.

"I don't know, Tyson, walking this late, in this part of town... He seems confident. Leave him, I'll find us a different mark." Ryan saw the blow coming too late and staggered back as Tyson's fist struck him.

"Enough boy, don't get in my way," the voice hissed at him

out of the dark as Tyson lunged forward into the alley, his cheap, worn knife clutched in his hand.

Ryan fell back onto the ground, the chill of the cold water seeping into his trousers, yet he didn't move. He watched, frozen, horrified as he felt a surge that told him the one in the alley was strong. Stronger than any of his kind Ryan had ever encountered.

The glowing figure swung around, one hand rising to block Tyson's strike as the fiery blade he wielded in the other plunged into Tyson. Ryan felt the anger that smouldered in the man, could see the eyes flickering from the depths of the hooded cloak, the power as it flared through him. Ryan could see the man's face from the glow thrown off the blade, his expression impassive as he looked down at the lifeless form of Tyson. He knelt down next to the body and made short work of searching him before appropriating the money pouch Tyson had stolen earlier in the night.

The man stood, his head swinging around to stare right into the damp alley where Ryan sat, frozen in fear. He seemed to know he was being observed by someone else out in the darkness, maintaining a confident grip on his flaring knife. The man stared straight at him. Ryan shook himself and scrambled to his feet, and dashed away down the cobbled street, not knowing where he was going. He only knew he needed to put distance between him and the man. Rough, mocking laughter followed him as he ran, but Ryan paid it no attention at all. Then he heard a voice in his mind as if the cloaked figure was standing right at his shoulder, whispering in his ear.

What am I becoming?

There was no anger in the mind voice, just pain and despair.

As suddenly as he had laughed, he stopped. Alex glanced around, taking a slow step in one direction before stopping and turning full circle, his head twisting around to look in all directions. The hood fell back from his face, and his knife hand trembled as the flickering light illuminated the dark liquid on the blade. The blood. His eyes flicked over to the dark crumpled form of the dead man on the ground.

Despite the circumstances Alex smiled. At least this time coming back to himself he was wearing clothing. That wasn't always the case. Although he had no idea where he'd obtained them from. The last thing he remembered was being naked in the middle of the forest after burning down a hunter's hut, and a decent amount of the surrounding forest with it. Unbidden a series of memories flashed into his mind; taking a deep breath, Alex ruthlessly shut them down. He'd worked out that trying to tease the memories out of his head about what he'd been up to while not quite in his own mind always sent him spiralling back down to madness.

Alex didn't know whether he preferred the moments when he was in his own head or the moments where he was absent—although he realised that even in those times, he was not really gone. There was a part of him that was there, just with no control or inhibitions. His emotions surged in ebbs and flows along with the flow of the surrounding veil. Alex shuddered. Cutting himself off from emotions hadn't worked. Transition hadn't turned him into one of the Sundered Ones, at least not all the time, but its effect had been worse. Unlike those he thought of as Sundered, he still had control over his actions. Cut off from emotion, he just didn't care, and he killed as easily as he once used to laugh, with no care, cause or mercy.

Alex looked down and patted his cloak, reassuring himself once more that at least this time he was wearing clothes. He also seemed to have armed himself again in the intervening time between the alleyway and his last memory.

He didn't even want to think about where he'd appropriated the clothing and weapons from, hoping their previous owners were still alive, although he had to admit it was unlikely. He'd just proved he killed readily and efficiently enough when out of his own mind. He looked down at the man he'd just killed, searching within himself for any sign of remorse, yet there was nothing there—not even pleasure or relief that his attacker was dead. Alex paused and smiled coldly.

His attacker. The man he'd killed had attacked him first, which had proved to be a foolish move for the would-be thief. It wasn't a mistake he would ever make again, and the world was likely a better place without this man victimising everyone he encountered. Alex laughed, bitter. It was amazing how he could excuse his own behaviour and the death of a man. Not convinced by his own internal monologue, Alex continued to stare down at the man, trying to feel something, anything other than the emptiness inside that seemed to be his constant companion.

ALEX SHOOK OFF HIS INTROSPECTION. Time for him to move, he'd spent too long here. Most of his thoughts were unsettling anyhow, and right now he didn't want to think about them. He suspected his blackouts were getting shorter, although with no real measure to judge that by it was hard to tell. If he ran around asking strangers what day it was, it would prompt concern and result in someone calling a healer. He'd rather avoid that for now.

He walked back towards the dead thief and finished wiping the blood off his blade on the man's clothes. Power still flared and flickered the length of the blade, and Alex absently extinguished the elemental fire, then sheathed the blade. It had perhaps been overkill, since he doubted the thief had any ability to control the power of the veil. If he had, Alex doubted that he would be dead in the alley right now after picking the wrong person to divest of his purse.

Dismissing his victim, Alex wrapped the veil around himself and walked down the darkened street. The guttering lamps flared, gaining new life as he approached, flickering merrily as he walked past, their flare throwing wide the pool of light. Not that there was anyone to notice their odd behaviour. If any had walked past or looked out of their windows, they would have seen the lamps flaring but they would not have seen him. Alex acknowledged that his powers had increased, and he'd learned to hide his presence not just in shadows, but in light. He moved through this world unnoticed when he wanted to, except by those others sensitive to the veil. Or others like him, with power.

That was another thing he was learning. He wasn't walking this world as alone as he'd thought. There were others out there that flared brightly at times before their glowing presence disappeared again. As a result, he spent considerable time trying to improve his own barriers. If he could spot their psychic flares out in the world across and throughout the veil, then they could likely see his. That they managed to shield themselves so thoroughly meant he could too.

Still, he sensed both Kyle and Jess on occasion before they too were shielded, although Alex had the distinct feeling it was others doing the shielding. That might have caused him some concern, except when he sensed them they seemed content enough with their current lives. That afforded him a little relief, knowing his friends were alive and had not come to any harm. He felt sure he would know it if they needed help, regardless of the presence of others and the shields they threw around his friends. They had both obviously sought out others like their own kind, other Kin, to help them get through and understand their transition.

Alex couldn't bring himself to do that. He knew he was being stubborn, yet a part of him needed to learn for himself. If he was being honest, he still had the irrational belief of being betrayed by the world. The thought made him snort. It wasn't as if the world particularly owed him anything. He'd grown up with every kind of advantage it was possible to have, unlike most others. Still, sense and feelings didn't always agree.

Yet another difference giving him reason to suspect he was not one of the Sundered was the pattern of his kills. Oh, he killed readily enough. The memories that burst and broke like bubbles in his mind told him that. Yet from what he gathered, each person he'd killed while out of his mind had been individuals that had sought to harm him first. Like the thief. Or other Sundered. He seemed to seek them out even while he was crazed. They were everything he'd thought they would be. Their minds were a scattered mess, the power seeming to stutter, turning off and on; they didn't even have the control that a child seemed to learn automatically. When the power turned on and raced through them, it caused them pain, driving them further into madness. When he killed them, it put them out of the misery their lives had become.

As much as he hated to admit it, perhaps he was correct. The Sundered were something else, even if he didn't quite know what. The best description he had for what he was going through, this transition, was Broken. He finally understood what the reference in his uncle's diary meant. The moments he was driven out of his own mind followed jumps in his own power. Until the growth in his own power levels had stabilised, he wouldn't risk going back to those he loved.

Alex closed his eyes and shuddered. Those moments where the power weaved around, intensified and charged into him were branded into his mind. The power levels became overwhelming, ending in him losing control, and his awareness sinking into darkness. Inevitably he would come back to himself in places like this.

Alex turned the corner and walked down what obviously passed for the main street in whatever town this was. A vague memory tugged at the edge of his consciousness, which irritatingly wouldn't be teased loose. A smile played across his lips, his eyes flaring with an inner light of their own. The power came as he summoned it, the dead lamps popping and flaring to sudden life down the street, racing ahead of him as he walked.

"Ah, big scary broken one I am. So scared of the dark I have to turn all the lights on." Alex chuckled. It occurred to him he was walking down the street talking to himself; he'd parted company with sanity some time ago.

He grinned and hummed to himself as he walked down the now well-lit street. At least he hadn't blown up the town with this pyromanic display.

The residents of this village were likely to be a little shocked when they woke. The lamps usually guttered and died an hour before dawn. He wasn't sure when these would die since they glowed blue, fuelled by the veil.

Alex's progress down the street halted, his eyes narrowed as he heard the unmistakable cry of the Sundered. Time for a little hunting. He shifted fully into the veiled world, speeding towards the mad presence of the others, using their mental howls as a beacon to guide him to them. He knew they weren't far away, still within the boundaries of this town.

4

HEALERS' RECORDS

*A*aron sighed, pushing the reports he'd been studying to one side. If someone had told him as a junior healer that if he reached the giddy heights of Master he'd spend a great deal of time buried in reports, he would have laughed. Yet the life that many in the Guild would fight over, Master Healer in the king's court, saw him spend the bulk of his time in paperwork and meetings. Hearing murmuring coming from the outer office, he wasn't surprised to hear his door open.

"Sorry to disturb you, Aaron, the dispatch from the Guild that you asked for has arrived." Cameron walked across the room and handed the sealed dispatch case to him.

Aaron took the case, seeing the unbroken seal of the Grand Guild Master of the Healers' Guild and knowing what the content would be.

"Thank you, Cameron. If this is what I suspect it is, it's the records I've been waiting for since Lord Kyle was drugged."

Aaron waited as Cameron left his office and closed the door quietly behind him before using a small knife to break the seal. He untied the bindings on the satchel and flipped the bag open. He removed the leather-bound records with care from the bag and placed them on his desk. Each volume bore the old seal of the Grand Guild Master. The records they contained were old, from a time before the Sundered War. They had been locked under the Grand Guild Master's seal and stored in the restricted archives. Given Aaron's rank and position, he'd known of their existence, although he'd never had cause to study them—until he'd tested the drug used on Lord Kyle. The results came back showing him the toxin used was not the same as the old folk remedy used in villages near the Great Forest.

As he stared down at the volumes, he felt dread settle in his stomach. Delaying the inevitable for a few moments, he cleared the reports he'd been working on from his desk, placing them back in their file.

Not able to delay any more, he took his knife and broke the ancient Guild seal on the first volume. The existence of the scrolls was known to all the Master Healers on the Healers' Guild's Council. The contents of the sealed accounts had been subject to speculation among the Master Healers but none had felt the need to break the seals. If rumours were correct, the records detailed a failed medical trial by Healer Katrina Lawrence in the era leading up to the Sundered War. The Healers' Guild at the time believed they had cause to conceal the accounts, however didn't wish to destroy them in case the research, failed or otherwise, was needed in the future.

Pushing back the old metal latch, Aaron opened the leather cover, settled back and proceeded to read the reports and details of that lost time it contained.

5

HOPE

BEFORE THE SUNDERED WAR

*K*atrina looked over her results, methodically triple-checking them, her excitement growing as her data told her what she thought it had the last ten times she had run them. Her results in the lab spoke for themselves; she had enough evidence to go to a trial. If this worked as she knew it would, she would help her people no end.

She'd seen how her brother had suffered through transition, his world transformed into a horrible nightmare. He didn't know where he began and others took over. They weren't a rich family, or connected. Those strong in the power, like her brother, were left to muddle on through by themselves, unless they were rich, a family with connections to get them into the palace. He didn't get the luxury of even being under the guidance of others who had been through transition before him, and as a result he suffered appallingly.

She was grateful that her own use of the power had guided her to the Healers' Guild. The Guild was extremely well set up, controlled with strict, proven rules. She, unlike her brother, had had her emerging powers bound as a small child as soon as the journeyman healer had detected that she had the gift.

5

Enrolment in the Healers' Guild when she came of age had been mandatory, like every other child who bore the gift. They had taken her in and guided her. She'd been under the care of the training healers as her powers grew and she'd battled for her hard-won control.

The memory of that made her shudder. What torment her brother must have gone through alone. She had long argued that the Healers' Guild should expand to accept those born with power like her brother's, or at least there should be a new guild set up to guide and train those born with that great power, not just the little powers that most grew up with that was handled from family to family. Children learned from their own parents just as they learned to walk, communicate and interact with the world. It had been accepted that it was impossible for her parents to guide, train and protect her as she learned to use her own gift. They had not been expected to. The Guild took care of that. And yet, for some reason her parents were left to try to help her brother. They were woefully unprepared and didn't have the skill nor power level themselves to understand. Her father and mother had the ability to heat their food or drink, push the salt bowl across the table. Her mother, with great effort, could speak mind to mind with someone she knew well. There was no way for them to understand and help her brother; he'd even destroyed the whole barn in spectacular fashion by accident.

The difficulty was getting someone to listen. Still, in the meantime there was the possibility Katrina could help those not born with privilege. She was too late to help her brother, but not too late to assist others like him, help them not to go through the torment that her brother had.

Katrina gathered up her paperwork and the small vial containing the medication she'd developed and scurried out the door. She most definitely didn't want to run, but she knew her last-minute double-checks of her data had potentially made her late. That wasn't desirable either. She turned the corner and took the stairs up to the Guild Masters' domain two at a time. Seeing the junior trainees on the boardroom door agitatedly gesturing at her to hurry, she left her dignity behind and ran the last distance to the doors that would determine the fate of her life's work so far, and indeed her own fate.

She tried to pause just outside the doors, only to have the juniors unceremoniously haul open the double doors to the boardroom and push her through. Katrina stumbled through the door, her hand outthrust to break her fall. As the papers she carried fell out of her hands and scattered across the floor, she juggled the medication vial in her other hand. Breathing a sigh of relief as she secured it before it fell to the floor and glancing up to murmur an apology, she scrambled after her paperwork. She stood up and made her way over to the table, paperwork crumpled and clutched to her chest, and dumped her research in the place before the chair waiting for her. She raised her gaze from the table and her paperwork, which she realised with dismay was now out of order. Her eyes darted around the Guild Masters, hoping she conveyed her apology, both for her tardiness and her undignified entrance.

The silence in the room stretched until she became even more uncomfortable than she had been to start with. Then she saw a small smile quirk on the face of the Grand Guild Master.

"Come, Katrina, relax. You are among friends here. You have, from what I have heard, remarkable results from your research. Take us through the pertinent details." His eyebrow rose as he looked at the mess of her crumpled paperwork on the table. "As best as you can."

Katrina closed her eyes, blocking out the stares from the Masters gathered at the table, and took a deep breath. Then, still clutching the vial of the medication, she ran through her results in a calm, clear voice, the words of her research appearing in her mind's eye just as if she were reading from her notes.

She could help those who channelled high levels of the veil with her medication. It would help to reduce their confusion and pain by controlling the incoming power they received. All she needed was the approval of the Masters and she could start the actual trials. Then, hopefully, no one else would ever have to suffer as her brother had.

6

ILARITH

*J*essalan stood in one of her favourite places in a high tower overlooking the mountain realm of Ilarith. It wasn't a city in the traditional way, nor a kingdom. Most of the land was wild and uninhabited as far as her eye could see, kept that way by the few that possessed the power to breach the barriers that protected this secret realm— the domain of the Elder, Kin and some humans. The few scattered settlements of humans who called Ilarith home lived their lives with little interference from the Elder they were beholden to. They assured her that while they were free to leave and seek a life elsewhere, most showed little inclination to do so. Merchant delegations left to trade occasionally and keep in touch with the world outside their magic realm, yet always returned. One of the Kin or Elder would go with them to ensure they were able to depart and return to Ilarith, and also to protect them while abroad.

Moving between places was difficult for the humans since there were only a few roads stretching between their villages. It was the Elder who had forged the roads through the wilderness for the humans living among them using the power of the veil.

Jess didn't understand how they had done so. The Elder had no limitations on their travel using the veiled paths, and could travel from place to place with ease. The villages paid tribute to the Elder both in food and with the occasional person to help maintain their own castles, towers and estates. Despite her initial concern, they assured her it wasn't something they demanded, just something the locals did. Given the Elder represented peace and prosperity for the locals that lived here, Jess could see why they did so.

She had been here for months now as Damien's guest, since this was the sprawling multileveled estate he called home. The floor-to-ceiling windows, a prominent feature of the estate, were to be found at every vantage point, affording incredible views of the surrounding countryside. It hadn't taken her long to track him down after she'd decided to do so, although it was more like he had tracked her down. Jess smiled, remembering; she'd been cast adrift, lost, searching for some sign of the Elder that she had known must exist, yet had not been having much luck.

SHE STARTED her search jumping from village to village around Vallantia, discovering when she widened her search a barrier in the veil that was impossible for her to penetrate. Jess remembered her shock; it had been like she'd run into an invisible wall. It had been frustrating and tedious when she'd found herself going around the outside of the barrier. Jess felt herself blush as she remembered how long she took to work out she could feel the barrier. Once she did realise, the process of discovery progressed much more quickly. She determined there was no way for her to pass it. Watching merchant caravans arrive and leave through one of the trade routes proved to her that those who were human, even some with power, could come and go as they choose. It was just that she was bound here. After some time testing the barrier, to no avail, she withdrew in frustration.

Still she continued to search, getting increasingly frustrated with her inability to find any sign of the Elder. Then, drawing the power to leave a small village, Jess transitioned to that place between, appearing as she always did on a makeshift road. She remembered looking around, uneasy, and seeing another standing near to where she was. He did not appear concerned that she had found him, and she had no doubt at all he had been watching her. Jess kept her sword drawn even when she recognised him: it was Damien. She noted that while he was wearing a sword, he did not have his own blade drawn at all. He was tall, with an athletic build and dusty blond hair; his eyes were the deep blue she remembered, and she noted his smile was as charming. His dress and bearing were no longer that of a hunter; Jess smiled cynically, wondering if he ever had been. His clothing was of a fine make, his body language confident, both of which placed him as someone with wealth. Still, he was no match for either Alex or Kyle in that department—they both possessed a certain self-assured easy flair that Damien did not. She suspected he was trying to emulate them, yet it wasn't something he'd been born to.

The part that made her gasp was something she had not noticed on her previous encounters with him, although she should have. When Jess looked at him with her mind's eye, Damien shone with power. He glowed and she could see the trails of power running through him and from him; he was bursting. In that arena Damien was in his element, at ease with his power, yet he didn't seem even slightly mad. Just as suddenly as the power flared, it disappeared as if shutters had been shut. Other than the fact that they were in the veil, Damien appeared like a normal human. Jess put the things her uncle had told her together and came to a conclusion.

Damien, I have been looking for you. You are of the Elder. Jess was surprised by how calm she was. She wasn't accusing, just stating a fact. *Is that even your real name?*

Jess sensed herself move through the veil under the other's will and fought to maintain her composure. They were travelling faster than she'd ever thought possible. They came to the barrier in the veil, and Jess only barely stopped herself gasping in shock as they passed through it. She knew Damien had manipulated something to get them through it, yet she hadn't been able to see what he'd done, nor seen his use of the power at all. She only knew he must have.

When they came to what was their destination, the veil blurred as they merged out into a comfortable-looking room. Jess knew it wouldn't be out of place in the finest mansions or even the king's palace, yet she had no idea where they were.

"Forgive my rudeness, Jessalan. I thought we could talk more easily here than elsewhere. Yes, my name is Damien, and yes, as you guessed, I am of the Elder. Please take a seat if you will. You will not come to any harm at my hands." Damien gestured to some high-backed leather chairs arranged in a half circle near large floor-to-ceiling windows. She felt a surge in the veil and the fireplace which had been empty moments before lit up, merry flames dancing and cracking on the wood.

Jess considered her options for a moment, then shrugged and put away her blade. She had the distinct impression that if Damien had meant her harm, she'd be dead already. In fact, he'd had the opportunity several times in the past. It certainly explained how he had tracked and rescued her during the kidnap attempt. On one of those occasions he'd moved to protect her. She walked over towards the chairs but did not sit immediately. Instead she walked over to the tall windows and looked out onto a village that sprawled down a mountain. The beauty of the mountain territory took her breath away. In the distance she could see tall towers and spires that caused her imagination to take flight and left her burning with curiosity. She'd never seen its like before or had even imagined such things existed. She was in a tower on what looked like the highest point, with mountains surrounding her and what looked like the deep forest below. Jess gasped and turned to stare at her unexpected host.

"Where am I? I don't recognise this place at all." Jess glanced back towards the amazing view out of the window, then back at Damien, who smiled.

"You may not have been here before, but I am sure you have heard of it. You are in the fabled Ilarith." Damien waited patiently, not concerned at all while she processed the information she'd just been given. He gestured around the room. "This is, well, one of the places I and the others of the Elder call home."

Jess couldn't help but laugh. "Ilarith? No one gets into Ilarith."

"We allow very few inside our borders, but on occasion exceptions are made."

"Ah, so the tales that Ilarith is a land of enchantment and magic are correct, rather than the monsters and your-trade-goods-are-possessed-by-evil variety." Jess's eyes sparkled.

Damien laughed and bowed floridly. "I think the monsters and possessed-by-evil rumours were started by people who wanted to drive the price of our trade goods down."

Finally Jess sat in the chair closest to her and noted, as Damien sat down on the chair near her own, that someone had set the table with food and wine. Damien took a fine green stained glass goblet that Ilarith was known for and picking up a bottle of red wine, then glanced at her, his lips quirked in a half smile.

Jess laughed and nodded, her mood switching in the erratic way it had been of late, realising that she wasn't going anywhere until her host let her go. She might as well relax and avail herself of his hospitality.

He smiled and poured the wine, handing her the goblet before he poured one for himself. He turned and, catching her eye, he raised his glass in salute. Jess fell back on court protocol and raised her own in response.

"What do you want with me?" Jess knew she was being blunt, but since Damien had brought her here against her will, she believed it warranted a little rudeness. Unconcerned at least to outward appearances, she took a sip of the wine and had to admit that he hadn't stinted on that score.

Damien smiled, amused. "I guess I deserve that. I want to help you, Jess. Besides, I believe you have been searching for me. You and your friends have fallen into a world you do not understand or know. The three of you are more powerful than you can possibly be aware of. You will each become Elder once you've passed through your transition periods."

Jess looked at Damien and held back a sob as pain and loss ran through her.

"How can you not know? Alex and Kyle are lost, sunken into their own madness." Jess stopped as Damien shook his head.

"No, Jess, they are not. Neither of them is of the Sundered, as you believe. The Sundered have a very distinct stamp of madness that neither of your friends have. They are in transition. They each have their path to follow, as you will choose yours."

"What do you mean not Sundered? I know they descended into madness, I shared their pain and anger, the confusion and loss. Alex killed that boy; he would never have done that if he were sane." Jess looked at Damien, her eyes wide with shock. "Kyle gave himself to another of his own free will, an act of treason he never would have committed if he were in his own mind." She noticed that her knuckles were white as she grasped the goblet in a vice-like grip and, taking a deep breath, she tried to relax.

Damien shook his head. "Alex does what he needs to do. There is madness in him, but he is strong enough that I believe he will rise through it. Kyle is under the protection of another, but not the Sundered Lord, as you believe. He is safe enough where he is for now. I will act on his behalf if I need to and he doesn't win his own freedom. I believe others have it in hand, though. Both Alex and Kyle are constrained by the path they are on." Damien paused to look out of the window, but Jess could tell his mind was far away before coming back to her.

Jess found she desperately wanted to believe her friends would recover. They had both been the centre of her world, her sanity, as far back as she could remember. Yet she couldn't shake the images she'd seen from them both.

"I can't escape from what I saw, what I felt." Tears welled in her eyes, and she made no move to hide them.

Damien stood and moved across the intervening space to sit in the chair next to her, and gathered her into his arms. He whispered to her in a calm, reassuring voice filled with certainty. "Both Alex and Kyle are what we call Broken. They go through periods of madness but there is still sanity in them, unlike the Sundered. Alex suffers—his power level is higher—and Kyle as well, due to the harmful effects of the toxin used during the kidnapping, but in my assessment, unlike many, they will recover and get through this period."

Jess didn't reply but allowed his words to comfort her. She couldn't contemplate a world where Alex and Kyle weren't there. If she only had a target, someone to take out in their defence. Yet right now she didn't have an enemy to aim her energies at; she was unable to help them and it hurt. They had both been there for her when she'd been a small girl, uprooted and transported into an unfamiliar world. Befriended her, taken her into their small exclusive circle of friendship.

Defended her against all of their peers until she grew to defend herself.

Jess struggled with a sudden rise of pain and anger at the world, a sense of helplessness. As suddenly as she had been overwhelmed, she felt herself return to calmness. She halted her inner monologue and glared accusingly at Damien.

"You're soothing me."

Damien grinned at her unrepentantly. "Of course I am. Those such as yourself and your friends born with great power do not appear very often. We have learnt such a one survives their transition in a much better state if given some guidance. Besides, I don't want you losing control and destroying my home. Come, let me show you around and you can pick a room that suits you. I've never had a student before. This should be fun."

Damien stood, hauling her off the couch with a grin. Not letting go of her hand, he led her farther into his home. Jess allowed Damien to drag her off, head spinning at the sudden change of topic. She wondered how she'd ended up with a tutor, since Damien had just appointed himself as just that. Jess shook her head and laughed, her mood swinging from the sudden anger she'd been experiencing moments before to euphoria.

JESS TURNED AWAY from the windows and walked through the tower complex towards Damien's sitting area. The walls threw off a blue glow as she approached, lighting up the corridor, fading as she walked past. The light caused the silver threaded through the fine silks of her gown to gleam. The fabric of her dress whispered as the cloth rubbed together with each step, her long blond hair held back with some ornately carved combs. This had been her home for months now and she had attracted her own servant, Clara from the village, within days of her getting here. Jess still wasn't sure how the system worked, except that Clara appeared and tended to her needs, even living here in the estate rather than the village.

Jess passed her days with some instruction from Damien on the veil and its uses. He'd taught her techniques on calming her mind. He'd explained that with her transition, she was one of the lucky ones. Still, she knew he considered her under his protection and for all intents and purposes restricted to the estate, at least until he gained confidence in her ability to protect herself. There was a way through the protective barriers of Ilarith, that much was clear. She didn't know what the key was to unlocking them, though. Damien had smiled at her when she'd asked about it, and advised her that when she was ready, she would possess the ability to come and go as she pleased.

Her reaction had been one out of character with how she would have reacted even a few short months ago: she'd made a conscious effort to batten down her emotions after her first day here. It seemed to work, since she'd accepted the restriction with an atypical calmness, without the anger she would have reacted with in the past. Now barely anything seemed to upset her at all. Of course there were explosions on occasion in training caused by frustration. It concerned her, abstractedly, that she was turning cold and remote, shutting herself off from what it was to be human.

Damien had explained to her she wasn't human as she knew it anymore. She would live far longer than any regular human would, and that required adjustments. Thinking through it, she realised that if the Elder raged and engaged in temper tantrums it would be disastrous. Kings could wreak havoc onto a kingdom or neighbouring territory. The Elder possessed the power to destroy the world.

Yet from what she saw they were remote, removed from the

concerns of the world, even from the fate of their own kind. When she thought about it, she realised that her uncle exhibited similar traits.

She also found it easier to wield the veil when she wasn't tripping over her emotions. How she'd managed in the past, bumbling through, reacting on instinct, was anyone's guess. Unfortunately Damien insisted she learn control, learn to consciously do what she wished with the veil. That was a sticking point that required concentration and practice. He'd pointed out to her that the Elder themselves built their own estates and towers. Utilising nothing but the power of the veil, they built their estates and access roads to assist humans to settle nearby.

Clara advised her that a new Kin took a group willing to settle in a new place with them when they resettled. The humans and Elder of Ilarith seemed to have a symbiotic relationship. At first the idea horrified Jess, suggesting that slavery was the way of life in Ilarith, yet Clara had disabused her of that notion.

The humans had their own guilds, interests and lives. The Elder, from Clara's point of view, were their rulers and protectors, unlike in Vallantia, where those with the power to become Kin were treated with fear and distrust. Her self-appointed servant told Jess that the Elder left them alone to run their own affairs, only distantly aware or interested in them. The humans paid tribute to their Elder. They provided produce and labour, yet it was up to them what and how much. Clara informed her bluntly that it was no different to the ruling family and class in Vallantia. She felt their system was easier since if a village had bad crops and couldn't spare the food, they would find that provender appeared by the grace of the Elder. Where the Elder procured the windfall from Clara didn't know. Jess suspected on those occasions that some merchant in another town or another kingdom would wake to find their supplies missing when they checked. Or perhaps they just willed it into existence from the veil. The thought amused her and Jess made note to ask Damien about the magically appearing food stocks.

The concept that she had the ability to construct an entire dwelling utilising the veil astounded her no end, so she practiced at wielding the veil every day. Practiced trying to form common things around her, everything from knives to the vase on her dresser. While Jess found spinning what she wanted out of the veil easy, unlike with Damien's ability, hers had no permanence. She observed Damien as he wielded the power and concluded that there were levels to the veil she couldn't perceive. Just as in the past, the veil appeared as grey wisps to her. After she'd pushed herself too far defending against an attack by the Sundered, burning the channels of her mind further open, she had discovered she perceived the veil differently. They were different colours and intensity, which she believed denoted different strengths. She'd also decided that whatever power he was accessing, it was what he used to trigger the barrier in the veil. He was using an aspect of the power that she couldn't perceive yet. It made her wonder how long this transition period was meant to last.

Jess walked into the wide-open sitting area where she knew Damien was. She could feel his burning, bright presence. It wasn't like he was trying to hide. Lessons didn't happen at the same time or even every day. She'd learned to seek Damien out when she thought she was ready for another lesson and, depending on what he had in mind, the sitting room was one room those practice sessions occurred in.

She stopped in the archway, shocked. She'd been so involved in her own thoughts she hadn't realised that Damien had company. Both Damien and his companion turned to gaze at her. Only years of training stopped her from gasping as the elegant woman dropped the barriers she'd been holding around herself. Her power flared, almost blinding in Jess's mind's eye, before she shielded again. This woman, like Damien, could hide what she was, giving off nothing to show that she was anything but human. The woman assessed her in return and Jess wondered what she saw. Unlike other women who had assessed her most of her life, at least this one wasn't showing the spike of jealousy. Jess smiled; she was powerful, self-assured and beautiful. Jess had a feeling that if the pair of them had walked into the ballroom at home together, the collective ladies of the court would have been murderous.

"Sorry to intrude, Damien. I was preoccupied and didn't sense you had company." Jess smiled and, bowing her head, turned to withdraw, only to halt at the low voice rippling with amusement.

"No need to leave, Jess. Please come in. This is Isabella." Damien smiled and gestured to his companion.

Jess had to admit that if Isabella and Damien currently slept together, she might just be a little jealous. It was obvious the pair had a history together, potentially a very long history given that Isabella was an Elder. Her display of power and ability to conceal it gave that away. Neither Jess nor Damien had tried to rekindle the time they'd spent together. He was the Elder, the Master, and she the Trainee he had taken into his care. Anything they had shared previous to that had been pushed aside, as it should. It was confusing enough going through transition without getting tied up in knots for all the wrong reasons when he remonstrated her for the smallest infractions. If they'd been sleeping together, those tense, sometimes fiery moments would on occasion quite literally get all mixed up and messy. As it was, she could distance herself from that and understood it was for her own good. Damien was teaching her the control she needed.

Jess shook herself and, utilising years of training at the royal court, she walked forward and paused before her mentor and his friend.

"Nice to meet you, Isabella. I hope you will show me that shielding trick one day." Jess compressed her lips and mock-glared at Damien. "He won't show me such things."

Isabella's startled laughter rang out. "If you do not work it out for yourself and this one does not instruct you, I promise I will show you." Isabella threw a glance at Damien, her amusement clear. "You have your work cut out for you."

"Oh, just you wait, you might wish to trade one day." Damien's blue eyes glittered in challenge and amusement.

The exchange left Jess confused, but she knew better than to ask. This was another thing she was destined not to know or understand, at least for now. Damien kept his own counsel, and it seemed Isabella was just as circumspect.

Isabella grinned impudently, dimples showing in her cheeks. "Possibly, from what I've sensed, I think this will be a challenging task you have asked of me. Yet there is need. I will leave you to your protégé." Isabella stepped forward and, to Jess's shock, hugged her. "Take care, Jess. Follow Damien's instructions no matter how infuriating he can be. He will teach you to be the best you can be. I will be away for some time, yet you have my signature now, so call if you need. I will come when I can."

Isabella stepped back and exchanged a look with Damien. They were talking to each other. It impressed Jess no end since she couldn't hear a word of the exchange. Then, with the only warning being the sudden draw of power from the veil, Isabella faded from view, drawing her shield around her. Again Jess was suitably impressed, since even though she tried, she couldn't follow Isabella's trail though the veil. It disappointed her a little since she was intrigued regarding where the woman was going

PATH OF THE BROKEN

and what she was doing. Still, she guessed she would find out
—eventually.

Finally she turned her gaze back to Damien, who looked at
her impassively, with only a hint of a smile on his lips.

"I guess teaching me how to shield like Isabella did is out of
the question?" Jess grinned, knowing the answer before he
spoke.

"I'm not sure you are ready for that. How about we go to the
training area outside and we work on your defensive shielding?
If you can master that, then soon we will learn the offensive
techniques." Damien held his hand out to her.

Pausing only to wonder what and where the outside
training area was, Jess grinned and took his hand. The veil
wrapped around them and he pulled her through.

7

BOUND

*K*yle sat, legs crossed on the training mat with his eyes closed, concentrating on the simple act of breathing. There were no distractions around him or on him. He was wearing a deep blue loose-fitting shirt and light trousers. His black hair had grown long enough since he'd left the palace to become irritating and was tied back to keep it out of his eyes while he exercised. For the first time since childhood, he was unarmed.

The breathing exercises helped to calm and focus his mind. The whispering voices of other Kin, and those in transition, echoed through his mind. He ignored them. Their conversations weren't for him.

Kyle inhaled deep into his lungs and held the breath for a moment. In his mind's eye he saw the veil, swirling around him, yet he made no move to control it. Exercising control, he exhaled, concentrating on the breath leaving his body.

He'd lost count of how many days he'd been here. He wasn't even sure where here was. It wasn't Vallantia, or even in the realm at all. Of that he was certain. Simon had not asserted control over his mind the way he'd expected. Unknown to him, another had been present. Irritation surged within when he thought back to those days and the consequences he now lived with because of his actions. Kyle pushed his aggravation to one side. His mistress ignored him for now, but if he worked himself up too much it would attract her attention, which was not something he wanted.

Instant recognition and shock warred within him as the former queen, Alex's mother, created a bond between them, though he admitted grudgingly that the bond restored calmness to him. Unlike the bonds that Alyssa had burned into his mind and body, the forging of these bonds did not hurt. They were simply there, and at times when he needed it he felt her presence, calming his mind and restoring his barriers. Then when he was calm again, she withdrew. It was perfect. Or at least he'd thought so at first, before he'd realised his new mistress was not sane herself. There were moments where he could feel the madness in her mind rise to consume her, even though it wasn't the madness he associated with the Sundered.

She had brought him to this place—her home, he guessed. He gathered it was a large sprawling estate all on one level since he'd seen no sign of stairs. He knew it was near the water since he could hear the waves crashing on rocks, although she refused to allow him out to explore his new surroundings. She'd had him disarm. He had seen none of his weapons since then. Weeks passed; months. That time was vague to him, almost like the memory of a nightmare. Slowly he'd come back to himself. She'd kept that part of the bargain. Kyle shuddered at the thought of trying to deal with the surging, increasing power of the veil running through him now by himself. To his surprise he was gaining control back, bit by bit, even more so when his mistress's attention turned elsewhere, and she was sane.

Demons still plagued his sleep at night. Memories of the innocent people he'd killed in his madness flashed in his mind.

Sometimes this brought despair; other times the need to kill rose. Those moments terrified him. At least now it did. Before he'd come under Alyssa's control, his kills had been clean, with clear treason against the Crown. After the toxin had been administered and Alyssa had inserted her insidious bonds, his kills had become sickening. She had been driving him to madness. In contrast, Joanna asserted her control when madness struck him, shunting aside the rising bloodlust, restoring balance. At his worst, she forced him into a deep, dreamless sleep. Other times the shocking images and feelings that bombarded his brain were not his own, but hers. He was powerless to block them out, to block *her* out when she succumbed to psychosis. On those occasions Edward, Kat or Cal would intervene when they could, allowing him some peace from her raging thoughts. Kyle vowed that if he managed against all odds to regain his freedom, he would never let another bind him to their will.

Worry about what he would become had driven him when he'd asked for Simon's help; worry about what he would be forced to do if he judged wrong; shame for not being able to bring himself to ask Kat for help. Yet Simon had been their friend and had fought with them during the Sundered War. Kyle had battled with himself, but believed that without help he would not have a chance. No one would have. He had been losing control of his power, of himself.

Taking a slow, deep breath, Kyle let his mind wander back to that moment he'd allowed Joanna to enslave his mind.

SIMON AGREED he would help but then another stepped from the shadows and intervened before Simon could take any action. Her calm voice indicated she believed he would be better with her and their alignment would not be treason. The

Skull Lord conceded to the other and backed up, showing not even a hint of emotion.

Kyle remembered he couldn't help the overwhelming relief that hit, and his legs buckled. His downward slump to the ground was stopped by the supporting hands of another. Kyle realised the hands that supported him were not those of the Skull Lord, who still stood in front of him. The delicate hands belonged to the yet unseen woman who had intervened.

Kyle looked up into the eyes of the one who held him, and his breath caught. With her dark brown hair and intense blue eyes that bore a startling resemblance to Alex's, he recognised her instantly.

"My lady, how...?"

"Shh, Kyle. I'm sorry I wasn't here sooner. Let me help you undo what that other did to you. Relax, let me in." A tear traced its way down his cheek. He knew what he was about to do and feared the consequences, but let down his barriers.

She was in his mind, delicate probes following the paths Alyssa had burnt into him. Yet this time it didn't hurt and, as he tracked her progress, she helped sections of his mind heal while still inserting her own control mechanisms—although not the ones relating to sex, he noticed.

Kyle felt that familiar calm wash over his mind, the kind he hadn't experienced since he'd first met Alyssa, and nearly wept. Except he knew it was the lady who imposed that on him, like she was placing herself between him and madness. When she withdrew, he knew she was still there in his mind.

Taking one more shuddering breath, he acknowledged his reality, standing to face the woman who had bound him and kneeling before her.

"My lady, Mistress, I pledge my soul to your service."

It had only occurred to him after it was too late to be a little concerned how Alex would react when he found out—not only that his mother was alive, but had taken his best friend as her mind-bound slave.

~

KYLE BROUGHT himself back to the present. Being taken by another was not what he'd thought it would be, what his first experience had taught him it would be. At least, up to this point it had mostly been the exact opposite. No one had lost their life under his blades since. Joanna had explained to him that he would remain here until he regained conscious control. The problems stemmed from when he discovered the former queen wasn't always quite sane.

Kyle remembered asking Joanna whether his brush with madness was purely due to transition or the combination of the toxin and Alyssa. He couldn't understand at all how he could have gone from who he had been to the mess he'd become. Joanna believed in his case that it was both, although she knew nothing about the toxin used on him. The insidious effects of the drug and the mental control Alyssa had installed on him shocked Joanna, and indeed Edward. It raised considerable debate amongst them regarding the origin of the toxin. The group, with the addition of Kat and Cal, had questioned the role of the Order and their true purpose. Eventually they had settled the debate, believing it had just been that small cell of people, headed by Daniel, spurred on by fear and jealously. Since they were already dead, no further action was necessary.

Kyle did not agree with their assessment, but kept his opinion to himself. He believed Alyssa and the Order would have kept dosing him with the drug until he became addicted to it and unable to function without it. He would have succumbed to madness or Alyssa would have full control of his mind. Probably both; at that point he would have become her puppet.

Fortunately, a moment of sanity where he'd been able to break away had saved him. Jess had found him and called Alex. Kyle realised how lucky he'd been that Alex had broken Alyssa's hold on his mind, even if he didn't know at the time what he was doing. He understood now that if Alex and Jess hadn't put their own minds between him and Alyssa, it was likely she would have regained her hold on him.

Kyle chuckled, although it held nothing but bitterness. His friends had managed to break him free of Alyssa's control of his mind. Almost the first thing he'd done was run to someone else and allow himself to be enslaved again.

Resolve firmed in Kyle's mind: he would gain his freedom again. First, though, he needed to heal. He needed to gain control of himself and his powers again.

Kyle cleared his mind, sensed the veil around him, and released his breath. He wasn't sure why the breathing exercise helped. He only knew it did. So it was an exercise he performed every morning and evening. His life was becoming routine, time slipping away, with nothing to indicate to him how long he'd been here. He was working on Joanna to allow him out into the world again, but he'd learned he needed to pick his moments. She confirmed to him she would allow him greater freedom when she judged he was stable and more accepting of his status. So he curbed his impatience and throttled down his anger at his own stupidity. He followed the instructions she gave him, the outward picture of obedience to her will. Any rebellious thoughts were exiled to the back of his mind.

He pushed aside other concerns and continued with the next phase of his exercise. Kyle concentrated as he drew in strands of power, selecting the ones he wanted with care, and he willed it to take form. A small flame appeared before him, dancing and flickering in the air at eye height in front of him, held there by strands of the silver-grey power. Manipulation of the two different powers to do as he wished took concentration.

It was an observation that caused him to smile. Oh, he was aware that lighting a candle was possible. A lot of people had that skill even if they didn't flaunt it. But to control the flame, to have it appear in the air in front of him and stay there, with nothing for the fire to consume... A few months ago he would not have even thought it was possible to do such a thing at all. Yet it was a small thing from what he'd seen Joanna and Simon do. Their feats were beyond what his imagination could conceive.

Every day he practiced and every day he was closer to winning his freedom. The day he could fulfil his retribution against the Order moved ever closer.

As the door opened, the flames went out and Kyle found himself on his feet, his whole posture defensive, only to relax at seeing Edward standing in the doorway. He expelled the breath he'd been holding. He shook his head and fought down his sudden burst of irrational anger.

"Edward, nice of you to drop in." Kyle had to admit his voice was cool even to his own ears.

The small smile that formed on Edward's lips did not help Kyle's temper.

"Calm down, Kyle. It's time for you to practice before you lose your edge." Edward's smile was sardonic as he offered the extra blade he carried to Kyle, his head cocked to one side, waiting for a decision.

Kyle felt his breath shake as he exhaled and, closing his eyes, he steadied himself before taking the few paces necessary to claim the blade that Edward offered him. One of his own blades, he noted. As he backed up a few steps to the centre of the room, his eyes flicked back up to Edward.

"Does Joanna know about this?" Kyle contemplated

Edward. His presence here had left him confused. He'd caught mixed messages and couldn't work out if Ed was keeping an eye on him or Joanna. He had to admit it seemed like a little of both.

"No, she's sleeping right now. She'll likely fish it out of your mind when she wakes. It's easier to beg forgiveness than get permission." Edward's tone gave away no hint of concern as he paced forward, raising his blade in salute.

"What about Alex? With all of you here he's having to stumble through transition alone." Kyle was worried for his friend, who shouldn't have to be facing transition by himself.

"Alex will be fine; *he* didn't run off and allow himself to be bound to another's will." Edward unexpectedly grinned. "He's not alone, or won't be for long. You need to concern yourself with getting better so you can be that blade at his side once more."

"I'm uncertain Joanna will ever allow that." Kyle settled himself as his old swordsmaster had shown him when he'd been a small boy. He smiled as he realised that what he'd been doing of late was just an extension of those lessons he'd learned as a child. Kyle flipped his sword up in salute to his sparring partner in that universal sign of one master to another that he was ready.

"We're working on it. Joanna is unstable, ranging from unreasonable to dangerous to all around her when she is not in her right mind. When sane, she's not dishonourable." Ed's words were more frank than Kyle expected.

"Ah. I thought you were lovers." Kyle hadn't just thought it; he was absolutely certain the pair were sleeping together.

A smile spread on Edward's lips. "Off and on, we are. Now concentrate, Kyle, and leave Joanna to me. Blade work today, to get you back into form. We'll work on integrating your powers later." With that last instruction Edward signalled his own readiness in kind and lunged.

Kyle's own blade rose to block in a long-familiar pattern that his body and mind knew well. Although he hadn't traded blows with Edward all that much, Kyle knew his opponent was also a master with the blade, a competent one. He allowed his world to narrow and leave other concerns aside, his blade becoming an extension of his arm, and Kyle lost himself in the exchange of blades.

8

EVACUATION

*B*ooted feet ran, doors slammed, people yelled, there was the distinct scrape of wood against the stone floors of the castle, and the sound of horses milling in the courtyard below. An energy, a feeling, panic. Scholar Clements stood at the window looking at the milling people, his people below. Despite the warning they had received, he didn't panic. The king's men would come for them due to the failed kidnap attempt, but he knew it took time to mobilise such a force.

It wasn't the first time he had been driven and forced to abandon his home. He ran his hand along the rough stone wall, evidence every block had been crafted by hand in a different era to this one. This keep would stand as it had for generations and he would come back one day. It amazed him the attachment that could be woken by coming back to a place.

He remembered a different time in these halls. The blue eyes of his sweet little Isa. He'd seen her in the village so long ago, dancing with some other girls. Her beauty had shone in her eyes and smile. He'd selected her to be his, taken her into his home. He still recalled her scream of fear as she'd been torn from his arms. All his girls taken from him as the screaming and yelling from an angry mob who'd mustered up the courage to attack echoed through these halls and rooms. As flames spread and thick smoke filled the rooms he'd fled then, too.

Turning from the window, he glanced around the now bare room that had been his home. Memories of a long-ago time still assaulted his mind. He'd never been able to forget so he'd come back, abandoned what he'd built elsewhere. Discovering the Killiam Order, he'd joined their number. It hadn't been hard to spin a tale of despair at the hands of monsters that they'd believed. An exercise in patience had allowed him to rise through their ranks. He'd learned lessons from his long-ago past.

He'd gathered people to him. This time the mob would be on his side.

SCHOLAR CLEMENTS RODE out the large gates of the keep with some of his people around him, yet he was isolated despite the company. As they had discussed, during the exodus they rode out in small groups rather than one big party, using the different exits to mask their departure as much as they could. The longer it took for word to get back to the king that they had evacuated the stronghold, the safer they would all be.

Their next base wasn't as salubrious as the Keep, but he'd been assured they'd made the village they'd taken over as comfortable as they could. Still, it was only a short-term solution. They would move onto a safer base on the lands of an ally, once they'd received word their intended home had been searched for their presence. Not all the high lords had turned their back on their duty, as they saw it, to the common people. Or forgotten their allegiance to him, to the Order.

Clements was aware that some of his people shouldered guilt at the villages and farmers who'd lost their lives as they had been cleared out of their homes. They'd organised multiple raids by the Sundered and their Controllers to achieve the panic and fear. That fit in with their goals. The population did not fear attacks by the Sundered as much as they should. It was time to change that, as the time of fulfilling his retribution on the people of Vallantia was close to being realised.

As fear spread throughout the two major sprawling cities overcrowded with people, Clements knew they would put pressure on the king to act. That thought made Clements smile. Kevin had assured him that their actions were being noticed, and it was only the king noticing his people suffer that would force him to act.

Kevin coming into the fold of the Order had been a turning point. The Order's progress had accelerated, and they had achieved so much since he'd come to them. A trained Master Healer, it had been his idea to recruit others with the mind control gift from the ranks of the Healers' Guild. That had proved to be a strategic move of pure genius. His work at refining their medication, continuing from the Order's founding father, the great Gail Killiam, had heralded a number of major breakthroughs, putting them in a good position.

It was in the annuals from the Founding articulating the path the Order should follow. They would keep refining the medication until they had an army of the Sundered under their control. Once that goal was achieved, they would take the fight to the monsters in this world, regardless whether the king approved the action or not. Once Vallantia was under their control, they would spread their reach, bringing safety to all the lands. Clements smiled, it was so nice that the Orders long term goals and plans happed to fit in with his own desires. He wanted it all back and he would use the Order to achieve it.

CATHERINE M WALKER

"Scholar Clements?"

Clements turned to see Stacey Frost frowning as she moved her horse closer to him and repressed a sigh. Some members of the Order really tested his patience. Stacey was one of them but she was a good follower. An organisation such as this could never have enough followers, even if he could wish that she didn't question so much.

"Yes Stacey, how can I assist you?" He kept his irritation out of his tone.

"I don't understand why we are abandoning the keep." Stacey's lips compressed.

"The king's people will come after us there."

"We're ready, we can fight them now! With the strong walls around us we'd have the advantage over the guard." Her back stiffened as she turned and gestured to the stronghold they were leaving behind them.

Clements smiled coldly. At least Stacey was one of his people that wasn't afraid to fight. Indeed, she and her partner were spoiling to engage in the war they knew was coming. Even if they were a little premature in that desire.

"The time is fast approaching, a few more pieces need to fall into place. Then we will take the fight to the king and his people."

"You keep saying that, yet year after year we hide rather than fight directly and now we run..."

Clements cut her off, his temper snapping. "Enough, Stacey. The steps we take are necessary. We have more allies than you know and we will need all of us in this fight."

Seeing others nearby turn, their eyes wide at the argument, Clements pressed his lips together. He turned his gaze on them all, waiting until they broke eye contact and looked away before he spurred his horse to a trot, putting some distance between himself and the others.

It took all of his willpower not to kill Stacey for questioning him in front of the group. At least Stacey wanted the fight and wasn't one of the ones who wailed over the death of innocents; those would have to be dealt with. He pushed down his irritation and remembered his goal. A smile spread on his lips.

Soon a time would come when none would dare question him.

9

LIAISON

*A*lex flashed through the veil, drawn to the surging power that called to him. He knew what he would find. It was the Sundered, the mad ones. He had no idea how long the last period of blackout had lasted. Alex wasn't even sure if he was in his own mind now. Although he thought perhaps he was. Generally, though, if his flickering memories were correct, at those times he was at his worst—times when he would kill someone he'd encountered for looking at him the wrong way. Well, to be honest, not quite for that; some unfortunate had to make the mistake of attacking him first or be Sundered. Still, as the dead thief in the alleyway had shown, it didn't seem to take much. It wasn't like money was much of a concern. He could get more from the palace anytime he wanted with no one noticing. Or by asking William.

He believed an increase in the surging power of the veil channelling into him was what caused his mind to overload and black out. It heralded an onslaught of pain and confusion, and pushed him out of control. Alex checked absently, once more reassuring himself that he was wearing clothes and had a sword. At least he hadn't blacked out with an unknown amount of time between the alleyway and now. Going up against the Sundered naked and unarmed probably wasn't the most spectacular idea

As he flew through the veil, Alex looked around and saw the thick strands of the veil arcing through the air, through him, from him. He winced, realising that in the past this would have been enough power to sink him into unconsciousness or madness. It seemed, despite everything, his impression that he was getting stronger was correct. Or maybe he was just getting used to the level of power. He smiled ruefully. Perhaps it was both. The thing that concerned him most was what he did while he experienced those black periods. Still his mind shied away, but the flickering pieces of memories told him things he didn't want to know.

Alex reached his destination and what he saw in the courtyard below gave him pause. It was a sight he hadn't seen before: three Sundered fighting against, well, he couldn't say who the fourth person was. The hooded figure fought against the Sundered, using a merged fighting style, incorporating the power of the veil with sword work. The hooded figure wasn't Sundered, he was certain about that, but seemed to be like himself, Kyle or Jess—someone he guessed going through transition. Or at least further along the path than himself. Whoever it was, they seemed to have a firm control both of their own power and ability to fight. The figure drew in an impressive amount of power. Alex shook himself out of his introspection and shifted into the courtyard below. Another thing he found odd: every other time he fought the Sundered it had been in more remote areas. Although, he could tell this place was situated on the forest edge, which might explain the unusual sighting.

Without giving it further thought, Alex threw himself into the battle, aiding the stranger in the fight against the Sundered. Now he was closer he could see that the figure was female, although he was suddenly too busy to notice much detail. Whoever she was, she made short work of the Sundered she had been fighting. She turned her attention to another of her attackers and it didn't take long before the head of the one she had been fighting hit the ground. He felt her probe him, then dismissed him as a threat, or at least not the most immediate threat. Alex dispatched his own opponent, then turn to help with the last remaining Sundered only to see she had already slain her enemy. Alex smiled, noting that she didn't sheathe her blade. Instead she stood watching him, waiting. She seemed so confident and self-assured, with good reason—both qualities he liked.

Alex knew she was assessing him, just as he assessed her. She reached a decision and pushed back her hood. She smiled, her mind voice low and somehow soothing.

I'm Isabella.

Alex licked his lips, then replied in kind. *I'm Alex.*

Isabella smiled, her head cocking to one side. *Thank you for your help against those.*

Alex glanced around the courtyard, realising they were in the back yard of an inn. If the noise coming from inside was anything to go by, it was a boisterous one. Alex assessed his current state, then grinned. He seemed to be stable, or at least as stable as he got these days.

Can I tempt you to a drink? We seem to be in the right place.

Isabella laughed and sheathed her sword, then turned with him, falling into step as they walked to the inn. The warmth and lively music hit him as they walk through the door. Alex barely paused scanning the room, spotting an empty table near the back. He placed a hand on Isabella's back and guided her through the crowded taproom towards the table. At their approach a group of men about to sit at the table froze; one horrified glance at Alex and they backed off hands raised in the air. Alex frowned, then noticed he still held his sword. He shook his head and raised a hand an apology, sheathing the blade. The men grinned at him uncertainly, but went off to find another table.

Alex sat next to Isabella on the bench, his back, as was customary, against the cool stone wall. He raised his hand to the serving boy.

Beer, wine or...?

Beer will be fine, thanks.

Alex ordered a pitcher of beer and a plate of whatever the food of the day was from the kitchen for them both. Out of habit these days he checked his pockets and belt for money. He breathed a sigh of relief when he discovered that he had money on him—the money from the thief he'd killed. Isabella, noticing his brief panic, chuckled.

"It's all right, Alex. I've been in the same position in the past more times than I can count."

Isabella was still assessing him, and he didn't blame her at all. Still, he could tell she liked what she was seeing. When the food and beer arrived, they both took time in between eating and drinking to exchange brief histories. Her full name was Isabella Katrina Hunte, and his eyes widened when she admitted to being from Ilarith. In the light of the taproom he took in her long blond hair, spilling around her shoulders, and her blue eyes he found he couldn't look away from. She intrigued him.

She took the news of who he was in her stride with only a faint look of surprise, her eyes widening.

"You're *that* Alex?" Isabella laughed as he nodded in reply. "Of all the people I thought might encounter someday, you were certainly not among them."

Alex smiled in return and, leaning back against the cool stone wall, he relaxed, placing one of his booted feet up on the bench.

"Why do I get the distinct impression you are not being terribly sincere?"

Isabella chuckled, the sound low and pleasing. "All right, Alex. Yes, I know who you are. I've been looking for you."

Alex looked at her appraisingly and realised to his shock she was not what he had first thought as he'd caught the flare in her power before it had dampened again. He guessed it had been deliberate, since she was remarkably good at hiding her true nature.

"So, you found me." Alex picked up his beer and swallowed a mouthful without taking his eyes off her.

"Yes, or rather you found me." Isabella reached across and picked up some cheese, nibbling the corner cautiously before smiling and taking a larger mouthful.

"Okay, I'll bite. Why were you looking for me?" Alex had to admit to curiosity.

"Damien thought you could use a mentor." Isabella smiled again at seeing the shock on his face.

"Damien?" Alex felt his mind racing, memories of things attributed to the hunter falling into place in his brain. "Ah, he is Kin?"

Isabella's eyes crinkled as she held back laughter. "No, Damien is of the Elder. He has taken in your friend, Jess, as his protégé."

Alex tilted his head to one side, amused despite himself. "I'm supposed to be yours?"

Isabella shook her head. "I'm a friend, if you allow it. More if you wish."

Alex unaccountably felt his cheeks go red; he had no doubt at all about what the more entailed.

ALEX WANDERED a little aimlessly around the village he found himself in. He'd stayed in control for a few days. The continuity of being in his own brain space for an extended period gave him hope he'd be able to maintain control of himself and his powers sooner rather than later. Isabella had left him to his own devices today with an injunction to call her if he needed her. Alex found he was a little confused as to exactly what Isabella was to him.

Friend?

Mentor?

Potential lover?

He had to admit, even if it was only to himself right now, he had a strong reaction to her. That realisation had left him restless and he'd resorted to wandering about the village to occupy his mind. He had enough presence of mind to know he'd found himself here in this village on more than one occasion, so there must be something about it that attracted him. After having breakfast and paying the innkeeper to keep the back corner room for him, he'd headed out to explore.

What he'd thought of as a small village hadn't turned out to be that small. Amberbreak was a bustling trade town on the tri-border Vallantia shared with The Heights and Sylanna. The marketplace was a hive of activity, filled with tradesmen from The Heights Protectorate and Sylanna. Some of the stalls were permanent three-sided wooden structures, others were just a series of portable tables arranged under tarps strung up to give them protection from the sun and rain. Traders from all over Vallantia converged on Amberbreak to swap, barter and trade. Towards the end of the week the numbers in the market swelled with performers and storytellers taking their places scattered throughout, entertaining any who cared to stop and listen, all for a few coins tossed onto a blanket they spread nearby.

Still, for all that the village sprawl was bigger than he'd thought. He realised the inn he'd been turning up at was in the quiet corner of town and was one of the few multi-storey establishments. It was surprisingly respectable for him, particularly remarkable since there was a less respectable part of town that in the past was much more likely for him to turn up in.

Alex found himself wandering along the dock that ran along the wide river to one side of the town. The Great Forest sprawled on the far bank, its expanse only broken by tributaries from the river. He was intrigued and distracted by barge trader families from Sylanna docked along the long pier, their large wooden barges utilised to not only haul their trade goods but to house the traders themselves as well. Suddenly he froze, hearing the wail of pain through the veil. It was different than normal and didn't sound like one of the Sundered. Moving out of sight into a side street that ran between two warehouses, he looked around and, not seeing anyone around, he pulled the veil around him and followed the pained screams like they were a beacon. He looked down on the scene in what looked like an abandoned warehouse, and Alex felt his face pale in horror.

1 0

MADNESS

BEFORE THE SUNDERED WAR

*C*olin screamed, struggling against the bonds that held him strapped to the bed deep in the heart of the Healers' Guild. At first, the medication that the healer had given him had seemed to help. He'd been a willing participant in the trial. It had cut his access to the veil, and had appeared to be a blessing. The healers had told him that with the control of his medication, they would introduce him slowly back to the power of the veil. That he would be able to learn control gradually, instead of just being opened wide to the energy as those who regularly went through transition were, as his sister had been—she had gone off into the wilds, lost time, and killed. She had eventually come back to herself, yet she had never forgiven herself for what she knew she had done during her transition.

He had been terrified that he too would be unable to cope during the transition. Everyone said the madness was due to going through the transition, and that those who broke ran in families, so he had been only too glad to agree to this trial. Yet something had changed. He begged the healers, pleaded with them to stop. The medication wasn't working as they said it would. Every time the antidote cut out, the power of the veil shot through his body in excruciating pain. It surged, along with the voices of the others around him, somehow amplified and worse than what he remembered. He found himself screaming in pain, begging for the tormentor to stop. Yet they didn't listen. They didn't stop. They continued with their trial.

Until now. Colin didn't know what had happened, but he hadn't been given his medication this day. He felt like his body was on fire; he felt sick, his body going into convulsion as the power was suddenly able to run through him. Even if they came and forced their treatment on him, it was too late, it would cause him excruciating pain. Where before his power had been steady and increasing, now he felt like his brain was erupting as the power surged off and on, totally out of his ability to control.

As power racked his body, he felt his back arch. He screamed his pain out into the veil as he heaved at the bonds, and a crack echoed around the room as this time they snapped. Colin leapt from the bed and staggered along the row of others like him, all of them begging to be released. Falling to his knees as pain racked him again, he grabbed his temples, screaming into the void with tears running down his face.

Colin felt himself be sick again, leaving a mess on the floor, but his stomach continuing to heave even when there was nothing for him to bring up. He staggered to his feet, making his way to one bed after the other, freeing those strapped down on the beds. They didn't stop, they didn't wait or help; some ran staggering from the room, while others seemed to have enough control to draw the veil to them, disappearing into the veiled world. As Colin released the last of those that had been in the healer's torture room, he looked around when the door opened to see the young medical student who'd been dosing them with the medication come in. The healer got halfway across the room before he realised that something was wrong. He stopped, looking up, startled to see Colin standing there. The young medical trainee dropped the tray, the medication smashing, spreading across the floor. He turned and started running towards the door. Feeling the surge of power, Colin grappled with it, then pitched himself forward to grab the trainee and snap his neck. Letting the broken healer fall to the ground, Colin threw his head up and screamed, releasing his pent-up pain and anger into the veil before transitioning into the veiled world to escape.

11

RYAN'S INJURY

*R*yan allowed the wadded-up cloth clenched in his teeth to fall out, cursing himself for a fool once more. As it turned out, he wasn't a great thief, no matter how much he tried. Not that he could see any other way out of what his life had become now. He hadn't thought his life could get worse until that fool Tyron tried to rob the man in the alley and paid for it with his life. After that moment Ryan's life had unaccountably spiralled out of control. He'd found himself living in an abandoned warehouse with the local thieves' guild. They'd taken him in and promised to teach him. Turns out so far he'd been a terrible pupil.

He watched as Ken heated the sewing needle in the fire, not ashamed of the tears that dried on his face from the fire. Ken nodded at Jyian, who picked up the wadded cloth and stuffed it back into Ryan's mouth. Ken threaded the fishing twine back through the eye of the needle and then, using clamps to pull his flesh together, shoved the needle through his skin, pulling the twine through to knit the jagged flesh together.

Ryan's hands clenched on the rails that ran around the edge of the shed, his knuckles going white, and screamed as Ken shoved the needle through his flesh once more. None of them paid him any heed. Jyian and Elsie helped to restrain him while Ken shoved the needle through his flesh over and over again, closing up the hole he'd made in his side.

It had been his own fault; his knife had been out, clenched in his hand, when he'd slipped on the roof of the merchant's they'd intended to break into. His knife had ended up lodged in his side as he'd fallen from the roof onto the cobblestone courtyard below. To their credit, Jyian and Elsie had come after him, helping him back to their base rather than leaving him for the occupant to find.

Feeling like the world was dropping out from beneath him, Ryan looked up in alarm and saw the glowing cloaked man appear. He hadn't seen his face that night in the alley when Tyron was killed, but he was certain it was the same man. Seeing him draw his blade and surge forward in a blur of speed, Ryan spat the bloody rag from his mouth to cry out a warning, pushing Ken out of the way. He screamed as the twine jerked at his skin, but was rewarded by the sight of the three desperately backing away from the stranger.

"No! Don't kill them, please, I'll give you anything you want." Ryan held up his hand desperately towards the cloaked figure, who stopped and swung his head back to him.

ALEX PAUSED and looked at the boy on the ground, blood seeping from his side and soaking dirty cloths he'd been sitting on. He was the one he'd heard screaming in pain through the veil. He could touch the veil, although clearly had little understanding of his capabilities and was too young to go through transition.

"You enjoy being tortured?" Alex frowned and absently put

a barrier up between him and the girl who had been trying to sneak up behind him.

"Elsie, no, don't. He'll kill you." The boy looked at the girl and shook his head.

Alex pulled back his hood, perplexed, trying to understand what he'd seen, given the boy's obvious concern for the three who'd been disfiguring him. He walked over to the boy and knelt near him, grasping him with one hand as he cringed away, wincing with obvious pain every time he moved.

"He's right, Elsie, don't test my patience. I have a remarkably short temper these days." Alex looked back at the girl as her knife she'd tried to throw at his back hit the barrier instead. She blanched as it stopped midway through the air and clattered to the floor. She looked at him, horrified, and backing up she spun and ran for the doors, followed by the other two.

"They were trying to help me." Ryan slumped back, defeated, knowing he had no chance of fighting against this man.

"You need a healer, boy." Alex frowned at the lad, still not understanding what he'd seen or why it had been occurring. That anyone would do that to someone who needed to seek the attention of a healer horrified him.

Ryan laughed, then stopped, grimacing in pain. "Healers don't have time or energy to tend to someone like me. Don't have the money to spare to pay them." Ryan pointed at the twine and dangling needle hanging from his side, with the clamp still grasping his flesh in its grip. "They were trying to sew me up, to stop the bleeding. It might give me time to heal."

Alex closed his eyes at the boy's simple words of explanation, appalled as the meaning sunk in.

"What's your name? I can't keep calling you 'boy'." Alex tried to look at the lad reassuringly, although given he was in pain and terrified, he wasn't sure he was successful.

"Ryan. It was you in the alley that night, wasn't it?" Ryan

was certain there could not be two people who shone like this man had in the village.

"In the alley?" Alex was thrown by the unexpected question.

"You killed Tyron that night. He deserved it, but he was all I had. It's how I ended up with them. They took me on. I'm a terrible thief, though. I fell and stuck myself with my own dagger." Ryan wasn't sure what had possessed him to blurt out all that to the man looming over him except that he seemed to be listening. While he was listening, he wasn't sticking that dagger that licked with flames into him.

Alex flinched as the memory of the man in the alleyway he'd killed flashed in his mind.

"He was your father?" Alex looked around the abandoned warehouse with the sinking sense of responsibility for leaving Ryan without a parent to care for him. Even if the man had been a bad one.

"No. My father died, but Tyron took up with my mother. Then she died." Ryan felt himself drifting and tried to wrench his wandering mind back the man in front of him, trying not to be wooed by sleep.

Ryan's words struck Alex like a blow. It meant he held responsibility for the position the boy found himself in. Alex shook his head, seeing Ryan was struggling to stay conscious, and gathered the weakly resisting boy into his arms, standing up smoothly.

"Stop squirming, Ryan. You need a healer." Alex pulled the surrounding veil around them both and, sensing the boy's shock, he sent soothing thoughts to the lad, trying to calm him.

ALEX GLANCED AT RYAN, concerned as he fought to stay conscious. The lad's breathing was shallow, tremors running through his body. He felt the pain stab through the boy any time he shifted his grip and Alex sensed his fear as he struggled to breathe. While it didn't take him long to traverse the distance between Amberbreak and the Summer Palace, despite the village being at the extremes of the realm, it seemed like an eternity, for both him and Ryan.

Alex made his way through the palace he knew so well, ghosting his way along the corridors. He arrived at Aaron's rooms and didn't pause or show any courtesy. He didn't have the time. As he entered the healer's rooms, the boy started to cough. Alex sensed the sharp pain shooting through him every time he did so. Bright frothy blood appeared on his lips.

Aaron looked up in shock as Alex dropped his concealment, any chastisement he'd been about to administer dying on his lips as he saw Ryan. He stood up from his desk, gesturing Alex over to the bed. Ryan moaned as Alex deposited him on the bed, grabbing at Alex's arm, trying to rise back up.

Can't breathe.

Alex helped hold his slight frame up as Aaron, hearing the comment and understanding the cause, piled pillows behind the boy. Alex stood back as Aaron placed his hands on the boy, detecting the surge of power. He took a deep breath, relieved, watching as Aaron did his work. While he could heal himself, Alex realised he did not understand how the healers accomplished their work.

Alex spun as the door opened, only to relax when Jocelyn walked into the room. She paused, looking at Alex before taking his presence in her stride and with a brief acknowledgement walked past him. Jocelyn assessed the scene before her, then moved over to the side bench to pick up a fine knife from the array of implements. She walked up to the bed and, after a moment's hesitation, went around the other side and crawled across the covers. Kneeling at Ryan's other side, she removed the clamp, holding it out without looking around. Alex stepped forward without comment and took it, placing the implement on Aaron's desk. He was fascinated as Jocelyn sliced through the fishing twine with the knife, and then, after handing him the knife, she pulled the pieces of twine gently from Ryan's flesh. Once done, she placed her own hands to either side of the wound.

Alex worried due to the long time the two worked, yet the boy's flesh knitted under Jocelyn's power and his breathing eased. As he'd feared there had been more damage than he could see.

Alex watched the power around the pair out of interest. Jocelyn had switched from healing the puncture wound caused by the dagger and was now channelling power to Aaron. He didn't quite understand why she did that or why it was needed. Then again, he still didn't understand healers.

AARON SAT BACK, a wave of exhaustion hitting him. He looked down at the boy Alex had brought to him and he placed his hand on his shoulder as he tried to get up.

"Relax, Ryan. I healed your body, but you still need to rest. You did quite a bit of damage to yourself." Aaron smiled reassuringly at the panicked boy.

"Thank you, healer, but I can't pay and this looks too fine for the likes of me. I'll mess your bed up." Ryan looked around in panic.

"It's fine, Ryan. His father already paid." Aaron's lips twitched in amusement and his head jerked in Alex's direction.

"I don't understand why his friends didn't just take him to the local healer. What they were trying to do was barbaric." Alex looked unhappy with what he'd seen.

Aaron sighed, wishing he was not familiar with the problem.

"Alex, there just aren't enough of us. Healing can be exhausting, particularly if the village only has a journeyman who might not even be in the village when problems occur." Aaron paused, sending a mental suggestion to his patient to sleep.

"Your Highness, it's a practice the Healers' Guild is aware of." Jocelyn looked sad, but not outraged. "Those who are less fortunate resort to these types of measures trying to stay alive long enough to heal or for a healer to see them."

"We have at least three healers at Master level here in the palace at all times, Your Highness, plus all the journeymen. The smaller villages share a journeyman." Aaron grimaced. "Still, if they'd taken the lad to the local healer, he would have been treated. We struggle to convince the poor that they can come to us. They see the more fortunate pay—it helps with food and upkeep so the healer can concentrate on that instead of where their next meal is coming from. Unfortunately, many of the poor think they have to pay, so they don't show up when they should."

Jocelyn nodded. "You may not be aware, but it's also why we help as many as we can during the Royal Procession. The locals all know they can come into the Healers' Pavilion to receive treatment." Jocelyn shrugged. "Our journeymen and trainees also run a clinic twice a week in the village either here or at the Winter Palace, depending on the season."

Alex looked a little pale. "How could I not know before now that people are forced to resort to this kind of practice?"

Aaron shook his head. "I wish I didn't. He must stay with us for a few days, Your Highness. I'll have him transferred to a bed in the recovery wing." Aaron paused and said hesitantly. "You recognise the power in him?"

Alex nodded. "I'll make arrangements. He's strong enough for transition to be a risk."

Aaron raised his hand as Alex drew the power. "Alex, how are you coping?"

Alex shook his head and disappeared into the veil. That wasn't something he wanted to ask himself right now, particularly when he felt more than a little responsible for the mess that the boy had ended up in.

ALEX LOOKED DOWN on the practice session going on below him and smiled. He waited patiently until the session broke up, then when the ones he wanted were alone he reached down and drew them to him.

The three guards spun, drawing their swords and the veil, only to freeze when they recognised him. Marcus stared at Alex, tension draining from him; he sheathed his sword, motioning for the others to do the same. James and Megan didn't question or hesitate as they put away their own weapons, breathing a sigh of relief, although they didn't release their hold on the veil, which caused Alex to smile.

"Marcus, good to see you are all still practicing." Alex grinned, knowing his guard well enough to realise he was being assessed. Alex waited, showing a level of patience that surprised him. In a way he enjoyed the experience, since it had been quite some time since he was capable of exhibiting such a trait. Marcus looked at his fellow guards and they both shrugged.

"Yes, Your Highness, we're still practicing. Just in case."

"Keep doing that and expand your sessions to all in the Fourth's Elite that are trustworthy and talented enough. You remember the attacks we went on?"

"We remember." Marcus glanced at Megan and James once more. "We have kept up our practice. It's just that without you, my Lord Kyle and my Lady Jessalan, we have little chance against the Sundered. We will do our best, though, Your Highness."

This time both James and Megan nodded agreement. It relieved Alex that the three guards were serious. They still trained even though they knew that to take up such a fight by themselves would mean their deaths.

Alex looked down at the ground before looking back up at the guards, his expression firm.

"You won't have to. I'll be back, I only need some time. Look after my father and William."

"Yes, Your Highness." Marcus nodded, along with assent from both James and Megan.

"There is a boy, Ryan. He is in Aaron's care. I feel more than a little responsible for him. Can you see to him in my absence, please? Arrange somewhere for him to sleep, training, something? He has power, enough that he will go through transition, but not for years yet, I judge." Alex stared at the three guards.

Marcus shook his head. "We're not set up to mind children, Your Highness, but we'll work something out."

Alex smiled. "If you need money, speak to William." Ryan's last occupation occurred to him. "It may not be prudent to give the boy money, though." Alex suddenly grinned at the guards, who knew him well enough not to ask, since they all knew they wouldn't like the answer.

All the guards straightened and stood at attention, their faces not showing any doubt at all as Alex moved them back to their barracks.

12

CONSEQUENCE

$\mathcal{K}$yle walked down the wide corridor, the cooling breeze flowing around him from the wide windows down at the end of the corridor. It was normally soothing, but on this occasion it barely registered on him as he made his way to what he thought of as Joanna's day room. Or at least it was the place she tended to be during the day. Kyle took in a deep breath, trying to calm his nerves. The conversation he was about to have with her would likely not come out the way he wanted, but he had to try.

He entered the solar and turned towards the windows that looked out over the cliff where his mistress stood. It was one of her favourite places, looking out over the grounds towards the bluff with the ocean beyond. Ragged cliffs were visible to one side towering up and ringing the estate, the tinge of green at the top hinting that a forest sprawled beyond the cliffs.

Kyle smiled as that sparked an idea. If he could convince her he shared her obvious love of the grounds and wanted to explore, even if it was just the immediate surroundings of the estate, it would afford him one small step to freedom. He kept the breathtaking view he could see from the windows in the forefront of his mind as if he were thinking of nothing else.

"Morning, my lady." A polite greeting to start was always safe.

Kyle watched for a reaction as he approached, trying to judge what her mood was like today. It would have a big impact on how the conversation would go.

"Kyle, you've done your exercises this morning?" She looked over her shoulder at him and smiled, holding her hand out to him.

Kyle didn't allow the relief he felt to show; Joanna was having a good day. He took her hand in his own, bowing to her and brushing his lips against her fingers. After growing up in the palace, courtly graces came as second nature even after all the time he'd been away.

"I'm about to, Mistress. I have not seen you for some time, so I thought I would greet you first." Kyle kept his tone neutral.

"Good, Kyle, you shouldn't neglect them. It's important for your recovery." Joanna turned her gaze back to stare out the window.

Kyle let the silence settle between them for a moment. He knew he had to take this in small steps if he ever wanted his freedom again.

"It looks beautiful out there. Calming." Kyle allowed a hint of longing to show in his voice, keeping his gaze on the crashing waves.

He was aware that Joanna turned to look at him, yet resolutely kept his gaze on the water as if that was all he was thinking about. He didn't want to give her cause to take over and search his mind. She would know what he was up to if she did that. As long as he didn't arouse her suspicions, she left him to his own devices. He'd been stable the last week, able to ride with the surges in the power without it adversely affecting him.

"It is beautiful. I keep forgetting you haven't seen the grounds yet." Joanna looked at him appraisingly.

"No, not yet. Could I go for a walk after my morning exercises?" Kyle again allowed a hint of longing to tinge his tone, turning to look at her. "Please, Mistress?"

Joanna looked at him, considering his request. The silence stretched between them and his face fell in disappointment. Without her approval to go outside, her orders to stay within the walls of the estate constrained him. She was his mistress, and he'd worked out he could not go against her direct orders.

Her hand reached up to stroke the side of his face, and Kyle closed his eyes, having no choice but to relax as a steady calm washed over him. He knew it was Joanna, willing calmness in him. He didn't fight her; he hadn't fought her control from the outset. Kyle smiled as a small burst of pleasure washed over him. It showed Joanna was pleased with him, with his acceptance of his status.

"I know you have worked hard to accept your servitude, Kyle. This change has not been easy for you to accept. You will see, it is for the best you belong to me." Joanna's voice and gaze were possessive.

"I am your servant, I understand that now, Mistress." Kyle fell to one knee, head bowed.

He wasn't lying; she owned him in a way he'd never thought possible, although he had no intention of allowing this current state to be permanent and hoped fervently Joanna did not search his mind for signs of rebellion.

"Complete your morning exercises, then you may go for a walk on the grounds. You will not go beyond the borders of the estate, Kyle." Joanna's eyes narrowed as she reinforced her new orders.

Kyle shuddered in reaction as the last command swirled in his mind and settled on him. She had enforced her words with a compulsion, and there was no way for him to breach her injunction. Still, it was more freedom than he'd had since he'd arrived. Kyle took several deep breaths, allowing her will to settle on him. Like a web settling all over his body and mind, it was disconcerting, her words placing a real binding of power on his body and mind. She didn't need to use physical restraints or keep him under guard in a cell. Her means of control over him was absolute.

Shaking off the momentary dizziness he felt at her alteration to her compulsions on him, Kyle stood. At her wave of dismissal, he bowed to her and retreated from the room. It was time for his morning exercises. He walked back down the corridor towards his training rooms, a hint of a smile on his lips. He kept the pleasure of the small victory to himself. One step at a time, little by little, he would win his freedom back.

KYLE CONTROLLED his impatience and concentrated on his breathing exercises. Now was not the time to show any kind of negligence towards his morning routine. Joanna granting him permission to the grounds of the estate was a victory—a small one, but still a win. If Joanna suspected even a hint of an ulterior motive in him, that small concession would be rescinded.

If he was honest with himself, in the beginning he'd had his bad days, days it had terrified him that the toxin was rising in him again. Uncontrollable power would surge into him, at levels he'd never experienced. His concentration had shattered under the assault, with pain and madness consuming him. As his control would slip, he would sink into darkness. It was Joanna that would force him into unconsciousness during those periods. She'd informed him the surges in the veil were a part of transition. He was changing, and right now his body and mind couldn't take the overload of power. For her care and help during those dark days he was grateful. Kyle shuddered thinking of the damage he could have inflicted, out of his mind and in pain due to power fluctuations.

Yet now he was doing much better, and even the power surges didn't knock him around as much anymore. But having lived a life, until now, of doing pretty much what he wanted when he wanted to do it, he was chafing under the restrictions. Inexplicably Joanna, who was perfectly reasonable about most other topics, turned possessive in the extreme about him. She would not consent to releasing him, she had maintained that standpoint every time it had come up. If the topic was pushed, unchecked fury would rise in her.

He realised Joanna could be the sweetest, most compassionate person, and she would have been an incredible queen. Yet there was a part of her that had broken in the Sundered attack all those years ago. In her mind he could see she tied releasing him to her inability to protect and defend Alex in that clearing all those years ago. Others trying to force her to release him spiked those memories. She would not abandon him the way she had abandoned Alex.

Kyle's eyes flew open as the floor under him rumbled and a loud explosion sounded. He pulled the veil around himself, reaching out to that cupboard where he knew she kept his weapons and drawing them to him through the veil—a trick he'd have to consider when he had time. Grateful that when she had relaxed her compulsions to allow him into the grounds she hadn't restricted his weapon use to the practice room, he dropped into the open space outside the estate house, appearing behind Joanna. One part of his brain noted that she was not fighting alone, but was still outnumbered. He noticed with concern that she was not a strong fighter, with Edward forced into a more defensive posture to protect her.

The next thing he recognised was that she and those with her were facing off against attackers who were all using the power. These foes might be more skilled in the use of the veil, but their blade work was shocking. His grin turned hard as he realised none of the attackers were paying any attention to him. They had sensed his arrival, but they didn't see him as the more immediate threat. More fool them.

Kyle drew the veil into himself while jumping into the battle, his blades a blur, moving in long-familiar patterns— except this time he also drew on his experience with the veil to help him fight, making himself faster and stronger. He willed the veil to take shape even as he struck with his blade, and a barrier like a shield formed in front of him. He braced himself for the metaphysical blow that struck his shield and absorbed the shock while lashing out with his knife.

That won't be enough to kill him, Kyle. He will heal even something you would normally consider a mortal wound.

Kyle ignored Joanna's panicked advice, and with an effort he tried to shield himself from the distraction her concern caused. It was something he already knew from previous fights with the Sundered. It was a little irritating, but unless you were careful, they would not stay down. Still, the physical blow was enough to cause his unsuspecting target to stagger back. He paused for a moment, concentrating on healing himself. Kyle used the opportunity to slice through his opponent's neck. With the force of the veil bound around his blade and enhancing his strength, his blade cut though his adversary's neck and spine like butter.

"Heal *that!*"

Kyle staggered as a blow struck him. He shook his head, trying to recover his balance, he turned to see a shaft of twined green, silvery-grey coming straight at his head. Reacting on instinct he threw his hand up, reinforcing what he thought of as his shield. It seemed the attackers had realised their mistake and half of them had turned on him. He staggered back, trying to hold back veil attacks coming at him from several fronts against people who were more experienced at utilising the veil than he was.

Joanna's panic flood into his mind, confusion welling up and tremors wracking his body. He almost groaned out loud; this was not the time for Joanna to interfere.

Joanna, please stop!

Kyle fell to his knees, battling to maintain his concentration and shield against multiple attackers raining blows on his shield. He saw a feral snarl and a gleam of triumph in the eyes of his opponents.

Kyle's eyes widened as he felt the ripple through the veil, a sure sign that someone was incoming. This was a signature he recognised, yet far stronger than he could believe.

Relief hit him.

Alex.

The incoming power was Alex.

ALEX SMILED at Isabella's joke. They had retired to a private, cosy sitting room at the back of the inn with a decanter of wine and food, to talk in private about the veil and its uses. Given its location in a border and merchant hub, the inn maintained several rooms where the merchant class could discuss business. He and Isabella had fallen into a pattern with an ease he didn't share with many people. For the most part Isabella let him explore and discover his abilities by himself. Then they would meet up in sessions like this and discuss any issues he might have. As a mentor she was excellent at explaining the subtleties of using the veil. That was a skill he didn't quite have the knack

CATHERINE M WALKER

for yet. More than anything, she had proven to be remarkably good company.

As he felt that tug of the veil on the edge of his mind drawing his attention, he stiffened and placed his goblet on the small table beside him. That signature was Kyle. A series of images came to him of his friend fighting, outnumbered, against those with power. Not waiting to explain to Isabella, Alex pulled himself into the veiled paths. His arms wide, fingers splayed, he drew power to himself as he rushed through the veil, closing the distance between himself and Kyle. The outside world blurred, but Alex paid it no mind, intent on his goal.

Alex materialised, placing himself between his lifelong friend and his attackers. The force of his arrival caused a shockwave of power to roll out, with him at the epicentre. Alex raised his head to pin his shocked opponents with his gaze. With a predatory grin, he reached out as far as his senses would allow and drew in even more power. In his eyes he could see the multiple thick bands of power arcing though the air, striking him one after the other.

Alex saw two of his enemies flee, there one moment then gone the next, before he blocked the remaining Kin from leaving. He saw their eyes widen in shock as they tried to leave but found they couldn't. Alex shaped the power he'd gathered and with a snarl hurled it at the four men in front of him. His power sliced through their attempt to erect barriers with ease. Then, with little time for their eyes to widen in shock and pain, just like the boulder in the clearing, they exploded. What had once been human disintegrated into ash, scattering in the wind. The stark silence that followed the explosive crack of power was absolute.

Alex relaxed with conscious effort, allowing the excess power to drain from him. He knew he would pay the price for his excessive display, but he'd sleep later. Alex's lips twitched as he turned to face his friend, standing there looking at him wide-eyed. Alex thought he might need to pay more attention to Isabella; he needed to learn some subtlety. He had to learn how to fight while not giving in to the anger that flooded his mind. He had to learn he didn't need to use every bit of power he could draw, pushing aside caution or any thought of consequences while he was at it.

Alex let the calm of the veil wash over him and let his anger at those who had attacked his friend drop away. It helped that the miscreants were dead or had fled on his arrival. He would deal with the ones who ran later. It was a puzzle he still had to solve. They were not Sundered, their mind signatures too controlled, too calm. They had also not been like himself, slowly healing from madness. At least now he could maintain conscious control of himself, even if he was still inclined to be ruled by his emotions.

"Brother, you know how to make an appearance."

Alex laughed and hugged his friend before stepping back. He ran his eyes over Kyle, assessing him both visually and with the veil. He was a long way from the man who'd been losing himself in a downward spiral to confusion and madness. Alex recognised now that his friend had been exhibiting some of the traits of the Sundered.

"Yes, well, I knew you were in trouble fighting and outnumbered. I have a feeling I've had a little more practice fighting than you have of late. You shouldn't play with them, Kyle. Just kill them."

Alex looked over his friend again with his other sight, then froze. It was almost second nature for him to check for signs of those malignant bonds in his friend after the mess with Alyssa. He stepped forward, grasping Kyle by the shoulders.

"What the hell, Kyle? Who's done this to you?" As tired as he was with his overcharge display, Alex drew in power, intending to take Kyle with him back to safety.

Alex staggered back in shock as multiple blows struck him and a sword plunged into his abdomen. He pressed his hand to his stomach and looked up at his friend, and saw him drawing power, ready to strike again.

The power seemed to gather around them both with the entire sky above them blocked out by the writhing mass, the crack of power rolling through the air. Alex hastily drew in power himself, throwing up a barrier between him and his friend. He held back his instinct to fight back.

Kyle, please. This isn't you, fight the control.

Kyle's only answer was to draw more power and launch it toward him. Alex deflected the blows, which exploded into the surrounding ground, with earth, rocks and grass flying up and out giving testimony to the strength of the power being used.

"You'll not take him! He's mine!" a woman's voice shrieked at Alex, almost unrecognisable in its fury.

Alex froze, staring at his friend. He had a moment to wonder why pain flashed across his face before he turned and caught sight of the woman—the one who his mind remembered talking to him, reassuring him, chasing away the nightmares since he was a child.

His mother.

Alex swallowed, his brain shrieking at him with instant recognition. Of all the people to have enslaved his friend, he hadn't expected to see *her*. He felt like he'd been hit again when he recognised she was being restrained by Edward. Her madness hammered at the shield on his mind as the power gathered and swirled around her. He'd known that his mother was alive but he'd never expected to see her alive in circumstances like this, certainly not with his uncle being present as well. Edward must have known all these years that she was alive.

"Why?"

Alex heard the anguish, the pain in his own voice. He didn't doubt what he was seeing. For once he welcomed the blackness that rose, and fled into the comforting darkness of the veil.

～

KYLE'S RELIEF at seeing Alex alive and well was momentarily replaced with horror when Alex realised that he was under control of another. As Alex's power surged, his intent to take Kyle somewhere safe to deal with Joanna's bonds surged in his mind.

Kyle tried to struggle as his own will was thrust aside, compulsion driving him.

Joanna, no! Stop it.

He continued to struggle against her control as he felt himself draw power and in a deft, practiced movement his body lunged, plunging his sword into Alex's abdomen. Kyle screamed, aware it was only in his own head as he drew power and attacked Alex, who only threw up a barrier in his own defence.

Edward struggled to restrain Joanna, conflicted and not wanting to hurt her yet watching the unfolding drama with a pained expression on his face.

"You'll not take him! He's mine!" Joanna screamed, her eyes burning in anger.

Kyle continued his futile struggle against Joanna's control, a part of him dying inside. He'd just committed one of the very acts that had given him nightmares before he'd submitted to Joanna's control: attacked his own friend, consumed by madness. Yet that madness beating through his brain wasn't his own.

As Alex called power and disappeared into the veil, Kyle slumped in relief as Joanna let her iron control of him ease off.

"Damn you, Joanna. That was Alex! You made me stab your own son!" Kyle's voice was raw with emotion.

He saw the moment his words and pain penetrated Joanna's madness, as she wilted in Edward's grip.

"No." The mad light retreated from her eyes, her head shaking in denial.

She covered her face, great wracking sobs shuddering through her slight frame. Joanna sank to the ground in Edward's arms, crying like a woman who'd just lost everything.

13

THE ABSENCE OF POWER

*R*elief washed over Alex as bit by bit the world around him intruded. It was dark, blessedly dark, and he couldn't hear anything either, not even the crackle of power that had been his constant companion from childhood. A complete absence, a void he'd never experienced. He rolled over onto his back and breathed a sigh of relief, his muscles relaxing one after the other like a wave travelling down his body. The last thing he remembered was rushing through the veil to help Kyle. He'd drawn more power to himself than he'd ever done before, courting madness to save his friend. Then, nothing.

Alex poked and prodded at his own mind, although he should have known better. Those memories would come back when they were ready, or not at all. Waking up with no recollection of his location or what he'd been doing wasn't a new experience these days.

He lay, eyes open, staring up into the nothing, content to let his mind wander, free from pain for this small space of time. Alex snorted as he remembered his uncle's astonishment when he'd found out months had passed since they had seen each other. While the absence of things seemed like a moment in time to him, he realised that this nothingness prevented him from knowing how much time actually passed.

It could be just moments, or weeks or even months. A vague thought crossed his mind: his lack of awareness of the veil, of power of his surrounds, should concern him. Yet it was the opposite—he felt content, warm, safe. Alex closed his eyes, noting that it made no difference, the blackness the same regardless of what he perceived around himself.

Alex's eyes flared open, and scrambling to his feet he turned around, seeking a point to use as a reference. There was nothing. Just a deep blackness. For all he knew he might be in a small contained room held by another, or perhaps in a great expanse in the veil of his own making.

Alex realised that the barriers in his mind were in place, more so than he'd ever been aware of doing before, so firm he realised that he'd blocked out his access to the power himself. That is what the absence was, this nothing he struggled to understand. It was new to him, something he hadn't experienced since childhood. To be honest, he didn't even remember experiencing this as a child. As far back as he remembered, the power of the veil had always been a part of his life.

Alex sank to his knees as the realisation came to him: he'd constructed this refuge in the veil. It was just that he had almost constructed a wall between himself and the power, which was the cause of the peace he experienced, the peace that normal people felt all the time. Or at least he figured this was what others experienced, except in their normal worlds. After a little consideration of his situation, he lay down and closed his eyes again. Relief washed over him, and he was content to rest, even knowing this wasn't a good idea; he'd tried it before and it had not ended well.

ALEX WOKE AGAIN, or at least he thought he'd been asleep. It was hard for him to tell. He moaned and rolled onto his side, one trembling hand rising blindly up to his face. Unlike the peace last time he woke, this time he was aware that something was terribly wrong. His body shivered although he couldn't figure out what it was in reaction to. He wasn't cold in this place, or hot or anything. Where the absence had been soothing the last time he woke, now he felt a terrible dread, as if something vital he needed was missing. Uncontrollable tremors wracked his body, pinpricks of sweat breaking out over every inch of his skin. Memory flashed in his mind: Kyle, his eyes blank, lunging forward with his sword, and the sudden pain in his stomach along with the realisation that Kyle had just stabbed him.

My friend, no. What have you done to yourself?

The surrounding void fragmented, pinpricks of light shining as cracks appeared in the black mirror. The background hum of power assaulted his mind, growing increasingly louder, and then the dark mirror shattered as piercing light drilled through and burst upon him. Alex bucked in agony as the power assaulted his mind and body at levels he hadn't known before, almost as if the veil was punishing him for locking himself away from its influence.

Alex screamed as wave upon wave of power charged into him. It was like he was exploding. The power channelling through him was overwhelming and even though he tried to grapple with it, to control it, he didn't know where to start. Just as he thought he was gaining control, pain assaulted him once more, power burning through every fibre from head to toe, over every inch of his body. His mind became confused and he lost himself and his battle for control.

The space around him seemed to change and merge from a vague something to nothing, colour receding until everything was a writhing, crackling mess, the whiteness of pure energy. Rippling out from him, the space transformed, with walls rising around him and a roof above. He felt constrained as the walls closed in on him, the power cracking everywhere as he writhed in pain. His vision seemed to explode in a mass of small glittering bursts of light. He screamed out into the veil, begging for forgiveness, for the pain to stop, for something familiar to intervene.

Alex, come back, stop torturing yourself. Isabella's mind voice was calm and reassuring as she separated from the whiteness and walked towards him. She knelt and gathered him to her.

Alex clung to her desperately, allowing Isabella to draw him back.

ALEX BECAME AWARE SLOWLY, realising he was comfortable and warm. He'd obviously found his way to a bed, and feeling movement he realised he hadn't found the bed alone. Alex shuddered as memory assaulted him. The nothingness, the lack of power. Then the pain as pure raw power broke through barriers he hadn't intended to construct. Then Isabella's voice out of the nothingness, reaching through the power, shunting it aside and drawing him back to her. He remembered he'd sobbed with relief as she'd drawn him back and soothed his mind and chased the pain away. He hadn't fought against her compulsion to sleep, certain he was safe as she watched over him.

Alex opened his eyes and turned his head to one side, and found Isabella curled up with him in the bed, her hand resting on his chest, one leg over his. Given they were both fully dressed and lay on top of the bed—even if they had slept in each other's arms—he gathered on this occasion he could trust his memory. They had just slept last night, Isabella offering him security and comfort.

Alex stifled a groan; he didn't want to wake her. This was a complication to his life he didn't need. Still assessing how he was this morning, he realised he didn't want to move either. This current calm and peace wasn't something he'd known for a long time. He realised that he felt safe to be with her and around her. In part he realised this was because she was strong with the veil herself, competent and sure of herself. He knew that if he got out of control, she would be fine.

He nearly sat bolt upright when the memory of the fight hit him in a series of rapid-fire images. First against a group of Kin. Then his shock at finding Kyle was once more enslaved to another's will. That shock compounded when he realised that someone was his mother. Alex closed his eyes, and the memory of his fight with Kyle hit him—or rather, the fight against his mother when he'd tried to free Kyle. She'd set Kyle on him. He knew his friend would never act like that on his own. Alex ran his hand against his midriff, noting that his injury from Kyle's blade had healed.

He knew when Isabella woke; her breathing rate changed, and she took a breath in, her eyes opening, a smile on her lips.

Morning, Alex. How are you feeling? Understanding shone in Isabella's eyes and was clear in her tone.

Isabella, please, I don't want that to happen again.

The bed shifted as Isabella moved closer. He didn't resist as her arms folded around him, her soft lips kissing him lightly on the temple.

Rest, Alex, you're safe. I'm here. You need to stop fighting who and what you are.

Alex relaxed again as he allowed himself to be soothed in

Isabella's arms. He didn't want to contemplate the mess with Kyle or his mother right now, content to allow the world to look after itself for a little bit longer. Isabella was correct in her assessment. He had to stop fighting against his own nature. It was easier said than done, though, having spent most of his life fearing he would become one of the Sundered.

14

FAILURE

BEFORE THE SUNDERED WAR

*K*atrina frowned, staring at the data in front of her, flipping from one page to the next, trying to make sense of what she was seeing. It made little sense and a lot of the data seemed to be contradictory. It wasn't what she'd thought she would see, nor what her initial small-scale trials had shown her should be the result. She raised her hands to her temples, using her fingertips to massage them before she loosened her hair from its strict bonds. Her face screwed up and she flung herself up from the chair with such force the plain wooden chair clattered to the ground. Katrina moved from behind her desk, her pace short and sharp as she moved back and forth across the room. It didn't make sense. It wasn't supposed to be like this. The internal monologue ran through her mind, over, and over again in a litany she couldn't stop. There was what she had intended, what should have happened. Yet the results on the pages of the report did not agree.

Katrina stopped halfway across the room, her hand moving from her temple to cover her face, trying to hide her tears. She didn't even know who she was trying to hide from, it's not like anyone could see her right now. Since this trial had started, she'd had her own office. She flung her head back and laughed, the sound bitter, even to her own ears. It was her brother's shade she had failed. She had wanted to set out something that would be his legacy, his gift to the talented. Instead her medication was making it worse. Obviously something vital was missing.

Unaccountably, many of her trial participants had sickened, and when they continued with the treatment, many of those had died. Others had suffered extreme pain, screaming for release. Then there were the ones that at first she'd thought responded well to the treatment, only for her to learn that instead of improving they'd gone mad, murderous, in the process.

Katrina closed her eyes, and took a deep long breath, holding that breath at her maximum capacity before slowly letting it out. Usually the exercise calmed her agitation. She opened her eyes, certain of what she needed to do. No matter what it meant to her, to her career, she needed to present her findings to the Masters. Her trial had to finish until she could establish what she had missed, why it had gone so horribly wrong. Her lips firmed and she nodded, then turned and stooped to gather results of her research one piece of paper at a time from her desk. After gathering them all up she rearranged them back into an order that made sense, even if the findings didn't.

She opened the drawer to the right, pulling out a fresh piece of paper and placing it on the desk in front of her. Without thinking or having to look, her hand tracked across to the pen off to one side of the desk and she made notes for herself. Brief, short, distinct; the highlights, the most important parts of her research to date that the Guild Masters needed to inform their decision.

Katrina laid down her pen and pushed her chair back, her hands rising to cover her face as tears tracked down her cheeks. The last thing she wanted to admit to was failure.

15

FREEDOM

*D*amien checked on Jessalan, finding she was preoccupied with practicing the exercises they had trained in the other day. He frowned, realising he was going to have to talk to her at some point about her bad habit of locking away her feelings. Nothing good would come of it. He'd seen plenty of examples of what happened to those who ranked among the Kin who did so. To say they turned into psychotic killers was a mild way to put it. Jess was Elder, or would be once she finished her transition, whether she knew it or not. At the power levels she would attain, what she would become if she continued on this path was a scary thought. Still, for now he could let it slide until an opportunity presented itself to broach the subject.

Right now, there was another more pressing matter he needed to check on. Shrouding himself in his shield, he pulled himself through the veil, passing the barrier that surrounded Ilarith without having to give it much thought. He smiled knowing that Jess was bound to work it out eventually; it was just a matter of time. By that time she would be Elder and coming fully into her powers.

He made it to his destination quickly. While he hadn't been here before he was well aware of its location. He was careful to keep his barriers in place—it wouldn't do for her to realise he was here right now. Uninvited guests tended to push her over the edge into madness. Damien scanned the estate below and smiled as he detected the person he was after.

Edward, I need to speak with you.

Damien smiled as he felt Edward start, followed immediately by guilt. As well he should feel guilty; Edward was well aware of his feelings on this particular topic. His eyes narrowed as Edward appeared in the veil without announcement. He was as capable of shielding his presence completely as many of the Elder were. Edward turned around slowly and, finally spotting his location above the cliffs, closed the distance between them, his expression wary.

Damien, it's good to see you, if somewhat unexpected.

You know why I'm here Edward. Joanna still has Kyle enslaved.

It was a circumstance that he could not abide. Even though his own experiences with the subject were more years ago than he cared to think about, he still held the practice of one person enslaving another as abhorrent. It was getting increasingly difficult to convince Isabella not to intervene. Thankfully, other than her brief communication with him, she had her hands full keeping track of Alex.

I know, please give me a little more time. It is not her fault. It will be better for her state of mind if she releases him willingly.

Edward was almost pleading with him. Damien knew Edward's own feelings were compromised where Joanna was concerned. You couldn't be attached and involved in a relationship for as long as the pair had been and avoid it effecting your judgement. He could feel for Edward, though. He was undoubtedly torn since he had watched over Kyle right alongside Alex and Jess since the three friends had been children playing in the veil.

Fix this, Edward. I will not allow this to continue for much longer. Regardless of the cost to Joanna's sanity, Kyle will be granted his freedom.

Damien stared at Edward, allowing his own growing anger at the circumstances to be felt by the other. Edward nodded in acknowledgement.

One thing: we've lost track of Jess. Please tell me she is with you.?

Damien smiled. *Yes, she is my guest at my estate in Ilarith.*

With that piece of information Damien retreated through the veil, heading back to his own domain, still troubled about the situation with Kyle but willing to give Edward more time.

16

EMOTIONS

*J*ess stalked down the wide hallways and checked out many of the rooms in the sprawling estate that Damien called home, yet she could not find her host and mentor anywhere. Looking with her mind's eye, as she'd learned to do, did nothing to help either. Not that it necessarily would, since her encounter with Isabella had shown her that the Elder could shield themselves remarkably well. All that remained to her was walking and searching. As fascinating as the exploration had been, she now found it a little disconcerting to be rattling around in the estate by herself. Not even the local villagers who normally came to help around the estate were in attendance today.

Jess wandered through the empty hallways, finding herself standing at the large arched window, her favourite viewing platform, yet today it failed to settle her agitation and frustration. She laughed, the sound echoing around the room. She was bored. It was a rather perplexing position to be in, and quite unfamiliar to her, to be honest.

In her old life, even trailing along in Elizabeth's entourage, while boring, had at least served a purpose. She could content herself with being on guard for a threat. Right now she would even jump at the opportunity to listen to the inane, mindless chatter of the other ladies.

She gazed down at the village below. Jess frowned at the atypical bustling, wondering what was going on. Then she spotted movement on the road and some tents going up in a large common area towards the centre. As she absently contemplated the scene below, a smile lit her features. The village was hosting a market and it looked like people from other villages were attending.

Jess spun and, lifting her skirts, she ran back towards her rooms. She yanked open the double doors to her wardrobe and scanned the racks of clothes hanging within. A long dark blue cloak caught her attention, hanging to one side with intricate woven designs in silver thread around the borders. She grabbed it off the hook and threw it around her shoulders, fastening the three ornamental clasps at the top. Jess turned to look in the mirror, nodding at her appearance. She'd noticed that while her wardrobe of clothes here had steadily multiplied, there were no hunting clothes. Even her original set she'd arrived in had disappeared. Clara only ever smiled at her and ignored her questions about where they were. Even Damien would only smile, observing she was unlikely to see them until she left, and would then change the subject. She'd given in and stopped asking about them. The last time, Damien had shaken his head at her suggestion he fetch some from her rooms back at the palace. He'd shrugged, saying that while he was capable of doing so, it was likely they would just disappear again. That had prompted a lesson on Ilarith and the locals, and he'd explained that it had nothing to do with her being a woman. Rather, it was what they deemed to be appropriate attire for the Elder. For her to be wandering around in trousers like a commoner was inappropriate by local customs. He'd raised his hands in defence at her outrage, informing her it wasn't *his* view. It was, however, the locals' view.

She'd even gone through her wardrobe looking for plainer dresses. That search had been in vain. Even walking into a high court ball, she would be perfectly attired wearing anything in her current wardrobe.

Pulling the large lined hood up onto her head, Jess smiled, although her face remained hidden in the depths of the hood. If she understood correctly, the locals would know by her attire that she numbered among the ranks of the Kin and Elder. Hopefully they wouldn't know exactly who she was, though. Then again, she'd gathered by now that there were not as many Kin and Elder as she had previously imagined.

When she had asked about this, Damien had smiled a little and observed that long life wasn't suited to everyone and that human nature didn't change because one had great power. When she'd looked at him, a little perplexed, he'd told her blandly that they fought amongst themselves. He'd then reassured her that they were unlikely to test her, since she was under his protection. Jess couldn't decide whether that was arrogance on his part or whether Damien was as powerful as he thought he was. It was very hard to tell. Still, she figured that was in part why her weapons, at least, had not disappeared.

She'd spent considerable time after that checking out her surroundings with a defensive eye. Damien had caught her at it and raised an amused eyebrow, but hadn't told her to desist. Which was just as well, since that was an injunction she wouldn't have followed.

Shrugging off her introspection, Jess grinned. She could explore the village, and was surprised that the idea hadn't occurred to her before now. Then again, she'd been kept busy training, always either trying to perfect what Damien had taught her or throwing herself into new lessons.

Jess pulled the veil around her and moved towards the

village below. Damien had spent considerable time, drilling her on moving safely through the veil. She'd understood her uncle's original injunction against appearing inside the walls of places she didn't know. Now, though, it didn't apply. The increase in her strength came with some advantages. Now appearing where she wanted—unless there was a shield to prevent her—was no hindrance. Still old habits held and she moved herself to a cobbled street after checking no one was standing there just as she'd been trained.

Keeping the folds of the veil around her to obscure her from the untalented eye, Jess looked around as she ghosted though the town, not bringing any notice to herself. The village looked like any number of prosperous villages from home, although she had to admit she'd never lived in one, not even before she'd gone to the palace as a child. Her family's estates had been in a remote setting, yet while nothing compared to the luxury of the palace, it had still been opulent in its own way.

Jess grinned at the children that raced past in a game of tag, as carefully she danced out of the way before chuckling to herself. They may not see her without talent themselves, but they could still run into her. She wasn't ready to make her presence known yet.

The cobbles in the street were well maintained with no sign that they were deteriorating or neglected. Flowers lined the windowsills of the single-storey houses, all nestled up close to each other, with herb and vegetable patches out front. She already knew the livestock were kept on the outskirts of the village. Clara had explained to her they were communal and tended to by the village. The children held the duty to care for the animals in the morning, under the supervision of some of the adults.

The hubbub of noise, laughter, excitement, calling and cheering alerted her she was drawing close to the centre of the village and the market. Hugging close to the wall of what she guessed was the local inn, Jess gave herself a moment to take in the sights and sounds of the bustling excitement of the market. Unlike the inns that she was used to, this one was a small single-storey stone building with a storage shed attached at the back. The building contained a kitchen and tap room just big enough for a few wooden stools along the bar. Instead of being inside, the tables from the inn were spilling out onto the cobblestones in front of the premises, with flaring tarps held up on poles to protect those frequenting the establishment from the elements. At the moment it was a beautiful afternoon without a cloud to mar the blue sky, yet she'd been here long enough to know the clouds could boil up quickly between one moment and the next. Still, she spied extra tarps and screens piled up nearby, and knew it was a circumstance that the locals were well equipped to deal with.

Beyond the inn a raised stage hosted some boisterous musicians who had struck up a popular tune. Adults and children alike danced in groups, bouncing and twirling around energetically in a series of concentric rings in time to the beat. On the other side of the large open commons, they had set stalls up to sell everything one could imagine—bolts of fabric, leather goods, shoes, kitchenware and children's toys. The variety spreading out and taking over that entire corner made her smile. She wondered if they had brought the goods up for trade from one of their regular trade runs to the world outside.

Her gaze tracked to the middle, and sprawling out in the centre were a series of food stalls, some with smoke and steam spilling up into the air. The smells wafting in her direction were mouth-watering.

Jess dropped her concealment and walked out into the bustling market, almost holding her breath as she wondered how the villagers would react. She would hardly blend in, which she would have preferred. Her gown and even the cloak would stand out. She guessed that was the idea.

Jess smiled within the depths of her hood, knowing none could see it. There were some startled glances thrown her way by the locals, although none sought to hinder her. If anything, they cleared out of her way as soon as they noticed her approach, even though not appearing particularly fearful. Some seemed curious, yet left her be.

Jess wandered around the stalls, almost wishing she had money since it would be nice to buy a few small things. She hadn't thought about asking Damien for any. It hadn't occurred to her before now. Back at the palace her money pouch had always been full, seen to by the servants at the orders of her aunt and uncle, she guessed, and then out of the royal coffers when she became a Companion of the Fourth. Still, she was content to look at the wares the traders had on offer and spent what seemed like hours weaving between the close-packed stalls.

She stopped at one stall with fabric. While she was not a clothes horse, some bolts were stunning and drew her eye. Bolts of silk and lace, all of them incredibly fine, dazzled her, and she trailed her fingers along a corner, appreciative of a bolt of patterned blue with white lace. It would make a beautiful dress. Then she paused, aware of the hush that had fallen over the market; like a wave, the once boisterous marketplace silenced. Jess turned, wondering what had happened, and made her way between the stalls. She noticed adults pulling children back, hiding them behind tarps and crates, anything they could find nearby. The sound of childish glee startled her, loud in the eerie quiet of the market. She spun to see a small child running, a panicked-looking woman chasing after him. The child thought it was a wonderful game. Stepping to one side, Jess scooped up the boy as he tried to run past her, passing him off to the worried mother, who bowed before running back between the stalls, hushing the child.

Then Jess sensed what she'd missed. Another with power had arrived, one that the locals didn't seem happy to see. That seemed odd, since none of them had paid her much mind at all. She was certain they had a good idea of exactly who she was, even though it was the first time she'd appeared in the village.

She had just arrived at the edge of the stalls to see a Kin, near the inn, that was the object of everyone's attention.

A middle-aged man stood up from a table out in front of the inn and walked across the square towards the man before stopping.

"You should know this village is under the protection of Elder Damien."

The interloper laughed, an ugly bark. "Your bluster is useless, he's not around right now."

The smile on the face of the spokesman of the village faltered. "You are welcome as long as you're not here to cause harm. Elder Damien will be displeased if you are here to cause trouble."

The man casually pulled in power and with an audible grunt lifted the spokesman into the air, with his feet dangling just above the ground.

"He's not here now and the likes of you can't stop me, little man. You don't have the power." His voice was oily, a sneer marring his features. "He's taken in a stray, and I want him. He's here somewhere, I sensed it when the whelp made the mistake of leaving the safety of the shields around the estate."

The spokesman compressed his lips and looked steadily at the man, although Jess guessed he knew full well she was here.

"Please, just take whatever you wish and leave—" His voice cut off, his hands clawing at his throat as if he were being choked by invisible hands.

Jess's eyes narrowed, and she walked forward, drawing power to her as she did so. She punched it forward as Damien had taught her and smiled as the other grunted and stumbled. It had the desired effect of him losing his hold on the spokesman, who looked at her wide-eyed as he lay sprawled on the ground. As the Elder spun towards her, two other villagers ran from the inn and helped the shaken spokesman back to the rudimentary safety of the inn.

"Enough, leave the villagers be." Jess concentrated on drawing more power to her, closing the gap between her and the man who had inexplicably come for her. "What do you want with me?"

Jess could feel the other's momentary shock at her appearance, then with only a split second warning, she felt him launch an assault in her direction. She deflected the blow and followed up with one of her own, grateful for the hours she'd spent on her shield work with Damien. Taking that as the stranger's answer, Jess wasted no time at all closing the distance between them. Using the veil to push herself forward, she raised her hand, deflecting yet another hammering blow from the man, and drew her sword. She threw a splash of fire at him and he flinched and raised his own hand in reflex to deflect. Without pause she lunged, plunging her sword into the man's abdomen. She knew it wasn't a killing blow, but he reeled in shock, clutching at his stomach. He gathered his power, and she knew he was about to flee into the veiled paths. Jess's eyes narrowed.

The power around her surged, the real world fading as if she was between both worlds. The channels of power filled her, sudden euphoria hit with flickers of raw white power. Bathed in power, she didn't want to let it go; looking at her attacker, she saw him pale as he glanced at her. She grabbed hold of the man with the power of the veil, wrenching him back into the real world and slamming him onto the cobbled ground, his breath expelled from his lungs in a pained grunt.

Jess strode forward, closing the distance between them. Reversing her blade, she slammed the hilt into his skull. His head snapped sideways with a crack, banging into the cobbled street. She looked at him dispassionately, watching as the blood splattered out and pooled on the cobbles, realising she'd perhaps hit him on the head a little harder than she'd intended.

Jess looked up at the frozen villagers, then concentrated to call out into the veil.

Damien, damn it, come back. I need you. She paused, not hearing a hint of a reply, and swore explosively. *Isabella! I need your help. A man attacked the village, he came for me in Damien's absence.*

The response this time was much more prompt. Jess felt the rush in the veil that indicated that someone was incoming. She had a moment to hope it was Isabella and not another who might want to kill her. There was no doubt that was what the man had intended, though his attempt had been clumsy.

She stood, drawing power, her sword raised and ready to strike, yet hoping that it wasn't someone intending her harm. Jess staggered off balance as something unexpected hit her from behind. Sword raised, she spun, blade following her movement as she swung to where she sensed someone behind her. She felt power not her own wrap around her and stood frozen in its grip. Instant panic hit her, and she started to struggle only to find herself spun around and Isabella's hand grasping her shoulders, shaking her.

"Jess, snap out of it! It was only a child running into you. He's no threat."

Jess turned her head and saw the small boy not far from her who stood frozen in fear, his eyes wide, with a thin trail of blood trailing down his neck from her sword. She sagged with relief as Isabella finally released her.

~

JESS SAT in the outdoor area of the inn at a table with Isabella. An assortment of food and drinks had appeared on the table without either of them making any request at all. The spokesman, Head Villager Dean, had been profuse in his thanks for her intervention, and then had promptly scolded her for putting herself at risk for him. Jess had endured his outburst, noting that Isabella was trying not to laugh, and had allowed him to usher her over to the nearest table. He'd scurried off bellowing orders that had resulted in the pile of offerings on the table for them.

Jess eyed the dead man again, flicking her gaze to her other sight once more to check he really was dead and not healing. Some of the villagers were rolling the body into a tarp to dispose of it. It had horrified them when she'd offered to help, and they'd waved her off.

She turned her gaze back to Isabella, who sat observing her.

"No, that one will not rise again."

"Mmm, I guess. Just making sure." Jess eyed the food, then picked up one of the small morsels of cooked meat and bit into it. She caught the juice from the meat on a napkin as the burst of flavour hit her, smiling appreciatively.

"Jess, you can't keep going like this. It's not good for you." Isabella looked at her kindly.

Jess looked at her companion, startled. "Continue like what?"

"As much as the surging emotions along with everything else hurts, you still need to allow yourself to feel, otherwise you'll turn into a cold, hard, psychotic killer." Isabella smiled to take the sting off her words.

"I don't understand what you mean. After dealing with the attack the boy startled me, that's all. I'm sure I wouldn't have killed him." Jess shrugged and brushed off Isabella's concern.

"Never mind, it will come to you, but I warn you it will hurt more." Isabella sighed, and pain flickered across her face. "I know from personal experience."

Jess frowned, a voice in the back of her mind whispering to her that she knew exactly what Isabella meant. It was like something had shut down deep inside since she'd learned of her mother's ultimate betrayal and she'd killed her. Jess shied away from the thoughts, deciding to change the subject. "I still don't understand why that one wanted to kill me." Jess nibbled at the edge of a sharp piece of cheese. Surprised, she smiled and picked up a piece of the sliced, toasted bread to add to it.

"It's not personal, Jess." Isabella grinned at her and after a moment's thought picked up a sliced piece of red fruit.

Jess felt her eyebrows rise. "He tried to kill me. Admittedly he wasn't very good, but when someone tries to kill you, I think it's a little personal."

Isabella's grin widened. "There are some who believe any addition to the ranks of the Kin and Elder dilutes their influence and power. He probably thought he could take you out while Damien was away."

"But how did he know I was here?" Jess winced at the grumbling tone in her voice and sighed, exasperated with herself. It wasn't like this was the first time someone had tried to kill her.

Isabella shrugged. "He probably didn't until you came out from the protection of Damien's estate."

Jess groaned at her own stupidity. She'd known that Damien's estate had extra protections, and unlike Isabella and Damien she still hadn't learnt the trick to fully shield herself from the other sight of her own kind.

"I'm an idiot."

Isabella laughed and sipped the last of her drink, her eyes narrowed as she observed her.

"Come, I think it's time for you to return to the estate. I'll wait with you until Damien returns. Your shields are erratic."

Jess smiled uncertainly, not understanding what Isabella meant, but stood anyway. She could admit she was still unsettled by the attack, that was probably why she'd nearly killed the boy. Jess sighed at the evidence that her emotions were getting her into trouble again and she ruthlessly pushed them down.

17

MEETINGS

*W*illiam tried very hard not to roll his eyes as the Lord Kastler trailed after him, wringing his hands and babbling about his fears regarding the Sundered. He wondered when the man would get to the point. Or if he even had one.

"Lord Kyle's accusations against the Order were preposterous! You need to convince the king he's a risk to us all. He should be stripped of the protection of his rank. He's obviously one of the Sundered now. The Order is right with their concerns." Lord Kastler halted as he realised William had stopped, a frown creasing his forehead as he looked back.

William's eyes narrowed, he closed the distance between him and the lord, whose eyes widened in panic. "Lord Kyle did his duty to the Fourth and the Crown. His loyalty is not in doubt. Be very careful of the accusations you make, Kastler."

William turned from the lord, making a conscious effort to release his grip on his sword. He signalled the Elite, who interposed themselves between him and Lord Kastler, preventing the man from following him further.

Recognising that his response to the lord had not been very

conducive to the meeting he was about to walk into, William attempted to calm down as he approached the meeting room. The doormen, seeing his approach, opened the doors, and William didn't fail to notice they exchanged glances as he passed them. They had undoubtedly witnessed the exchange just down the hallway. Thankfully, the personal staff who worked closest to members of the royal family were discrete. While William was sure they gossiped amongst each other, they spread nothing to the wider population of the palace. If they were found spreading gossip of what they saw and heard about the members of the royal family, they would lose their jobs. The fact that all of them received better rooms, pay and conditions than the rest of the staff helped maintain their loyalty.

William walked across the room aware that everyone was watching him; with an effort he tried to contain the irritation Lord Kastler had caused. The only bright side he could think of was that his official day was nearly over. Ignoring the blank looks of those in the room, indicating they had picked up on his anger despite his best efforts, William took his seat. He gathered his exchange with the lord outside in the corridor had been loud enough for those inside the room to hear it.

"Report. Have you found him yet?" Even to his own ears his voice sounded terse. He cocked his head to one side as Marcus grinned.

"Yes, Your Highness. The guard report we've found him, or at least a place he keeps going back to." This grin was Marcus's first since Alex had gone missing.

William felt relief wash over him. "Where is he? Is he safe?"

Marcus nodded. "He keeps going back to a small inn, The Last Stop. It's in Amberbreak, a trade town on the tri-border in the east. Reports suggest he appears to be fine but is mostly keeping to himself."

William felt himself relax. Finally he'd have something

positive to report to his father; it had been rather depressing in his daily briefings until now.

"Do the locals know who he is?"

Marcus nodded. "The report suggests that they may, Your Highness. They say the villagers seem awfully protective and reticent. The innkeeper nearly threw them out when they asked after Alex."

William couldn't help but smile at the image that provoked. He shook his head. He wasn't sure how Alex seemed to make himself welcome and accepted in bars amongst the commoners no matter how disreputable the places might be.

"Please tell me the inn isn't populated with the more unsavoury members of our community."

"No, Your Highness. I'm told it is quite respectable." Marcus's lips twitched, even though his tone was respectful, as always.

William sat back, relaxing in his chair, and thought through the options. He knew Alex. If he tried to put too much pressure on him, Alex would resist and move elsewhere, and the elsewhere may not be as pleasant.

"Send a protection detail. Strictly hands off unless needed or Alex requests help. Get money off the chamberlain, and instruct the Elite you send to make sure the innkeeper is well paid for a room and full board. Get the chest Joshua prepared and make sure it goes into Alex's room at the inn." William paused in his rapid-fire instructions, fixing Marcus with his gaze. "You and James will stay put here at the palace, Marcus."

A fleeting look of disappointment flickered across Marcus's face but he was too well trained to object.

"Yes, Your Highness."

William shifted his glance from Marcus to the Captain of the Guard, nodded and stood.

"Thank you for your work, gentlemen. The king appreciates

your efforts." William paused as he walked towards the door, looking back at them. "I appreciate your efforts."

William left the meeting room, grateful it was at the end of the royal wing so he didn't have far to go to get back to his own suite. It had been a long, eventful day, but at least he'd had good news that they had found Alex alive and well. That had lifted a weight off his shoulders.

He waved off the household staff and opened his own door. Closing the door behind him, he had stripped his vest off before noticing a rhythmic slapping noise, and he froze. He looked up, his attention drawn to the couch and the spinning knife that slapped into the hand of the person sitting in it.

THE DAGGER SLAPPED into Alex's palm as he sat waiting. Having lived in the palace his whole life, appearing here from the veil hadn't been difficult. He knew these rooms in the palace almost as well as he did his own. Better, actually, since he'd spent more time in these rooms than he had in his rooms at the Complex of the Fourth. Moving back into the complex was something he'd toyed with and discarded many times over. He wasn't ready yet. If he was honest with himself, he wasn't sure he wouldn't kill everyone. Restraining his temper, his increasing powers, was not an easy proposition. Although he didn't think he'd kill William. Alex tossed his blade again, catching it as it slapped into his palm.

The door to the room opened and his brother walked in. He was halfway across the room, stripping off his formal vest, before he stopped in his tracks, suddenly aware that he had a visitor. Alex smiled at William's obvious shock and reaction to his presence.

"Hello, brother. It's all right, I won't kill you. Or at least I don't think I will." Alex waited, impatient as his brother stood, still frozen.

Alex felt his anger rise and let it build. He was still confident he wouldn't lose control. At least, he wouldn't lose his temper with William. Alex smiled as William decided, dropping his vest on a nearby chair. He watched as his brother walked over to the drink counter and poured two drinks in tumblers. Placing the stopper back in the bottle, William picked up the glasses, handing one to Alex.

Alex sipped the drink, savouring the strong, smooth liquor. It was much better than he had been drinking of late, bringing back strong memories of better times.

William sat down in the chair next to him, regarding him for a moment. Alex returned the gaze. His older brother looked well but tired; it was likely that he himself was the cause of some of that stress. He knew they looked much alike, both inheriting their father's height and broad shoulders. He smiled. He knew he had more muscle on his frame than his older brother, courtesy of William spending more time sitting down in council meetings while Alex trained. That and constantly using the veil burned energy, managing to strip all the spare flesh from him. All of them—including his sister, he now realised, since he'd recently come face to face with their mother —had inherited their dark brown hair and blue eyes from her.

"How have you been?"

Alex laughed, closing his eyes, the bitterness clear in his tone. "I've been better. How much did you know, William?"

"That's a broad question, Alex. How much did I know about what?"

An instant hot flush of anger ran through Alex.

"Don't play games, William. How long did you know our dear brother was trying to kill me? The Killiam Order, Kin and Elder. How much do you know?" Alex took a deep, settling breath, feeling anger roll over him, as it often did.

Transition—such a simple word, yet its effects were dramatic, hard for normal people to understand. His access to the veil, or perhaps just his ability to use it, had increased. It pulsed and thrummed through him, different power lines swirling around him. That was a change he could track back to that first major attack on his party as they'd ridden between the Winter and Summer Palace. He'd drawn so much power he'd burned out his mind and nearly killed himself. That moment had heralded the start of the disintegration of his life. Or, more rightly, the kidnapping attempted that had preceded that moment, but it had been that attack that had been the start of his powers increasing and getting out of control.

Alex steered himself away from this dangerous train of thoughts. Thinking about that time and all the people he'd killed, even in his own defence, triggered a burst of memories which made him shut down. The cycle of madness then continued.

William sat, not saying anything. He waited for Alex to regain control. If anything, that told Alex he was correct. His big brother was not shocked. He'd known more than he'd ever let on. Whether he had known before or after Alex had broken was another matter. William spoke, his assured, familiar voice causing Alex's mind to settle and calm.

"Daniel always had an issue with the Sundered, and so with you. He sided with the Killiam Order when he was young, under the influence of Scholar Clements. Please believe me, Alex, neither I nor father were aware he'd joined the Order." William closed his eyes, pain flashed across his face before he took a breath and steadied himself. "We would have stopped him if we'd known. You were the one who killed him?"

Alex smiled, yet there was no humour in it, the flicking memories of those last few days at the palace playing across his mind's eye. The events had left him feeling betrayed. It had been an inescapable realisation that his father and brother had known far more than they had ever let on to him. They had kept him in the dark, not trusting him or how he would react.

"Yes. How could I ask anyone else to? You realise the Order was behind the assault on Mother?" Anger flared through him again, as it always did when he thought about Daniel's actions and his mother. He closed his eyes, battling to stay on that tightrope of emotion without falling off either side.

Once again silence stretched between them as William gave him time to battle his demons. Alex heard the cork come out of a bottle, the flow of liquid into his glass. He waited, hearing the creak of the leather seat as his brother settled near him again and opened his eyes, taking a sip, savouring the taste as it slid down his throat.

"Only when Kyle accused the late Lord Vannen in court. The man had enough time to confirm his involvement before he begged forgiveness. Kyle snapped his neck for treason." William watched Alex and, assessing he was calm enough, continued. "We did not know about the Order's involvement in Mother's death. It was attributed to the actions of the Sundered because of your testimony. As unbelievable as some found it, your account was verified by Aaron when he arrived at the palace to take up his post. There was evidence of other involvement, with the arrow wounds, and the guards scoured the countryside. Other than clearing out some unsavoury types, the search achieved nothing that pointed back to involvement in Mother's death. We are still uncertain how they managed it, but we accept your word."

Alex shook his head, took another sip and contemplated what William had said for a moment. He almost whimpered as power surged through him again. He took a shuddering breath; his hand shook.

"Kyle and Jess confirmed other involvement when I showed them what happened from my memories. The Skull Lord, Simon, one of the Kin, is one of Great Uncle Edward's contemporaries. He denies they were involved. The involvement of the League of Skulls never made sense. Jess followed Daniel to one of the Order's meetings. He engaged with the other conspirators about their plans and came away with more of the toxin, and with a promise to dose us all again so they could attempt to take us again." Taking a deep breath, Alex opened his eyes. "She overheard them admit to getting away with having a hand in the attack on Mother. They kept that piece of information from Daniel."

"I wish we'd realised sooner. Things might have been different."

"You know more about the Kin, Elder and me than you have ever let on." That last was a statement rather than a question; he could tell by William's reactions he was aware of a great deal more than the average person. When he thought about it, it was not surprising, yet it still hurt that they had cut him adrift, left him to muddle through on his own.

"Records have been kept in the locked Royal Archives for generations. I'm sorry, Alex." The last was said softly.

Alex finished his drink in silence and placed it on the low table beside him. He looked at his brother, then nodded.

"In hindsight, we should have told you more. Father thought you were under enough pressure and didn't want you worried." William didn't look all that sorry, not that Alex really expected him to be. As the heir to the crown, there were many matters that he knew and kept his own counsel on. It was expected; their father took William into his confidence on most issues of state. He had been doing so increasingly for years now.

Alex sat for a moment, staring off to the far side of the room trying to gather his scattered thoughts. "Great Uncle Edward, as in, the one that I can blame for that ridiculous legend of the Fourth? He's not dead. Neither are Lord Callum Barraclough or Lady Leanna Katrina Shaddin."

Alex found it was his turn to smile as the small plate of food William was holding hit the floor. Clearly, while his brother knew a great many things, that had not been one of them. It was nice some things could still shock him.

"What do you mean, not dead?" It was clear that William, usually so quick on the uptake, was struggling to understand.

"The usual meaning of not dead, William. They never died. I was a little disconcerted when I worked it out myself." Alex felt his lips press together. "That little deceit is something I intend to discuss with them next time I run into them."

"Alex, they lived generations ago." The concern in William's voice was clear. Alex didn't know if he was amused or irritated by William's disbelief.

"I know that, William. Imagine my surprise—and Kyle's and Jess's—when our dearly departed ancestors kept showing up to talk to us and give some basic instructions on the veil." Alex paused, observing his brother. "William, you already know that the Kin and Elder exist, yet you are struggling with Uncle Edward and his friends being alive and among their number?"

William opened his mouth, then closed it again, laughing weakly. "You have a point. I didn't say I am consistent. They're immortal? *You* are immortal?"

Alex couldn't help the laughter that erupted from him. "I'm sorry, William, you should know better than most that those with power can die. You know I've killed enough of the Sundered. Let's just stick with the potential to live longer than most, with the ability to possess great power."

They sat for the longest time in silence while William processed the information he'd just been given. Finally, William stirred again.

"You never mentioned it before, none of you did." The accusation in his tone was clear.

"If our situations were reversed, would you have admitted that to me?"

"Of course, I—" William rubbed one hand over his face. "Sorry, you're right, I probably wouldn't have."

"If the healers had found out, I would have been medicated until I was insensible. Besides, I was worried for some time that it was a sign I was going mad. That all of us were. I only worked out that they weren't actually dead right before things got messy." Alex's expression closed down a little as he thought back. "Transition—they call it transition. It hit, William... you have no idea. I could access power before, but it was nothing compared to the power I can reach and use now. The power levels surged. There are times where I black out... I think it's just too much, and my brain just shuts down."

William's voice was soft. "The ancient ones couldn't help you?"

Alex smiled as William shied away from using Uncle Edward's name.

"I really don't know. I was a little preoccupied the last time I saw him. I needed to get some control and calm down first," Alex admitted candidly.

"Understandable, I guess. In your shoes, I'm not sure I'd be terribly happy." William grinned, the mood in the room lifting.

"Believe me, given the circumstances, that is an understatement." Alex pushed the memory of the last time he saw Edward firmly to one side. He looked back to William to find his brother watching him.

"You haven't asked about Amelia." William's voice was quiet.

Alex winced. Before his transition, Amelia had been the only thing he could think of, she'd become his whole world. Since their enforced separation when he'd fled the palace after killing Daniel, it was like all the feelings he'd had for her had disappeared. If anything, when he thought of Amelia he'd reverted to thinking of her with the affection as if for a little sister. The realisation caused him guilt and embarrassment now, since unbidden the images of their time together flashed in his head. He'd thought he was in love with her and their relationship had certainly not been platonic. He was under no illusion about his growing attraction for Isabella, so this change wasn't just a side effect of going through transition. None of this was a confession he wanted to make to his big brother right now. Or rather, the crown prince, since the whole circumstance had potential political mess written all over it.

"How is Amelia?" Alex did his best to smile as if nothing was wrong. The way William looked at him, he wasn't certain he pulled it off.

"She misses you. You should come back, Alex."

"No. I... can't. Not yet. I still have too many periods where I black out, it's too dangerous until I'm back in my headspace all the time." Alex heard the hesitation in his own voice and stood up, knowing it was time to leave.

"Look after yourself, Alex. You are welcome back home anytime." William stood and walked across to the sideboard, withdrawing a heavy-looking money pouch from a drawer. He threw it at Alex, smiling as he adroitly snatched it out of the air. "I'll make sure the supply is checked regularly and replenished. Take it when you have need."

Alex paused and closed his eyes before looking back at his brother. William had always supported him. Still, it was too soon to speak of the things he had done, even if William guessed a great deal of what he was going through.

"I'm tracking the other Sundered, when I can. There is something odd about many of them, things that make little sense."

Alex contemplated the other pressing issue that weighed on him. Kyle and William had always been close and, if he could break away from his new mistress, it was likely that he would show up here. William had the uncanny ability to fix all kinds of unusual problems.

"Be careful, William. Kyle is... well, compromised. He is bound to another as he was with Alyssa. I doubt he'll show up here, but do not try to separate him from his mistress. She is not as psychotic as Alyssa was, but she will not take interference well." Alex tried to hide his concern, yet he had to warn his brother.

He didn't wait for a reply, simply pulling in the veil and disappearing down the paths he was now as familiar with using as breathing. He didn't have to think or concentrate on travel within the veil anymore, he just did it. Still, it was on his list to analyse the process one day to see what he was doing. Right now it was not a high priority.

18

RYAN'S BENEFACTOR

*M*arcus grimaced as he watched the men bumble their way through the new drills; attempting to use the veil was distracting them all. Even knowing they would do better with consistent practice, he still found it frustrating.

"Matthew, enough. You already have those drills down, so I have a task for you." Marcus kept his focus on the training grounds

"Captain?" Matthew sheathed his sword as he walked towards him.

"There's a boy, Ryan, that his Highness Prince Alex left with the healers. They tell me he is ready to be released from the medical wing." Marcus turned his focus to Matthew. "Go fetch him and put him in a room in the empty barracks we just had cleaned out. Then see that he gets to the scholars' training rooms, they are expecting him."

Matthew raised his eyebrow, grinning. "Sure, Marcus. Do you want me to see he gets outfitted? I take it since he is staying with us he'll be doing blade work as well?"

Marcus grinned. That was one of the traits he liked about Matthew: he was quick on the uptake.

"Joshua has organised the lad's wardrobe, but yes, blades if he doesn't have any. He'll do blade work with us and some rudimentary training in control and use of the veil. According to His Highness and the healers, the lad has power. Make sure he settles in this week and can find everything he needs here in the palace." Marcus waved a hand in dismissal as Matthew snapped a salute and turned, heading off to attend to the tasks he'd been given.

RYAN SAT on the edge of his cot, his hand running nervously over his new vest and shirt. The new clothes had just appeared this morning, and his old clothes were nowhere to be found. The old healer, Aaron, assured him that everything had been settled and he didn't need to worry. Of course, that didn't stop him from worrying. He may have come from an incompetent failed merchant family, but even he could tell the fabric was of much finer quality than he'd ever worn.

His mind turned to his unexpected benefactor and who he could possibly be. This room with its stark white utilitarian walls and no windows didn't help at all; it was a small utilitarian room without much more than his sleeping cot. Whenever he'd asked the healer who the man was, he had just smiled and ignored the question. This morning he'd been told he was being released and that he should wait, someone would be by to pick him up.

Ryan looked up expectantly as the door to his small bare room opened. A young man stood there, one who looked a few years older than he was, yet they couldn't be more different. Ryan swallowed. His visitor was wearing a uniform that bore what he was sure was one of the royal crests. He just didn't know which one.

"Ryan? I'm Matthew. Come on, I've been ordered to show

you to your room and then to the scholars' classes. You'll be late for today's lessons, but that certainly isn't your fault." Matthew stood aside, smiling encouragingly.

"Thank you, Matthew." Ryan stood and followed Matthew. Looking around a little wide-eyed, he realised he'd been in a private room off a larger room that had a long line of cots spaced down the wall.

Matthew glanced at him. "Don't worry, you'll be fine. It won't take you long to learn your way around."

"Where is here?" Ryan swallowed, hoping that Matthew wouldn't think him strange for not knowing.

Only the raising of his guide's eyebrows gave away his surprise at the question.

"You're in the Summer Palace in Callenhain."

Ryan stopped in astonishment, staring at Matthew, trying to work out if he was kidding, yet he couldn't think of a reason why Matthew would lie about something like that.

He swallowed nervously. "Who is he? The man who brought me here?"

A slow grin spread on Matthew's lips. "I believe it was His Highness, Prince Alexander."

Ryan felt sure he'd gone pale, his mind repeating the name of the man who'd saved him in his head over and over again. Ryan realised he'd been correct about the crest on Matthew's uniform. He wasn't just any kind of ordinary guard. He was one of the Elite.

"He's the youngest son of the king, why would he save my life? I'm nobody." Ryan was incredulous, continuing along the hallway as Matthew placed a hand on his back to gently guide him forward.

"His Highness obviously doesn't think so. Come on, the barracks isn't far." Matthew continued to lead him through the palace, pointing out things of interest along the way.

Ryan, for his own part, barely paid attention, his mind still grappling with the knowledge that the dangerous man in the cloak had been Prince Alexander. His eyes widened as he realised that Tyron had tried to rob the prince. Not that he'd known who the man in the cloak had been; he'd just wanted the money he was sure his mark was carrying.

RYAN PACKED up his lesson book and pen from the table at the end of the day's lessons. His life had settled into a routine here in the palace, although his head still spun when he thought about the changes in his life. He had a small room to himself in what he'd learned was the barracks of the Fourth's Elite. It was just big enough for a small bed, a desk and wardrobe. The wardrobe had been filled with clothes—they'd just appeared— all of such fine quality he knew he'd never be able to afford to buy them.

He had lessons with the scholar a couple of days a week, and he was doing much better with his lessons with the scholar than his other classes. To his amazement, he was being drilled in sword work, including practice with the use of the veil. He'd been shocked to discover all of the Elite used the veil, and even more stunned to learn he was much better with the use of the power—once he started practising—than he was with a sword. It had been hard to go from hiding what he was and could do to openly practising. Well, openly at least in the company of the Elite. It was strange for him to think there was something he could do that others could possibly value.

Walking from the room, he felt himself jostled and stumbled into the wall, looking up to laughter as some of his class-mates sailed past him.

"Careful, orphan boy! I doubt you can afford to pay for my clothes if you damage them." Branton sneered at him as he passed, his friends clapping him on the back and laughing.

Ryan looked up as some of the girls swept past him, sniffing in disdain and laughing outright at Branton's quip.

"Don't get too comfortable here, boy. I've told my father that we have a peasant boy in our classes. You won't be here long." Kelly flipped her hair over her shoulder, her skirts rustling as she went back to ignoring him.

He'd learnt that those he shared classes with were the sons and daughters of the peers of the realm. They'd found out he didn't share their lofty heights quickly and had set about trying to make his life miserable. Ryan had chosen to ignore them all. He didn't know how long he would be allowed to take these lessons here in the palace, but he was determined to make the most of it. Little did they know their sniping had little impact on him. He had a roof over his head, as much food as he wanted to eat, he had lessons with the scholar and learning a valuable skill training with swordsmen that were counted among the best.

Ryan straightened his shoulders and nodded. He wouldn't let them distract him. He had a goal in mind, but to get to it, he knew he'd have to work as hard as he could to prove himself worthy.

19

FAMILY TRAIT

*A*melia ran through the garden, fleeing back to the only thing a part of her mind perceived as safety. She looked around as she ran, the colours in the garden merging from a washed-out grey to the colours she knew and back again. She sobbed as a greyed-out figure rose in front of her, on his knees, his head flung back and mouth open wide, screaming out.

No, what have I done!

The voice reverberated in her mind, along with a ricochet of other voices one after the other, their grey washed-out bodies appearing before her as she ran.

Blood, no! It can't be true.

Please, please help me!

One after the other the spectres appeared and their whispering voices merged over the top of each other, rising to an overwhelming crescendo. Her hands rose to her temples and she sobbed, her head shaking from side to side trying to negate what she was seeing and hearing.

She stumbled as she ran, falling to the ground, where she

curled into a ball and screamed as the voices rose in intensity, drowning her in their pleas and madness.

Then hands picked her up and she struggled and screamed, still lost in the greyed-out world. The voices ringing in her head and those belonging to the hands that picked her up merged, causing more pain and confusion. Amelia couldn't tell the difference between what was real and what wasn't. Strong hands carried her, held her and didn't let her go; they carried her through the garden and into the house. All the way voices screamed in her head, merging with the voices urging her to calm down.

Amelia was passed from one person to another. She recognised the second person as her nanny, Kate. While that calmed her a little, the screaming voices in the grey world flickering in and out continued to upset her, and she didn't understand what was happening.

Then, as suddenly as it had begun, it stopped. The cool voice entered her mind, and this time she recognised the owner of that voice. It was one of the healers here at the estate, Healer Bates.

It's okay, Amelia, I'm here. Healer Bates reached forward and brushed a tear from Amelia's eye. The healer held a beaker to Amelia's mouth and Healer Bates's voice said in her head, *Here, drink this, it will make you better.*

The sweetness of the medication didn't quite hide the bitterness underneath, yet Amelia drank it because she knew from experience she would get in trouble if she didn't. She felt herself drifting off to sleep as Kate tucked her into bed. She could hear the adults talking but didn't quite know what it all meant.

"She's tainted just like her brother, isn't she, Healer?"

"Yes, she is. It's all right, though, this medication should help her. She is young enough that it should work. She will need to have to have it on a regular basis. I'll leave the bottle with you along with instructions." The healer's voice was calm and soothing, and as she drifted off to sleep, Amelia heard the clink of bottles being put in the cupboard, the drone of the adult voices continuing as she fell asleep.

~

AMELIA'S EYES FLARED OPEN, a scream on her lips that she managed to muffle. She sat up in bed, looking around and trying to get her breathing under control. Relief washed over her as she realised she was in her room in the Fourth's Complex. Emotion welled up in her as she realised the world still looked how it should. Her hands trembled as she grabbed one of her pillows and, pressing it against her face, she sobbed. She hadn't had the old childhood nightmare for a long time, yet it still had the ability to terrify her—as did the whispering voices that had intruded on her mind again.

"Alex, where are you? I can't do this alone." Overwhelming loneliness welled up in her, tears trailing down her cheeks. The pillow muffled any sound that escaped her lips.

Climbing from the bed, Amelia crossed over to the windows and drew the curtains open to reveal the garden beyond. Walking back to one of the comfortable chairs, she curled up in it, her feet tucked up on the chair. She leaned against the armrest, pillow still clasped in her arms. Amelia let her mind wander. It was almost hypnotic watching as the early dawn light lit up the garden. She felt her muscles relax as the early morning calmness and beauty of the gardens soothed her.

~

AMELIA WALKED through the garden with Elizabeth, a gaggle of ladies following in their wake a discreet distance behind. To all outward appearances, she knew she looked calm and in control. She was dressed immaculately, her black hair piled on top of her head with a small curl running down the side of her face, the necklace of the Consort Elect around her neck and the bracelet, as always, around her wrist. Both declared her rank as the Consort Elect of the Fourth to everybody—not that anybody here at the palace would ever forget who she was. Yet she moved as if in a dream world; she spoke, smiled and made conversation, but she felt removed, as if she wasn't there. There was another version of herself looking out from her eyes, colder and harder than she had ever been. At times she felt she was just a passenger in her own body.

Even though Alex wasn't here, hadn't been here at the palace in months, she was still the Consort Elect of the Fourth. Life went on, as those around her seemed to ignore the fact that Alex was gone, along with Kyle, and Jess. It was as if everybody avoided the subject, thinking she was made of spun glass and would break at the mention of Alex's name. The thought made her laugh. They weren't far from the truth, although not for the reasons they might think. Yet William, Elizabeth, and even the king behaved as if they expected he would be back. It was only a matter of time. Amelia didn't know whether to have hope or to scream at them. She knew Alex had Sundered. Still, she couldn't help but have hope. She had to believe Alex would be back, because to think otherwise would drive her mad.

She was jolted out of introspection as Elizabeth spoke.

"How are you coping without Alex?" Elizabeth voice was low as she glanced across at Amelia.

"I... I don't know." Amelia thought of all the things she could say and discarded them all. If Elizabeth knew how much her world was falling apart, she knew she'd end up in the healers' hands.

With their father being the main advisor and friend to the king, Kyle had spent most of his life from early childhood in the palace, companion to Alex. Unlike her brother, Amelia had spent most of her life in the family estates with her mother. She had visited the palace, of course, yet her life growing up had been very insulated. That was something she was only just learning. Her brother's words warning her of the life she was entering came back to her. It made her laugh to think she did not understand what life as the Consort Elect of the Fourth would be like.

Since she had fallen into Alex's world, she hadn't been home. Her life had been one unending string of commitments to balls, dinners, parties. If you'd asked her before she'd entered this world, she would have told you it was what she wanted. It sounded like an amazing life; it was a goal she'd kept in her sight her whole life. Now she was living it, the centre of attention, always watched no matter where she went or what she did. The only moments she could ever be alone was in her bedroom, and even there she had to order the servants to stay out when she wanted time alone. Even here, on a simple walk in the garden, the ladies in attendance watched and listened avidly, the Elite trailing and always watching not only her and Elizabeth but everyone around, constantly looking for a threat. She realised what Elizabeth must have been going through her entire life.

"I'm sorry, Elizabeth." Amelia's eyes flicked to one side before tracking back to the woman who was becoming the grounding of her current existence.

Elizabeth smiled, hugging her closer. "For what?"

Amelia smiled bitterly. "For not understanding."

She stopped herself from squirming as Elizabeth regarded her, then released the breath she'd been holding as she saw the smile spread on her lips.

"You need not apologise, Amelia. I don't know any different. Neither does Alex." Elizabeth bit her lip, glancing at her. "Or Kyle. He's grown up in our world. Don't regret that you didn't."

"I don't know how you do it. You always seem busy, never having time to yourself." Amelia smiled.

Amelia thought about telling Elizabeth what was happening, that her mind was disintegrating, piece by piece. Then she discarded the idea. She didn't want to add a further burden for Elizabeth; she bore enough worry already. Hearing the cluster of ladies that trailed behind them gossip amongst themselves, Amelia thought about the rumours she'd heard regarding Alex. She grimaced. Some of the ladies had been only too pleased to pass on that particular piece of gossip onto her.

"I've heard about Alex." Amelia glanced at Elizabeth, yet her face didn't betray anything that she might be thinking.

"He's shown up a time or two, talked with William. He's not ready to come back yet." Elizabeth's face was neutral.

Amelia shook her head. "I've heard about the woman."

This time she noticed that the inane chatter of the trailing ladies halted. Elizabeth turned to gaze at her, the hand on her arm stopping their progress through the garden. Amelia allowed Elizabeth to draw her into an embrace and, despite herself, drew comfort from it.

"I'm sorry, Amelia. Alex is my brother, I love him dearly. Yet he's —"

Despite the situation, Amelia chuckled, surprised that she wasn't as hurt as she thought she should be. This was one occasion her brain being insulated by a fog was helpful.

"I've always known what Alex is, Elizabeth, even though I didn't spend as much time here in the palace as Kyle. The pair of them have a reputation. I'm not angry, although it would have been nice if the madly-in-love part had lasted longer. Alex and I had an agreement. Although I would have preferred it better if he'd been a bit more discreet in his liaison with another woman."

Elizabeth drew back and looked at her for a long moment

before looping her arm through Amelia's and recommencing their stroll through the garden.

"Isabella. The reports suggest the woman's name is Isabella." Elizabeth paused as Amelia laughed.

"I don't care what her name is. She's a beauty, I'm told, and that Alex spends all his time with her. That he's sleeping with her." Amelia smiled, her own reaction perplexing her. She realised that she genuinely didn't care that Alex had taken another woman to his bed.

This gave her pause. There it was again, evidence of this other woman she didn't know that well peering out from her own eyes, making herself at home in her head. Amelia wondered if this cold version of herself meant she was growing up.

Elizabeth shook her head. "We've heard, but haven't spoken to Alex about it." She took a breath and looked at Amelia, clearly judging her mood. "Yes, and we've heard those reports as well."

Amelia closed her eyes and breathed in the sweet aroma of the roses in full bloom—her favourite flower of all those in the garden beds—as her hair ruffled in the soft warm breeze. It was soothing.

"My lady mother warned me his infatuation with me might fade. That we'd have to find a way to make it work. There are worse fates than a political union with the Fourth." Amelia smiled sadly and took a settling breath. Despite her words, she still wished for a moment that she could go back to that time where she and Alex had been happy.

"Political unions between high-ranking families go with the rank, unless we are exceedingly lucky."

"Does he intend to break our proposed union?" Despite everything, she cared for Alex, that she was certain of, and it was a good thing in a union like theirs.

"I don't believe so, Amelia." Elizabeth's voice was low and

calm as if they were discussing the evening's dinner. Of course Elizabeth faced a similar union of her own, a political one, as did William. It was the life they had all been born to.

Amelia smiled faintly. "If he could manage to be a little more discreet in his liaisons in the future, it would be better." She glanced across at Elizabeth.

Amelia waited until Elizabeth nodded understanding before turning her gaze back to the well-manicured gardens. She breathed in the scent of the flowers, trying to settle the agitation caused by the conversation. She had no doubt that the message would be passed on to Alex when he next paid a visit to William.

OUT OF THE corner of her eye, Amelia saw the world flicker. She almost groaned and had a hard time suppressing her terror as the world merged between the world she knew and a washed-out grey. She remembered this from childhood, yet the medication her family healer had given her had kept it under control. Until now, she'd been at the palace so long her own supply of her medication had run out. Lately, she heard the voices again—the screaming, pleading voices of people who weren't there. The world flickered and merged between what she knew and the washed-out, colourless place she remembered from childhood. A place that terrified her. Yet she hadn't dared to tell anyone, not even the healers now responsible for her welfare here in the palace. If only her old healer back at the family estates was here, she knew Bates could help her.

Amelia smiled and nodded at a comment from Elizabeth, hoping her reaction was the correct one. She had been too distracted by the screaming in her head and the world fading from her sight to hear what Elizabeth had said. Since Elizabeth smiled and they kept walking at a steady pace through the garden, Amelia guessed her response had been correct.

Amelia concentrated on trying not to let her inner turmoil show. She had toyed with the idea of requesting Aaron, the healer who had attended Alex, Kyle and Jess, for help. Yet she didn't trust the palace healers after what had happened. Amelia wished she could be sure it wasn't the care of the healers here at the palace that had driven Alex mad. Whispering voices clamoured in her mind, yet none of them was her own. Amelia only realised she'd come to a stop when Elizabeth's words hit her.

"Amelia, what's wrong? You've gone pale." Elizabeth looked at her, concern written on her face, still standing with her arm wrapped around her shoulder.

"I'm sorry, Elizabeth, I'm fine. I think I need to rest. This fuss about Alex... I haven't been getting much sleep of late." Amelia smiled at Elizabeth but knew that it wasn't very believable.

"It must be hard. Give it time, things with Alex will sort themselves out." Elizabeth smiled, her understanding and sympathy making Amelia feel guilty that she'd lied. "Come, let's get you back to your rooms. You should try to get some rest. Don't come to dinner tonight, take the night off. I'll explain to Father."

Amelia nodded, placing her hand on Elizabeth's and noticing the tremble in her hand. She hoped that the trembling was due to exhaustion. They turned without a further word and walked back towards the Compound of the Fourth.

AMELIA CURLED up on the bed, her hands pressed against her temples, body shaking. She kept her eyes firmly closed so she couldn't see the room around her flickering between the world it should be and the horrible washed-out grey world. The tremors and feeling so sick were new. Amelia had barely been ill in her life and didn't know how to cope now that she seemed to be. It was like her life had been turned upside down since Alex had left, resulting in a downward spiral that she couldn't halt, and now even her own body was betraying her. As the whispering voices increased in tempo, Amelia moaned.

"Leave me alone, please leave me alone," she whispered, tears trailing down her cheeks.

This, she knew, was what it felt like to start going mad. She had thought, after all these years, that she had missed out on the burden of the Taint that her brother bore. Now she knew that she had been wrong. Unlike her brother, who had suffered from it most of his life, for her there had been only those few occasions. Her memories from childhood came rushing back to her. This is what it had felt like as a child, worse than what she remembered. As a child, she had been confused, not knowing what was happening to her, yet now she knew it was the Taint. However, of all the things that Kyle had told her, that Alex had told her to expect with the Taint, they had never mentioned feeling sick, wrong. Amelia rolled onto her side, grabbing the bowl she'd put next on the bed next to her as a contingency, unable to stop herself from being sick. Sweat broke out on her body as the tremors shook her, and she moaned as a stabbing pain shattered her concentration. She felt herself heaving again, and was glad she'd thought to get the bowl before she had collapsed into bed.

The only thing Amelia had to be grateful for was that she wasn't expected at court tonight. She also doubted that the servants would disturb her; instructions left that she needed to sleep before she had retired to the inner chambers should take care of the inconvenience. That was something to be thankful to Elizabeth for. Amelia was sure that Elizabeth had reinforced the orders that she wasn't to be bothered. Still, lying there in her misery, Amelia only hoped that she would have regained her composure by tomorrow.

Amelia shoved the bowl she been clutching onto her bed's side stand before falling back into the pillows. Even though her stomach still felt queasy, she doubted there was anything left to come out. The sweat trickling all over her body was uncomfortable. It felt like her body was on fire, and rolling onto her side, she muffled her sobs with the pillow. Regardless of the orders not to disturb her, she knew that if servants heard her crying, they would come in to see what was wrong. If that happened, they would send for the healers. Amelia didn't know why she was terrified at the thought of being tended to by Aaron, but she was. A small part of her mind knew that fear was irrational.

Knowing that her mother would be here at court soon, Amelia had left instructions that Healer Bates and Kate, her old maid, be given access to her quarters. She only hoped that they arrived before anyone else thought to check on her. Hearing the door to her rooms crack open and scolding voices without, Amelia opened her eyes and breathed a sigh of relief.

"There is no need, I tell you, we'll tend to Amelia. We've looked after her since she was a child." The scolding voice belonged to Kate, her maid and nanny when she had been younger.

Amelia was relieved to see that Healer Bates was a step behind her. Trembling, almost doubling up as pain assaulted her, she still sobbed with relief at the sight. Amelia couldn't help the moan that escaped her lips as the pair bustled around. She knew the bowl she had been sick in was removed, as the pungent smell disappeared, and then the healer was there, propping her up, holding a bottle to her lips. She almost gagged at the sickly-sweet taste she remembered too well as the medicine slid down her throat.

It's all right, Amelia, you know it'll make you feel better. It's been too long since you've had your medication. The healer's cool mind voice reassured her, and she drank as she was bid.

The healer continued to talk to her, urging her to sleep and rest.

You can trust only me.

A cool cloth wiped across her brow, instantly making her feel better. As the healer spoke to her, whispering in her mind, she felt herself relaxing.

That's it, Amelia. Only I can protect you.

This was familiar, known. Bates had been looking after her since she was a small child, since the very first time she'd encountered the Taint. Amelia trusted Bates more than she did anyone else. As she drifted off to sleep under Bates's urging, a small part of her mind wondered whether it was Bates herself that caused her to distrust the other healers. Yet somehow that thought did not seem necessary. As always, Bates had made her feel better.

Sleep, Amelia. Your medication will make you well again.

As Bates's mind voice compelled her, she drifted off to sleep, her body relaxing, the shaking stopping, the pain drifting away. More importantly, other than the whispering voice of Bates, she couldn't hear any other mind voices.

Thank you, Bates. Please, please don't let the Taint take me.

Amelia let herself drift off to sleep as the healer had directed her to, relieved, knowing that under the healer's ministrations she would be okay.

20

THEFT

BEFORE THE SUNDERED WAR

*J*unior Healer Gail Killiam backed up, feeling the sharp bite of the edge of the cupboard in his back as Healer Katrina stormed out of the office. Her step was even and precise, face closed, and she gazed straight ahead without looking at anyone in the office. He watched her as she walked out the door, closing it behind her. Killiam had been watching the research with interest, not sure even within himself whether he wanted it to fail or to succeed.

He judged from Healer Katrina's actions that the research was failing—as far as she was concerned. Gail had been tracking the research himself, meticulously reading over every piece of information as it came in from the test groups, before he placed it on her desk. Unlike Healer Katrina, he felt the research had value.

Gail frowned, looking around at the other staff in the room, all of whom pretended to be busy. He stood for that moment, frozen, and then he realised this was his moment. This was the moment he could act, do what he knew needed to happen. The others would be unlikely to register what he was doing. They were too busy trying not to come to the attention of Healer Katrina.

Gail took a deep breath. He wasn't proud that he could hear his breath catching in his throat. His nerves were evident, at least to himself. Smoothing down his robes, being careful not to glance around, he walked towards the office door. He opened Katrina's door, passing inside and closing it behind him, careful not to slam it in his hurry. He didn't even have to guess; he knew what he needed. The cupboard he wanted was off to one side, and contained the samples of the trial medication he needed. As he opened the wooden doors of the cupboard, he smiled in triumph as he saw rack upon rack containing the vials of the medication, each bottle stamped with its own date and batch number. Smiling, he looked around the room and saw a discarded bag off to one side. Walking across the room, he picked up the bag and looked inside, and found that it was Katrina's day pack. He upended it, spilling the contents—a pad, book and pencils—to the floor. He stood and walked two paces back towards the open cabinet before he stopped and gazed back, looking again at the plain leatherbound notepad, there on the floor with the pens and the papers. A grin spread across his face and he stooped to pick up the notepad and flip it open, his eyes scanning the familiar, precise hand writing. A grin lit his face: it was her diary.

Gail moved to the cupboard and grabbed the vials, knowing he didn't have much time. He placed one after the other in the bag, hoping they wouldn't break.

Stepping back from the cupboard, he noticed the small drawer below. On an afterthought he reached and tried to open it, but it was locked. Damn the woman. Then a smile spread on his face; there would be only one reason to lock the drawer in a personal office. Killiam grimaced and wrenched the drawer open, hearing the snap of the lock, and then watched the contents of the drawer spilling onto the ground around him with a dull thud—a bunch of paperwork bound in leather. Gail licked his lips and looked around, waiting to see if anyone would come into the room to investigate the noise. Relaxing when no one came, he reached down to grab the bound paperwork and place it in the bag.

As he moved towards the door, he paused, hands moving down to the edge of his tunic. He tugged at it, then smoothed his hands down the front. Running his hand through his hair, he took a breath and then reached out and grabbed the doorknob. He walked through the outer office without stopping, walking with purpose, as if he had an important task. Gail walked through the room past the others, none of whom paid the slightest bit of attention to him, and into the outer corridor. Trying not to run, he went down the stairs at a trot before making his way across the open gardens of the Healers' Guild towards the exit. He took another deep, calming breath as he walked away from the Guild. It really was that easy.

21

SUBTLETY

*A*lex felt himself stiffen as one rapid-fire image after the
other hammered into his mind. Finally they stopped,
and, taking a breath, he looked up as he realised he must have
just come out of a blackout period. It was always confusing and
unsettling finding himself in unfamiliar surroundings,
although this time he was in a bar—a bar that he recognised.
Alex chuckled, not that the particular thought was terribly
helpful. He had been to more bars with Jess and Kyle than he
cared to count. Of course, a great many of them were disreputable and in the run-down parts of the villages.

The other part that perplexed him was how he'd ended up
here, sitting in the back corner of a bar he vaguely recognised
in the first place. The last thing he remembered was leaving
William, intent to hunt down some Sundered... and then, here.
Prodding at his memory didn't reveal anything except blank-
ness. Sighing, he gave up, confident that some memories would
come back to him eventually. They usually did. Reaching down
to his belt pouch, he pulled out some coins, remembering that
this money had at least been given to him from William. Alex

slid them across the table and signalled to the barkeep he wanted a drink.

The portly man nodded and poured a mug of ale that he passed it across to the serving girl with a nod in Alex's direction. The girl walked across the taproom floor and placed the mug on the table in front of him, her cheeks flaming red. She looked at the coins and picked them up, looking at him through her lashes. She blushed even more as she took the payment with a shaking hand before she turned and walked back to the bar, glancing back at him several times on the way.

Alex chuckled. He'd obviously been charming enough to make a friend, even if he couldn't remember. There was so much that was swallowed in darkness. It worried him what he might have done in that time, but he knew better than to prod at the emptiness.

Back at the palace, he'd thought he was in full control of what he was doing. Yet now he knew that he hadn't been at all. The gaps in his memory were significant and startling enough that he knew he was losing time. Still, he had more moments like this, where he seemed to at least have some control over himself. While he hoped that this lucidity would last, he knew enough now to see that hope was futile. Someone would say something or an event would trigger him, and he would be lost again—lost in the confusion of overpowering emotion, voices ringing in his head, power surging through him that he grappled to control, but failed due to the turmoil in his own mind.

Alex pulled himself up sharply from that train of thought. It wasn't helpful and would likely set him off into a spiral that would lead to someone dying at his hands.

He was beginning to learn in these moments between that he could exert some control, for a space of time. These were the moments he searched for the others like him, the Sundered. He was learning that not all of the Sundered were the same. There seemed to be degrees of madness in the ranks of the Sundered.

It was a circumstance that he found strange, as the difference was stark.

Right now he didn't know enough, and going off the rails himself didn't help. It did give him something to investigate when he was sane enough to remember. He knew that going back to the palace was not an option; he didn't have the control. Alex just hoped that in his moments of madness he didn't just take himself back there anyway.

Reflecting on that concern, he realised that he couldn't really say with any certainty that others wouldn't perceive him in the same way as he saw some of the Sundered ranks, yet he could hold off the madness for more extended periods of time, sometimes managing to divert himself entirely.

Alex also took hope that he apparently wasn't always murderous, even if he wasn't always in total control. He'd somehow gotten here, to the bar where he was known. No one was apparently dead or running screaming from the room. That had to be a good sign, even if he didn't quite understand how he got here, how long he'd been here or why he was here. Indeed, the barmaid seemed to like him, so he'd probably done something to impress her. If she only knew the truth about him, she wouldn't be so happy about that circumstance.

Sipping his beer, he was pleasantly surprised at the quality of the brew. Alex pulled in a small amount of power, gazing around the room casually. No one here flared with power in his mind's eye. All of them were normal. He was also incredibly surprised at the bar he was in. It was decent.

Alex shifted his gaze towards the doors as they creaked open, and in the flare of light from the lamps out in the street a figure walked in, a dark outline against the lights outside. As the door closed, Alex found his attention was caught immediately by the woman who'd entered.

Isabella. The woman's name was Isabella and Alex had seen her before, yet he couldn't say right now when or how. With the recollection of her name, the memory of their meeting had flashed in his mind. They had been in a bar, this bar; they'd been sitting together, and had slept together many times.

Memories continued to flood his mind, and he allowed them to play out one after the other. He knew better than to try to resist or force this bombardment. Alex reeled at the memory of Kyle stabbing him. He remembered it was Isabella who'd brought him back from his spiralling madness. Alex smiled, his eyes drinking her in. He firmly ignored that part of his mind nagging at him that it would be better if he avoided entangling her in his world.

Isabella looked around the bar, and a spark of recognition lit her eyes. Walking through the crowded bar, she made her way to the back. She sat down opposite him without saying a word, raising her hand to the barkeep, gesturing for a jug to be brought and a platter of food. Isabella said nothing until the pitcher and food arrived, and paid the barmaid. Alex nearly snorted at the disappointment on the barmaid's face as she glanced between him and Isabella before retreating to the bar. Isabella pushed the sharing platter onto the table between them and refilled Alex's mug. Her gaze didn't leave Alex, and the woman was clearly assessing him.

"Back with me, I see, Alex."

Alex raised an eyebrow at her and swallowed a mouthful of the brew. On second taste, it was even better. Then again, perhaps Isabella had ordered a jug of something better than the contents of his original mug. The series of images flashing through his mind finally stopped.

"Just... I'm still a little confused, but yes, I'm back in my own head."

Isabella nodded and poured more beer into Alex's mug before topping up her own. There was no judgement at all in her.

"You are coming back to yourself sooner, I think. It's the

sudden rise in power levels that overwhelm your mind. You remember me?" Isabella took a long sip of her ale, not seeming concerned with the answer she was going to get.

Alex smiled and nodded. Reaching across, he grabbed her hand, and he kept his eyes on her as he kissed her palm. He decided even her blush was pretty, and pulling her gently across the bench, he wrapped his arms around her. He closed his eyes, sighed and relaxed.

"I remember enough. You've saved my sanity and my life more than once."

Isabella relaxed into his arms, and they sat in silence. Alex was grateful she knew him well enough to allow his mind to catch up with being back. It was always disturbing, with his memories fragmented, coming back in bits and pieces like he was trying to put all the parts of a shattered mirror back together.

ALEX LAY BACK on his bed at the inn he seemed to keep returning to even when he was out of his mind. This time, even though he'd spent a delightful evening with Isabella, he hadn't ended in bed with her, although that was more Isabella than him, since she'd practically pointed out he needed more time to come to terms with being back first. She didn't want to take advantage of him, he realised, and he chuckled in amusement. At least none of the flashing images filling in the gaps in his memory indicated he'd killed anyone this time. These days he had to take the small personal victories when they occurred. Isabella's face flashed into his mind—mentor, friend, lover and all-around complication in his life that he didn't care to avoid. Last night, by mutual agreement, they had both decided to put the *lovers* part on the back burner. At least until he'd settled down to being back in his own head. As much as he didn't want to admit it, Isabella was correct. Coming back to himself was always a little unsettling.

Absently he willed small flames in and out of existence. It was one thing to practice in the middle of nowhere with no risk at all to anyone, yet here he had to exert control over himself and his power. If he didn't, the inn and all occupants would likely end up dead in an unexplained fiery death. He knew that *he* would live—his first unwitting experience had proven that.

Frowning, Alex remembered his encounter with the Sundered when he'd gone to try and help Kyle and the blow he'd received from his opponent. He'd instinctively copied what the Sundered had done, yet he still wasn't sure how he'd done it. Alex sprang up from the bed and shifted from his room at the sleepy little village back into the depths of the forest where he'd learned how to use fire. He'd come to think of the blackened area as his training ground.

There wasn't much left standing in the large blackened circular patch—a few blacked tree stumps and some boulders were about it. Alex looked towards the edge of the forest but didn't want to cause more destruction on the old wood than he already had. It had stood impervious to the devastation that was humankind, until he had come along and changed that in an instant. Switching his view, he saw the swirl of colourful power flows around him more clearly, in stark contrast to the black place he stood in.

Concentrating, he pulled some of the silver-grey strands that he associated with wind and speed—or at least he knew that to travel faster on the veiled paths he used more of that colour. He frowned as he formed it into a ball and sent it at a large boulder a few paces away from him. The result wasn't spectacular; his efforts just rolled over the rock.

Biting his lip, Alex paced a few steps before turning and walking back again. Finally he turned, drew in more power, and flung it at the boulder. His eyes narrowed as this time his efforts resulted in the boulder rolling over. Not what he'd had in mind, yet better than his first effort. Conscious that his anger level was rising, Alex pushed his concern aside. This time he drew in both the silver-grey and wove some of the green strands, the earth, through it. Compressing the power into a smaller, tighter formation, he hurled it at the boulder.

Alex's eyes widened in shock, and he hit the ground, covering his head as an explosion rocked the clearing, booming over the forest in a loud crack. Alex instinctively raised a shield of air around himself to block the shards of rock flying through the air, shunting the projectiles on a different path. Leaves fell to the ground from the distant trees as the missiles shredded them off the branches. Alex looked up, saw a hole and rock shards where once the boulder had stood, and let his barrier fall. Looking around, he noted the eerie silence that had fallen over the forest. Not even so much as a single bird call could be heard. Finally, he hauled himself to his feet and looked at the devastation he'd caused.

Hearing delighted laughter ring out behind him, Alex spun around to see Isabella, hand covering her mouth, which did nothing to hide her mirth at all. Alex groaned and covered his face with his hands, knowing that his whole face was burning red.

"How about we try that again, Alex. This time with a little more control?"

Alex looked up at the sky and shook his head, then spun, and crouched reflexively as another explosion rang out. He realised he didn't need to dive to the ground as the pieces of the boulder Isabella had exploded flew through the air. Isabella walked towards him, absently throwing up her own barrier to keep them safe.

Alex looked down at the ground, then back up at her, unable to help the grin that spread on his lips. He shook his head self-deprecatingly at her display and turned, looking for another boulder. Spotting another large one off to the side, he took a deep breath and concentrated on what he wanted. This time he attempted what Isabella called 'control'. It wasn't as easy a thing to achieve as she made it seem. Sometimes it felt like the veil had other ideas. Alex felt the warmth of her body as she pressed up against his side, one of her hands on his back, the other resting on his arm. Her voice whispered in his mind.

Now concentrate, Alex. Draw what power you need to perform the action you want, and no more.

Alex took a deep breath, blocking out everything except the sound of her voice, and began to draw in power, this time making a conscious effort not to overdo it.

The forest around them was teeming with creatures. All of them stayed frozen in place, quiet, knowing predators when they heard them.

ALEX SAT in the back corner of the inn that was fast becoming his regular. At least he'd finally worked out its name. The Last Stop was a surprisingly comfortable inn in the village at the edge of the forest in what many considered a forgotten corner of the realm. It had the added advantage of being close by to his favourite practice ground, and was surprisingly civilised. He threw back his hood and removed his cloak—he'd given up trying to hide his identity. Given a chest of his own discreet, unadorned clothing had arrived at the inn along with a couple of the Elite, and that the bill always seemed to be paid, he guessed the publican knew precisely who he was, or at least guessed. The regular patrons certainly didn't pay him any more attention than to nod welcome as he entered. If they knew who he was, they certainly kept their own counsel and didn't seem all that bothered. Then again, he'd never caused them any trouble here, that he was aware of. The Elite kept a discreet eye on him but didn't interfere—he guessed they had strict orders. Either way, he was glad that they let him be.

One of the evenings not long after the Elite had arrived, a caravan master had offered the Elite on guard a job. The regulars in the bar had laughed in amusement, and even Alex had smiled as the pair politely turned it down. That, if anything, told him that the local residents knew exactly who he was. They knew full well that the two well-armed, quietly confident and watchful men propped in the corner were not mercenaries waiting around for a job on a caravan. The clearly oblivious caravan master had then sized him up and begun to walk in his direction. The Elite hadn't needed any orders. Alex's face had obviously conveyed to them he wasn't in the mood to be approached. They had reacted swiftly enough, without any requests at all, and headed off the caravan master, suggesting to him it wouldn't be a good idea. That had caused even more amusement to the patrons. The caravan master had been clearly confused by the reaction of the bar to his offer, and Alex had no doubt that he'd left even more confused, with no one willing to clarify the situation to him.

Alex wasn't sure what to make of his gear and some of the Elite taking up permanent residence, other than that William had obviously located him, and, rather than try to have him hauled back to the palace, was giving him the space he needed. Alex sighed as the familiar feeling of guilt settled on him. A visit to his brother, if not his father, was overdue again; it was something he had recognised he'd been putting off. Still, now that he was a little bit more stable, it was a risk he should take more frequently. He knew that he could relocate himself easily, yet that would worry his brother, and then he'd only send people out to locate him again. If he was honest with himself, it also showed him that perhaps the door wasn't as closed as he'd thought it was.

Alex grinned as the owner's lad brought a jug of wine and a

plate of food in his direction without having to be asked to do so. Feeling the low-level surge of power, then seeing the steam rise from the plate of food, Alex realised that the boy had heated it. It surprised him a little, and he looked at the boy curiously. Not that the lad had much power. Small, low-level uses of the veil were a part of daily life that was often discounted, although generally kept hidden from sight in this day and age, like the dirty little secret that everyone was keeping from each other. People thought—incorrectly, as it turned out—that it wasn't the same type of power that made the Sundered.

Power was power, and it all came from the veil. It was just that the more common usage was akin to comparing a tiny droplet of water dripping from a water glass to a waterfall. Yet here in this small, remote village far from everywhere else in the realm, they seemed to have very little stigma associated with those little abilities. Alex wondered whether it was their very isolation that helped them maintain their way of life. He'd also not seen any sign at all that they were killing children detected to have abilities like his, as happened in the bigger villages. Still, there also hadn't been any sign at all of any of the Sundered nearby that he had detected either nor any stories of farmers' children going mad from the Taint.

Alex thanked the boy and picking up the fork. He tasted a mouthful of the stew—big chunks of tender meat, vegetables and fragrant herbs—and he smiled in appreciation. The kitchen staff made good use of the provender from the edge of the forest. Alex realised he'd made short work of the plate of food as he wiped up the last of the rich gravy from the dish with the last of his bread and popped it into his mouth. Sitting back contentedly, he polished off the last of the wine he'd been served with it. It was a local variety that they were extremely proud of, and well they should be. It would be entirely in place on the king's table. Contemplating the empty pitcher, he caught the innkeeper's eye and held the empty pitcher up with a hopeful smile. The man grinned and filled a fresh pitcher from the cask behind the bar before making his way across to Alex, quietly refilling his goblet before placing the pitcher on the table. Alex thanked him and gestured for him to sit. The barman scrutinised him a moment, then nodded agreement and settled on the bench opposite. The innkeeper's boy darted across the bar with another goblet for his father and moved back to look after the bar.

"I take it my brother has been paying you well?" Alex sipped his wine, keeping his eye on the man, deciding a little bluntness was in order.

"Yes, Your Highness, but you were always welcome here even before then. You never caused us any problems." The man's voice was sincere.

Alex smiled sadly. That meant that even here they had heard about the trouble that had occurred.

"You weren't ever worried that I'd go mad and kill you all?" Alex felt he might as well be forthright. Apart from everything else, he was curious.

"No, Your Highness." He looked up at Alex and took a sip from his own goblet before continuing with care. "Even when you weren't quite so well, you never tried to harm any of us."

"You knew who I was?" Alex glanced around, aware that many in the bar were trying to look like they were not paying attention to the conversation and failing miserably. He'd liked the idea of being anonymous for a small space of time, but that apparently hadn't happened even though he'd thought it did.

The barman chuckled in amusement, his eyes lighting up. "Yes, Your Highness. We're a small village at the edge of the realm, but you are the son of our king and word travels, even out here."

Alex considered those words for a moment and absently filled up the man's goblet before refilling his own from the pitcher. He hardly noticed when the boy, at a gesture from his father, came and replaced the pitcher before retreating once more. Finally, Alex stirred.

"Thank you for the refuge this place has been and the risk all of you took in taking me in." Alex relaxed back into his seat, noting that the Elite sitting quietly in the corner did so as well. They were always vigilant, even if they didn't look it; he knew they wouldn't have been happy about the distance between them and him. The guards never were in bars, particularly after the kidnap attempt.

The portly man shook his head. "No thanks needed, lad. You'll always find refuge here should you need a break. We'll defend you like you're our own kin."

Alex noted the amusement in the guards' eyes although they carefully didn't laugh. The barman was obviously sincere in his claim. He glanced around the bar and noted that they all seemed to be. Alex felt overwhelmed that these strangers would take him in, regardless of hearing the various rumours that he'd gone mad, and was death on two legs for any that confronted him. They had ignored all warnings and taken him in regardless.

"You don't fear the Sundered?" Alex was genuinely confused. Everyone feared the Sundered, or so he had thought.

The man shrugged. "We've heard about them. You're not that, if it's what you've feared, lad."

Alex turned his attention back to the barman, took a sip of his wine, then licked his lips before replying. "What do you mean?"

The barman looked at him sincerely. "You're just a mite confused with the gift and all. We've had some turn like that. You're not the murderous kind."

A harsh bark of laughter escaped his lips before he could stop it, he could hear the bitterness in it. "I've killed. My memories show me I have."

Hearing the creak of a chair nearby, Alex flicked his gaze up and caught the eye of the woman who'd moved to face him.

"I'm sure you have, lad. I'm sure your guards over there have killed when the occasion warranted it as well. Yet I'd rather them sitting over there in the corner than some others who think of themselves as respectable." The old woman nodded her head emphatically and, much to his bemusement, so did others in the bar.

Alex realised they accepted him not because they didn't know the risk he represented, but because they *did*. Yet they didn't fear what he might do. That gave him hope that perhaps he might be better and safer than he thought he was.

Alex was drawn out of his introspection as the door to the inn opened, and without having to look, he knew exactly who it was. The barman looked over and, smiling, he raised his goblet to Alex before standing clear of the table as Isabella drew near. Alex held out his hand to her and she took it without hesitation, sliding into the seat next to him. She smiled at the barkeep as he poured her a drink before retreating to the bar. She didn't say anything; she didn't have to. She simply settled back into his arms. Alex found that was one of the things he really liked about Isabella. They could sit there in companionable silence. She knew when to speak, to draw him out, and when to let him be.

They sat and enjoyed the evening and each other's company, finishing off the food and drink between them. Keeping his eyes on Isabella, he stood, backing up towards the stairs that led to the rooms above, tugging on her hands lightly. Isabella laughed. Rising from their table, she joined him in retreating upstairs to his bedroom.

THEY ROLLED APART, spent. Alex took a breath and chuckled.

For the first time in a long time, he was calm and happy in his headspace. The power threaded around both him and Isabella, yet he didn't feel over powered by it. He just let it be.

"Thank you, Isabella. I haven't felt this good..." Alex stopped abruptly and chuckled. "Well, in a long time."

Isabella rolled over onto her side to look at him, a smile on her lips. Alex found himself distracted by the sight of her. He couldn't resist reaching out one arm, gently snaking it around her slim waist and pulling her closer, lightly kissing down the side of her neck. He knew the thrill of pleasure went through her since she shared the feeling with him.

"You can't possibly be ready to back up already, Alex." Her elegant eyebrow rose and she laughed with him before contently lying in his arms as his hands gently stroked her body.

"I like feeling the thrills of pleasure in your body. Learning what you like. I'll stop if you want me to." Alex was earnest, although he hoped that she didn't want him to stop.

He was rewarded with her lazy laugh. "Not to put a dampener on things, Alex, but we should talk about it. Our display was hardly subtle last night."

Alex smiled, shaking his head. "Subtle or otherwise, it wouldn't matter. I'd be surprised if reports about you being in my company haven't already made it back to the palace."

"But we were discreet, or we were before last night." Isabella's cheeks flamed red.

"Being seen with me, discreet or otherwise, doesn't make a difference. I'm sorry, Isabella, I should have thought to warn you of the consequences of being in my world."

"It's me who should be sorry. You're only newly transitioned, and I know the confusion that can cause." Isabella laced her fingers in his long dark hair at the back of his head and pulled him down to meet his lips with her own.

They lay for a while, content in each other's arms, before Alex chuckled softly.

"You know, it occurs to me you know just about everything about me, but other than you being from Ilarith and of the Elder, I know very little about you." That would cause some issues since he knew his brother would ask for details before too long.

"What do you want to know?" Isabella looked at him, not seeming worried in the slightest.

"You were born in Ilarith?" Alex shifted, settling them both a little more comfortably with the pillows piled up behind them.

"No, I... I was from around here before Vallantia was Vallantia. It was a long time ago." Isabella shuddered in his arms.

"You don't have to tell me if you don't want to." Alex pressed his lips against her forehead, sensing a wave of distress from her as she thought about the past.

"Only a few began to emerge with true power back then, closer to what we now think of as Kin. My master was such a one."

Alex's eyes widened. "Your master?"

"Mmm... He was cruel with powers that no one else had. People were scared of him. He was the war chief of this whole area. He observed me playing with the other girls in my village and took me as one of his bed slaves."

Alex felt his breath catch in his throat as images and feelings flashed in his mind from Isabella as she spoke.

"I'm sorry." Alex hugged her, his mind whirling.

She shook her head and drew closer to him, seeking comfort in his arms as she continued in a soft voice.

"He always took what he wanted, people, food, even if it was just to let it spoil while the villagers starved. It was his undoing in the end. There was an uprising. My brother had just come into his own power and used the resulting mayhem from the rebellion to take me from him. We fled far away to escape my master. I was scared for a long time that he'd come for me again. The place we ended up is now known as Ilarith. My brother found out years later that many people died during the uprising but they were free of that evil and in its place Vallantia was born."

They lay in silence as Alex struggled to process what she'd told him.

"Now you are of the Elder and nobody's slave." He kissed her gently, pleased when she responded. "What happened to your brother? Is he alive and still in Ilarith?"

Isabella suddenly laughed, her mood lightening. "You know my brother, you've met. It's Damien."

Alex realised as soon as she said it that he should have known or guessed, particularly since he already knew that Jess had gone to Damien. That had prompted the man to send Isabella to check on him.

"I will understand if you don't want to be pulled into my world, Isabella. If you'd rather we just met each other here or elsewhere, then that is what we will do. If you'd rather never see me again... well, I'll be miserable because I do really like you, but I will abide by your wishes."

Alex turned his head to see Isabella smiling at him. She pulled him to her, kissing him, leaving no doubt at all in his mind that she at least wanted to be with him.

22

BARRIER

*J*ess frowned and sat back into a comfortable chair that hadn't been there moments before. She filed the information of the chair and how she made it away for when she had time to consider it. Rolling out from her the veil pulsed and throbbed as if in tune with her concentration as she stared at the shield. At least she could see it now, even if it was even more perplexing. It was constructed in power—not just any power, but a power level that could only be wielded by another of the Elder. Jess guessed not just any Elder either. An extremely powerful one.

She suspected that Elder was Damien but she couldn't bring herself to ask at the moment. He'd been badgering her about the need to stop cutting off her emotions. He'd blown her nearly killing the boy in the village right out of proportion when he'd returned and was filled in about her exploits. Having had her fill of being lectured, she'd left early before Damien woke up. She'd wandered aimlessly for a little before ending up here, looking at the barrier that surrounded Ilarith.

The power it would have taken to construct it was something she was struggling to understand. Yet she needed to. Jess

155

flung herself from her chair and started pacing—a habit she recognised with an absent part of her mind, one she seemed to have picked up from Alex, although she remained calm. At least that was something she could be grateful for.

The pulsing of the veil around her grew more erratic, bands of power striking and exploding, sending sparks, tiny motes of light into the air around her. She frowned, wondering what was causing the instability, then dismissed it. She didn't have time right now to ponder the peculiarity of the veil.

Right now she needed to understand the shield.

As THUNDER RUMBLED and lightning stuck through the veil, Damien sprang out of bed. He knew the upheaval was caused by Jess, he just didn't know why. A quick scan told him she wasn't here in his estate. That much he could sense. He folded the veil, travelling the distance between where he'd been and her location easily and quickly.

She stood there in a centre of calm while the veil roiled and churned out from her. Damien swallowed as he closed the distance between them. The disturbed energy flowed over him, through him, but it didn't hurt him, so he gathered it wasn't directed at anyone in particular. He stood behind her, yet she hadn't even noticed his arrival as she stared ahead of her. Damien looked over her shoulder, seeing Ilarith's shimmering curtain of power that had captivated her attention. Still, she should have known he was here no matter how fascinated she was by the curtain of power.

Jess?

Damien's arm flashed up in an automatic response, deflecting her strike. She froze, looking at him, pale, her eyes wide in shock. The veil around them cracked and rumbled in response.

Damien, you startled me.

Damien reached out, placing his hand on her shoulder, trying to get a sense of what was going on with her. He'd been battling to get through to her about the consequences of locking away her emotions. She'd dug in, stubbornly resisting, unable to understand what was so wrong about what she was doing. She could not see herself; she maintained steadfastly that she was fine. Yet the reaction of the veil around her, responding to her, showed she wasn't. Not really.

I'm sorry, I didn't mean to startle you. Jess, you need to rein in whatever it is you think you are doing.

Jess looked at him, perplexed, then glanced around the veil, finally noticing the upheaval around her. She smiled slightly, clearly not understanding.

I'm not doing this, Damien. Why would you think I am? Her tone was defensive as she had been for days and she backed up a step.

Damien glanced around, assessing the veil again. It had her mark threaded all through it, yet she seemed to be telling the truth—as far as she knew it. As unbelievable as he found it, she clearly didn't realise that the veil was responding to her.

Yes, you are. It is responding to you. Your signature is threaded all through this. Jess, snap out of it. Stop what you are doing.

Damien walked forward, scanning her shields and noting they were leaking although he could tell she didn't realise. He also knew her shields weren't like this all the time. It was a recent deterioration. He placed his hands on her shoulders, expanding his own shield to cover her as well. Jess's eyes widened but she didn't back off or take any action to stop him. As his shields covered her, the agitation in the veil stopped.

Jess glanced around, her confusion written on her face.

I don't understand. I had my shield up.

Damien nodded. He could see that she did, except she'd leaked, badly. Without asking, he drew them both away back to the relative safety of the sitting room at his estate. He knew she like the sitting area and the view it afforded. Damien hoped it would settle her.

Jess slumped into one of the chairs, curling up in it and looking confused and miserable. Refusing to look at him.

"Your shields are almost non-existent." Damien sat down on a nearby chair, maintaining his own shields around her for now.

"I... I don't know why that happened. I guess I was letting my emotions get the better of me. The shield and how it was made is frustrating me. I'm sorry, Damien, I'm normally better at pushing my emotions down." She winced, biting her lip. "I'll do better."

Damien groaned. "Jess, I keep trying to explain this to you. You can't lock away your feelings, it doesn't work that way."

Jess shook her head. "Damien, it's too dangerous to get out of control."

"You are *already* out of control. Refusing to acknowledge your feelings the way you are, well, they are finding another way to express themselves." Damien held up his hand, stopping her protest. "What I saw from you in the veil is not someone who is in control."

Damien threw images at her of the veil and how it had reacted to her lack of control. Another of her being unaware of his presence, when she should have sensed him since he hadn't been hiding his power from her. Lastly he threw the image of what her shields had looked like to his other sight, broken and leaking out into the veil around her, leaving those around her vulnerable. Leaving her exposed to anyone else with power. Damien sighed, seeing her lips tremble, her emotions raging inside the shield he maintained for her.

"I don't understand."

Damien stood and walked over to the couch she was sitting on, pulling her into his arms. She remained stiff for a moment before she broke down. Emotions she'd tried to lock down since she'd killed her mother rose up, seeking an outlet, overwhelming her. He could sense that even though she didn't understand how she'd been wrong, she was now listening. Damien rocked her and let her cry. Time for instruction could come later.

JESS SAT CURLED up on her favourite lounge chair in the sitting room, looking out at the mountains beyond. She found the sight soothing. She took down her own personal shield, then painstakingly reconstructed it again. Over and over. It was remarkable how difficult it was to rebuild something that had at one point come naturally to her. She sensed Damien enter the room and smiled at that small victory.

She felt his approval wash over her and turned to look up at him.

"Oh, stop it. If I hadn't been so stubborn and I'd listened in the first place, I wouldn't have had to work to get back what I had previously." Still Jess smiled, allowing herself to bask in success.

Damien sat down in the large high-backed chair next to her and shook his head.

"It was my failure for not being able to get the problem across to you until you started falling apart."

"How did you come to be so wise?" Jess rested her head against the armrest, looking up at him.

"The same way anyone does. The hard way. With much worse results than you." Pain flashed on Damien's face.

"What happened?" Jess bit her lip, sensing the sadness and guilt that rolled off him.

"The world I grew up in was brutal and under the control of a warlord. He promised the village they would be safe if I joined his war party. They didn't see any other way to protect everyone, and it seemed like a good deal: trade me for everyone else in the village. I became a killer for him. The only way I could do it was to cut myself off. Not to feel or empathise with those I tortured for him." Damien closed his eyes as he recounted that time, his face a mask.

"Did it keep them safe?"

"Yes, for a time. The things I did. It was he who ordered it, but I was the one who committed the atrocities. It gave him great pleasure. He liked owning people. We belonged to him. I didn't much care, I was incapable of it, or so I thought."

"What changed?" Jess knew something must have and almost dreaded finding out. Damien today was not the man he was describing. She knew people didn't change that much without something to cause it.

"My little sister was beautiful, and my parents mostly tried to keep her out of sight, but because he'd taken me and promised to leave them alone, they relaxed." Damien opened his eyes, taking a shaky breath.

Jess felt horror well up in her. "It wasn't the village, it was your parents who gave you to him to protect themselves, to protect your sister?"

"They didn't have a choice. He was Kin. If they didn't give me up, he would have taken me anyway and killed them along with the whole village as punishment."

Silence fell between them and finally Jess prompted. "So your sister?"

"The warlord ordered me to kill a boy, I don't know why, something happened that day, but despite the death and cruelty I'd committed in his name, I refused. He saw my sister playing with the other girls at the edge of the river. She was not a little girl anymore but not of age yet. Still, she was attracting the eye of more than one man in the village. As punishment for my disobedience, he claimed her as his own. To use her as his bed slave."

Jess gasped, her hand flying up to her mouth in shock.

"I'm sorry, that isn't adequate, I know."

Damien laughed but there was no warmth in it. "He chained me in a cell across the courtyard from his bedroom, so I could hear her cry and beg him to stop as he took her. It broke something inside of me. I didn't know what it was at the time, but I went through transition. All that I'd done came back to haunt me, and I thought the pain was my punishment."

"That is when you became Kin, so you escaped?" Jess spoke quietly.

"He'd finally done enough to break the villagers, and they rose against him. Despite his power he was a coward, really. He ran out, releasing those of us he kept to terrorise others from our cells, ordering us to fight for him. We all turned on him as well. I used the distraction to grab my sister off him. I promised I would keep her safe and we fled as far as we could run."

"You ran here to Ilarith. Isabella is your sister."

It wasn't really a question, but Damien nodded.

Jess rose from her own chair and slid into the seat next to him. Wrapping her arms around him this time she comforted him until the bad memories the conversation had brought to the surface faded into the background.

23

PERVERTED BONDS

*A*lex restlessly hunted for the Sundered when he sensed that roiling mess of madness that was not quite the same as some others of his kind. His movement through the veil slowed, and he concentrated moving from that place in between the worlds back into the real world. He did it smoothly and slowly, never taking his eyes off the sobbing man, who sat with his back against the tree and his head cradled in his arms. Alex just stood there quietly, waiting for the Sundered One to notice his presence; he was sure he would eventually.

If he didn't know it would startle the man, Alex would have laughed. Even a couple of months ago, a couple of *weeks* ago, he never would have contemplated doing this. He'd always viewed the Sundered Ones as being dangerous, like rabid animals that had to be put down. Now, because of his own path, he knew that perhaps going through transition wasn't as simple as he'd thought. Not everyone sank to madness, or at least not everyone descended into madness and stayed there. This man was not totally crazy, yet his mind imprint glowed and stuttered, similar yet not so similar to the crazy ones of their kind.

162

Alex frowned and wondered if he could be reached rather than just killed.

Finally, the man started and sprang to his feet, immediately going into a fighting crouch, his hands raised in front of him, balled into fists, yet empty of any weapons. An inarticulate growl escaped from his mouth, echoed by his mind voice as he looked at Alex with wide eyes.

Alex drew in a little of the power of the veil, using it to put a barrier between him and the man and, remembering how Isabella had pulled him back from madness, sent soothing thoughts out, trying to get the man to relax. The Sundered in front of him seemed to lose some internal struggle as he screamed and ran at Alex. Alex didn't even flinch as the man came to a halt, impacting with a barrier he couldn't understand, and fell to the ground, obviously stunned.

Alex filtered through the jumble of images and rambling thoughts from the man's mind and had a moment of recognition. He'd seen this man before, had watched as he'd succumbed to madness, killing his family before running off into the forest. It had seemed like almost a lifetime ago now. He was shocked that he was still alive.

"Calm down. Devon, isn't it?" Alex spoke calmly, projecting authority, looking sadly at the seemingly broken and confused man. Alex frowned once more as Devon struggled with himself, searching for words. Then Alex smiled slightly and imposed a barrier around his mind, cutting him off from what must be the constant whispering voices of the other Tainted running through his head. The difference was almost immediate and Devon cried out in relief, almost curling into a ball on the ground.

Alex felt a surge in the veil and smiled as he recognised Isabella; she'd found him, as she often seemed to do. How she managed to track him so well was a conversation he needed to have with her another time. He knew she was there and sensed her sudden interest and sadness at the quivering mess of what had once been a man. Alex moved forward, one foot carefully placed before the other, closing the distance between him and Devon. He sank down on one knee near the sobbing man, ignoring the bite of twigs and a stone from the forest floor through his trousers. Alex placed a hand on Devon's shoulder as he sobbed and just sat there, letting him cry out his fear, sorrow and anger. Alex wasn't sure how long he sat there, projecting soothing, calming thoughts and emotions at him, but eventually he calmed down. Alex was under no illusion, though. His calm was artificially imposed in part due to the barrier that Alex was maintaining. His mind was still switching between healthy, sane and angry, chaotic.

"You don't know what I've done, what I am." Devon's voice was low and gravelly with raw emotion. "I couldn't stand it anymore. I killed them. I didn't mean to..." The man stopped and looked up at him, frowning. "How do you know my name?"

"I know who and what you are, Devon. You bear the Taint, you succumbed to madness." Alex paused as the man groaned and he caught the flashing images from his mind as he flashed back to his killing frenzy. "Shh, you were not in control. No one taught you how to control what you are. It's not your fault."

Alex continued to project calmness and keep his barrier on Devon's mind, sheltering him from the whispering, screaming voices that were not his own. That, at least for now, seemed to be helping him stay reasonably calm. Alex grimaced as he felt Devon stiffen at the realisation that he was being controlled.

Devon glared at Alex, his sorrow fading fast to the anger that was bubbling up in him.

"What are you doing to me, how are you doing it?" Devon started and pushed himself back away from Alex, then froze, staring behind Alex.

Alex grinned, knowing that the broken man had just noticed Isabella behind him. He knew how startling it was to see. She also had drawn in her not inconsiderable power and he had no doubt that she would use it if she needed to.

Devon snarled, his mind snapping, spiralling into turmoil. He lurched and, in a surge of raw, uncontrolled power, wrenched himself from Alex's control, fleeing into the veil.

Alex sighed, looking over at Isabella.

Isabella closed the distance between them. Placing her arms around his shoulders, she pulled him into an embrace.

He is Broken, Alex. There isn't much that you could do that would reach him.

"I'm not so sure, Isabella. There was something wrong. I don't think he was Broken, as you put it."

"Not all the Broken are capable of mending, Alex."

Alex heard the sympathy in Isabella's tone. Suddenly he felt guilty, certain she remembered all the times in the past where a piece of her had been crushed to discover yet another Broken that she couldn't help. Yet he couldn't help that niggling part of his brain that insisted that this wasn't the same.

"I can't help but track the Sundered down, Isabella. Something about him is similar to the Sundered."

"I'm sorry, Alex. I have other things I must attend to. I'll catch up with you later." Isabella pulled his head down and brushed his lips with her own.

Alex sighed, sure that he'd upset her with his own uncertainty. He pushed a little of his remorse at her and was rewarded with her smile before she turned, heading off into the veil.

SIMON SWORE as he saw a woman, obviously Kin, with Alex. He wanted Alex to see him as a friend, to trust him without another getting in the way. Simon sighed. Today was not the day when that was going to happen. Pushing his irritation aside, he watched as Alex departed through the veil and, shrugging, decided to follow. He had a little more time before he had to be back.

Simon stiffened, barely aware in that split moment before he was hauled back to face the woman that had been with Alex. Only this time he gasped. She *glowed*. A part of his mind froze. The woman who'd been with Alex wasn't Kin. She was Elder.

"Who are you? Why are you prying where you are not wanted?" The Elder's voice was cold, the hint of anger not that well restrained.

Simon licked his lips, his mind racing. "I'm sorry. I didn't mean to interfere. I'm a friend of his uncle's. I said I'd check in on Alex, look out for him."

Simon allowed himself to babble, shunting aside the knowledge that it was not far from the truth. He may have been numbered as a member of the Cohort in his day, but that didn't mean he wanted to go up against an angry Elder. He swore internally, keeping his annoyance to himself.

The Elder's eyes narrowed as she looked at him. "Go. If I catch you around again, I will kill you."

The anger glowing in the Elder's eyes left Simon with no doubt that she was serious in her threat. Feeling her release her hold on him, Simon wasted no time in fleeing through the veil, determined to put as much distance between him and the Elder as possible.

ALEX FELT the battle rage surge inside him, the power pouring into him, and a predatory smile spread on his lips, his eyes lighting up as the rage rose deep within. He was stronger than the mad one below him.

Then he froze, eyes fastening on one who came out of the tent. Human. Not Sundered.

Watching the scene as it unfolded below him, Alex saw the Sundered try to back away. His power flared as if he was about to fight, then his knees buckled, and he screamed, begging for mercy from the human. The human snarled, his hand holding out a capped bottle to the kneeling man in front of him. As Alex watched, he saw the Sundered's hand shake as he took the bottle.

Kill me, please kill me. I'm lost. As soon as I take this, I will fight you. Kill me.

Alex stiffened. He watched as the mad one swallowed the contents of the vial. The Sundered One crumpled in pain and screamed, his body shivering in reaction. Then Alex saw it— the insidious bonds he recognised from Kyle. They pulsed as he watched, filaments reaching out from the primary connection and binding their way around the broken man like a spider's web. His skin glowed in a pattern that crisscrossed his body, melding with the balefully glowing lines, the power coming from the man—the human man—in a way that was both familiar and unfamiliar. Alex couldn't work out what it was about the power of the human that was triggering his memory.

Shaking himself out of his introspection, Alex transitioned into the glade where the pair camped, drawing his sword as the Sundered rose from his knees, madness in his eyes. Alex called fire, wrapping it around his blade, cutting through the fiery bonds that he could see. He was learning, to use power to fight the power, and the genuine sword to follow through against the flesh. As his sword followed through and up, he saw the mad one stumble, like a puppet cut from its strings.

Kill me, they'll retake me. Kill me.

Alex felt hopeless rage well up in him as he slashed his blade back down, using the strength of the wind and earth to cut through his opponent's neck, severing the head from the body. Alex watched, like the moment was in slow motion, the head falling back, tumbling to the ground. The body stood for a moment as if not realising that its life had just been ended, then toppled bonelessly, sprawling next to the separated head. Alex didn't pause to think as he spun, looking at what appeared to be a man. Wanting the kill, he drew power to him and screamed. Instead, he pulled back and cast it at the man, holding him in a cage of fire and earth. Alex paused, knowing his eyes lit with the inner flare of power as he teetered on the edge of madness.

Alex saw a questing trail of power reaching out toward him and snarled. He reached out with his own power, hauling that malignant thread to him, then extinguished it. It was the power of the veil, yet wielded differently to how he did. Still, power was power, and that was something he had more of. The other's abilities seemed somewhat constrained and limited compared to what he was able to do. Strangely enough, that was enough to settle his mind and bring him back to a semblance of stability.

"Nice try, that won't work with me. Now how about we find out who and what you are?"

THE BOUND and gagged man stumbled as Alex hauled him back with the rope crafted from power tied around his neck and waist, his lips curled back.

Not too far ahead, little man, we're nearly where we need to be. If you don't behave, I might leave you here.

Alex had no patience for the quivering wreck of a man who only hours before had been tormenting a Sundered One. Alex didn't pause to assess his own anger at that. He himself killed the Sundered easily enough; they were monsters. They had tormented and haunted his dreams as a child. Yet somehow, that scene in the clearing of the forest in the middle of nowhere had shaken him. He may have killed plenty of the Sundered, yet he didn't torment and torture them—they were tortured enough. After securing the man, he had ransacked the camp. He'd found a leather bag filled with familiar brown bottles, the same type of container that Daniel had been given to poison them all.

Eyes narrowing, he realised that there was definitely more going on than the Order trying to kidnap a prince and his friends. The reaction of the Sundered One—he had been almost normal for a brief time, he'd known Alex was there. Instead of attacking straight away, he'd begged for death. Then in pain, trembling, he'd taken the drug. After that his mind had closed off, and he'd become the killer Alex had expected, that he was used to encountering. Alex had no regret for granting his request.

The snivelling companion, however, he was another matter entirely. Alex had been about to kill him when he'd remembered that the man wasn't Tainted. He had access to power, yet not like Alex's own. This had given him pause. The feel of the man's ability was familiar. It was triggering a memory, yet it took Alex some time, finding the brown bottles to remember. The power was the same that he'd sensed from Aaron. His failed attempt to reach into Alex's mind had solidified his course of action.

Shifting into the veiled paths, he hauled his captive along to the palace, covering the distance with remarkable speed. Pausing, Alex was glad to see his brother alone in his room.

Not giving any thought to how William would react, Alex, dragging his prisoner, appeared in his brother's room.

William stiffened, dropping his coffee mug as he spun to face him, swearing.

"Damn it, Alex, you startled me." William's eyes tracked the cowering man behind Alex, who got as far away from Alex as his bindings would let him. William looked at Alex, his eyebrow raising as he stooped to pick up the mug he'd dropped.

"Sorry, William. I need Aaron to look at this filth. He's not Tainted, but he was controlling one of the Sundered, like what Alyssa tried to do with Kyle."

Alex dumped the leather bag filled with what he suspected was the toxin on his brother's couch. His anger simmered below the surface as William went to the door and requested Aaron be summoned immediately. Turning back, William refilled his mug from the flask of coffee on the side bench.

"Coffee, Alex?"

Alex shook his head, and contented himself with glowering at his captive. It didn't take long for Aaron to arrive—it never took anyone long to come when summoned to attend to a member of the royal family. Aaron entered the room, then froze when he saw Alex and the bound man cowering behind him. His eyes wide, he looked at William.

"Your Highness?"

"Alex needs your assistance with his prisoner. He apparently did to one of the Sundered what Alyssa tried to do to Kyle."

William nodded his head towards the gagged, trembling man. Aaron turned to look at the man, his interest spiked. Any sympathetic feeling for the man he'd initially had died with William's explanation. Alex smiled as he recognised the change in attitude in the healer.

"I believe that one isn't Tainted, but someone with the healer's gift."

Alex positioned himself behind his captive, hauling him to his feet, restraining him as the healer walked towards them. Aaron used his own power and shut down the man as he tried to speak mind to mind with the healer.

Enough, I don't need to listen to your lies to find out the truth.

Aaron placed his hands on the temples of the sobbing man,

his eyes drilling into him. While Alex knew that Aaron was exerting power, he still couldn't quite follow what he was doing. Yet there was no doubt that it was effective. They stood, eyes locked for long enough that Alex traded glances with William. He was about to intervene when his prisoner slumped into unconsciousness. Alex let him fall unceremoniously to the floor in a crumpled heap.

"I'll take charge of him if you don't mind, Alex."

The healer held up his hand as Alex's eyes narrowed to forestall the objection that he knew was coming, not that it worked.

"Well, Aaron, am I right?"

"Yes, Alex, your assessment is correct. He was a healer." The healer's face dropped. "Unlike Alyssa, he was formally trained by the Healers' Guild. I need to investigate this. It should not have been able to happen."

Alex looked at Aaron, trying to decide whether he trusted the healer. His instinct was to kill his enemy now that he'd learned that the man was a member of the Healers' Guild. Pushing down his anger, he tried to approach it logically. If Aaron had meant him harm or to kill him, then the healer had had plenty of opportunity over the years. Aaron could likely extract more information from the corrupted healer than Alex could. If he tried, the man's mind would probably melt. Alex closed his eyes, battling with his own instinct.

"All right, Aaron. I trust you. Find out every detail from him."

"I will, Alex." Aaron's lips compressed, his eyes narrowing as he glanced at the captive.

William stepped forward, glancing from Alex to Aaron, then to the unconscious man on his floor, apparently concerned.

"If the Healers' Guild is involved somehow, if its members are being subverted... We need to know. Do not let your guild know anything until we get to the bottom of this, Aaron. The Fourth's Elite will assist you to get him to a cell and keep guard over him." The command in William's voice was unmistakable.

Aaron opened his mouth, then closed it again. Frowning, he nodded.

"Yes, Your Highness."

"You think I'm harsh. People are dying, Aaron. The rise in the number of Sundered, the viciousness of them, hasn't made any sense. If the Healers' Guild is involved in this, we need to know what they are doing."

Aaron nodded assent, bowing to William, acknowledging the order even though it was clear that he was not happy with the situation. The Healers' Guild took steps to ensure the compliance of its members to the Guild's orders, yet clearly someone had found a way around them. He had a duty to tell the Guild. Yet being assigned the primary responsibility to members of the royal family, he also had a sworn duty to them.

Even with just the brief insight into the broken healer's mind, he knew that the Guild—or at least someone of high ranking—was involved, and that there were likely more healers involved than one; there would have to be to have accomplished this. Their guild instilled compulsions, yet their controls had somehow been broken. Until he knew more, he could not trust that the Guild Masters themselves or at least one of them were not involved.

Alex crossed the room and picked up a leather satchel from the couch and handed it to him. Aaron undid the buckle to look inside. Seeing unmarked brown bottles inside, he glanced up at Alex.

"That's what they are using, on the Sundered Ones. I saw him give some to the Sundered he controlled as well."

Alex was careful not to look at the man on the floor. He knew that he would be tempted to kill him. The rational part of his mind knew that the current plan would give more information as to what was going on. That was the most important thing right now. Alex felt like he was drowning. Something was wrong. He just didn't have all the pieces. The rise of the Sundered, the Order, corrupted members of the Healers' Guild —it was all forming a picture that he didn't like.

Still, he didn't want to run off and kill members of the Healers' Guild randomly in the act of retribution. The healers could have just been targeted individually, or there might be someone in their own guild selling them out. If that was the case, it was likely they were high-ranking. Alex needed to know who it was. Then he would track them down and kill them. Alex drew his attention back to the healer when Aaron spoke.

"How are you, Alex?"

"I'm... getting used to this. The surges in power drilling into me, extremes in emotions, blackouts. Yet I'm not losing as much time as I was in the start. You have no idea what I'm capable of." Alex shrugged, laughing. "*I* don't know what I'm capable of."

William walked forward and pulled him into a hug before stepping back.

"Stay safe, Alex, and come back when you feel you can. The Fourth's Compound is still operational. Or use my rooms, you know when I'm likely to be here." William frowned, catching Alex's arm before he disappeared. "Try to come back a little more regularly, even if it's just to sit and talk. Father is worried, and I can at least assure him that I've seen and talked with you."

Alex looked at William. Feeling guilty, he nodded. Somehow his big brother always knew how to get to him.

24

JEALOUSY

IN THE TIME OF THE SUNDERED WAR

*S*imon slumped onto the bench next to Kevin after his own practice bout, exhausted but trying not to show it. He took a deep, slow breath, glancing around and hoping no one actually noticed how much practising combining fighting with the veil cost him. He knew he could do better, he just needed the time to get stronger. If they found out they would kick him from the inner circle, and he would lose the advantage of the training that he gained by being in this particular set.

After all, how many in the realm could claim to be in the inner circle of a prince? And not just any prince, but a powerful one, even if he didn't know it. Then there were his closest friends, scary beyond belief, yet somehow they rated him in their number. Still, there was Ed, then his inner circle, Kat and Cal. No one was breaching that friendship. Then there was the circle beyond that. That was the circle Simon was in. Even if others didn't realise the difference or notice that the layers existed, he knew that he wasn't quite in Prince Edward's actual inner circle.

Feeling a surge of the veil, he looked back at the fight that

174

was still ongoing. Edward was fighting, and doing superbly well, as he always did. Simon fought down his own jealousy and anger. How could one man be born with so much advantage over everybody else? It wasn't as if he actually deserved all the attention or accolades that he received. Still, he put a pleasant look of approval on his face; it wouldn't do for Ed, Kat or Cal to realise how he really felt. If that happened, he knew he wouldn't be in any circle of the prince—regardless of how good he was using the veil—for very long. Being kicked out of Edward's company was not in his plans.

"Careful, Simon, your expression might be pleasant but you're leaking how you really feel." Kevin spoke in an undertone.

Simon glanced around, noting the noise in the training grounds would have been sufficient to cover the comment. He was grateful everyone else was too busy watching Ed fight to pay attention to him. Concentrating on strengthening his personal shield, he shot a grateful glance at Kevin. He was the closest he had to a friend in the Cohort.

Simon chuckled as Ed stumbled. "Come on, Ed, you can do better than that!"

Simon grinned, quite enjoying the fact that Edward, for once, was being run around the work ring by the weapons master. It was rare to see Ed actually have to exert himself. If he spent as much time practising his skillset as he did running away partying and drinking, it would be sensational. The only indication that Simon had that Edward had heard his taunt was a slight flicker of amusement on his face that was quickly replaced by a tight grin. It was clear that Ed was actually enjoying this fight with the weapons master.

He concentrated and switched his view. Now the world was overlaid by the veil. He could see the strong colours thickest around Edward, passing through him and coming from him. It was one of the ways you could tell how powerful someone was.

The power of the veil was always drawn the most to the individual that was the most powerful. That person in these training grounds was Edward. If only Edward stopped pretending to be so noble, he would realise that he would be a much better ruler for Vallantia than his untalented normal sister, the crown princess who would be queen when their father the king died.

Still, there was always potential. There had been rumblings of late that some of the people going through transition were going totally mad. Rumours were flooding in of entire families being slaughtered. The king and his council were contemplating how they would react and what that would do. As with all things related to a committee decision, it was taking time. Simon was hopeful that Edward would be sent to investigate. If Edward were dispatched to investigate, that meant Kat and Cal would go with him. That in turn would mean that Simon would be going with them as well. Their entire circle would, since they were the ones who could combat the Kin. This might mean the chance he was looking for, for Edward to realise that he could take control of the realm. Ordinary people couldn't hope to stand against them if they chose to rule.

A smile spread on his face as he contemplated that potential future where he would be the power behind the throne that controlled the realm. He just had to nudge Edward in the right direction.

25

___

DRAWN

*D*evon emerged from the fragmented confusion and pain his world had become into an area that was somewhat familiar. He was near his childhood home where he'd grown up. His mind shied away from the associated images of his family, dead on the ground by his hand, amid flickering flames that reduced his family home to ash. Yet as painful as those memories always were, and no matter how far he tried to flee from them, somehow, eventually, he'd always find himself back in the vicinity of the village that he'd called home.

Devon looked through the trees to the nearby home. It was the journeyman healer's hut, one of many spread throughout the kingdom. As the light faded from the sky, he saw light flare within the cabin and the familiar figure of Healer Jenny Medcalf's silhouette in the window. He sat watching her hut as the light completely faded and darkness set in. Healer Medcalf had been away visiting the surrounding villages when he'd finally succumbed to the Taint. She had been trying to help him, even leaving a supply of the medication. He remembered his little sister had been playing and bumped into the cupboard, and the bottle containing that vital liquid had fallen to the floor, the precious liquid seeping into the floorboards and disappearing between the cracks lost forever.

Devon whimpered, curling up on himself and sliding down the tree trunk he'd been leaning on, barely noticing as the harsh bark cut through his tattered shirt into his skin. The memory brought up others, a flickering succession of images, feelings and smells as if he was reliving the moment over again. His little sister, Emma, he'd been so angry with her, the anger and fear growing, boiling up inside him. Then out in the yard, a scythe in his hands, her scream resounding in his head. Her crumpled, bloody, lifeless form on the ground. His father, mother and brother nearby. The smell of smoke and the crackle of fire burning his home. Blood, all over him. Their blood.

Devon sobbed, his fists pounding into his head as the images kept flickering in his mind's eye and the voices all around whispering to him, echoing in his head.

Please stop. I didn't mean it.

Devon's broken, pleading mind voice joined the chorus of others carried through the veil.

DEVON WASN'T sure how or why he'd crossed the intervening space between the forest and the healer's door. Caught between fear and desire to be healed, he froze outside her house, his hand raised to knock on the solid wooden door. He swallowed, eyes squeezing shut, lines of pain etched across his face. She would hate him for what he'd done, turn him away.

The door creaked, light flared on his eyelids. Devon's eyes flew open, wide-eyed he looked at her, still frozen. The instant flash of fear in her eyes hurt. The compassion that followed, with her hands reaching out to him to draw him into her home, caused great wracking sobs to come from deep within him.

Help me. Please help me, don't let me kill anyone else.

26

PRISONER

Simon turned as one of his people, Keith, walked into his rooms. He grimaced. Alex had killed a great many of his good people when he'd come hunting him. Thankfully, since Alex's rampage had been contained to Vallantia and he also had a base in Callenhain, he hadn't managed to find and kill all of them. Simon smiled. Not that it was taking long to fill the ranks of the League of Skulls, human nature being what it was.

"My apologies for the interruption, Skull Lord." Keith grinned at him, pushing his unkempt red hair out of his eyes.

"I'm sure you aren't sorry. What is it?"

"You did ask to be notified of unusual goings on at the palace."

"What is it?" Simon growled at the man, impatient.

Keith grinned at him, not concerned by his display of temper. "One of the maids that works in the kitchen sent word back about a prisoner."

"People ending up in the cells are not unusual, Keith." Simon went to turn his back on the man in dismissal.

180

"It is when it's Elite that guard him and he's a healer that is also a member of the Order."

Simon swung around, his eyes wide. "How does she know this?"

"She had to prepare a meal for him and the servants are all gossiping about it." Keith shrugged.

Simon's eyes narrowed as he contemplated that small piece of information.

"Send Blake to deal with the healer."

Simon turned his back on Keith as the man nodded and went to do his bidding. If he understood correctly, the healer should have already been dead. If he was alive and a prisoner of the Crown, it meant something had gone wrong. It wouldn't do at all for the healer to give up his secrets.

BLAKE KEPT the veil wrapped tightly around him as he walked carefully through the palace. He shivered. The temperature was noticeably cooler down at this level given it was underground. It wasn't common for him to have a job at the palace, although this place was just as easy to infiltrate as most places, at least for him, unlike most of his contemporaries, who were human. Having even limited power like he did still gave him many advantages over a normal human.

The only concern was that the Elite were reportedly on guard over his target. Still, the lords and ladies were all busy attending a banquet where the king and crown prince were in attendance. If the Elite were on duty over the special prisoner, he doubted it would be anyone powerful. They would be on duty in the ballroom.

Seeing the locked metal door with ordinary guards on duty on the other side, Blake stopped and waited. He wasn't powerful enough to appear in the cell but he could hide himself with the veil and walk through the doors when they were opened.

Hearing a noise, Blake looked up and grinned, seeing the servant bearing a tray of food. Just in time. As the man walked past him, the guards inside opened the door, pushing the bars back. The servant mumbled his thanks and Blake, keeping his step light, walked behind him through the doorway into the cell blocks. He gave no mind to the door as it clanged shut behind him, his attention on the two members of the Elite sitting at a table halfway down the row of cells. These ones were for special prisoners of the Crown. Blake looked around at the small windowless rooms with three solid rock walls and metal grates for doors.

He eyed the Elite and smiled. The Skull Lord had been correct. These men were not strong and unless he did something stupid they would be unlikely to detect him. One of them looked up and grunted. He stood up, taking a key off the table and walking down to the next cell.

"Move back to the wall," the guard barked at the occupant of the cell that Blake assumed was his target, particularly since the rest of the cells appeared to be empty.

Blake heard the metal clunk as the bolt drew back and the Elite pushed the door open. The servant placed the tray on the table, picking up the bowl with spoon and a metal mug and nodded at the guard who remained at the table.

Blake nearly laughed out loud in amusement but stopped himself in time. Obviously the rest of the food on the tray was for the guards. That should keep them preoccupied long enough while he did his work. Once again he walked behind the servant into the cell. He stood out of the way as the servant placed the bowl of what looked like oats and the mug of water on the small table without ceremony and turned to leave without comment.

Given it was usually high-ranking prisoners of the Crown

who graced these cells, they had a few more amenities than the cells for the common criminals—like the privacy of their own cell, with a basic cot, a table and a small wooden chair that adorned the otherwise stark stone cell. Still, it was a luxury compared to the regular cells.

Blake paid the clang and rattle of the key that signalled the cell door being closed and locked no mind at all. He grinned; they'd be back soon enough. He eyed the man he'd come to kill. The man had been huddled in a miserable ball against the far wall. He'd obviously learned not to disobey his keepers. He'd been stripped of everything except a basic linen shift, even his feet bare on the cold stone floor.

As his target walked forward to reach for his food, Blake moved quietly behind him, keeping his concealment.

Shhh... be still, traitor.

The healer froze as he'd been ordered, trembling. These corrupt healers were so open to compulsion if you knew how to target their broken bonds. Thankfully Blake was fully aware of how to deal with them. This wasn't the first of these he'd been sent to kill over the years.

Taking the coiled rope over his head, he stepped carefully up onto the stool, then table. Having prepared the noose earlier, he made short work of stringing it up on the chain that held the lamp hanging from the stone ceiling. He knew he had to hurry; the guards would probably be back for the bowl and mug soon.

Step up on the stool.

Blake watched, his eyes glittering as a sweat broke out on the man's forehead, shaking as he complied.

You know what to do. Don't worry, it will be quick, you don't want to compromise the Order.

The healer reached up and grabbed the noose, and standing on his toes he placed it around his neck. A tear trailed down his face as he trembled and tightened the noose without requiring direction. Without ceremony Blake kicked the chair out from under the man. It smashed into the wall. His victim fell the short distance, jerking on the end of the rope as the distinct noise of his neck snapping sounded. Blake backed up and positioned himself to one side of the door.

The Elite on duty walked up to check on the prisoner, his bored expression melting as he saw the healer dangling from the ceiling. The guard swore, calling for his companion as his key rattled at the lock and he yanked the door open. Blake waiting long enough for the second guard to enter before he eased out the door, careful not to make a noise as he made his way to the next door at the end of the corridor. He didn't have to wait long. He grinned as one of the guards pelted up to the door at a run, keys rattling at the door he burst through it, bellowing for assistance.

Blake sighed happily at a job that had gone to plan and made his way carefully out of the palace the way he'd gone in. Of course there was a servant who was going to have a very bad day trying to explain that he hadn't dropped the rope off to the prisoner when he'd left the food. That, however, wasn't his concern.

27

LOCKDOWN

*M*aster Healer Kevin Meagher walked through the ancient halls of the Healer Enclave. He smiled at a young healer trainee that almost fell over himself trying to clear out of his path.

"Trainee, I've heard good things from your tutors. You'll be joining me in the Journeyman Healer ranks before too long, I hear."

He smiled as the trainee blushed with pride at the compliment and continued on his way. The smile disappeared from his face as soon as he passed the trainee. They were so irritating with their abject obeisance, yet it was enlightening to point out the ones who were more useful as journeymen. While it was helpful information for future planning, it wasn't his primary purpose today. His own assigned Journeyman kept him apprised of the best candidates, yet he did think it was essential for him to keep tabs on and have a personal connection with the potential new recruits.

Walking along the hallways, with benches and small tables at conveniently spaced locations along the old corridors, he had to acknowledge that the ancestors knew what they were doing when building the Healers' Guild. The benches were convenient for healers to take a rest if they had just exerted themselves, or if masters needed to stop along the way between destinations to consult before heading on their own paths.

He just felt it was a shame the Healers' Guild had strayed so far from their original purpose. Here in the heart of the Guild, where they swore to protect life, they turned their back and didn't do anything about the cancer in their own society that threatened everyone.

There was once a time that he'd been young and naïve, and had believed wholeheartedly in the cause of the Guild. Then he'd returned to his home after seeing to healing needs of the locals in his zone. He'd found his wife and children slaughtered in their small back yard. It had made no sense to him. They were just torn apart and left, scattered, forgotten. No one had defended them even though the villagers in the surrounding houses must have seen and known what was happening. Yet even after the monsters had left, none of them had made an appearance, not even to cover his wife and child with a blanket to protect them from the scavengers.

Still, that was long in his past, and he'd made his own road. Devastated and disillusioned, he'd gone to the Killiam Order. He'd known about their existence, of course. All journeymen were alerted to watch out for the Order. They were told that the Order was filled with misguided individuals. And yet, the founder had been a healer himself. Much like him, the founder had lost his family to the blight on their society that was those with the Taint. It didn't help that Kevin knew that he and every other healer used power from the veil as well—yet it was not to the same degree as the monsters. The healers helped people, or they were supposed to, and not just help the individuals that history had shown them over and over again meant them all harm.

The Order had welcomed him into the fold with open arms,

grateful to receive someone of his stature and training. The current leader, Scholar Clements, had been particularly sympathetic to his circumstance as his own history, with his wife and child being slaughtered, had been similar to his own.

Still, he'd found a way to help drag the Healers' Guild back to what they should have been, what they'd been formed to be. It was hard to walk through the halls with no acknowledgement of that, but the time would come. He'd made it to the Healers' Council now, and that at least meant he had more control over what the Guild did. A day would come—soon, he hoped—when all would know what he'd done to fulfil his healer's oath and protect the people.

The Order, with his aid, had helped him break the healers' compulsion. That had been an integral moment in his past. Still, unlike most, he'd had the spine to go and find a solution. He'd spent his time since helping others break free of the Guild's compulsions and move forward toward a future of helping humans against the monsters in their midst.

Master Healer Meagher smiled and nodded at another healer in acknowledgement as they walked past each other. It interrupted his internal monologue. Not that it mattered anymore; he knew who he was, he just found it useful to run through his fictional traumatic history in his head, so he wouldn't forget it. It wouldn't do for anyone here at the Healers' Guild or from the Order to realise he wasn't the person they thought he was.

Master Healer Kevin stood behind the journeyman, his hands splayed on either side of the young man's temple. He could feel the trembling running through the boy's body, as the talented journeyman tried to fight back against Kevin's will. A cruel smile twisted his lips; he always enjoyed this part—the part where the skilled journeyman realised that Master Healer Kevin wasn't just inserting a training bond into his mind, but that he was subverting the old binding and instilling his own. The truly talented always tried to fight back. If Kevin hadn't already seized control of the journeyman's vocal cords, he'd be screaming in agony. Not that he had to inflict much pain in this process, but he enjoyed breaking them more when he did. They either lost, or they died. Generally, they lost. The only issue was that when they died, he had to find some plausible excuse as to what had happened to them. It was such a waste of a good slave.

What he did to the journeyman healers—breaking their compulsion and binding them to his will—was similar in nature to what he did to those who bore the veil. He had learned through experience that those with actual power had more ability to fight back and heal. Or they would if they weren't drugged first. The properties of the toxin thankfully made resistance impossible. Unlike his emerging brethren, the healers were primed for him to take over their minds. They'd already submitted to another's will, their gifts being bound from childhood before they grew old enough to fight back to ensure they didn't hurt anyone. The Guild helpfully instilled controls over their mind to ensure their trust and loyalty to the Guild, to ensure they didn't go back on their oaths, that they didn't kill another human being. All he had to do was twist and manipulate the compulsions that were already implanted in their head.

Kevin laughed as he felt the young journeyman collapse under his mental assault with one final soundless sob escaping the boy's lips. He smiled grimly and finished laying the bonds in the boy's mind, before laying him back and compelling him to sleep.

Kevin turned as his door opened, unsurprised to see one of his aides, Eric, come through the door, a look of concern on his face. That, if anything, caused some alarm, but he just waited patiently for his aide to tell him what was wrong.

"Master, the Grand Guild Master has issued a lockdown. None of us can leave the Guild." Eric was wringing his hands, sweat beading on his forehead.

"Slow down, what's happened? Why has the Grand Guild Master issued a lockdown?"

"I don't know, Master." The young man shuddered. "A messenger came, rumours said that it came from the king."

Kevin kept his face calm even though he wanted to rage. Just when things were going according to plan, something had apparently happened to turn those plans on their head. He couldn't afford to be locked down in the Healers' Guild at this point in time. Their plans were too close to fruition. Still, it was too early to show his hand at this point; he had no choice but to comply with the Guild Masters' orders. That didn't mean that he couldn't speak to the Guild Masters and try to convince them he needed to leave the grounds, out of concern for his journeymen. Kevin felt himself relax as a plan formed in his head. He just had to go to the Guild Masters to find out what the cause of the lockdown was, then find a way around their injunction.

"Calm down, stay here and watch our newest recruit. He should sleep for a while yet. I will go and see if I can find out more about the lockdown, then I'll be back."

Kevin gathered his things and left, quietly closing the door behind him. He made his way down the hallways he knew so well, seeking the other Guild Masters who, like him, were the heads of the various sections and sat on the Council. Although at this time of day, with an alarm raised, he knew where he would find them.

~

As KEVIN HAD THOUGHT, it didn't take long for an out-of-breath healer trainee to find him. Breathlessly, he imparted his message that the Grand Guild Master requested Kevin to attend the Council. He thanked the boy, who barely paused before continuing on his way to find more of the people he had been tasked to find and give his message to.

Kevin felt his mood darken even further; it showed the gravity of the situation that he'd been called to Council. He couldn't remember anything that had happened previously that could be serious enough for the Guild to be on lockdown. The last time that had occurred was when a contagion had broken out. There was no contagion this time; if there had been, he would already know about it.

Kevin continued on his way, although he didn't change his pace. It was not customary for him to run and he wasn't about to start now. Turning the corner, he made his way over to the rather ornate staircase that led to the upper floors, the home of most of the Guild Masters, their offices and the boardroom. He kept his pace measured as he climbed up the stairs, twenty of them. He didn't even have to count, he'd climbed them so many times. On both sides leading up the staircase were portraits of the previous Grand Guild Masters that had served the Healers' Guild. It was an impressive display, showing exactly how long the Healers' Guild had been around. A Grand Guild Master's portrait was never placed on these walls until after he was dead. Kevin wondered idly, where the next paintings were going to go since there were already forty portraits, twenty on each wall, evenly spaced all the way up.

Kevin admired the view from the expansive windows that looked over the healers' grounds as he walked down towards the boardroom. The well-manicured gardens could rival the ones at the Royal Palaces. It was a soothing sight, yet today it did not have that effect. He was way too agitated, wondering what had gone wrong and hoping that it was nothing to do with his plans. At least he couldn't see any of the King's Guard out in the gardens. It was important to find the positives when things went wrong; that was a fundamental lesson he'd learned long ago.

Kevin smiled and nodded at the youngsters on the doors as they acknowledged him and pulled the doors open. He entered the room without pausing, walking down the side of the table to take his usual seat, noting that those already present turned to stare at him as he entered. They all looked flustered and slightly panicked. He had never seen any of these men and women look like this before; they were generally a confident bunch of people. As Kevin took his seat, the Grand Guild Master cleared his throat.

"To fill you in, Kevin, the Guild is on lockdown by order of the Crown." The ageing Grand Guild Master stared around the table before looking back at him. "The king's Master Healer, Aaron, advises us that healers have been implicated in attacks on people, and in somehow using the Sundered."

Kevin felt his heart sink—it was worse than he'd thought. He felt his anger starting to burn, and with effort pushed it down. It would not help for these men and women to see how much this information got to him. How the king's healer had learned of his journeyman healers' involvement in running the Sundered he could not even begin to imagine. It should not have been possible for the man to find out about the plot.

"Grand Guild Master, surely there is some mistake. If this is true, then my journeymen would be at risk. I cannot stay here safely within these walls. I must seek them out and check on their welfare."

The Grand Guild Master shook his head. "The instructions from the king are clear: we are on lockdown until we have checked every member here to ensure their healer's bonds remain intact."

Kevin carefully kept his face blank. He knew he couldn't

afford to allow the Grand Guild Master or anyone else into his mind, he'd have to kill them. It was too soon, he was not ready to leave his position here at the Healers' Guild. If he couldn't divert their attention elsewhere, he was going to have to kill his latest recruit and get rid of the body before they found out.

"If you will allow a suggestion, Grand Guild Master?" Kevin made sure to keep an appropriate expression of concern on his face.

"Of course, Kevin, anything that may help in this situation." The Grand Guild Master turned to give him his full attention.

"This will take some time to clear the whole Guild. In the interest of expediency, you could start with those Masters who have smaller departments to look after. The rest of us could go back to our offices and as heads of our departments muster our people so they are ready. Once you have finished clearing, say, Master Darius, he can then in turn come and clear me. Once I'm cleared I can in turn start checking those who look to me." Kevin looked up, a pleased smile on his face as he saw the Grand Guild Master nod.

"Ah, excellent suggestion, Kevin. It makes sense. You might as well all go to prepare your people. I'll start with Master Darius and we'll then move around to check you all. Remember, don't start checking your own people until you've been cleared by either myself or Darius."

Kevin stood, careful to keep the relief off his face as the Grand Guild Master turned to Master Darius. He thought furiously as he walked back to his own domain. Hopefully it would be old Darius who came to clear him. The doddering old fool would be easier to deal with than some of his other fellow Council members.

Kevin sat at his desk in his office. He had paperwork everywhere indicating he was working hard but it was an illusion. While he was relieved that the Grand Guild Master had decided to implement his suggestion, it was still playing at his nerves to wait. They were only humans, but some of them were stronger than he'd thought possible. He had learned a surprising amount about how to maximise the power that he had from how the healers worked with their limited power supply.

Kevin looked up as his door opened and smiled as Master Darius walked in. His assistant glanced at him, then closed the door quietly.

"My turn already, Darius?" Kevin stood in greeting and moved around his desk.

"Yes. You're the last of the Masters who sit on Council to be checked. I don't know what the king is thinking. I don't believe any of us is compromised." The old man was clearly grumpy that he had work to do rather than relaxing in his office or the gardens like he was more inclined to do these days.

"I agree, but he is the king so it's best to humour him." Kevin smiled at the old man.

"Let's get this over with, shall we?"

Darius raised his hands at Kevin's nod and went to place them on his temples, his own mind shields lowering so he could probe Kevin's bonds. Before he could complete the action Kevin's own hands shot up, grasping the old man's head in a firm grip. The old man's eyes widened in shock.

An unarticulated gurgle came out of his mouth as Kevin put niceties aside and sent his own mind probe piercing into his mind. He froze his victim's vocal cords as he quickly took over, careful to scrub this moment from the other healer's mind and put in its place a series of fleeting images he copied from the multiple times the old healer had performed this act on his fellow healers this day. Finally he constructed the memory of Darius finding nothing out of the ordinary in his mind.

Finishing up, he removed his own hands, standing quietly in front of Darius. As he withdrew from the other's mind, he shook his head, as if disconcerted by the other healer's search of his mind.

Darius looked momentarily confused before he smiled. "Ah, I'm sorry, my boy, it's always a little disconcerting, having another in your mind that way. Take a rest, and you are clear to vet your own people when you are recovered."

Kevin smiled and complied as the old man courteously directed him to rest on one of his own lounges before leaving his office to return and report the all clear to the Grand Master Healer.

The smile dropped off Kevin's face as the old man left, his eyes narrowing. It was such a shame he had to invade the old man's mind cleanly and quickly. He much preferred to play with his victims; inflicting a little pain and torture on them always put him in a good mood.

KEVIN WALKED out of the gates, entering the outer gardens of the Guild. He looked around and spotted the man he'd come to meet. He was angry since he knew that all in the Healers' Guild were being watched now. He just didn't know why. That detail had not been revealed, even to those of them on the Council.

Walking across the manicured lawns, he noted the immaculate garden beds; even the trees were well trimmed, and the leaves raked every morning. There was nothing out of place.

Simon had taken a horrible risk coming here, of all places, particularly now, while the Guild was alert for anything that was strange or out of order. Still, there he stood by the tree waiting for him, not looking concerned in any way as to his fate. Surely he should have known to stay well away if Kevin was late reporting back. There was a reason. Simon turned and smiled as he recognised him.

"Kevin, it's good to see you."

I thought I'd check if you needed a hand. Some of these Master Healers are too sensitive for me to shout at you over great distance.

"Simon, what are you doing here?" Kevin kept up their verbal conversation for the sake of the observers in the garden to disguise their double talk.

I'm fine, at least for now. What is going on? The Grand Guild Master hasn't been very forthcoming.

Master Healer Meagher looked around and saw that there were a few within the boundaries of the outer gardens that looked at them curiously. He wasn't known to have friends or family visit at all—in fact, he wasn't known to have any family; it wasn't in his carefully rehearsed backstory—so to anyone who recognised him, this was unusual.

Frustratingly, Simon smiled at him, unconcerned by the attention that they were drawing. "You missed our family meeting. I became concerned."

Alex cleaned out many of my people in his temper tantrum but I still have some eyes and ears in the palace. One of your pet healers was taken, he was in the hands of Master Healer Aaron and the Elite.

Kevin nearly ground his teeth. "I've been busy, Simon, I am a Master Healer, Head of Journeyman Healers now. I've been vetting the new journeyman healers about to go out into the realms. I have responsibilities. You should realise by now that I will certainly drop by when I can."

How much do they know?

"Ah, of course. My mistake. I just worry about you. I heard there was a fuss here at the Guild. You do understand?"

Don't worry, I've had people take care of it. He's dead and can't reveal more than he already has. If your identity had been revealed, the king's men would already be here to take you.

Kevin could see that they were still drawing the keen attention of the others in the gardens, yet at least some had turned away, dismissing the meeting. He breathed a sigh of relief, trying not to let it show when he realised what he'd done.

"I know, Simon, it was resolved easily enough. I'm sorry. You know I will come and visit when I can." Kevin kept a pleasant smile plastered on his face.

Thank you, I should be fine for now. I'll leave this place if I must. Simon smiled and nodded.

Be careful, Kevin, this is a dangerous game you are playing. If Edward finds out what you are up to, well, I doubt you will live very long.

He kept his eye on Simon and nodded acknowledgement of the warning as the man then turned and walked back down the road. He smiled. Despite the risk, Simon had come to see if he needed help.

His pleasant smile faded from his face. He was right about Edward's likely reaction if he found out. Of course Simon failed to see he'd be just as dead for helping him. His friend needed to stop being so scared of Edward and pick a side.

28

THE SAME?

IN THE TIME OF THE SUNDERED WAR

*E*dward sat on the windowsill, one foot dangling down towards the ground, his other leg propped up against the other side. He looked down into the courtyard below as his father's advisors droned on in the background. It was rare for him, as the fourth son of the king, to actually be involved in one of his father's meetings. Still, he guessed they would get to why he was asked to attend this meeting eventually.

If he had to guess, it was likely to be about the rumours spreading that those with access to the veil were going mad and killing people. The tales were wild, everything from single people to entire families to villages being slaughtered. The one thing in common between all of the recent deaths was that the acts had been committed by someone who bore the talent.

Forgetting himself, Edward chuckled as one of the young guardsmen below in the training ground fumbled his sword, dropping it to the ground. It was the trials today, the day young men around the realm could try out for the guard, or even for selection to the Elite if they were good enough, though it was rare for anyone to progress straight to the Elite from such trials. It was clear that the young man who'd dropped his sword wouldn't even get into the guard. Edward hid a smile behind an upraised hand, as some of his father's advisors glanced at him, clearly irritated. Edward didn't much care.

Aware of a silence that had grown in the room, he finally looked over to see that everyone was looking at him, including his father, who at least seemed amused, and his sister Jocelyn, who was biting her lip, looking suspiciously like she was trying not to laugh. Edward gathered he'd missed his cue.

"Sorry, I was watching the training session below. You finally need me for something?" Edward smiled, trying to put all the charm and sincerity that he could muster into his voice.

"We were talking about all these recent deaths, Ed." Jocelyn's voice didn't give away a hint of her amusement.

"Specifically, whether you, your friends, and guard could go out and investigate the claims?" While his father's request was phrased as a question, he had no doubt that there really wasn't a choice involved.

Edward looked away out the window, although this time to the forest he could see beyond the palace walls, thinking of the rumours. He also wondered whether this was the time to admit that he could hear the mad ones. Their screams rang out, day and night; there was little sense he could make from them other than pain, and rage, like an animal that had been provoked and driven into a frenzy. He doubted that either he or his friends could help them.

"We will, of course, go to investigate, Father. I think you need to consult with the healers, though." Edward kept his gaze out the window but knew all at the table would be trading glances.

"I have talked to our Master Healer. He told me there wasn't much that he knew or that he could do. Unless you had more information for me...?" His father's voice was calm, but Ed could hear the firmness and the surety. His father, as always, knew he was hiding something.

Ed closed his eyes, letting his head sink into his hand, his fingers absently massaging his temple.

"I can hear them, Father."

The silence in the room was deafening, the only noise coming from the clash of blades down in the practice ring below.

Edward heard the wooden scrape of a chair being pushed back, the rustle of skirts and the clip of court shoes, telling him without having to look that it was Jocelyn who was coming to his side. He didn't look even when a hand was placed on his shoulder.

"Are you all right, Edward?" Jocelyn's voice was soft, a hint of concern escaping her usual blandness.

Edward couldn't help it; he flung his head back and laughed. He turned his head to look at her, only seeing the concern in her features.

"Yes, Jocelyn, I'm fine. We all are. But you need to understand what you're asking us to do." Edward kept his gaze on her, the coolness of the stone wall soothing to the skin. He was aware that the rest of the board members were almost holding their breath, listening avidly to their exchange.

"So explain it to us, Ed. You know none of us has enough of the talent to understand this."

"They scream. It's like a never-ending wail of confusion, pain, rage. They just want the pain to stop, so they kill those around them. Sometimes they come back to themselves, and they discover themselves covered in blood. They're horrified, sister. They have no understanding of what they've done except that they must've killed their family and friends. They must've slaughtered those that were closest to them. Then the cycle begins again—the shock, the wailing, confusion, pain, rage." Edward shook his head, still ignoring all the other advisors, noting absently that none of them had moved. "We've been blocking them out; it's the only way to keep our own sanity."

Ed turned away from his sister's concerned gaze to stare at the distant trees. Taking a deep, steady breath, he opened his barriers just enough, and he could hear them: crazy ones crying out in pain, in confusion, begging for what they'd done to not be true. Edward winced, slamming his barriers back in place. Rubbing his temple once more, he chuckled. It had been a while since he'd tested. Still, at least he knew that he could track them down. It didn't seem like the mad ones, the broken ones, were trying to hide their presence at all. That would have taken some intelligence behind the madness. Ed pulled his attention back as he heard his father's voice.

"Is it different from what you went through with your own transition?"

One of his father's councillors leaned forward to stare at him intently, waiting on the reply.

"Yes... no..." Edward shook his head, trying to think. "You don't understand, it's different for everyone. More power charges into you, your shields falter, opening you to other thoughts not your own, you know nothing but pain and the increased power can cause you to black out."

"You think it is normal?" Jocelyn frowned, clearly trying to understand what he was having trouble explaining.

"It could be. I can see how it could drive some mad."

"Mad enough to kill their entire family?"

"I didn't suffer from it, but I've heard transition can cause blackouts and in that state some have been known to kill. Although it is usually when someone makes the mistake of confronting the person in that state. Sometimes the power can explode out of control, destroying everything. There really are not many of us at this power level, not like the healers. We call some of our own the Broken. Some recover eventually, some do not, transition is enough to break their minds" Edward looked away from the intent stares of the entire council and returned his gaze to the window.

"If it's too much for you, Ed, for all of you, if it's too dangerous, then you shouldn't go. We will think of something else." The king looked around at his advisors, receiving nods all around. He was about to launch into a strategy when Edward interrupted them.

"No, Father. My friends and I will go, and most of our guard. It's too dangerous for you or any of the others to go after them. They kill not just with their own hands, not just with weapons; they kill using their talent as well. No one else that you send will be capable of standing against them." Ed put his hand on the windowsill and jumped to the floor in one smooth motion. "I will leave half my guard with you, otherwise you will be unprotected should any here at the palace and surrounds who bear the power of the veil suddenly go mad." Ed strode towards the door, pausing just before walking out. "With your permission, Father, I need to do some planning with my men. We shall leave in the morning." Seeing his father's nod, and a look from his sister that said they would be speaking later, Ed turned and walked out the doors that were hastily opened by the servants.

29

CONFESSIONS

*A*lex sat quietly as William issued instructions to Shaun that he wasn't to be disturbed until morning, waiting quietly for acknowledgement and the door to close before turning back to him. He resisted the sudden urge to leave. When William left instructions that he wasn't to be disturbed, it meant what he needed to deal with was serious. Since Alex himself was the current issue his brother was dealing with, it didn't bode well.

"What is going on between you and Amelia?" William crossed the room and sat in the chair opposite him.

Alex was taken back. He had expected this talk to be about Isabella, since he was certain William would have been briefed by now.

"Nothing, I haven't seen her since before I killed Daniel and left the palace." Alex looked down and swallowed.

"There was a time when you two were almost inseparable. Now you are avoiding her. Don't try to say it's because you are afraid you will kill her. It isn't true and you know it. You haven't killed me." William sipped his drink, sighing and relaxing back into the cushions of his chair.

"Would you accept it's because I'm an idiot? It's my fault, I don't know what I was thinking."

"You could have just had a torrid affair with her and gone your separate ways. She is your Consort Elect now, Alex, there is no getting around that." William rolled his head to one side and pinned him with his gaze.

"I know. I remember how I felt back then, and it bears no resemblance to how I feel now. If anything, when I think of Amelia, I feel mild affection and a little embarrassed." Alex felt his cheeks heat.

"Do you think it is a side effect of your transition?" William frowned.

Alex shook his head. It was so tempting to jump at that excuse for his behaviour, the only problem being he knew it was a lie. However tempting it was to fall back on that lie to make things easier for himself, he couldn't do it to himself or Amelia. He knew she deserved better.

"Thank you for giving me an out, but no. Going through transition does not kill off the ability to feel for other people."

"Since you brought up feelings for other people, tell me about the woman you've been seen with." William shifted in his chair so he was facing Alex directly, his stare uncompromising and disturbingly implacable.

Alex squirmed in his chair. This was the conversation he'd been expecting, and he still wasn't ready to have it. Although he had to admit it would probably never be an easy conversation to have.

"You've never bothered to quiz me on women I've been with in the past, William." Alex recognised his stalling tactic for what it was and knew it wasn't going to work. It rarely did with William when he wanted to know something.

A smile spread slowly across his brother's face as he obviously recognised the deflection for what it was.

"You've never had a fling with the same woman for this

length of time before Amelia. I didn't need to ask about Amelia." William's tone was dry.

Alex looked at William above the rim of his glass, taking a sip, considering his options. He was better off just talking with William about it. Otherwise, knowing his brother, he would utilise other methods to find out what he wanted to know. Of course, it made it much easier that unlike some occasions in his past he didn't have to ask which woman he was asking about.

"Isabella. Her name is Isabella." Alex couldn't help but smile.

"Well at least the reports I receive on a daily basis got that part correct." William's eyebrow rose, his tone dry.

"She's Elder. I owe my sanity and life to her. She pulled me back from moments of madness I don't think I would have myself."

Alex shuddered at the painful memory that admission provoked. He looked at William and saw no judgement at all. Running his fingers through his hair, he stood abruptly and started pacing across the room.

William sighed. "She's your, what? Mentor?"

Alex heard his brother stand up and walk across to the sideboard, and he watched him refill his glass. He turned and held up the bottle in a silent question to Alex.

Alex looked at his glass, surprised to see it empty and walked towards William, holding out his glass to be refilled. Recognising the tactic to bring him back in, to divert his mind momentarily, Alex made an effort to calm his own agitation. He should be used to everyone's obsessive prying into his life by now. Indeed, if William was asking, that meant that his father knew as well and wanted answers. If Amelia knew, the court gossips were hard at work, and he could only imagine the spin that they had put on it.

"Mentor, friend and yes, William, as I'm sure your reports have suggested, my lover. I like her." He shook his head and took a breath, thinking bluntness was the better option. "I like her more than I should." Alex noted that William hadn't stinted in refilling either of their glasses. His brother was serious about not wanting to be disturbed, which was a rare thing.

Alex looked at William, who was watching him, still calm, not judgemental. That was one of the things Alex really did like about William. He was always quiet and never judgmental. Even when he was angry, William just tended to get even calmer, which was scary when you knew him.

"Where do you see this liaison with Isabella going?" William turned and leaned against the sideboard, watching Alex as he continued his pacing around the room.

Alex felt his mixture of emotions swirl and rise, threatening to overwhelm him. He took the time to breathe slowly before trying to reply honestly.

"I don't know, William. We haven't discussed that. I live day to day between moments of madness." Alex swallowed some of his drink, savouring it before looking up at his brother, a lopsided smile on his lips. "I knew I didn't need this added complication in my life, yet I come back to myself, and inevitably, more often than not, I find I'm with Isabella. Please don't ask me to cut ties with her. I don't think I can go through this alone."

William walked across the room and sat back down, gesturing to the chair opposite himself, waiting patiently as Alex struggled with himself before finally deciding to comply and slumping into the chair.

"I thought you were getting better?"

"I am. I have more time when I am present in my head, and the periods of memory loss are getting further apart."

William's gaze didn't waver. "I need to meet her, Alex. Father is concerned and wants details although he won't lend weight to the rumours that you have taken a mistress by meeting with her. Which puts this in my court. He needs to know if your continued relationship with Isabella is any risk to the Crown. Or to you."

Alex tried to breathe normally. That framed the request more as a royal order. It didn't mean he had to like it. Finally, he nodded. He knew William would not give up, given it was his father's request.

Isabella? William wants to meet you.

It didn't take long; it never did when he reached out to her. He couldn't help the smile that lit his face as her familiar signature sang across the veil, and she solidified in the room. She unerringly faced him and smiled in return. Alex stood and crossed the room to greet her, holding out his hand. With a slight hesitation as she glanced at William, she took his hand.

"Isabella, this is His Highness Crown Prince William."

William's head tilted to one side and he threw an exasperated glance at his brother. Alex nearly panicked for a moment, then saw his brother smile as he put his drink aside. William rose from his chair and walked a couple of steps to close the distance between them. He reached down and took her free hand in his own and kissed her fingertips.

"Isabella, thank you for coming. There is no need for formality, call me William." He waited until her eyes rose to his own. "Thank you for your part in helping my little brother back to himself."

Isabella smiled in return, her gaze darting to Alex before going back to William. "He did that mostly by himself, I've just lent support when I could."

"Come, take a seat." William gestured to the chairs as he turned and led the way, waiting for Isabella to take a seat before he took his own.

Alex watched the byplay a little wide-eyed and noticed William smile at his hesitation. He stalled, aware that William knew it for what it was, and walked over to the sideboard. Taking a glass, he filled a fresh drink. He quickly checked his

PATH OF THE BROKEN

brother's glass and noted that William had barely touched his own. That, if nothing else, told him that his brother had flipped back into official mode. Alex walked over and placed the drink for Isabella on the table next to her. With a barely visible hesitation, he gave in and slid into the chair next to her.

"So what do you want to know?" It seemed Isabella had decided there had been enough pleasantries between them.

"Where is home for you?" William smiled.

Isabella smiled in return. "Ilarith."

"Ilarith? The mysterious land that none from outside get to enter? A place of magic, good or evil depending on which tales you listen to?" William looked so startled that Alex nearly laughed.

"The very same. My brother made it as a sanctuary for me many years ago. Since then many others of power call it home."

"Sanctuary? So you weren't born there?" William's head tilted to one side as he considered her words.

"No, I was born in a different era in a small village at the base of a high hill where the warlord's castle sat. Vallantia did not exist back then."

William leaned forward, seemingly fascinated. "Do you know where it is? I'd be interested to hear your account of that time one day, and I'm sure the scholars would as well."

"No, I could probably find it but I've never been back." Isabella shivered.

Alex shook his head at William, who took the hint and changed the subject. He launched into being as pleasant and charming as he possibly could be. The conversation moved smoothly from topic to topic, all under William's guiding hand. He didn't bring up Isabella's ancient history again, although Alex was under no illusion he wouldn't be grilled for the information later.

"Not that I don't appreciate it, but why did you seek out

Alex?" William's gaze and expression was casual, but Alex wasn't deceived at all.

"My brother, Damien, became aware that Alex was going through transition and asked me to check in on him and help if I could. We have learned over the years that in particular for those as powerful as Alex, the outcome is much better for everyone with some guidance." Isabella met William's gaze, candidly answering without any hint of deception.

At hearing Damien's name, William visibly relaxed. While there was much that he didn't know, Damien was a known entity.

"Ah, so it seems Vallantia owes Damien yet another thanks for helping to save my brother's life again."

Alex felt himself relax as it became apparent that William approved of Isabella. He breathed a sigh of relief. For now, at least, he wasn't going to be ordered to break off his association, his relationship with her.

AMELIA LOOKED UP, irritated as the door to her inner chambers opened. Her maid, Carla, entered and curtseyed.

"I'm sorry to bother you, my lady, but you asked if I heard anything about His Highness to let you know." Carla kept her eyes down as she babbled.

Amelia's interest was aroused. "What have you heard, Carla?"

"He's here in the palace right now with Crown Prince William." Carla's eyes looked up from her study of the floor to meet Amelia's before sinking once more.

"Thank you, Carla." Amelia went to turn, but frowned as she noticed Carla was staying put. "Is there more?"

"Prince William has asked not to be disturbed for the night, but those orders don't apply to family." Carla blushed and curt-seyed before retreating from the room.

Amelia considered the information her maid had given her, and then, with a decisive nod, she stood. It was time for her to take action rather than sitting in her rooms in the Complex of the Fourth waiting for someone to bother to advise her what was going on. She swept out of her rooms, leaving the Complex of the Fourth, taking the passageway that led to the Royal Wing.

Amelia smoothed down the front of her dress before raising her head just as the doors to William's chamber opened when the staff on duty saw her approach.

Be careful.

Amelia nearly faltered as she heard the voice, whispering caution in her mind. Other than Healer Bates, he was the one who whispered to her the most. She couldn't afford for William to see, to discover how unhinged she was becoming. The only person worse would be the king. Yet William was dangerous. He spoke with the king's authority and voice.

You must not let him see.

Amelia felt a light sweat prickle her forehead as she wondered what she'd been thinking coming here to confront Alex. As if that wouldn't be difficult enough; now that the whispering voice in her head had returned, she wished it would retreat. This meeting was going to be difficult enough as it was, yet that presence in her mind did not withdraw, as it sometimes did. That made her even more nervous, but the next moment, unaccountably, she felt reassurance wash over her.

Do not fear. I am with you, I have always been with you.

Amelia walked into the room with a pleasant smile on her face, hoping that it reflected in her eyes. It should, after all her years of practice since childhood. Yet she knew William was schooled in the same mastery, one that Alex, while he could do the same, most of the time discarded entirely. The thought of

Alex made her smile in truth, although it was tempered with sadness.

Amelia made her way across the room, heading unerringly towards William. She paused, placing her hand on her heart and bowing her head. She was taken aback as she saw the momentary flicker of panic on William's face before he hid it smoothly behind his official mask.

She steeled herself when she looked up and saw Alex, but the thing that made her heart freeze was the presence of a woman she didn't recognise. An incredibly beautiful woman, standing with her body pressed close to Alex.

Amelia almost gasped as she felt the presence surge within her, narrowing into the other woman's blue eyes, blond hair and delicate features. She felt a burst of desire mixed with ownership, possession that was not her own, flood her.

Mine!

The desire that followed that one hissed word caused her to stumble, then the presence fled and she was saved from falling by William grasping her arm, and then with one hand around her waist supporting her, walked her to the couch.

"Sit, Amelia. I'm sorry. Elizabeth told me you'd been sick." William sounded more concerned than usual.

"I'm all right, William. It's been a little stressful lately, and the sight of your visitors shocked me." Amelia steeled herself to deal with the woman, anxiously trying to think of a way to keep Alex and his mistress from coming too close. As much as she wanted to confront him earlier, she now desperately wanted to escape his presence.

"I'm sorry, Amelia, I know this is a shock." William went to the sideboard and poured water from the pitcher into a glass, placing it in her hand, not withdrawing his own until he was sure that she had a firm grasp on it.

Amelia took a sip of water, grateful for the small delay it gave her in responding. She glanced across at Alex, then to the rather stunning woman standing at his side. The rumours that had been reported to her surfaced in her mind. She smiled, although this time she didn't care that it didn't reach her eyes. As if it wasn't bad enough Alex had chosen her over him, that voice that had always been with her, since she was a small girl, desired and wanted to possess this woman as well. She felt jealousy spike in her.

"So, is this the woman I've been told about? The one you've been sleeping with, Alex?" A part of her died inside to see the pain in Alex's face, yet it didn't stop her from wanting to cause him pain.

"Amelia, please—"

"Oh please, Alex, we both know you grow bored quickly and dispose of your women as easily as you drink and kill." Amelia heard the bitterness in her own voice and realised she half believed her personal accusation. She hardened her own heart, seeing it was the last barb that had hurt him more than anything, as she had known it would.

As Alex took a lurching step towards her, Amelia stood abruptly and headed towards the door, genuine tears streaming from her eyes, only to have her hand caught by another just as she was reaching the door. Amelia nearly fainted as she felt the thrum of power emanating from the woman at her touch.

"Please, Lady Amelia." The woman's blue eyes bore into her own.

Amelia quailed inside, understanding the warning she had received from the voice; the power in the woman was unbelievable.

She tore her glance away and looked back at Alex, biting back a sob before returning to the woman's intense gaze.

"Keep him safe." The last was said quietly as she wrenched her hand free and stormed out of William's rooms. She hauled up the folds of her dress and ran down the hallway, retreating to the dubious safety of the Fourth's Complex.

ISABELLA FROWNED as Alex's consort ran out of the room.

"Alex I thought you said Amelia didn't have power?"

"She has a little. The healers say it isn't enough for her to go through transition, though." Alex looked at her, still distressed by the run-in with Amelia.

"Ah, perhaps that is what I sensed."

Isabella stood for a moment longer, staring at the door that Amelia had fled out of. Her signature had been odd, with a strange ebb and flow to it.

30

WE CHEAT

*M*arcus strode into the training ring, James and Matthew in his wake. He nearly let a bark of laughter escape as the general guards lazing around the edges of the yard hastily moved out of their way. It wasn't typical for the Elite, let alone the Fourth's Elite, to attend the general training sessions, especially not on one of the open days where they tested new aspiring entrants to the King's Guard. Still, Prince William had given them the task of expanding the ranks of the gifted within the Fourth's Elite.

Now that Alex had reemerged, Marcus would rather be on his shoulder once more, or at least at the inn where they knew he returned to on a regular basis. Yet he had his task, so the assignment of watching over Alex had been designated to others for now. Meg would be with them, except that today Lady Amelia had emerged, which was rare these days, so she was on duty. That meant Matthew was the next most powerful in the use of the veil after himself and James. That, of course, had meant the poor lad had been hammered in training to bring him up to standard, rapidly. Not that he really needed much work. He really was brilliant with a sword, he just needed seasoning. Being attached to the Fourth and his Companions meant that generally happened more quickly. Or it had, until recently. Still, according to the Elites' own records, this period of withdrawal would likely be short. Until then, Marcus had a job to do.

He made his way over to the padded bench towards the centre of the extensive open practice grounds. The current occupants took one look and vacated the seat without being told to move. It always amazed him that even without the crest of the Elite—or the Fourth's Elite—blazoned on their vests, everyone still knew exactly who they were. He made that observation under his breath to James and Matthew. James smiled at him sardonically, and Matthew snorted. The lad had settled down remarkably well after his encounter with Lord Kyle; that had not gone well.

"You mean they recognise *you*." Matthew traded amused glances with James, who grinned openly.

"Get used to it, you're legendary." James's eyes were already scanning the training grounds.

Marcus shook his head and applied himself to the business at hand. The regular King's Guard were holding their own training on one side of the vast grounds, while the aspiring applicants had been corralled off to one side and were trying out on the other. It was part intimidation—some, seeing the standard they would need to attain, left without continuing with their application. That at least saved the guard some time with weeding out the timid ones.

Hearing a consistent heavy thump drew Marcus's gaze over to the side of the training ground where a solitary guard was practising with a training blade, hammering it time and time again into the training dummy. Marcus frowned and glanced at James.

"Do either of you know what that one is trying to achieve?"

Both James and Matthew shook their heads, both a little

bewildered. It was an odd training session for one of the King's Guard to be engaging in. Marcus noticed that even the weapons master's attention had been drawn, yet he merely shook his head, sighed and shrugged his shoulders at him. His eyes narrowing slightly, Marcus couldn't help himself. He stood, aware that the eyes of the other guards were on him as he made his way across the ground. He was also aware that both James and Matthew followed, yet paid it no mind. He doubted that he'd need any backup in this company, yet habits were hard to break. No one in the Fourth's Elite went by themselves while on duty.

Marcus paused, watching the lad as he beat away at the training dummy. Sweat drenching his body, giving evidence to his exertion. The lad swung at the reinforced dummy once more, grunting as his practice blade landed. He wilted slightly, and taking a deep breath, he raised his sword.

"Stop." Marcus didn't bellow—he didn't need to—yet the boy jumped and lowered his blade. "What are you trying to do?"

The boy looked at him, his eyes suddenly widening as he recognised who had interrupted his practice session.

"I'm, I..." The boy swallowed convulsively. "I heard that Lord Kyle, Prince Alex... well, all of you, can cleave a body in two with a single blow." The boy glanced back to the training dummy before his gaze slid back to the trio confronting him.

Marcus didn't have to look to know that James was trying to mask his laughter. Matthew didn't even try. Marcus controlled himself with effort.

"Trying to do that is likely to get you killed, lad." Marcus assessed all the eyes from the King's Guard and smiled grimly; it was time for a lesson. "Stand aside."

Marcus strode forward, drawing his own blade from its sheath. Bringing in the veil, he used it to both brace himself and augment not only his own strength but to run the power along the blade. In one smooth strike, his blade sliced through the practice dummy. Aware of the stunned silence and audience he had attracted, Marcus turned his gaze around the practice ring.

"We cheat. All of us, every man and woman in the Fourth's Elite, can channel the veil." Marcus turned back to the lad who'd been hacking away at the dummy. "You don't have that ability, lad. Learn what the weapons master can teach you. Trying to emulate us will get you killed."

With that Marcus turned and strode back to their place on the bench, James and Matthew on his heels, aware he'd just outed all of the Fourth's Elite. Of course, rumours had always flown around the guard about the 'secret' training sessions and abilities of the Elite. Rumour was one thing, knowledge was another. Unless he was very much mistaken, they were heading into a different era, one where those who bore the ability to control the veil were needed once more instead of feared. Marcus smiled grimly. Perhaps both.

The Elite, in particular the Fourth's Elite, had always been more than just good swordsmen. Maintaining their traditions and training over the years since the time of the Sundered War had been difficult, yet they had managed. There had always been a core group of their number who maintained their old ways. Now, on the direction of William, and indeed Alex, they were to grow their numbers. He doubted the Elite would grow to what they had been in their glory years in a hurry, yet grow they would.

Feeling and hearing surges of power around the training grounds, Marcus traded glances with James and Matthew. Their little display had been useful. As he suspected, there were some with ability already hiding what they were within the ranks of their fellow guards. He suspected that many had been trained by their own family members, tradition being secretly handed down through the generations. James and

Matthew stood and, going opposite directions, they circulated around the training men and women. Marcus glanced up as the weapons master approached, sitting on the bench next to him.

"Thank you for ending that particular idiocy." The weapons master kept his voice low, his eyes still intent on his training charges.

Marcus grinned, finally letting amusement show. "Well, it was our fault."

"Like any of you had much choice but to step up with that mess surrounding His Highness." His tone was even, without even a hint of criticism.

"To be fair, Prince Alex didn't really go looking for any of that trouble, particularly the attack of the Sundered during the migration to the Summer Palace." Marcus carefully kept any censure out of his voice.

"I know Marcus, and he along with Lord Kyle and Lady Jessalan did a remarkable job, by all accounts, of using their own abilities to protect everyone. That story has grown to become legendary, prompting foolishness like you just stopped." The exasperation in the weapons master's tone was evident.

Marcus chuckled. "Sorry."

They sat in silence for a time, just watching the practice session and trials continue. The weapons master's own seconds were sufficiently trained that they could continue admirably on their own without his intervention.

"So what do you need from me? Do you want all the new ones with talent?" It was clear from the man's tone that he didn't think that was a good idea.

"No. Take the new ones into the regular guard, see what you can make of them. We will take some of those already in who also have talent." Marcus finally looked at the weapon's master. "With your guidance, of course. We don't need any troublemakers in our ranks. I fear we don't have time to knock it out of them."

The weapons master gazed back at him, he then nodded. "Have a look around and bring your list and men to the back room of the Arms tonight. I'll bring my deputies, and we'll discuss your hopefuls."

With that, the weapons master stood and went back to prowling around the training grounds. Marcus smiled. The back room of the Arms was notorious hangout for the higher ranks of the King's Guard. It was not somewhere that the Elite was generally invited to. There had always been a divide in their ranks. It seemed the weapons master was intent to end that divide, at least in the upper levels. He doubted the animosity bedded in jealousy and the need to prove who was better would ever truly disappear in the lower ranks.

31

TREATMENT

*D*evon woke groggy and confused, unsure of where he was or what had happened. He groaned and rolled over, recognising that he was in a comfortable bed, then he surged up in panic as he realised he was shackled. The chains were bolted to the wall, giving him limited room to move. He started to shake, not understanding what had happened; there were too many blanks in his memory, too many images of blood and death, atrocious acts that he was sure he had committed.

The door to his cell opened, and a man and a woman walked in, smiling at him. Devon recognised the woman, Jenny; she was a healer that his parents had consulted about him having the Taint.

"It's all right, Devon, you're safe now. Do you remember who I am?" Jenny smiled at him as she crossed the room to sit in a chair by his bed.

Devon nodded, unsure of himself. "You're Jenny, the healer. I'm not safe to be around, I don't want to hurt you."

Jenny smiled sympathetically and reached for a bottle on the nearby table. She pulled the stopper out and poured a measure of the dark liquid into the mug before moving to his side.

"It's all right, Devon, the medication will help keep you safe, will help keep everyone safe from you. You can trust the Order. The medication will help you control the power and yourself. It will take some time, there will be pain and adjustment. Eventually, as long as you stay on the medication we give you, everyone will be safe."

She placed the mug to his lips, helping to prop up his head so he could swallow the medication. She withdrew as he felt himself start to tremble, breaking out into a sweat. As her hands grasped either side of his head, he stiffened, feeling sharp stabbing pain explode in his skull. He screamed as her mind whispered words that he didn't understand, and fire raced through his veins like a burning web all over his body. As he bucked on the bed, the shackles bit into the skin at his wrists and ankles. All the while Jenny's voice dominated his mind, agony pulsing through mind and body in time to the pitch of her voice.

Devon didn't know how long the pain went for; a minute, an hour, an eternity. Gradually it subsided, and he sobbed, and as he felt nausea rise up, he struggled to roll over. Then he felt her cool hand on his forehead.

"Shhh, Devon, it's all right, don't be sick, I'm with you now, I'll help you. If you are sick, I'll have to compel you to have more medication." Jenny's mind voice was soothing, and he felt himself starting to drift off under her ministrations.

Devon finally became aware again, not sure if he'd passed out or not. He felt strange, wrong, but he couldn't put his finger on what it was that was different. Then he realised he wasn't feeling the surging power that he associated with the Taint flowing through him. He still felt sick, wrong somehow, yet relieved all at the same time. He moved his head to one side to see that Jenny had returned to sit on the stool next to his bed, as had the man who finally stood and came closer, placing one hand on Devon's still sweating forehead. He frowned in concentration before smiling.

"You'll make a fine addition to our team when the treatment takes hold, Devon. We'll discuss that another day soon, when you are feeling better and under Jenny's full control." The man turned to Jenny and nodded. "Good catch, Healer Medcalf. Continue with his treatments. Notify me when he is under control."

Devon watched the man walk out, confused about the conversation that he seemed to be a part of yet missing half of it. He licked his lips and looked at the healer.

"What was that you gave me? Who was he? I don't understand." Devon felt drowsy, but heard her answer as he drifted off to sleep.

"That is Scholar Caine, he is in charge of recruitment here at the Order. You are fortunate, Devon. You are one of the ones to receive the new treatment for the Taint. The medication will install control on you and your power. When I'm done with your treatment, you will be able to trust yourself again. Once controlled, you will go out into the world under Scholar Caine's direction, to kill and capture monsters like you were, to help save the people." Her intent brown eyes swam into his view. "You want that, don't you, Devon? You want to stop the monsters in the world?"

Devon nodded, and seeing a sweet smile on her lips in response made him feel unaccountably good. He decided the medication, no matter his reaction, was worth it if it helped him become less of a monster.

"Good, Devon. You will never kill uncontrollably again once we have you under the control of the medication. You will only kill as we direct. You will become a weapon against those who would hurt others."

Devon fell asleep feeling a cool cloth, wiping his face, then down his chest and arms, relaxing, and he felt reassured under her ministrations.

32

BARRIER IN THE VEIL

*J*ess checked on her personal barrier again; it had almost become a fanatical habit after she lost control of it. She shuddered. Losing control like that was never something she wanted to risk again. It had taken some time but once they were back in place and not leaking, she realised how unstable she had been. A slow gradual slide into becoming someone she didn't like very much.

With Damien's help she had tracked down the boy she had nearly killed, would have killed without Isabella's intervention, and apologised to him. At the time she hadn't cared about her own behaviour and the very real consequences that would have resulted. The death of the man who had attacked her didn't concern her, or it hadn't—she'd been defending her own life. Except she hadn't really intended to kill him. She'd meant to disable him and hold him for Damien to deal with. Ilarith was his domain, she was just a guest. When Kyle had gotten out of control and killed without real cause it had been because of the drug and Alyssa. She didn't have any such excuse.

Standing in front of the barrier again, Jess looked up at it, her eyes narrowed in frustration. Then she laughed at herself.

At least she was making progress. She wasn't trying to suppress the fact that she was frustrated by it. Damien was frustrating on the issue, simply smiling and indicating that when she could work out how to get through it by herself she would be ready to go out in the world. Although it wasn't as though she was in a burning hurry to leave Damien's hospitality and tutoring. She knew her access to power had been increasing; flicking over to the pure, raw power took a little concentration, but she could access and use it. It was that power she'd discovered that was utilised to make things permanent if she willed it so. Practising with creating permanent objects for wielding that power was what had caused her curiosity about the barrier. She had a hunch that it was formed from the pure white power source, which was why she couldn't do anything about it when she'd first encountered it. Now that she could sense that power and was starting to use it, Jess was determined to see if that had changed.

Jess paused when she felt the glow of power, like a cool unseen force pushing her back. Concentrating, she switched her other sight to view the pure energy source and gasped in awe. The shimmering curtain of power sprang into her sight, moving and scintillating in undulating waves. It might have been irritating, but it was beautiful.

Jess moved forward, not even bothering to simulate walking, she was that intent on the barrier. Reaching out, she grasped hold of the curtain wall and willed it aside. Meeting resistance, she narrowed her eyes and pushed herself forward, and gripping the curtain with the mental fingers of her mind, she compelled it to peel apart. Jess shivered as she felt the power moving and enveloping her like a fine mist, pinpoints prickling all over her skin as she passed through it. Even though passing through it took only moments, it had felt longer, and as she popped out the other side, Jess felt herself trembling from the exertion. She'd discovered that while she could perform a great many feats, she was still constrained by the limits of the power she could draw at any one time. Jess chuckled as her stomach rumbled at her, letting her know that drinking in power was all very well, but her body still required food, particularly after burning through so much energy. She could use the veil to re-energise, wash away fatigue, but it didn't replace the need to eat.

JESS THOUGHT ABOUT HER OPTIONS. She hadn't actually thought about what she would do if she managed to get through the barrier. Coming to a decision, she willed herself through the veil towards the Summer Palace.

Jess smiled appreciatively as she stared at her target from the veil. He stripped off the formal blue vest with the gold and silver braid of his rank that he hated so much and dumped it on the couch as he walked past it. As he started unbuttoning his shirt to reveal his chest, Jess unaccountably blushed. It wasn't as if she hadn't seen him take his shirt off before—and a good deal more than that—but watching him this way when he didn't know she was there wasn't what she'd intended. Jess passed though the veil, appearing in the room behind him before he pulled his shirt off, and cleared her throat.

William jumped in fright, spinning around, a look of relief on his face as he saw her.

"Jess, you nearly gave me a heart attack." William pressed his hand against his chest and sighed.

"Sorry William, I arrived just in time to see you stripping off. Didn't feel right to peep at you through the veil that way." Jess knew her cheeks had gone red.

William laughed and closed the distance between them, pulling her in close and hugging her. Finally he looked down and kissed her.

CATHERINE M WALKER

"Well, it's not like you haven't seen it all before," William teased, his eyes dancing.

He drew away but kept possession of her hand, leading her through his suite and out through the private side of the Royal Wing. Glancing around, he led her down the stairs and out the double glass doors into a private courtyard garden. It was a pleasant evening, the light breeze ruffling his short brown hair. The light shirt he was wearing did nothing to hide his physique, particularly since it was half unbuttoned. Not that William needed to, she admitted. He pulled her over to one of the large reclining couches, lounging back onto it as he tugged her into his arms.

Jess sighed happily and relaxed. For a moment she could pretend her life hadn't been turned upside down.

"It's good to see you again. I'm sorry if you were worried by our disappearance." Jess rested her head against his chest, content to just sit.

"It has certainly caused a little stress, but it's fine. I managed. How are you?" William's voice was low, even though there was no one around to overhear.

"I thought at first I was perfectly in control, but turns out I was wrong. Damien helped me pull myself together before I did something unforgivable."

"Damien? I'm glad you are getting some help."

Jess's eyes narrowed. "Why do I get the feeling you already know I've been in Ilarith with Damien acting as my mentor?"

William was quiet, then chuckled. "Alex came to see me and I had to insist on meeting Isabella. Father was insistent about knowing more about her due to the rumours surrounding them both. Your whereabouts came out during that meeting." William winced. "Then Amelia heard that Alex was here visiting me and descended on us to confront Alex, and it turned into a mess."

Jess's eyes widened. "Oh, that would not have ended well."

226

William groaned. "It didn't. I'm taking the coward's way out and have co-opted Elizabeth to speak with Amelia."

Jess turned in his arms, her hand resting on his chest, taking comfort from his familiar embrace and presence. They lay there together quietly before William spoke again, his voice filled with compassion.

"I'm sorry about your mother, it must have been a shock."

"You know I killed her?" Jess swallowed but didn't try to push down the sadness and anger that betrayal had caused.

"We put the pieces together. She was a member of the Order and involved in the kidnapping attempt." An undertone of anger threaded William's words.

"Yes, I followed Daniel to their meeting. I knew she didn't like me after the display at court in the Winter Palace, but I didn't think she would be involved in such a plot."

Jess felt a wave a sadness crash over her again even if she never got on with her mother. If she was honest with herself, she'd barely known her, but the woman had still been her mother.

"Any more than I would ever have believed Daniel would engage in such a plot."

"Scholar Clements is still a loose end. However did he manage to get a position at the palace?" Jess frowned. Now *he* was someone she wanted to track down, and she doubted she would feel badly about killing him.

"He came with excellent credentials from the scholars, he trained at their Great Library in Vallantia before he was appointed as a tutor to us. I did send some people out to locate him, but he's disappeared."

"Hmm... I might drop in on the scholars in Vallantia and ask a few questions." Jess suddenly found her attention diverted as she felt the top of her dress loosen.

Pulling William's head down, she kissed him, then shifted

to make it easier for him as his fingers continued undoing the fastenings of her dress.

"Ah, wait, is Damien going to get insanely jealous if he finds out you are here in my arms?" William looked down at her.

"No. He laid down the ground rules from the start. He is my mentor, nothing else." Jess chuckled at the satisfaction in William's expression.

"Good. I was jealous when you were with him. It's wrong of me, I know, but I wish I wasn't the crown prince. I wish Elizabeth had been born first." William leaned down and kissed her, leaving no doubt at all where his thoughts were going.

"William, don't do this to yourself. Even if Elizabeth had been born first, I would not be considered high enough rank for your father to consent to our union. As it is, you are the crown prince, you will be king" This was an old conversation they'd had before.

"I don't want to be king."

"You do. You will be a great king when it is time. Your father will pick someone of suitable status. She will be your consort and Queen."

"Just once in my entire life I wish I could have something for me, rather than a life of duty." William turned his head to the side, refusing to look at her.

Jess reached up, placing her hand on his cheek and gently turning his face back to look at her.

"Well, there is tonight."

Jess tugged his shirt out of his pants and pulled it off, running her hand up his chest. William pushed aside his bout of depression, his lips closing on hers, his fingers busy at the fastening of her dress again. Jess chuckled and, pulling the veil around them, transported them to William's bedroom, grateful she was as familiar with it as she was her own.

33

RESCUE

IN THE TIME OF THE SUNDERED WAR

*S*imon followed in Edward's wake as they travelled in the veil towards yet another village where they could hear those driven to madness by the veil screaming in pain. After so many communities, he had no doubt what he would see. He was finding it increasingly hard to hide what he honestly felt. None of the hints that he made that Edward was born to rule, that this—the Sundered War, they were calling it —could propel him to take the crown had had any effect on the man. The people were chanting his name, grateful when he showed up to rescue them from the Sundered hordes.

The reports of the realm being overrun with Sundered were highly exaggerated. In reality, when they arrived to investigate they usually encountered one or two sick, mad people of his own kind. Yet this was enough in the minds of the villagers to believe that there'd been a veritable army of Sundered who swooped down on their village and killed them all.

Despite the accolades, the adoration of both his peers and the commoners alike, and from his men—and they were his men, heart and soul, particularly his inner circle—Edward sought no advantage. He still firmly supported his father, and his sister who would take the crown. Simon had to stop himself from sneering. He couldn't understand Edward's attitude. They had been born with power. They were born to take the lead to rule this world. Edward just couldn't see it.

Still, one thing this little war was doing was culling the competition amongst the ranks of those born with the power. The fewer there were that could control the veil, the more likely it was that *he* could wrest control. Or at least he could if he could convince Edward and his inner circle to his way of thinking. Simon found it interesting that the ordinary people adored Edward and his men. To a person, they knew that Edward and his people all utilised the power of the veil, yet they overlooked it. They adored them all, saw them as their saviours. Without even realising their own hypocrisy, they had started to hate those born with the veil. Reports were coming in—of mothers smothering their babies, of fathers killing mother and baby both all for the crime of being born with something that only months before would have been regarded as something to celebrate.

Simon smiled. The common folk were doing his work for him. He didn't have to go after his own kind, not really—the average person would do it for him. That, and the sudden influx of those turned mad from the veil. No one could quite say how it had happened. The healers indicated that they were at a loss. Rumours were spreading that something had gone wrong with the veil, or perhaps people had changed somehow, were becoming incompatible with the power, which was now driving them mad.

As they transitioned from the veiled world to the real world, Simon drew in his own power. You could never show too much caution with the Sundered around. They would attack those who bore power just as quickly as those who didn't. Sure enough, there stood one of the Sundered holding a woman, about to kill her. He could hear a baby wailing off to one side, as the Sundered, feeling their approach, snarled and tossed the woman aside.

"Now is that any way to treat a lady?" Edward's voice was scolding.

Simon watched as Edward showed once more his mastery over the veil, showed him why he didn't dare let Edward know what he intended. Edward drew on the power, and it ran down the length of his blade as he drew it, chopping off the Sundered One's head in one smooth motion, before he allowed the body that he'd been holding in the air to fall to the ground.

With the Sundered One dispatched, Edward walked over to the common farmer woman, held out his hand, and helped her to her feet. Cal had walked over and retrieved the crying baby from the bushes beside the road, and he handed the swaddled bundle back to its mother.

"Simon, take the woman and her child to safety. Join us in the village to clean up when you are done." The prince turned to gesture to his other men to follow.

Kevin lingered, glancing at the woman and child, his eyes glittering and cold as they met Simon's in mutual understanding.

Ah, you get all the luck. He smiled and turned to follow Edward.

Simon ignored Kevin's parting shot and spoke to Edward's retreating back.

"Certainly, Edward, as you wish. Save some of the fun for me." Simon nearly winced as he heard the mocking tone in his own voice, but managed to smile reassuringly at the woman as he grabbed her shoulder and wrapped the veil around them both, disappearing from sight.

Simon didn't have to take them far, only into the bushes, far enough from the road that no one would hear anything. He doubted that she would be discovered. The woman looked up at him, perplexed at where they'd ended up, apparently having expected that she would have been taken to the nearby village. Simon let the coldness he felt show on his face. She tried to step back, fear replacing the relief from moments before. She clutched the child to her, and it wailed in response to her fear. Simon grabbed his knife, and a quick, simple strike slit the woman's throat, and her child's, all in one smooth motion. Their bodies fell to the ground, the woman's blood spurting, yet he paid it no mind.

The woman should have been grateful it was he that killed her. If it had been Kevin, he would have played and tormented her first. Simon drew in the veil and closed the distance between him and Edward. He didn't want to miss out on the fun.

3 4

SUSPICIONS

*I*t took conscious effort after the mess with Amelia to come back to the palace again, although Alex had taken William's request seriously to visit regularly so he could report to their father that he was at least alive and getting better. That was another meeting he'd been putting off. He had to see his father himself. Eventually. He was almost afraid of what his father would say. Just as he was pulling one side of his life together, he was promptly making a mess of the other.

At first, he'd stayed away from the palace because he didn't want to inadvertently kill someone he loved. He had to admit he was probably stable enough to start moving back, at least for a few days at a time. Except now he wanted to give Amelia time to calm down from her run-in with Isabella.

Alex frowned, pushing his relationship issues aside and dragging his attention back to William.

"Now that I'm going through it, William, I don't think it is the veil causing the Sundered to go mad. There is something else happening. The mad ones I've encountered, so far, their signature..." Alex paused, frustrated with his inability to say what was swirling around in his head. "I've encountered it before. It is similar to what happened to Kyle when he was under the effects of that toxin and Alyssa. Except worse."

"What do you mean, Alex?" William sat back in his chair, his attention caught by the sudden change in conversation.

"I can show you mind to mind, I think." Alex glanced at William for permission. "With your permission, if you would like the insight?"

Alex watched as his brother considered the offer, but wasn't surprised by the quick, decisive nod. William was generally quick to assess the information he had and make a decision based on the information available to him. That decisiveness was something that he loved about his brother. He made choices and accepted the results along with the responsibility, good or ill.

"You can do that? I've always wondered what it was like." William put his drink aside and settled back in his chair more comfortably.

Alex took a steadying breath, trying to ignore his uncertainty, and he concentrated, contemplating how he could draw his brother into a mental exchange. It wasn't something he thought about that often; talking that way with Kyle and Jess had been second nature most of his life.

He knew William had a limited ability with the veil, but he honestly didn't know if it was enough to be able to show him what he knew. Reaching out to that glowing signature that he knew was his brother, Alex drew him in, forcing a connection between them. The first indication that he had that he had succeeded was William groaning, both physically and mentally. The fact that he'd caused his brother pain sparked some guilt, yet he pushed it aside and sent reassurance towards William.

It's all right, William, try to relax. Although you may want to clear your schedule tomorrow. I feel like you are going to have the worst headache of your life.

Alex knew his brother heard, even if he couldn't respond, or perhaps just didn't know how. He waited until he felt William's anxiety levels decrease.

Taking a breath, Alex concentrated, bringing the memories from Kyle to the forefront, sharing them with William—Kyle's increasing bloodlust, loss of self, pain and anger bubbled to the surface, flashing with images of the cool, calm and collected Kyle; the two together didn't make sense. Then the flashing images in quick succession that he'd gained from Jess—of the Order, the vials of the toxin, and what they had intended. Next, he moved on to what he had encountered with the various Sundered that he had fought. Bringing forward that mental signature—bloodlust, loss of self, pain and anger—he flashed the dual memories at William of what he knew: Kyle under the influence of the toxin, under Alyssa's control, and the mental signatures of the Sundered he had fought, under the command of a healer.

Alex took a breath and sent comforting thoughts to his brother's mind, trying to soothe the growing pain he felt coming from him. Wincing, Alex sensed that William was clinging to the connection between their minds, although he doubted he was aware of it. He finally pushed William from the contact with his own mind, realising that his brother didn't have the power or knowledge to do it himself.

Alex shook himself from the violent disconnect. He needed to check on William. Finally getting his eyes to track, he saw that William was curled into a ball on the couch, waves of distress emanating from his mind.

Alex lurched from his chair and landed on his knees at his brother's side. Placing his hands gently on either side of his brother's head, he sent his thoughts into his mind. Offering reassurance and comfort, he drew William back to himself.

"Shaun!" Alex knew that his brother's servants were always within calling distance.

He was proven correct by Shaun's prompt appearance. He

could see the servant's alarm as he saw his master unconscious on the couch with his supposedly mad, murderous brother leaning over him. Alex dismissed what the servant thought from his mind.

"Get Aaron and alert my father. William will be fine, but he'll need to be excused from his commitments tomorrow, maybe a couple of days. I doubt he will be capable of fulfilling them." Alex looked up from his brother to the servant, the command in his voice obvious even to his own ears.

To Shaun's credit, he bowed smartly and responded. "Of course, Fourth."

Alex cursed softly, wondering why it always seemed to take longer waiting for the healer to show up. Being the one who'd summoned the healer was a rarity for him.

ALEX STOOD to one side of his brother's room, keeping out of the way as Aaron tended to him. Both his father and Elizabeth had shown up promptly, which wasn't unexpected given the sudden nature of William's collapse. Still, he'd done what he could while waiting for Aaron to attend, even if it was only to maintain a mental barrier between his brother and the veil. He didn't want to make mental contact again to attempt to soothe the pain he felt emanating from his brother's mind. The genuine fear that he could burn out William's mind gripped him.

Looking at the raw energy emanating from his brother's mind, it seemed to Alex as if a part of William's mind had been torn open. He hoped he hadn't done irreparable damage.

His father greeted him softly and embraced him, asking how he'd been. Alex decided now was not the moment to be candid with his father—although he had the sneaking suspicion that, as always, William had briefed him fully on all of the visits that Alex had made.

"I've been worse, Father. It gets easier. I think I'm getting used to the overload of power." Alex pulled back and turned to greet Elizabeth, who merely hugged him. He knew that she would speak with him later. He could tell she was torn between wanting to pull him aside and check on him and concern for William. He was her twin, and he knew there was still a strong connection between them.

All of them fell silent, watching as Aaron treated William, who had descended into unconsciousness. That was probably a blessing for him.

"What happened, Alex?" Elizabeth's voice was soft.

Alex glanced at her but saw she hadn't taken her gaze off their brother. He closed his eyes briefly and took a deep breath.

"I take it he's been briefing you?" Alex's voice was bland, despite the circumstances, as he turned his gaze between his father and Elizabeth.

His father nodded, and Elizabeth threw him an exasperated glance.

"Of course he has. He said your stability was improving, and told us about your run-in with some of the Sundered, and about his meeting with Isabella."

Alex couldn't tell from Elizabeth's tone whether she was disapproving or not. He plainly heard the unasked question in her tone when she said Isabella's name.

"My ability to make a mess of things hasn't changed. Seriously, it was innocent enough to start. Isabella was my mentor. I was floundering until I met her and then, well, I take it you already know we started sleeping together." Alex turned and stared intently at his father, who reached up and squeezed his shoulder.

"It's all right, Alex, we'll sort things out. Lord Strafford and I had already agreed before Amelia became your Consort Elect that even if your mutual infatuation with each other died it would still be a good political union. What happened with William?" His father returned his gaze to the bed where William lay unconscious before glancing back at him.

Alex released a breath he hadn't realised he was holding. His father had just essentially given him tacit approval to continue his association with Isabella. Of course he'd also indicated that Amelia would become his consort on his return regardless. No amount of wishful thinking or regret was going to change that circumstance. While he might have been confused about his own behaviour, it appeared that neither his father nor Lord Strafford had been caught off guard.

"I was discussing the Sundered with William." Alex shrugged, a little uncomfortable. "Given my own experiences with transition, I don't believe that what the Sundered have gone through is the same thing."

Alex suddenly found he had the attention of both his father and Elizabeth.

"Go on," his father's calm voice prompted him when he paused too long. Alex suddenly realised where his brother got his own calm tone in the face of adversity.

"It... They reminded me of when Kyle was drugged that time." Alex lapsed into silence and gathered his thoughts.

This time it was Elizabeth who prompted him. "Alex, I swear if you don't tell me what happened..." She left the rest unspoken, although took the sting out with a soft smile.

"I didn't know how to say what I was thinking, so..." Alex swallowed. "I drew William in mentally and showed him."

Elizabeth gasped. "You could draw William into your mind?"

Alex shook his head. "It is not quite like that, it's more... It's hard to explain. I used the power to link my mind with William. I could then show him what I meant. William has talent—not much, but it was enough that I could communicate with him that way."

His father nodded, not looking at all surprised. "Ah, yes, the healers told me that he had more power than regular people, although they said it was minimal enough it would never be enough to cause him harm."

They all lapsed into silence and just waited for Aaron to finish. Thankfully, for all of their sanity, it didn't take much longer before Aaron sighed, his fatigue evident as he stepped away from his patient.

Noticing the three of them waiting to one side of the room, he approached and bowed his head in acknowledgement to the king.

"Your Majesty, William will be fine." He glanced across to Alex, then back again. "Being drawn into mental communication with Alex has burnt out some of the channels in his mind. The ones associated with power. I won't know until he wakes, but I believe he is more susceptible to the veil now, although still not enough, I believe, to cause him to suffer through a transition."

Relief wash over Alex as he bowed his head, vowing never to communicate with his brother that way again.

MANOEUVRING JOANNA

*E*dward steeled his heart, knowing what he was about to do was cruel, yet it needed to be done. When Alex had shown up at the battle with the Kin at the estate, he'd been horrified, yet he'd quickly seen the potential. He knew that Alex, if he took the time to look, would understand that Kyle had been taken. Again.

If he knew his nephew—and after all these years he liked to think he did—he guessed that Alex would react badly to Kyle being bound to another's will once more. He hadn't been disappointed; Alex responded precisely as expected.

I'm sorry Alex. I hope you will forgive me. I will make it up to you, I promise.

Edward had to make a decision, in that space, in time, one that he knew would have ongoing consequences. He'd watched as Joanna had taken control of Kyle and turned him against Alex. Watched as Kyle thrust his blade into the stomach of his best friend and drew his power, raining strikes down on him, all against his own will and struggling within himself. That, if anything, had given Edward hope Kyle wasn't completely lost, that he still retained some of himself that was separate from his mistress. Yet if he didn't act, soon, he knew there would be no hope that Kyle would ever be capable of being independent again.

All of it played on Edward's conscience. He could have intervened, he could have stopped Joanna. Yet that would not have aided Kyle in gaining his freedom. The consequences of that act, of finding out she had tried to kill her own son, could be leveraged to force her into releasing Kyle. He just needed to find the right fulcrum.

He could feel the dark swirling confusion and guilt of Joanna's emotions. Smiling grimly, he walked into the front room, his eyes locking on her. She stood staring out to the crashing waves, dark clouds boiled in, thunder rolled across the skies, the rain almost sideways as it struck the window. As if nature itself was echoing Joanna's mood, her shoulders shook, as she cried. He knew that she was aware that he'd walked in, yet she ignored his presence.

"Damn it, Joanna, see what you've done? You had your thrall try to kill your own son." Edward's voice and words were deliberately cutting and harsh.

Joanna gasped, a trembling hand flying up to her face.

"I didn't mean it, Edward, I didn't know it was him." Joanna's voice shook. She looked at him, quaking, wanting his understanding.

"Release Kyle. Cut him free before it is too late." Edward sent a soft mental nudge, aware that she was so tied up in her own guilt and pain that she wouldn't notice it.

Joanna stiffened and stepped back, her face closing down. "No. He's not ready. He's mine. Kyle is better off with me. All of you need to understand that. You don't know what those people did to him, what they drove him to."

Edward closed his eyes and shook his head. "What? Worse than having him turn on his best friend and try to kill him?"

CATHERINE M WALKER

Joanna cried and turned her back on him. "I didn't know, I swear I didn't know," she almost wailed.

Edward's lips thinned. He made an effort to contain his own anger at her obstinance. Shaking his head, he decided to change tack. As imperative as Kyle's release was becoming, a series of small steps was probably easier to achieve.

"At least let him go to explain what happened to William. If they hear of what he did to Alex without explanation..." Edward smiled grimly. He knew she wouldn't budge and let Kyle go to Alex. She would dig her heels in, thinking that he would take steps to free his friend from her influence, and rightly so.

Joanna turned to face him, confusion evident on her face. "What do you mean?"

"Trying to kill Alex is an act of treason, Joanna. William needs to understand what happened from Kyle before he hears it from other sources." Edward kept his expression clear and a careful guard on his thoughts. William would no more countenance Kyle's enslavement than Alex would. "You told me one of the reasons you bound Kyle instead of Simon was so that he didn't commit treason."

Joanna looked stricken as she considered his words and her head bowed in grief. Edward kept strict control of his emotions, not allowing his triumph to show as he felt her capitulation.

SERVICE

*D*evon walked along the pathway of a village he didn't recognise. He walked as instructed slightly behind Healer Medcalf. He'd felt some trepidation when Jenny had told him they were going to slowly start withdrawing him from the medication. Yet his treatment held, the compulsions and controls she'd instilled in his mind and like a comforting web over his whole body stayed in place. He grew more relieved as the days passed since he'd last had his medication and he didn't descend into madness. He could feel the power of the Taint, yet it didn't corrupt him anymore the way it used to. Jenny had told him that was the effect of the treatment, that the destructive power could not hurt him anymore.

He was aware that it was Jenny who had full control over him. He moved and performed as she willed it, yet within constraints, she allowed him a certain amount of free will. It was hard for him to comprehend; he was in his own mind, the same as he'd ever been, yet somehow he was changed and not truly himself anymore. He was not a free man as he had been. He was connected and bound, subservient to whatever Jenny willed of him.

Devon contemplated that thought for some time as they continued their progress to what he guessed was the main meeting hall. He felt Jenny's presence in his mind, cautious yet not intervening. She was allowing him to work through his new status himself. Devon remembered who he had been, the pain and suffering he'd inflicted. He remembered, yet he didn't feel the trauma of it anymore. It was remote and different from where he was now. Then he thought about himself now, bound to Jenny. Compelled to obey. Yet Jenny had been right. She'd promised him that the treatment would help him, that he wouldn't kill undirected in an uncontrolled fashion again.

He would be one of the weapons the Order used to fight against the ones who were what he used to be, or were about to become what he had been. He would fight against the monsters.

Devon smiled. It was a form of redemption for the terror and destruction he'd wrought on others. He basked in the burst of pleasure that flooded through him. He'd pleased Jenny, and that in turn gave him pleasure. He wanted her to be happy and proud of him. He lived now to serve her. To serve the Order.

SCHOLAR CLEMENTS MOVED from where he'd been observing the newly bound Sundered, Devon, who stood calmly without a hint of madness in him. He walked up to him and placed his hand on Devon's chest, feeling the well-placed bonds that Healer Medcalf had meticulously forged in place. They spread like a spider web through his entire body and mind, just as she had been taught. This refined batch of medication had worked, finally. He was not fighting, sickening or an insane thing to be kept drugged insensible until needed. He was enslaved to her will, entirely.

Finally, Clements moved back, and smiled. "Well done,

Healer Medcalf. The Order will never forget your service and achievement."

Jenny blushed, her head ducking, and she lowered her eyes. "I just added to all the work that others had painstakingly done before me, Scholar Clements."

Clements nodded. She was modest as well; that pleased him. "You have documented every step you followed to fully enslave the monster without destroying the mind?"

Healer Medcalf's eyes shone in pride and accomplishment. "Yes, Scholar Clements."

He nodded approval, then looked at Scholar Caine. "We must send word immediately of the success we've had. See if we can use this current batch of medication and Jenny's method to salvage some of the other monsters."

Scholar Caine also nodded his approval at Jenny before acknowledging the instruction from the head of the Order. "Of course, Scholar Clements. We'll start immediately." He gathered Jenny and her slave in his wake and walked from the hall.

A slow, triumphant smile spread on Scholar Clements's face. Finally everything was falling into place. The Order would be in a position to take over and instil the control over the realm and people that was needed for everyone to be safe. As the leader of the Killiam Order, that would rise him to primacy in Vallantia.

LOOSE ENDS

*J*ess relaxed as she walked down the cobbled laneway in Vallantia that she knew led into the Scholar's Quarter. Not that she'd spent much time in this area; the conversations in the bars and coffee houses tended to bore her. Today it suited her purpose.

She wore her deep blue cloak from Ilarith, the edges decorated with the concentric patterns in silver around the edges, with its deep hood drawn up to obscure her face. Underneath she wore one of her formal gowns, a deep blue with silver thread to match the cloak with the crest of a Companion of the Fourth. She would much rather be wearing her old familiar set of hunting leathers but on this occasion she guessed she would get more cooperation by appearing as the Lady Jessalan, Companion of the Fourth, complete with Elite trailing along behind her. James had appeared promptly when she'd sent for him from William's suite, barely pausing when she requested him to come with her, and hiding his shock admirably.

Coming to the end of the laneway she walked out into the big common square, ringed on three sides with coffee houses, bars and book shops. Patrons sat at tables that spilled out into the courtyard and at tables on the balconies above, taking advantage of the beautiful day. Trees grew in the centre, and people lazed around in the shade, reading books, chatting animatedly. The whole square was dominated by the multi-storey building that took up all of one side of the square. Jess paused, staring up at it: the Great Library of Vallantia. Home of the scholars. It was more than a library, though; it contained training rooms as well. All scholars spent some time in these halls proving their worth at their chosen profession before being accepted into their rarefied ranks.

Jess walked across the large common area heading straight for the large wooden double doors of the Great Library. The stone steps that led to the doors were irritating, a little too wide to walk up smoothly from step to step and too narrow for two full paces. She modified her step accordingly; no lady brought up in the circles she had would struggle with the stairs. As she approached the doors the Elite trotted up the final steps in front of her and opened the doors for her. She thanked them as she passed within. She took a few steps in and paused, looking at the long path that ran down the centre of the room, tables and chairs spaced down the length. Row after row of massive wooden bookshelves ran down both walls. Staircases curved up to a second-level gallery that ran around the whole room, filled with row after row of floor-to-ceiling bookshelves.

In the hushed chamber, robed figures sat at the tables with tomes open in front of them, scribbling notes, while others browsed the shelves. An elderly female scholar hastened towards her, hand outstretched towards her in a warding gesture as if she was about to lay hands on her.

"I'm sorry, my dear, the library isn't open to the public today." She stopped, wide-eyed, as James stepped in front of Jess, blocking the scholars path.

"Careful, Scholar. Lady Jessalan, Companion of the Fourth, goes where she wills, and it would be best if you cooperate."

James's tone was firm although he didn't feel a need to place his hand on his weapon to underscore his point. His presence was enough.

Jess smiled as she drew back the hood of her cloak. That was the other reason to bring the Elite with her, since she was being official. It was amazing how polite people became in their company.

"I need to speak with Scholar Beacham." Jess stared at the flustered woman. William's servant, Shaun, had been terribly helpful finding out who was in charge.

"Lady Jessalan, my apologies, but this is most irregular." The woman gripped her hands in front of her.

Jess continued to stare at her, keeping her expression neutral as the scholar started to look uncomfortable.

"Scholar, unless you want me to order the guard in here to lock this place down to locate and drag Scholar Beacham out, you'd best take us to wherever he is located." James's stare was flat.

The scholar's eyes widened as she looked around, but finally she turned and started scurrying down towards the rear of the building. Jess followed, refusing to increase her pace. It forced the scholar to stop every table or so and turn and look at her, wringing her hands in agitation.

Finally they passed the last row of bookshelves and the woman turned and hastened to a door in the corner. With a brief knock she opened and whispered to the person inside, glancing over her shoulder at Jess as she sauntered closer.

As Jess approached, the scholar flattened herself against the wall as James darted past Jess into the room first, then stood aside himself as Jess entered. His fellow member of the Elite staying outside the office and unapologetically closed the door so the female scholar couldn't enter.

Jess looked at the middle-aged man behind the desk whom she had been informed was in charge of the scholars. It was interesting since they didn't seem to apply titles to differentiate each other, all of them just using the uniform title of scholar. He stood with a smile on his face although she could see he was bursting with curiosity as to why she was here. He, at least, did not appear to be in the least upset by her invading his domain.

"Welcome, Lady Jessalan, please take a seat." He paused as she inclined her head and sat. "Please forgive Scholar Michaels, she is good at keeping the junior scholars in line but not with dealing with those outside our order."

"I took no offence, Scholar Beacham. My presence here today was unannounced, and I can understand how it may cause some to be unsettled." Jess smiled at the man, instinctively liking him.

Beacham eased himself back into his seat, glancing briefly up at James, who stood discreetly to one side, refusing the seat.

"This *is* unusual. How can I be of assistance?" Beacham returned his earnest gaze to her.

"I find I am curious about Scholar Clements." Jess settled back and saw a flicker of sadness run across Scholar Beacham's face.

"Ah, that is before my time leading the scholars, but I am aware of him. It is tragic how things worked out."

"In what way?"

"He was a brilliant scholar, very learned, well-travelled, and an expert in ancient history in particular. He was driven to fanaticism by tragedy. My predecessor was shocked when he separated himself and joined the Killiam Order." Scholar Beacham leaned forward, his hands clasped together loosely on the desk.

"Tragedy? You mean the death of his wife, was it?" Jess tried not to shift uncomfortably in her chair; it wasn't the most comfortable she'd ever sat in.

"Yes, she lived in a small cottage in Barinth, I think it was.

I'm sure he never forgave himself for leaving her there rather than bringing her to the palace with him where she might have been safe." The scholar nodded, clearly saddened by the event.

"He was from Barinth?" Jess hadn't been able to find a reference to where Scholar Clements had been born, just that his wife had been slaughtered by a Sundered at their home in Barinth.

"I... I'm not sure, my lady. It's just the part of that story I'm aware of." He smiled at her apologetically.

"Do you know what kind of ancient history he specialised in?" Jess found she was curious.

"Oh, well I heard he was an expert at all of it. The details he could ferret out of the ancient accounts was apparently astounding. He is a sad loss to our ranks."

"You said he was well-travelled; didn't you find that odd for a scholar?" Jess frowned at the small detail. The scholars she'd met were perfectly happy staying in their libraries and schools surrounded by books and learning.

"I guess it is a little out of the ordinary. I believe he'd travelled and lived in a number of other countries. The Heights Protectorate, Sylanna and beyond. Places I've only read about." Scholar Beacham laughed.

"So he became a scholar late in life?" Jess tilted her head to one side as she considered what he was telling her.

"What? Oh no, he was a young man. He'd done his initial training in Barinth. Many of our scholars do their initial training in the home villages. Then he came here to become a full scholar. Later he was appointed to be the scholar to the members of the royal family. It was felt with his experience with travel and his knowledge of ancient history he was a perfect candidate." Scholar Beacham chuckled.

"So when did he fit the extensive travel in?" Jess shook her head, confused by a personal history for the man that didn't make sense.

Scholar Beacham frowned, his smile fading as he contemplated her words.

"I don't know. I must have the timelines confused. I'm sure we must have his records somewhere, I can have them looked up and dug out if you like, my lady. It will take a few days, those records will be buried in the archives." To his credit Scholar Beacham now looked perplexed himself, realising the details he thought he knew didn't seem to track.

"Thank you, Scholar Beacham, I'd appreciate it. Your discretion on this enquiry would be appreciated. If you could have the records taken to the palace for me as soon as you locate them, please?" Jess smiled but had the sinking feeling that the records she was looking for wouldn't be located.

"Of course, my lady, I'm only too happy to help. I'll bring them myself." Scholar Beacham stood in haste as she stood and bobbed his head as she turned.

James opened the door and she walked out. This time she strode back the way they'd come towards the doors. Scholar Michaels scurried after them in her wake. Jess paid the woman no mind at all as she mulled over the limited information she'd been given. Her eyes narrowed as she drew her hood back up just as she walked out of the doors, opened in haste by a startled young scholar. There was definitely something odd about Scholar Clements's known backstory.

38

ROYAL ORDER

*K*yle sat at the window looking down into the courtyard below, waiting. It was a familiar pattern that was soothing. He spent some idle moments wondering what had convinced Joanna to agree that he could visit William. He'd risked a glance at Edward, who stood with his arms crossed, observing as Joanna relaxed her injunction, yet the man had his emotions, face and body language under strict control. He guessed that Edward had something to do with her backing down, although if Edward thought it prudent to keep his own counsel, then he wouldn't force the issue. He hadn't wasted anytime at all on taking Joanna at her word. Wrapping the veil around him as soon as she was done, he fled to William's rooms at the palace. He had to admit, even if it was only to himself, he was nervous. That was a new experience. He'd always been self-assured as far back as he could remember.

Still, the scene below was fascinating. The Elite were training below with new recruits. He could see and feel the surges of power that they utilised while training—the more confident and assured patterns of the regulars that he recognised and the fumbling attempts of the new ones. Kyle grinned, wishing he could spare the time to go down and give them a lesson.

Hearing the door open, he turned his head away from the scene below and watched as William walked into his outer rooms, stripping off his formal royal blue vest with the gold and silver trim as he made his way across the room. Kyle grinned; William always hated the vest because it was so fussy, yet because he was almost always on duty he was stuck with it. At the noise William suddenly froze, turning.

A look of relief crossed his face. "Kyle, is this some form of payback?"

Kyle grinned. "William, you have years of payback coming your way."

William threw his vest on the back of the brown leather couch and walked over to the window where Kyle was sitting, looking to see what had attracted his attention.

"They have orders to recruit more men who can fight with the veil." William placed his hand on Kyle's shoulder. "How have you been?"

Kyle looked up at William, seeing his genuine concern. "Better than I was. I've had help stabilising. That toxin I was drugged with messed me up more than anyone knew."

Kyle stood up as William prompted him by gesturing to the sitting area and walked across to the seats. He flopped bonelessly onto the couch, throwing his legs over the armrest, grinning as William shook his head at him, observing him intently.

"Talk to me, Kyle. What's happened to you?" William's voice was calm, as it usually was, with no hint of censure.

Kyle hesitated. There was something in William's tone that warned him that the prince already knew or suspected something. Yet if William had information on his life between the events in the ballroom and now, that left a tiny group who could have been his informant. He felt a burning need to explain everything; William's opinion mattered. Taking a deep breath, he reassessed what he'd been about to say, deciding that honesty and throwing himself on William's mercy was his best course of action.

"Will you hear me out?" Kyle glanced up at William, troubled despite his efforts at being nonchalant.

William's own face closed down to a mask, apparently recognising that his request heralded an explanation he wasn't going to like.

"No matter how bad it is. Just tell me. All of it, my friend." William leaned back in his chair patiently for Kyle to continue.

"I could feel myself spiralling out of control, so I went seeking help. I found it." Kyle paused and bit his lip. "I am not entirely my own person anymore. I have a mistress. I gave myself willingly to her control."

"You're foresworn?" William rubbed his temple lightly with the fingers of one hand.

"I thought it was the only way. I was afraid that I'd kill you all." Kyle looked away from William's implacable stare.

"Go on."

Kyle sorted through what he wanted to say, seeing no way to tell this story without letting William know that his mother was not only alive but at times a little psychotic. Still, right now he didn't feel that he had any choice, so taking a deep breath, he plunged on.

"Do you remember what Alyssa tried to do?"

William nodded. "Aaron said she was trying to control your mind and turn you mad."

Kyle smiled lopsidedly. "In effect, what Alyssa tried to force with the aid of the toxin, my mistress has achieved through my willing consent, which is much worse in its own way. She has control of my mind, and I didn't fight back." Kyle held up his hand as William surged from his seat, a protest on his lips. "Please just let me finish, or I'm afraid I won't tell it all."

William sighed and nodded once more, although it was clear he wasn't happy with the direction the conversation was going.

"At first it was working. My mistress helped me gain control, taught me. The fact that I have the control that I do is a credit to her." Kyle closed his eyes. The next part was painful to consider. "Then things started going wrong. She adamantly refuses to release me. I have more control than I've ever had, yet no control at all." Kyle shook his head ruefully.

"That is quite often how things work. Come on, Kyle, spit it all out. I'm not happy about any of this. You will tell me who this person is." William shook his head, kneading his temple lightly with his fingers.

Kyle frowned, noting the pained expression on William's face and his tenseness. He finally realised it wasn't all because of his own story.

"William, are you all right? Should I call Aaron?" Kyle was genuinely concerned.

William winced. "Alex drew me into his mind to show me some of the things he suspects. It worked, but according to Aaron I am now a little more susceptible to the veil's influence." William relaxed marginally back into his chair, closing his eyes. "Not enough for me to turn, like Alex, Jess or yourself, but Aaron advises against any more experiments with the veil, sometimes it causes headaches."

Kyle stood. "I'm sorry, William, I'll let you rest—"

William's eyes flew open, a rare hint of anger flashing in them. "Sit down, Kyle. Nice try. You will finish telling me everything."

Kyle swallowed. He'd seen William use his authority as the crown prince to enforce his will before, but he'd never had it turned on him. Then again, he hadn't really given William cause to have to command him in anything before. Kyle shook his head. William was correct, he was stalling.

"You know about the Kin, the Elder." This, Kyle was sure, was a reasonably safe bet.

"Yes. There are records, and Alex came to see me as well. He advised me that Edward, Kat and Cal are all alive. That Mother didn't die." William's face was back to being inscrutable.

Kyle blanched, swallowing. "Did he tell you what I did? What I was forced to do? I'm sorry. I tried to fight her, to stop, but I couldn't." Kyle leaned forward, covering his face with his hands, trembling as the emotion, the images, the horror of what he'd done ran through his mind.

"Alex has been very circumspect. Damn it, Kyle, just tell me! I can't help if you won't tell me everything."

"We came under attack at the estate by other Kin, badly outnumbered. Alex came to help in the middle of the fight." Kyle was surprised that his own voice was steady. "He noticed the bonds in me, and he wasn't happy about it and tried to take me with him."

"Go on." William's voice was low and calm as if he didn't want to spook a terrified child.

"My mistress is a little possessive, and she became angry, didn't recognise Alex, and turned me on him. I struck him with my blade and with power. I tried to fight her, William, I tried. She won't let me go." Kyle felt the silence in the room stretch between them. He couldn't bring himself to look at William.

"Who is she, Kyle?" William's voice was hard.

Kyle groaned, not knowing how to soften his next words. "Joanna."

"Joanna?" William's eyes narrowed to slits. "She used you to hurt Alex?"

Kyle opened his mouth to speak, then closed it again. "She didn't really mean it, William, she didn't realise it was Alex. Some days she's fine and others not so much. The incident in the glade all those years ago with the Sundered didn't just mess up Alex."

William stood abruptly and started pacing. It was a habit he shared with Alex, or perhaps it was Alex who'd picked it up from him.

"I'm going to have to insist on seeing her, Kyle. There are a few things that need to be discussed, faking her death being one of them." William's voice had turned hard and determined.

Kyle groaned, thinking of what was to come, there was never going to be a good time for this conversation to occur. The only bonus was that Alex wasn't here as well.

Edward? Can you bring Joanna here, please? William is insisting on seeing her.

Feeling Edward's satisfaction, he had cause to wonder how much of this had been set up by Edward in the first place.

Relax, Kyle, I'll bring her.

Edward broke the communication between them, although Kyle sensed trepidation and remorse through his bond to Joanna, so he guessed Edward was talking with her. Kyle got up and helped himself to the sideboard, topping up his own drink and William's while they waited. He knew it wouldn't be long; he'd felt her acceptance of the request.

WILLIAM TRIED TO RELAX, a difficult proposition given the current mess.

"Can you call Alex?" William didn't look towards Kyle, although he could feel the misery coming from him in waves.

"No. She's forbidden me to contact Alex." The weariness and defeat in Kyle's voice was unmistakable.

William frowned. It would be better to resolve this mess while Alex was present rather than go through the upcoming drama twice. After a moment of thought, William frowned in concentration.

Alex? Can you hear me?

The reaction was quick enough that it made him catch his breath in shock as he felt his brother's presence.

William? Are you alright? What's wrong? Alex's concern was evident in his tone.

I'm fine. Can you come here, to my rooms? There is a mess that needs sorting out, and it will be easier with you here as well. William hesitated then added, *Bring Isabella if you wish.*

William, feeling Alex's acknowledgement, knew it wouldn't be long before he arrived.

Alex arrived with Isabella at his side with such promptness it was apparent that he was concerned. William shivered as the power from their arrival rolled over him. He'd noticed all sorts of changes since he'd strained the part of his mind that deals with the veil. Detecting people arriving by those means seemed to be one of them.

Alex opened his mouth to speak, then noticed Kyle sitting on the couch, slumped, managing to look hunched up and miserable all in one. Alex traded glances with William, then a long glance with Isabella, before he walked over to Kyle.

"Kyle, you managed to get away? You're still bound to her though, I can see it." Alex looked at his friend with not even a hint of anger.

"I'm sorry, Alex. I tried to fight her, but she was lost and couldn't hear me." Kyle looked up at Alex, dejection in every line of his body. "I seem to have done an outstanding job of messing up my life."

"That was always *my* speciality." Alex ducked his head before looking back at him.

Kyle smiled, but his unhappiness was clear. "I think I've more than made up for it with this one."

William was relieved that the two didn't seem to be allowing what was between them to ruin their lifelong friendship.

"I thought it best to try to sort this all out. Joanna is on her way, or at least I hope she is." William transferred his gaze from Alex, whose face suddenly became guarded, to Kyle, who nodded.

"I sent your request through Edward. If anyone can get her here, it's him." Kyle groaned, trying to relax back into his seat and failing miserably.

Isabella walked over to him. "I'm Isabella, a friend of Alex's."

Kyle looked up at her, a smile appearing on his lips despite everything. "It's a pleasure to meet you, Isabella."

She sat on the other side of Kyle, in a seemingly casual move, yet William wasn't deceived in the slightest.

Feeling a surge in the veil, he looked unerringly at the spot where Joanna materialised from the veil and noted almost absently that she wasn't alone. William regarded the two who stood there frozen, looking at him—waiting, he realised, for a response from him or some kind of indication as to how this meeting was going to proceed. Kyle groaned softly and picked his drink back up from the table where he'd placed it.

William regarded Joanna. He knew that Alex was equally focused, he could feel his brother's turmoil. Looking at her, he realised he couldn't bring himself to call her *mother*, not even in his own headspace. She looked just like the portrait of her hanging in his father's rooms, not appearing to have aged. Her long dark brown hair was trailing down her back, held off her face by a couple of combs. She wore a long blue gown which highlighted her blue eyes, so much like Alex's and his own. Finally, William gestured to the remaining seats, grateful that Kyle had warned him that he'd put the summons through their Uncle Edward, since that was clearly who accompanied Joanna.

"You feared my reaction so much that you brought backup with you, Joanna?" William heard the displeasure in his own voice and almost winced. He'd have to try better to hide how he was feeling. Of course, it would be more helpful if he understood that himself.

Joanna's gaze darted between Edward and Kyle before settling back on him. She walked gracefully across the intervening space with Edward trailing her and sat on the seat. After a brief hesitation—and, William guessed, silent communication with Kyle—Edward complied and sat in the next chair.

"I'm sorry, William. I know this must be a shock." Joanna's voice was low and soft, her own pain clear.

The silence grew between them, Kyle stirring in his own chair, clearly unsettled and not knowing how the meeting was progressing.

"Why? Why did you fake your death? Do you understand what your apparent death did to Alex? To all of us?" William heard the pain in his own voice, the anguish that he'd thought he'd long gotten over.

Joanna's lips parted, and a tear trailed down her cheek. She looked up at Edward, who nodded at her. Reaching up with one hand, she brushed the tear away.

"The attack was real. I had use of the veil, but not much. Alex was much stronger than me even as young as he was then. I didn't know how to fight the Sundered. I pushed Alex away from me. I still remember the feeling of the blade as it ripped through my throat." Joanna shuddered, her hands clutched in her lap.

"I heard Joanna's call, her fear as she slipped unconscious," Edward interjected, giving Joanna a little time to settle herself. "It was all over by the time I arrived to see what was wrong. She should have been dead. The guard thought she was; a normal woman would not have survived that attack. I didn't check as carefully as I should have. I was more concerned that Alex got back to the palace safely. It was evident that he was Elder Born and needed protection."

"The old Master Healer in the royal court had died, and

his replacement was still on his way to the palace," Joanna put in. "I didn't know I would heal. I don't think anyone did. I woke up, in the tomb." Joanna shuddered at the stark memory that provoked. She remembered the cold, smooth stone she'd been lying on, seeping into every pore of her body. The dark isolation. The howling wind outside with rumbling and cracks of lightning giving evidence of a storm outside.

William felt his eyes widen in shock. He wasn't sure what he had expected to hear, but not that she had effectively been buried alive.

"You woke up in your own tomb? It took you that long to heal?" William glanced at Edward, who nodded confirmation. He also noted that Kyle wasn't shocked at all.

"We believe the shock of the attack heightened Joanna's abilities with the veil, which happens sometimes," Edward said. "Even unconscious, her own body started to heal, but slowly, and outward signs of life would have been minimal. Without a Master Healer here in the palace, it would have appeared to all that she was dead." He took Joanna's hand in his almost absently.

"Edward, Kat and Cal heard my scream and came to help me. They convinced me that I was better off letting my death stand. That it would be better for everyone." Joanna looked at Edward as she spoke, tears welling in her eyes as she remembered.

William sighed, a pained look on his face, looking at his brother. "The night of the storm, Alex heard you scream. His nightmare...He kept insisting you were alive."

Joanna sobbed and buried her face in her hands. "I swear, I didn't want to leave you, Alex, to leave any of you, but you all thought I was dead already. I wasn't well. Much worse than I am now."

Edward stirred. "I was checking on Alex when I heard her

mental scream. I could sense her mental state even then. Joanna's shock transition broke her mind."

"I woke up in the tomb. I was confused and in pain. I didn't know who I was, but I was intent on slaughtering everyone. All those responsible for burying me alive. Edward stopped me." Joanna ducked her head.

"Joanna has improved greatly, but she is still a risk to all when she is having a bad day." Edward chose his words with care, squeezing Joanna's hand gently.

William closed his eyes again, trying to sort out his feelings and failing. He could see that Alex was struggling. He had seemingly closed down, apparently concentrating on supporting his friend instead.

"When did you start to appear to Alex?" William switched his attention to Edward, allowing Joanna time to get herself back in control.

"After the attack. I hadn't realised that he was Elder Born." Edward's eyes slid over towards Kyle, then back again. "Kyle and Jess were not quite as powerful but definitely Elder as well. It was a bit of a shock when they showed up as well. Elder are rare but the Elder Born are rarer. For three to be born in the one generation is unheard of."

William found his interest piqued despite himself. "Elder Born? What do you mean?"

Joanna dried her eyes on one of her sleeves. "Most of us born with power are Kin, those who are Elder are stronger and much rarer. We can grow in strength over time if we survive long enough. Some even gain strength close to that of the Elder." Joanna looked up at Alex, her lips trembling as he refused to look back at her. "Some, though, some very few, are the Elder Born, their strength apparent from very young, and when transition hits them, they grow to a full strength that the rest of us can barely imagine. Alex, Jess and Kyle are all Elder Born."

Edward nodded. "Transition is not easy for any of us. The level of power that suddenly starts racing through us spikes dramatically during the transition, and it can be overwhelming. For the Elder Born, while such children have been born before, to my knowledge they died young. I'm not aware of any that survived before Alex, Jess and Kyle."

William glanced at Kyle, who sat quietly listening to it all; none of it appeared to be information that was new to him.

"It can't have been easy for you. Any of you." William kept his eyes on Kyle and saw him shake his head.

"It wasn't. It isn't. The added complication of that damn toxin did not help at all." Kyle's face hardened as he thought of the Order. That was unfinished business.

William straightened and looked back at Joanna. "I haven't forgiven you. It will take time, but I do understand. I don't ever want to be Kin. I suspect it would be enough to drive me mad as well."

Joanna looked almost hopeful, he noticed, and that caused him to smile sadly, wondering what life would have been like growing up with her still alive in the palace.

Joanna looked almost relieved. "I understand, William. Now that this is out in the open and you know, well, we have time to work on issues like trust. I don't expect that to happen overnight."

"Now there is the issue of Kyle." William stared at her unwaveringly.

Joanna looked back at him, suddenly uncomfortable, looking like she would flee the conversation if Edward hadn't been there as well.

"I bound Kyle to me. I could see someone had done so before. He was lost and needed help." The words tumbled out of Joanna's mouth as she attempted to explain herself.

"Kyle tells me you were attacked at your estate and that Alex came to help." William glanced across at his brother and

Kyle before turning his gaze back to Joanna. "You controlled Kyle and used him to attack Alex."

He could clearly see the shame and guilt race across her face, and she sobbed, the tears now flowing freely. She raised her free hand to her mouth.

"I didn't know it was you, Alex, I swear. I was angry and confused. You were trying to take Kyle from me. He's mine—"

Alex's face flushed red. "Kyle is not yours to keep!"

Joanna recoiled in shock at Alex's clear condemnation and loathing.

Isabella spoke, confident. "There is a reason we who are Elder do not bind others to our will, Joanna, apart from the fact the practice of enslaving another to your will is abhorrent. The bound lose themselves, they become a thrall. Something in that act also changes the one who bound them, regardless of their intentions to start with."

Joanna frowned, looking at Isabella with wide eyes. "You are Elder?"

Isabella simply nodded

"I'm not happy with a lord of the realm being bound to another's will, let alone a Companion of the Fourth. Even when that person in control is you, this skates the very edge of treason. You will undo what you have done to Kyle."

Joanna tried to stand, but firm pressure from Edward kept her in her seat. She looked at him as if he had betrayed her and anger warred with guilt on her face as she alternately flushed red, then paled.

"You need to understand that I can and will stop you. It will be better for all concerned if you release Kyle willingly." Isabella's voice was low and confident, without a hint of doubt.

Joanna looked up at Edward, her eyes narrowing as she spat her words at him. "You knew they would take Kyle from me! You *planned* this!"

Edward looked down at her sadly. "You need to listen,

Joanna and do as William commands. Isabella is right, this is not good for Kyle, nor for you. This sick bonding you have made is already clearly affecting your judgement. Release him so you can both heal."

Alex stood, straightening; he was the Fourth, and as he gazed down at Joanna, his tone was even without a hint of compromise. "Kyle is the Fourth's Blade. You will release him."

"Please Alex, I didn't mean it—" Joanna stopped as Alex's face hardened.

"Enough, Mother! This is not about me or you, it's about Kyle. Release him, and perhaps then we can all start to work out the years of hurt between us all. That will not occur at all while you hold Kyle as your slave."

Tears welled in her eyes as she looked up at Alex and William, neither of them showing her any sympathy. She then looked at Kyle, almost pleading.

"Kyle, please, you know it's better for you with me. I've helped you." A tear slid down her face as he shook his head.

"Joanna, yes, you helped me when I needed it. Now it's time for you to let me go. This bond is hurting us both." Kyle kept his face clear of judgement, aware that she could sense his turmoil anyway. His fear of what he would become was still there, but so was his determination to face his fears, to become his own person again and trust his own judgement, not just to rely on another.

Joanna seemed to battle against her internal demons, finally bowing her head.

She stood up, her eyes empty. "Lie down, Kyle."

William wondered for a moment if he would have to order Kyle to do as he was requested. Finally, he closed his eyes and took a deep breath and shifted to the long couch, where he lay down as instructed, pulling one of the cushions under his head. William watched, fascinated, as Joanna went up to Kyle, kneeling at his head and placing her hands delicately on his temples. As Kyle's back arched and he cried out in pain, Edward moved to the other side and assisted in restraining him. He looked over at William.

"The binding of another's will is done with subtlety. If done well and the subject's barriers are down or compromised, the person being bound shouldn't notice." Edward's expression turned grim. "Withdrawing those bonds, however, causes pain, as they are burnt out. Joanna cannot leave Kyle open for another to take advantage of."

With that explanation, William settled back as Alex went to assist Edward in restraining Kyle. William felt momentarily guilty at the pain this was causing Kyle, yet he knew it was better for his friend to be his own person, or he'd never gain back his confidence or respect himself again.

As his doors opened and worried guards burst in, William got up and placed himself between the guards and his guests. He glanced over his shoulder and breathed a sigh of relief as he realised that the position of the couches obscured both Joanna and Edward from full view. He turned back to deal with the guards.

39

DISBELIEF

ATTACK ON THE QUEEN

Kevin's eyes narrowed, and he grinned in anticipation. Petty of him, yet the knowledge that the Order had decided to go after the queen and her son gave him some pleasure. He didn't have the strength to go up against Edward; in fact, he'd worked hard to avoid it. Still, it would be interesting to see how they went. Of course, he fully expected them to fail. The queen didn't travel anywhere without a full guard detail. Still, he was interested to see why they thought they could pull it off. Simon informed him that rumours in the shady underground world he mixed in suggested the Order had a secret weapon to use against those born with power.

That is also what had drawn his attention, even though he doubted that they had any such thing. Survival, if nothing else, had him out here in the forest masking his presence from everyone. He already knew the queen had power, or at least a little of it—she was quite an active mind-speaker despite her insignificant power level. He made a point of keeping tabs on the royal family, which was the only reason he knew. He would love to know how members of the Order had found out, though.

From the outside, the Order just seemed like a bunch of humans, paranoid and scared about people who weren't quite like them. Of course, they had the right to be, and if only they really knew the whole truth, they would be too terrified to take the action that they were contemplating now. Yet here they were with a plan in place to kill the queen and her youngest son. They were aiming way above their supposed capabilities.

Kevin's attention was drawn by the arrival of the royal party. The pleasant time that mother and child spent together almost made him impatient, wondering when the Order was going to act. Kevin rolled his eyes watching the child mirror his mother's movements, showing the perfect protocol. Another useless prince in the making.

Kevin split his attention between the queen eating her lunch with her youngest child and the members of the Order that were moving closer, surrounding the clearing. It amazed him that the guard didn't seem to notice. A condescending smirk crossed his face. They had grown complacent since his time as a member of the Elite.

Frowning, he started to draw in power to leave this place. It was apparent the outing was nearly over as the queen stood and grabbed the young prince's hand, leading him towards their mounts. Kevin froze and turned his attention back to the glade in the real world, and the singing of arrows in flight caught his attention. His mouth opened as servants and guards started to slump where they stood around the clearing.

Kevin stiffened as he felt the Sundered One enter the battle, his hand going to his blade despite himself. The mad ones were a plague on the world that remained unexplained. He held himself in the veil, watching, knowing that the other sensed his presence yet discarded him for the closer prey before him.

The Order's ranks halted their own attack, waiting. The

mad one used the veil to jump the intervening space between himself and his target. Drawing his blade, Kevin nearly forgot himself and cheered as the queen's head was yanked back and her throat slit, but not before she used the power herself to attempt to order the prince to run, and even gave him a mental shove, her fear giving her a power surge.

Yet even at a young age, he was showing those noble traits of his ancestor. The boy unaccountably held his ground and refused to abandon his mother. Kevin smiled softly to himself as the Sundered picked the boy up, knowing it was all over. The next Fourth was about to die unceremoniously at the hands of one of the Sundered.

Kevin gasped, his eyes wide as he watched the scene in the real world unfold. The boy unaccountably pushed at the Sundered One's mind with his own, forcing at the mad one to be released. He was too young to accomplish such a feat, yet the Sundered considered and suddenly swerved from his intention to kill the boy to let him live.

No.

Kevin backed up a couple of steps in shock. The boy was Elder Born, already a strong mind-speaker and wielding power he shouldn't have even if he didn't know it. Kevin snarled and drew his own blade. He had no intention of allowing another to rise and challenge him. He pulled in power to shift into the glade and finish the job that the Sundered had failed to do, then stopped as he felt another surge of power.

Kevin saw the Sundered hadn't fled as he'd expected. He had appeared in front of a group of the members of the Order, who backed away, fear written on their faces. Kevin smirked, expecting them to die, only to be hammered with shock. The Sundered one just stood there, looking at them. Waiting. The members of the Order looked at each other, seeming just as shocked as Kevin was himself.

Then his eyes moved back to the clearing, at the members

of the Order, quickly and methodically retrieving their arrows and cleaning up any sign they had been there. Somehow they had some control over the mad one.

The knowledge that there was a connection between the Order and the Sundered made him pause in his flight to safety. Perhaps it was time for him to investigate the Order in truth. Despite how much he couldn't understand, didn't believe, the Order controlled the Sundered. Or were at least trying to.

Kevin wracked his brain trying to understand what he had seen, trying to put it into some sort of order that made sense. As always it was a mystery, yet now he was leaning towards the opinion that the rise of the Sundered wasn't a natural phenomenon. It had been thought in the days of his youth that something had changed in the veil that caused humans who had contact with it to go mad, or that humans had somehow changed so that they were no longer compatible with the power of the veil, that they were weaker and now overwhelmed by the power quickly.

Still, back there in the clearing there had been an abnormality. One of the Sundered arriving in company with members of the Order. That was a connection he had never made before or ever seen. Generally, the Sundered killed everyone, or tried to—human and others with the power they targeted equally, and showed no discrimination in their killing. Yet this one had allowed the members of the Order to survive.

The boy had also somehow turned the Sundered from his murderous intent. That shouldn't have been possible either. Kevin's eyes narrowed. He had much to discover and learn. He might have just found the information he needed to rise to prominence. He just had to work out what it was that he had actually learned.

HIS OWN MASTER

Kyle became conscious of his surroundings in degrees, the first thing he became aware of being his pounding head—it throbbed like red hot pokers were being driven through his brain. He almost wished he was unconscious again, and reaching for the veil caused him to groan. He decided that perhaps it was better to let the headache go away naturally. It reminded him of that time Alex, Jess and he had burnt themselves out after being attacked by the Sundered.

Kyle only realised he must have drifted off to sleep again when he opened his eyes to a dark room, and his head felt marginally better. Hearing soft talking to one side, Kyle idly looked over to see William talking with James and Matthew, who were stationed by the door. He then realised that the lassitude he was feeling was likely to be from healer's drugs, which his body was burning through at a rapid rate. The bottles on the side table and Aaron sitting in the corner gazing at him intently confirmed it.

"Your Highness, he's awake." Aaron's voice was soft but loud enough to cause Kyle to wince.

CATHERINE M WALKER

William turned and, smiling, walked across the room to his bedside. "I seem to say this to you a lot, but how are you feeling?"

Kyle took a breath, considering the question. "Like chopping my head off would be a distinct improvement, but I'll survive." Kyle frowned, looking around the room, and levered himself up into a sitting position. "I take it that I managed to kick you out of your bedroom?"

William nodded gravely. "Yes, I thought it best. Very few know that you are here, and I wasn't sure whether you wanted to be back here officially or not yet." William looked around the room, them back at him. "These few know, and Shaun had to know as well, and of course Father has been briefed. That is it."

Kyle looked around and realised that Joanna and Edward had left and probably gone back to Joanna's estate. He was relieved she was gone, and even though she had finally conceded and released him, he didn't trust her good sense to not retake him. He was also ashamed to admit, even if only to himself, that he wasn't sure he'd resist her if she tried. Besides, Joanna was still mad more often than not. Her nightmares alone would inflict terror on residents of the palace who wouldn't be able to block her out.

"Thank you. The fewer that know right now, the better. I'm not ready to wade back into the intrigue of the court just yet." Kyle relaxed back against the pillows that had been piled up magically behind him and thanked Aaron for his assistance.

"I was assured that once you regained consciousness you would heal rapidly, but it might take a couple of days and it wasn't wise for you to travel through the veil or be moved too much until you woke." William looked at him candidly noting his friend's consternation.

"You think she might have mentioned that little complication before commencing." Kyle decided that he was going to have words with Joanna. At least, he was when his head

272

stopped pounding and he was certain he wouldn't give himself to her again.

"Even if she had told us all, I couldn't have allowed the process to be delayed. Isabella told us the longer the bonds were in place, the harder they would be to remove. She said in your case the damage was nearly irreversible." William looked at Kyle gravely.

Kyle contemplated that, noting that Aaron did not contradict anything he'd said. He realised, assessing his own state before Joanna had cut him loose, that he had to agree. Kyle settled and sighed. There was no point in arguing with William; he knew the man well enough and it would be a futile effort. So he decided to change tack.

"Who is Isabella? A friend of Alex's, I take it. She's powerful and a lot older than she looks." Kyle wasn't sure how he knew, only he was sure it was true.

"She is somewhat of a mentor to Alex, and before you hear it elsewhere, they are sleeping together. Your sister has heard all the gossip about the pair. Someone told her Alex was meeting with me and she came to confront him. She came face to face with Isabella. That went about as well as you'd expect." William was watching him carefully.

Kyle sighed. "I'm certain that isn't a conversation I want to have with Amelia right now, but I'll speak with her."

William's eyebrow rose. "Given Amelia is your sister, you are taking Alex having an affair with another woman extremely well, Kyle."

Kyle's eyes flashed open, and he shifted his position to roll over onto his side. "I did try to warn Amelia about getting mixed up in our world. To be honest, I'd be shocked if she hadn't strayed herself. If I know her, she's probably more upset about all the rumours, and that Isabella is stunning."

William chuckled. "Elizabeth indicates that you are correct. She just wants Alex to be a little bit more discreet. Now I'll let you get some more rest. The sooner you do, the sooner I'll get my bed back." With that parting shot William, true to his word, left the room.

Noticing that neither Aaron nor the Elite showed any sign of going anywhere, Kyle sighed and closed his eyes to rest.

~

KYLE SIPPED HIS COFFEE, amazed at how much better he felt having bathed and changed into fresh clothes. They had been obtained—discreetly, he'd been assured—by Joshua and the Elite. The pounding in his head had receded, and he felt human again.

William had ducked in and out the last few days, performing his regular duties, since it would be noted if he suddenly disappeared and the court would wonder why. The only difference was that the Elite were under strict orders and no one was gaining access to his rooms right now. Instead, he was seeing petitioners that couldn't wait for the regular court sessions in the meeting room down the hallway.

Kyle looked up and grinned at William's irritated expression as he walked back into the room and poured him a coffee from the flask on the table, handing it to him without comment. William grunted his thanks and slumped into the chair opposite him, the steam that suddenly started curling from the mug he held giving evidence that he'd warmed his drink. Public displays of the little powers were not the done thing in either the high society or in the working class, yet in private it was a matter of everyday life. Still, Kyle assessed that William had grown stronger, even in such small things.

"Lord Castlemaine is an idiot." William's stormy expression hadn't settled in the slightest.

"Of course he is. Why is he an idiot on this particular occasion?" Kyle found he was curious despite himself to discover what had gotten under William's skin.

"He brought all kinds of inane subjects up, but it seems he thinks I should marry his daughter." William looked at Kyle in disgust when he laughed in response.

"His daughter is barely in her majority, what made him think you should marry her?" Kyle tried to contain his amusement. William was always getting subtle and not-so-subtle hints from just about every lord and lady with a daughter that he should marry their daughter. He generally took it all with good grace, probably safe in the knowledge that his father didn't see the need to rush him into marriage, and that having the crown prince in an unmarried state gave a certain amount of leverage in not only their own realm but the neighbouring countries.

"Recent events. Apparently he thinks the Crown is in a precarious state right now, with Daniel dead, Alex gone. Well, you know how those discussions usually go." William sipped his own coffee, yet didn't seem any less irritated.

Kyle groaned in memory. He did know. His own lot in life wasn't quite as bad as that of William, Alex and Elizabeth in that regard, but it wasn't far off. All the lords paraded their daughters in front of him. Of course, because he tended to be near Alex, quite a few of them managed to become confused about who their main quarry was. He'd had no compunction at all against throwing Alex to the wolves on more than one occasion—yet another reason to delay his return to the palace.

They sat in companionable silence for a time, the only disturbance when Shaun bustled in and refreshed the coffee flask and added a selection of fruit to the sideboard before quietly withdrawing.

"Thank you, William." Kyle was genuinely grateful for William's intervention. At least, he was now that his head wasn't pounding anymore. He doubted Joanna ever would have been convinced to release him without William's help.

William shook his head. "You've always gone above and beyond what anyone could reasonably expect, Kyle. The least I could do is cover your back when you needed it and give you this sanctuary while you recovered."

"Father impressed duty on me when he first had me brought to the palace, and I was not impressed. Thankfully Alex and I worked out early on that we get on and understand each other." Kyle chuckled in memory. "I remember all the young hopefuls that he pushed away and wouldn't have a bar of. Still won't."

William's expression turned bland. "None of you will. The three of you have been a solid unit since you met and no one was breaching that friendship."

Kyle grinned at him and shrugged. It wasn't like he could refute the statement, they *did* tend to push others away. "All three of us grew up knowing we were Tainted." Kyle gestured to William's steaming cup. "Not just access to a convenient level of power, but the much rarer might-go-insane-and-kill-people variety. Tended to draw us together, a shared secret."

William shook his head. "One of the worst-kept secrets, you mean. The court, at least those with brains, were all aware of the power the three of you possess."

Kyle's smile became self-deprecating. "It was that thing we had in common that none of our contemporaries could even hope to understand." Kyle shook himself, determined to change the subject. "Anyway, I'll get out of your way today. You mentioned a task for me when I was feeling better?"

William sat looking at him for a moment before nodding. "After everything that has happened, I think the Killiam Order bears checking out." His expression hardened. "Agitating for protection and change and attempting the lives of others, or whatever it is they are up to, are entirely different things. Father was assured that Daniel's group was rogue, but with everything that is happening, I don't believe it."

Kyle's smile turned hard and cold. "Oh, I'm ahead of you there, that isn't something that you have to request. They are definitely on my list."

William nodded, his own eyes narrowing. "Don't kill them." He held up his hand as Kyle went to protest. "Yet. I want to know the extent of their actions against the Crown and who else they are dealing with. I can't help but feel there is more going on than we know or suspect."

Kyle considered it, then sighed and agreed to the request. While he really, *really* wanted to kill every last member of the secretive order, he had to admit it was probably smart to find out exactly what was going on first.

"I'll go to my rooms at the Winter Palace first, and when I've got myself settled again I'll go and investigate." Kyle put his coffee mug aside and stood up.

"Take as long as you need. Get used to being yourself again without being constantly watched. The Killiam Order's stronghold isn't going anywhere. Please call in regularly." That last, although gently said, sounded more like an order.

Kyle ducked his head before looking back up at William. "Am I that transparent?"

"You've been through a great deal. Don't rush things, and don't risk yourself at the Order's Stronghold. Investigate and report back." William levelled such a stern gaze at him that it made Kyle chuckle.

"As you command, Your Highness. With your permission?" William shook his head in mock disgust and waved him off. He breathed a sigh of relief as he disappeared into the veil, his own man for the first time in what seemed like an age.

AN OFFER

*M*arcus stood inside the door of the Arms, glancing around the suddenly quiet pub with the eyes of every man in the place on him. He felt his lips twitch in amusement. Anyone else would probably be intimidated and back out of the situation, and he was sure that many had. James drew his attention to the doorway to the side of the bar and without further prompting they made their way across the room. A man—undoubtedly one of the guards, though Marcus wasn't familiar with him—was propped up against the wall and nodded as they got closer.

"Carson. The weapons master's primary second." James's voice, although low, was clear in the quiet bar. His tone, however, didn't show any concern for the reaction of those in the bar.

"My apologies, we didn't actually advertise you were coming, but the three of you are a little notorious." Carson scanned the bar, one of his eyebrows rising in amusement.

He pushed himself off the wall and opened the door to lead them through. Marcus glanced at his companions and promptly followed Carson towards the legendary back room.

"Why do I get the distinct impression that I'm not the one with the reputation in these circles?" Matthew was clearly amused and not put out at all.

Megan chuckled. "You'll get there, lad, particularly if you keep getting tapped to assist Marcus. They all tend to notice such things, even if Marcus is oblivious to the attention."

Marcus smiled at the exchange but didn't correct the assertion that he was oblivious to his reputation. How could he be? He'd been trained and groomed to be on Alex's shoulder since he was a child. Out of fifty hand-picked candidates, he had been the one to win through. Of course, being trained by his father, who had been a legend in his own right in both the use of weapons and the veil, had probably helped. That small but influential core of the Elite who had always maintained the traditional training of their unit were always on the lookout for those with the talent.

Sadly, the force that had been the Elite was not now what it had been in the time of the Sundered War. It was time to change that. The rising number of the Sundered gave those with the duty of protecting the royal family nightmares. It was only a matter of time before one of them appeared in the palace or went after one of their charges. Unfortunately, the Elite didn't have the numbers to be everywhere they were needed. Yet.

Carson opened the door at the end of a wide hallway with lamps evenly spaced down its length throwing bright, warm light along the wooden walls. Marcus nodded his thanks and walked in, assessing the room automatically for exits and trouble spots. He smiled at the well-ingrained habit when he noticed he was doing it. It's not like there wasn't enough of the guard here at the present time to make this the last place anyone would attempt to cause trouble.

The back room, as it was called, was very comfortable indeed, very different from the immaculately clean public taproom at the front of the bar. Couches were spread around the room, and a large fireplace in one of the walls was dormant, but Marcus was sure it made a welcome addition to the place in winter. A long wooden sideboard was well stocked with all imaginable drinks and glasses down one side and a selection of finger foods on the other. That left Marcus wondering if it was a standard order here in the back room, or whether the leadership of the King's Guard had decided to have it put on for this occasion.

Carson directed them to a cluster of seats where the weapons master, captain of the King's Guard, and commander all sat waiting. The commander smiled a welcome and gestured to the remaining chairs. Marcus had barely had time to settle himself before Carson, who'd been busy at the sideboard, came back handing out drinks.

Marcus took a sip of his drink and realised that it was one of his favourite spirits. He raised his eyebrow appreciatively; the members of the Guard must have been paying closer attention to the members of the Elite than he'd realised. Commander Janson smiled faintly at his hesitation.

"Relax, Marcus, enjoy the hospitality. I've assigned a couple of my men to make sure you all get back to barracks safely tonight." Janson raised his own glass in a salute to his guests, his peers around him following his lead.

Marcus smiled and nodded at James, Megan and Matthew, who were all waiting for his cue before raising their own glasses in answer to the commander's salute.

"My thanks, Commander. I would hope none would be foolish enough to attempt our party, though." Marcus grinned at the thought.

The weapons master laughed. "Take the opportunity to relax, Captain. Besides, how often are all your charges either already in bed for the night or, well, elsewhere and not your responsibility?"

James made appreciative noises after tasting his own beverage, which Marcus took to mean his own drink was of equally excellent vintage.

"He does have a point, Marcus. We'd normally still be working at this hour and likely will be again soon enough." James shrugged at him and took another sip.

Marcus noticed that Megan hadn't hesitated in following James's example, but with Matthew being new to their company, after the initial sip had he his eyes on Marcus, as tradition dictated, doubtlessly waiting for permission. Marcus sighed, admitting that the weapons master and James had made an excellent point.

"We'd probably be turning the city upside down and shaking it trying to find them right about now, to be honest." That last dry comment elicited a chuckle from all those close enough to hear. Marcus settled back more comfortably in his chair and took a large swallow from his drink, nodding discreetly at Matthew.

Commander Janson smiled as he noticed the interaction.

"Carson has a list of likely recruits for you and some recommendations. There are a couple that, while good in the guard, we don't recommend for advancement at this stage."

"Life in the Elite, let alone the Fourth's Elite, is not suited for everyone." James's tone was a matter-of-fact without a hint of criticism.

Matthew leant forward and accepted the list from Carson and, at a gesture from Megan, placed it safely in the internal pocket of his vest for later consideration.

The weapons master grunted in acknowledgement of the statement. "Not that some of those fools don't think it's all glory and sitting on their laurels."

Matthew chuckled, amused at the acidic tone of the weapons master, and found himself the object of the sudden attention of all in the select but influential group.

CATHERINE M WALKER

"One training fight with Lady Jessalan, or worse, Lord Kyle, will knock that idiocy out of them." Matthew smiled at the memory of what he'd thought was one of his most humiliating moments in the Elite. Both Marcus and James laughed at his comment, remembering the one-sided fight well.

Megan shook her head, clearly amused. "Be grateful Prince Alexander didn't join in that fight as well. Of course, their first all-night stint running around looking for that trio would also be educational."

Matthew groaned, but took the ribbing of his senior officers with good humour. If anyone had told him back then that he'd be in this position now and on tap to the three most important and senior of the Fourth's Elite, he'd have laughed at them. Of course, mostly it was him scurrying around performing various errands for the three, but the experience this early in his career left him amazed.

Marcus shook his head at the lad. Not that he'd tell him, but the boy was shaping up well. He thought of that first fight with Lord Kyle as a failure, yet there were not many who could stand against the lord with or without weapons in their hands, particularly when he was channelling the veil while fighting. The three usually did, although Marcus suspected they did it mostly without thinking. It would be interesting to see how much they improved when they returned and weren't trying to hide what they were. Personally, he didn't know why they had bothered. It had been the worst-kept secret of the palace. Still, he and the rest of the Elite had kept the knowledge to themselves, since that was the way the trio had wanted it. Of course, it was taboo, and out amongst the commoners they would most likely have ended up dead. In the high society they were born to, that was less of a concern.

"So, this is all very nice and unexpected. Forgive my bluntness, but I take it there is a reason why you asked us here, other than the new recruits we need for the Elite?" Marcus accepted a refill of his glass by the commander's steward with a nod of thanks.

He watched in amusement as the commander and his men traded glances. The commander, while the ranking member of the King's Guard, had no real authority over the Elite. They had different roles. Still, courtesy was the order of the day between the two services. After all, they all served the king and the best interest of Vallantia.

Commander Janson looked at him appraisingly before coming to a decision.

"We've heard that His Highness Prince Alexander has shown up again."

Marcus's eyes narrowed and his back stiffened at that. "Yes, he has."

Janson held up his hand. "There's no need to get defensive. I mean no disrespect." Marcus relaxed with an effort and gestured for Janson to continue. "I know the Elite are stretched a little thin at the moment. I've taken the liberty of sending a squad of my own men, experienced ones, out to the town His Highness is reportedly holed up in. They have orders to report to your own men but keep their distance unless required or requested."

Marcus contemplated the unexpected information, trading glances with both James and Megan. While the two services showed each other courtesy, this amount of cooperation was unheard of, at least in this day and age—unless the king or Prince William issued an order, which he knew hadn't occurred.

"I trust they will be discreet. We've just located Alex, and he seems to be tolerating the hands-off Elite presence. If he gets irritated, he's just as likely to go elsewhere, and we'll have to track him down again." Marcus chose his words carefully, throwing James a frown when he groaned softly at the thought of having to track Alex down again.

James grinned at him unrepentantly. "Seriously, Commander, we expect that Prince Alexander will be back at the palace soon. When he returns, I doubt Lady Jessalan and Lord Kyle will be far behind. Then you'll have to haul your men all the way back here."

Carson blithely shrugged off the inconvenience. "It does them good to get out of the palace and surrounds. That town has a major trading fair and is on the caravan route. Lots of outsiders pass through it. Familiarity with the area won't hurt."

Marcus contemplated his drink and held it up. If he was having a rare night off, then he was going to make the most of it. The steward, taking the hint, made the rounds, filling up all the drinks. Finally, Marcus looked at the commander and nodded his consent for the extra protection detail. The Elite was responsible for the personal protection of the members of the royal family, and the Guard for the external and general security of the realm.

Marcus sighed. "Even when Alex returns, I have a feeling it may be good to maintain people out that way."

James grinned. "You think he'll keep disappearing and end up back there?"

Marcus was aware that the rest of the company was listening to their byplay with avid interest.

"Knowing Alex, it's a distinct possibility. We'll all find out eventually." Marcus considered the commander and shrugged. "Of course, knowing Alex, he might just bring your men and ours back with him. I hope those men you sent are aware of that possibility."

Commander Janson's expression turned serious. "I briefed them personally. They know the possibility might occur. They are all steady men."

Marcus gazed at the commander, then finally nodded. "Alex does seem to be ending up back at The Last Stop on a regular basis." Marcus took a sip of his drink, considering his words carefully. "Prince William has requested we keep our distance and not crowd him, but to be nearby if needed."

Carson grunted in surprise. "I'm shocked Prince William didn't demand you drag Prince Alexander back here."

James laughed. "With which army? William knows his brother well. Alex will return when he is ready, not before."

Megan shrugged. "This isn't the time to pressure Alex, he'll just pick up and move elsewhere. At least this way we know that he is returning to that inn and we can keep a discreet watch on him."

Marcus considered Janson, smiling. "You didn't really request that I come here to discuss our wayward charges."

Janson relaxed back in his chair. "I've seen the reports coming in through the security council. You don't have enough men. Let us help. Integrate some of ours with your own."

The weapons master stirred. "They don't have your skill with the veil, but some of them are equal with the blade. We can relieve some of that pressure. Small groups, perhaps, trained to work with a core cell of your own men."

James glanced at Marcus. "It might work. Use some of our strongest, with similar formations that we normally use around Alex, except with a core of the Elite at the centre working with a unit of the guard."

Marcus considered the offer, wishing he could turn it down. Not because he thought the Elite was better than the Guard, but because he knew that it would likely mean certain death for members of the Guard. The bulk of them didn't even have the rudimentary power to protect themselves from anyone baring the power of the veil.

"You know the risk you'd be placing your own in?" Marcus kept his gaze steady on Janson.

"I know, and my men know, or at least the ones I would put forward." Janson's regard was unwavering.

The weapons master suddenly grinned at him. "Perhaps

you now have an insight of how His Highness feels, Lord Kyle and Lady Jessalan, knowing the guards who surround them don't have the power to truly defend themselves."

Marcus glanced at James and Megan, both of his seconds nodding.

"Volunteers only. They'll need to pull double duty with training, your own and ours." Marcus looked at the steward, who filled up his glass without prompting. "I have a funny feeling this will be our last night off for some time to come. Let's make the most of it."

Janson and his fellows raised their own glasses in salute, sealing the accord between the Elite and the King's Guard.

4 2

PLOT

AFTER THE ATTACK ON THE QUEEN

evin looked down and growled in the back of his throat, seeing the prince curled up near the cooling body of his mother. He could hear the trumpets blare in the distance. The guard had been turned out, and he had no doubt that they were coming to find the queen, and find her they would. He desperately wanted to kill the boy.

Most of the members of the Order, however, had fled once the Sundered had killed the queen. He doubted they'd believed the prince would survive the encounter. He watched in disbelief as the members of the Order who'd stayed behind crept into the clearing, cleaning up after themselves, removing the arrows. Kevin felt his lips curl in contempt. The Master Healer stationed at the palace would know as soon as he saw the bodies that arrows had killed everyone besides the queen.

Kevin watched the Order members search around the clearing, apparently trying to find something and failing. Perplexed, Kevin glanced again at the boy, curled up asleep next to his mother's body. The searchers scoured the clearing and the nearby bushes, but as the call of the horns from the approaching guard sounded even closer, they gave up and retreated from the death they'd helped wrought. Kevin shook his head and looked back at the boy, lying there in plain sight, sure it was the lad they had been trying to find.

Kevin felt his breath catch in his throat. No. He shouldn't be able to do that.

Kevin felt as if his world had been rocked. Now that he looked, he could see there was a definite barrier around the boy. He may not understand what he was doing, but he had apparently pulled the veil around himself to hide. Impossible —it should be impossible at the boy's age, yet he was clearly doing it. Kevin licked his lips, feeling a small thrill of fear. Powerful indeed, Elder Born. He hadn't really understood what it meant until now. The child would be a power in this world. If he survived.

Kevin shook his head and curbed his immediate instinct to kill, a smile settling on his lips.

Or the child would be a great tool. Young and impressionable, Kevin had time to either bring the prince over to his own viewpoint of the world, or kill him.

As the guards arrived in the clearing, Kevin withdrew. Let them have their prince for now. This was his opportunity to track the Order and find out what they were up to. Now more than ever he was convinced that they were up to something and he needed to find out what. Coming to a decision, he spun around, scanning the surroundings as he sped through the trees. He found them quickly with only a few false starts.

His lips spread in a predatory grin as he followed the trail of the members of the Order. Travelling along the veiled paths as he was, it wasn't even a hard task. They were obviously intent on getting as far away as possible before the King's Guards found the dead queen. Not that he could blame them. Their act had been one of treason, and their deaths would be swift at the hands of the guard should they be caught. With the death of the queen and the welfare of the prince at stake, that was all the reason the guard would need to summarily execute them.

Kevin needed to know how the members of the Order had managed to coordinate the attack with one of the Sundered. By everything he knew, the Broken one should have killed them. Yet they lived still.

As he tracked the small band of men and women, he had plenty of time to think. It was not like it took all his concentration to follow them. After checking them out, he was satisfied they were all fully human. Finally the group made it to a clearing where horses waited, tethered to the low-hanging branches. Kevin was impressed despite himself; they were well organised for such an untrained, motley-looking crew.

"Now remember to keep going well through the night to get well clear of this place. Return to the Killiam Sanctuary. Do not speak of this night to anyone until you get within the safety of our Orders walls." The man who had spoken, although not old, obviously had the respect of all the others who nodded assent.

"Yes, Scholar Clements. We will do as you order." The woman who spoke looked over her shoulder, back in the direction of the palace. "Are you certain you will not return with us, Scholar? If they work out your role in this night's activities.... If they find out how important you are to the Order..." The woman stopped, her voice faltering, her expression closing down.

"Be at peace, Berna, and may Killiam guide you. I will be safe enough. As a tutor to the royal family, I am all but untouchable. I do us more good by staying in place for now." The man looked at all of the members of his party until they nodded acceptance of his order.

"Should we take another of the monsters on the list that have been pre-dosed on our way back to the Sanctuary?"

Scholar Clements frowned, then nodded. "Yes. We'll need to keep our stockpile up. Make sure you medicate it well, it's the only way to keep them under control until we need them." The man nodded to his companions, then spurred his horse away, heading back towards the palace.

Kevin shook his head. That explained a great deal. How the Order had managed to place one of their members not only in the palace but as a tutor to the royal family was anyone's guess. Yet that was how the Order had been able to plan the attack. The scholar would have known where the queen and her son were planning to picnic that day. All such events were planned well in advance. The fact that the man was obviously of high rank in the Killiam Order, important to them, was information Kevin filed away for later.

His eyes narrowed at the talk of monsters and medication, his mind baulking at believing what he'd heard. He shook his head. They couldn't mean what he thought they did. There wasn't a known medication that had any effect on those with power, yet the implication he got was that not only had they found one, but they were also using it.

He shook his head at the impossibility, though. A misbegotten bunch of humans could not possibly have something that allowed them to control those with power. Yet if they did, the potential for such control over his own brethren was breathtaking.

It would also mean their inevitable death. At least, it would once he managed to get whatever it was himself. Shaking himself back to the task at hand, he continued to trail after the group, even taking it into his own hands a time or two to make sure they weren't stopped or hindered along the way.

Kevin was grateful he'd chosen to follow them and not try for the prince. He had plenty of time to go after the boy, yet if he'd done so this night, he probably would have lost track of this group.

Still, following them was a tedious task. He'd almost forgotten how slowly normal humans moved through the world. It took them the better part of a week to get close to the Sanctuary, and that was with them riding hard.

Kevin's interest finally picked up when the group diverted off their path to head down a small road leading to an isolated farm. The woman, Berna, dismounted here, followed by a short, stocky male. They didn't have long to wait before their knock at the door was answered by a weathered-looking man, who immediately turned his head and bellowed back inside. It didn't take long—it was a small farmer's cottage, and Kevin was sure the bellow of the farmer could have been heard at the next farmhouse. The young woman who appeared instantly had Kevin's attention. He could feel and see the ebb and flow of the power around and through her, although strangely stuttering. Kevin winced and increased his mental shield. The roiling, tumultuous mental state reminded him of the Sundered. She was terrified, yet unaccountably relieved to see the members of the Order.

Berna raised a hand to the side of the girl's head, her expression dripping sympathy that Kevin recognised as a sham. The woman was a viper if ever he saw one. He watched with interest as Berna uncapped the small brown vial that she'd taken from her saddle bags, moving in closer to the girl, speaking in a calm and reassuring voice.

"Please, please, I can't..." the girl half sobbed, hand rising to her mouth.

Yet Kevin noticed that she didn't back away. Not that she could, as her father braced her from behind while Berna stepped forward. She gripped the girls head in a strong hand-hold, and her father helped prise her mouth open. Berna poured the vial's liquid into the girl's mouth, the fingers of her other hand pinching the girl's nose shut, compelling her to swallow. It didn't take long for a reaction to set in. The girl shrieked, her mental voice screaming out into both the physical world and the void. She convulsed, sinking to the floor, held by her father whose face had closed down, with tears unashamedly running down his cheeks. Then, as quickly as her power and mental voice had surged, it shut down and the girl slumped into a stupor.

Berna and her men talked quickly to the farmer, who looked distraught but handed the girl over to them. After strapping the now insensible girl to a horse, the party left the isolated farm, returning on their path to the stronghold of the Order.

Kevin stayed, frozen, his eyes wide, breath coming in short, sharp bursts.

They would die, all of them, for what they had done. He could kill and torture his own kind as much as he liked. That didn't mean he condoned humans doing so. First, though, before he arranged their downfall, he'd learn the secret of the liquid in the brown vial. For that, he needed to follow them further, to make sure what the Order was doing and that he was interpreting what he had seen correctly.

43

KEVIN MAKES A MOVE

*T*he sounds of the everyday life of the Healers' Guild passing by in the corridor and the courtyards and gardens outside could be heard dully in the office. Kevin sat at his desk, staring at the wall but not paying any attention to it at all. Outwardly his demeanour seemed calm, as if he was contemplating some medical mystery that still needed to be solved. Internally he was seething. All his plans had spread out through the years, just as he'd envisioned. It had been a long game plan, and so many things could have gone wrong. Yet he prided himself that things had gone well. He scowled, before smoothing his features once more to be the epitome of contemplation.

All his plans had gone well except for one.

The Rathadon boy.

His teeth gritted as anger surged through him. Always the Rathadons standing in his way. Unaccountably Alexander Rathadon and his friends had managed to slip the nets he'd cast. With his knowledge and their lack of it, he knew that he could have subverted them. In his hands, the three would have been a powerful weapon.

Somehow the Healers' Guild had been implicated; the lock-down by order of the king had been evidence of that. He'd managed to mask his true nature in the systematic clearing of those within the confines of the Guild. He'd managed to protect his own people since the Guild Master had ordered that each of the masters who had been cleared in turn test those who looked to them. He and his own people were secure enough for now, yet unaccountably the Guild remained in lockdown. That was something the Guild Master would not budge on.

Kevin knew he could leave the Guild any time he chose, taking his people here with him through the veil, yet he wasn't ready to give up his position here just yet if he didn't have to. It lent a certain amount of legitimacy anywhere he went and to anything he did. As the Guild Master in charge of all Journey-man, he was expected to move around and check on his charges. People quickly forgot what they perceived as usual, so his presence would likely be overlooked. Even in the midst of extraordinary events, people would not see his appearance as something to comment on.

Kevin frowned, chewing at his bottom lip. He'd left his run for the Rathadon boy too late, and now he and his friends were in transition and being protected by others. Still, he had another play. His features smoothed and he smiled. This one could not escape him, it was more than time to take her. He could disappear from the Guild for the time it would take to claim his prize and bring her back to finish her enslavement. Kevin smirked. What better place to bring her, now that the Guild had been locked down and cleared? In the inevitable search that would result from her disappearance, who would think to check here?

With her as his willing slave, he could make one more attempt to gain control of the Rathadon prince. If that didn't work, he would still gain one more willing slave, a powerful one, to do his bidding.

Kevin stood and nodded, his decision made. It would be hours yet before he was expected anywhere. It was time to take his property before she too slipped through his fingers.

Opening the door to the outer office, Kevin left concise orders with his assistant for one of the old long-forgotten holding cells, deep within the bowels of the Guild, to be readied for a new arrival. They had proven to be very useful for his purposes over the years. His assistant nodded understanding, displaying not a hint of shock. It was a drill that he knew well. Kevin had brought all of his special slaves here over the years, to break them to his will, and not just the journeyman healers that he broke. Their tortured screams went unheard by any but his own people.

The assistant handed the report he'd been checking over to Kevin, a smile on his face. "You'll want to see this, Master Meagher. It's a report from Healer Caine on the new medication trial." With that, his assistant turned and scurried out of the office, carefully closing the door behind him.

Kevin turned and walked back across the utilitarian room that was his office and sat down in his chair behind the desk. The serum that the Order referred to as the 'medication' had been refined and tested over the years, steadily getting better with each successive batch, with fewer of those who could channel high levels of the veil able to resist it. Fewer of them died outright, particularly when bound in time by a healer with a keen mind-gift. Leaning back in the seat, he propped his feet up on the desk and finally began to read the report.

As he read the initial summary, a smile spread across his lips. He suddenly sat up straight in his chair, placing his feet on the floor. Healer Caine reported that the latest batch of the medication had achieved amazing results. They had treated several of their subjects that had previously been treated with older versions of the medication, and in combination with binding, they returned to some semblance of sanity. They were calm and under the complete domination of their controllers. There had been no deaths as a result of the new batch of serum.

Kevin stood, leaving the report on his desk, still smiling as he looked out to the gardens below. It was a perfect day.

KEVIN STOOD in an alcove in the Summer Palace gardens, waiting for Healer Bates. It had been ridiculously easy to appear there unnoticed by any due to the trysting spots conveniently spaced around the gardens. It galled him that he needed the healer to gain access and claim his new slave. While he could whisper in her mind readily enough, due to the medication level she was on, he couldn't simply command her to come to him. The medication she'd been drugged with since she was a child blocked her from accessing her greater powers. They'd had much greater success and survival rates finding and medicating those who would be Kin from childhood than dosing them later in life. Even though he had a certain level of control over ones who'd been treated this way, he still needed to get his hands on her to finish the process. This property was too important to leave to his corrupted healer to finish off. Besides, he wanted her for himself.

It was safer to wait for his healer to bring his new slave to him rather than to try to appear somewhere he was unfamiliar with, even though he hated waiting passively in the garden this way. His lips curled in a snarl. He knew that Edward was strong enough now to emerge anywhere he wanted, yet while his own powers had grown, he was still lacking. He needed to be familiar with the places he was going if he wanted to appear behind closed walls. Always the Rathadons were stronger, had more than they were ever entitled too. It rankled him even more that it seemed to be a generational trait.

Hearing the approach of another, he opened up his own mind and sensed his healer approaching. She was one of the first thralls that he'd taken and managed to place in the Strafford household. That had been a stroke of genius, spoilt a little by Lord Strafford taking his son Kyle to live permanently at the palace, companion to the young prince. The boy had been extraordinarily gifted, even when only young. If he'd just had a few more weeks before the relocation, he had no doubt that Kyle Strafford would be his now. As it was, as soon as the boy entered not only the palace but became the constant companion to Prince Alex, Kevin had had no opportunity to get one of his healers near the boy.

It wasn't something that he could risk with a Master Healer in residence, bonding all healers to him and ensuring their loyalty to the king. One of his slaves with their compromised healer's bonds would be found as soon as the king's Master Healer examined them. He was still surprised that Healer Bates had gone unnoticed, although he'd given strict instructions to the woman to stay well clear of the palace healers. It had been worth the risk of exposure to ensure his access to his property. He'd invested too much time to be thwarted yet again just before he could triumph.

Healer Bates appeared around the corner. Glancing around, she bowed her head in greeting.

"Master Healer Meagher, are you sure this is wise?"

Kevin dismissed the woman, his eyes settling on his new slave standing docile by her side, just as she'd been ordered to. His eyes raked her possessively, tongue licking his lips as the desire to have her as his own rose in him. No one could take this prize away from him.

AMELIA STARED, transfixed, at the man standing in front of her.

The man she didn't know. She was suddenly terrified, yet couldn't bring herself to look away from his eyes. He compelled her to stay where she was and not to call out. She felt him in her mind, a forceful, dominating presence that made her shiver. A part of her mind shrieked as he eyed her with greed and possessiveness, his desire evident. He looked like a young, handsome, yet cruel-looking man. He looked at her as if he owned her already. In a small part of her mind, she recognised that he already did.

Amelia knew that Healer Bates was nearby. She tried to turn to speak to the woman that she had trusted her whole life, yet she found she couldn't turn away from the man in front of her.

Be still, child, you are already lost.

His strong and commanding voice compelled her not to fight. Amelia fell still, and even that back part of her mind seemed to go entirely under his control. It didn't even occur to her to fight. She realised absently that she recognised the voice as one of the commanding mind voices that often spoke to her these days. Although it was a different voice to the one that had warned her to be careful of Alex's lover.

"You've done well, Heather. The Order will never forget what you've achieved." His voice was smooth. "Go, return to the fold of the Order. Do not return to the palace."

"Yes, Master. It will be dangerous, they will come after me. With Amelia going missing, they will find out I had been visiting her." Amelia recognised the faintly worried tone of Heather Bates, although she still stared straight ahead, not looking either way, waiting for the next command from the man that she didn't know.

The words that Bates had said echoed through Amelia's brain; she knew that she should be concerned, yet somehow she wasn't. She knew she wasn't meant to leave the palace without the Elite, it wasn't safe. Yet their words that flowed over her indicated that they intended to take her somewhere. She felt in control, even though a part of her recognised that that control was held elsewhere. It had always been elsewhere. That control was carried now by the man. Because he had told her to be still, she was.

"Go, Heather, quickly. Get as far away as you can before they miss her. Remember, you can utilise the journeyman healer huts as you travel."

Even though it wasn't aimed at her, Amelia knew command when she heard it. While she didn't see Bates leave, she heard the woman walk away, just as she was commanded to do. Still, Amelia wasn't worried. She seemed incapable of it right now.

Come, Amelia. Even though you don't know it, you belong to me already.

Amelia didn't blink or draw away as he grabbed her arm. She felt the power draw in and then they shifted from the world she knew into that grey world, disappearing from sight.

44

HEALER'S GUILT

*A*aron's hand trembled as he closed the last journal, the guilt of his organisation settling heavily on him. The papers they had contained were diverse, including accounts of the medical trials itself, the adverse effect the trial had on those with power, the detailed description of the volunteers, their descent into madness and murderous rage. Stories that sounded very much like the Sundered.

There had been reports on the rise of a scourge that seemed to be sweeping the ranks of those who would be Kin, report after report of more people breaking entirely and not recovering from the transition. The healers in the day even had reports of the initial response to the rise of the Sundered and the lead-up to the Sundered War. The final report was from the Grand Guild Master, finding the Healers' Guild had been responsible for the Sundered. Fearing the response of the people and the Crown, the records of the medical trail and its consequences had been sealed.

Aaron covered his face in his hands, shaking.

"Forgive us. What have we done?" His whispered words died in his empty office, with no one to hear.

Aaron flipped the cover of the first journal open, pulled a pad to him and jotted notes regarding the composition of the medication that had been used back in Healer Katrina's trial. Closing the book, he gathered them both and locked them safely in the drawer of his desk.

Aaron picked up his pad and walked purposefully towards the door. There was one more series of tests he was determined to conduct on the bottles of the toxin that was being used on those with power. He knew it wasn't the same as the folk remedy, but it remained to be seen if it bore a resemblance to the medication that had been used in the trial all those generations ago. He was determined to get all his facts; he knew he would need them before he reported his findings to the king.

45

AMELIA'S CONVERSION

*A*melia became aware bit by bit, as if her mind had been bound in fog. She could barely make sense of her surroundings. She went to sit up and found she couldn't. She breathed in sharply and tried to struggle against the bindings that bound her to the bed. Her breathing started coming in short, sharp breaths; there wasn't enough air. The world around her began to merge, flickering and grey compared to the natural coloured world that she knew. Amelia sobbed. She couldn't help herself. She couldn't remember how she had gotten here, nor what had happened. She remembered being in bed at the palace. She remembered Healer Bates coming and giving her tea. Then they went for a walk in the garden. Bates had told her that the fresh air would make her feel better. Then nothing. She woke up here in a stark room strapped to a bed. A scream rang from her lips, and she sobbed again, fear overwhelming her.

Amelia didn't know how long she screamed or cried. No one came. No one cared, or at least, no one who could hear her. Her breath catching in her throat, she looked around the room, taking in as much of it as she could see. She could move her head only a little. She could see that each of her hands was bound to the side rails of the bed, and her feet were strapped with leather bindings, each trailing to the corners of the bed. There was another wide strap, she noticed, bound around her stomach, with each end tied to the bed frame. That was when she realised she was wearing a simple white linen shift; all the symbols of her rank, of being the Consort Elect of the Fourth, had been removed. Amelia started crying again, terrified, wondering who had taken her and why.

Amelia woke again, realising that at some point during her sobbing she had fallen asleep. Unfortunately, it had not been a nightmare. She really was in a plain, unadorned white gown and bound to a bed in a room she didn't recognise. Hearing a noise, she turned her head and saw a man she didn't know, yet who somehow looked vaguely familiar, sitting on a chair next to her. Her breathing stopped, her eyes widened, and she started to struggle against her bindings only to hear him laugh.

"Relax, my dear, there's no point in struggling. You can't escape me."

As if to prove his point, the man stood, came over to the bed and sat on its edge. As much as she tried to cringe away from him, all she could manage was to turn her head away. The panic rose, as she felt his hands on either side of her head turning her so that her eyes looked into his. Under his gaze she found she stilled and couldn't look away.

"Please, please don't." Amelia hadn't meant to show her fear, yet the defiant words she'd planned to utter escaped her.

She felt a vial pressed to her lips and swallowed convulsively as the liquid spilled into her mouth. She recognised the faint bitterness that was similar to her medication, and then she felt her body stiffen, straining against her bindings as fire raced through her whole body.

The man chuckled, cruel and low, his eyes drilling into hers, as the room faded away until all she could see was his eyes glittering with malice. His voice was in her mind, and her terror rose to new heights. She recognised the voice, yet not the words being said. They whispered through her head, and stabbing agony throbbed through her in time to the cadence of his voice.

She knew without even understanding how that he deliberately left a small piece of her mind conscious so that she could understand what he was doing to her. Yet she recognised that she was blocked and unable to do anything without his consent —merely an observer in her own head.

His hands trailed the length of her body, causing her to tremble in both fear and longing, as pleasure shot through her body. Her eyes flickered, and she heard a soft moan escape her lips. His voice spoke to her softly in her head.

You don't know it yet, but you are no longer the Consort Elect of the Fourth. You are no longer a lady. I'm going to enjoy breaking you. You will become my most devoted and willing slave. You will call me Master.

Amelia felt her body trembling as she warred with herself. As she disobeyed him, Amelia felt the pain flare and intensify, wave after wave flooding her mind and body.

She started screaming again, begging him to stop, to let her go, for someone to help her. Yet he didn't let her go, he didn't stop, and no one came to intervene.

AMELIA LAY IN HER CELL, staring up at the ceiling, her face vacant, eyes dull, not a hint of awareness showing. She had retreated to a small corner of her mind. Away from the excruciating pain, her world had narrowed to when her master was present. At first, she had believed that her master didn't realise that she was still there and aware. Then, by degrees, she worked out that it was yet another method he used to torment and crush her will. She learned that he could control her, force her to act. Images flicked in her mind of the things she had done, causing tears to trickle down her face.

She had found herself over the fallen bloody body of a man who'd been viciously stabbed and slashed multiple times. He'd almost been dissected with surgical precision. She hadn't just been unaware, or a spectator in her own body. She'd been there, in her own head—cold, inhuman. The man's pleas for her to stop had meant nothing to her, nor the fact that he had not been armed.

Yet his screams haunted her now, along with his pleading broken voice asking what he'd done. She'd had no reply. Even now. How could she tell a man she didn't know that his death had been a lesson for her?

She didn't know now what was real and what was imposed. Under her master's prompting she had remembered one of the first nights she'd spent with Alex. Her master had taken control and used her to forge a bond between her and Alex as he slept in exhausted slumber. He'd explained to her that it was a small, subtle bond likely to go undetected. Even if someone had noticed they would probably discount it as the bonds forged between lovers.

Then he'd pushed her aside, reaching out to Alex through those bonds, sending memories they'd shared: the time when they'd come to an understanding on the couch at her brother's bedside; fleeting moments they'd managed to steal together within the palace grounds; the moment deep in the forest where they'd made love in the waterfall. Small bursts of memories. At first, she thought that he was tormenting her with the memories of her past. Memories of her relationship with Alex that had been fake even though at the time she hadn't known that it was all engineered. Then, as the torment of the memories continued, she realised that he wasn't torturing her, at least not with those memories. He was after Alex, and she was the bait.

Why, Master? Alex has been through enough. He is going through enough.

It didn't take long before he appeared. It never did when she was prompted to reach out to him. She watched his soft, almost gliding walk, followed by the faint smell of astringent soap. She knew he was a healer. He'd told her as much.

"I'm trying to help him, Amelia. Just like I'm trying to help you." His voice was low and smooth.

No. You want to turn him mad. Like you're trying to torture me.

"I'm trying to help you, Amelia. That is why you are here at the Healers' Guild."

Amelia heard the scrape of wood against the stone floor, the rustle of robes and faint creak of the chair as he settled in it next to her bedside. More tears flowed down her cheek. He always sounded so reasonable and caring, as if he really did care and was trying to heal her. She still doubted herself after his visits.

You made me kill that man.

Amelia threw the memory of the man in the shop that she'd killed at him.

"Child, do not inflict this pain on yourself. You spiralled down into madness and killed that man. I'm trying to help you gain control." There was only concern in his voice.

No, I couldn't. I wouldn't. It was you in control. Amelia heard the doubt in her mind voice and sobbed, suddenly terrified that he was right. That it had been her who was out of control, and she'd done that terrible thing. She heard him sigh and then his hand stroked her cheek, brushing the tear away.

"Amelia, you need to gain control, and I can help you. If not, you will be the monster that you fear." His tone was sad, his face coming into view with concern written on his features.

"Your own fragmented memories show you what you become without my help."

You've been torturing me. Amelia clung to the words, trying to hold onto reality.

"No, Amelia, you've been fighting your own treatment. That causes you pain, not me. Let go, Amelia, let me help you, so you don't hurt anyone else."

Amelia stiffened as on queue memories of people that she'd killed flicked into her mind one after the other. She screamed, rolling onto her side, the only movement her bindings to the bed allowed her.

"Master, please stop, I don't want to see any more." Her voice was cracked and rough from disuse.

She felt his hand on her chin as he lifted her head gently until she was gazing into his eyes that, despite everything, shone with compassion.

"It's your own mind and memories of your actions that hurt you, Amelia. Not me. Let down your barriers, give yourself to me. Let me help you."

Amelia closed her eyes, trembling. "You'll hurt Alex."

His hand stroked her cheek. "No, Amelia, Alex isn't here. I can't hurt him. It's *you* who are flinging your memories of the time you spent together at the prince. It must be causing him considerable distress."

As his words sank in, Amelia felt despair settle on her mind, weighing down her body. She had been certain before that it was all her master's doing, not her own, yet no matter how she searched her own mind, she could not find any trace of him forcing her to his will or using her. The restraints fixing her arms and hands to the bed prevented her from reaching up to cover her face. She opened her eyes and looked up at him from the bed.

"Help me, Master. Please, I don't want to be this." Amelia

heard the defeat in her own voice, mixed with a thread of certainty.

All she knew was that under Healer Bates's care she had been stable. She hadn't suffered the way many of those with power did. The way her brother, Jess and Alex did. Then her own power had increased, and she had gone past Healer Bates's ability to contain. She wilted back onto the hard mattress, feeling the tension drain out of her. That was why her dear old healer had called in Master Healer Kevin.

"That's it, Amelia, stop fighting me. Let me help you get better. Then, when you are well, you can help us treat others who still suffer." Master Healer Kevin's voice spoke to her, soft and caring, his hand holding her head in a vice-like grip, tilting her head up to look at him.

She found herself staring up into his eyes, her vision blurred by tears as she stared up at the master healer. Trembling, she pushed down her instinct to fight, knowing that was what caused her pain. Amelia dropped the barriers around her mind that she hadn't known she was using, choking back a scream as she heard his mocking laughter. His presence in her head strengthened as he smoothly invaded her mind, and her will to resist crumbled. She knew she was lost, then, and her distress drained from her under his ministrations.

That's it, Amelia, relax and let me help you. You're doing well.

Amelia felt herself drifting off into unconsciousness with her master's reassuring voice soothing her fears.

If thinking of me as your master helps you, then by all means, Amelia, I am your master. Trust me to help you.

Amelia lay on the bed, exhausted. At least now she wasn't bound, although she had no desire to leave this room that was her life. She pushed away thoughts of the past and the life that she had led—that would only drive her mad. Right now, the only world she could contemplate was the one she found herself in at this time. This bare, stark room, grey rock walls unadorned with anything to break the monotony.

After what seemed like months, she had finally been given some peace. She had stopped trying to fight Kevin; though she shuddered at the thought, she had to acknowledge that Kevin was actually her master. Even when she had conceded to his will, her treatment had been an agony, her mind and body bathed in fire as he stripped the layers of her mind like stripping the petals of a flower to reveal its true heart. The presence of the weak 'Lady Amelia' had been stripped away. Her life had been more comfortable since she had come to accept that, since she had stopped fighting him. The time that she dreamed that Alex or Kyle would come and save her seem like a distant memory. She knew now that that was unlikely to happen. As soon as she had acknowledged that, her life had gotten a whole lot better. Her master had stopped tormenting her.

Amelia levered herself up from the bed, reaching across to grab the bottle that contained her medication. Measuring a small amount into the cup that had been placed there for this purpose, she took her morning dose without complaint or anyone else to force her. She had to admit, with the medication she was more under control. It worried her a little that her master had started cutting down on her dosage. Still, she had to trust him, trust that he knew what he was doing. Amelia grimaced and put the small cup back on the side table. She heard the sound of metal against metal, the metallic clunk that indicated that her door had been unlocked. She knew what that meant. Without even having to look she knew that Kevin had come to check on her, as he did every single day. Despite herself, she found that she was looking forward to seeing him. He was the only person that she ever saw. Even her meals were pushed through a small outlet in the wall, she never got to see who was on the other side since the small door to the alcove on the other side was always shut before she could get to her food. Her master was her entire world.

She felt herself smile as the door opened and she found she was correct. It was her master, Kevin.

"Master."

He smiled. "Good afternoon, Amelia. You see? Everything is much clearer when you don't fight. I'm pleased with you."

Amelia felt a thrill of pleasure at hearing her master was pleased with her. She couldn't understand why she had fought when she was first brought here. It was becoming clear to her that her master had only been trying to help her. She just couldn't see that before.

"I'm sorry I was so much trouble, Master." Amelia dropped her eyes for a moment as he sat down.

"It was not your fault, Amelia, you were sick, you had to get better. It won't be long now before you are able to join me outside of this room. You'll be well enough to be trusted."

Amelia smiled back at her master, grateful that he had been helping her. She felt sad that neither Alex, Kyle or Jess had the help to overcome the evil inside themselves. Her master had explained to her that the healers had kept them away. That confused Amelia. She didn't understand why the healers didn't want any of them to get better. The confusion and madness that being able to reach the veil without help caused was torture. Without the medication, she couldn't tell what was her and what was other. Yet now she was slowly gaining control, and she was happy that her master showed her she would have a life again eventually. Her master had even been getting her to practice using the veil. She had been terrified at first, thinking it would drive her mad. With his guidance, his control, she found she was getting good at that too.

"Now it's time for our practice session, Amelia. Drop your barrier just as I taught you, let me in."

Amelia sighed in pleasure. She always enjoyed their sessions together. A small line appeared on her forehead, and she dropped her barrier just as her master had shown her. She knew he could control her even with her barrier in place, but he had explained that this was part of the learning process. It would help her gain acceptance, and help him take full control of her so she wouldn't have to risk going mad. If something went wrong, he would always be able to help her.

She felt her master's presence in her mind, and she was comforted by his strength and control. Amelia felt a burst of pleasure run through her. Her eyes fluttered and her lips parted slightly at the thrill. It was her master's way of showing when he was pleased with her. It was rare these days for him to have to punish her like he had in the early days. It had been hard at first, to allow her master to control her. She hadn't seemed to be able to stop herself from trying to fight back at first, yet now she was able to allow him complete control without fighting. It just seemed reasonable to her now. Her other life was fast retreating from her mind, fading just like a dream.

Under his guidance, she stood, walked to the middle of the room and began her training exercises. He ran her through them one after at the other; she drew the power of the veil under his guidance and formed what he had told her were shields and blows that she would be able to use when fighting one of the Tainted that were not under control. Fighting strangers that bore the Taint did not concern her at all anymore. They were a threat to themselves and everyone around them. They would go mad; they would kill. The thought of having to confront Alex caused her some trepidation. She knew in that other life that she loved Alex that she would never want to hurt him, but she also knew that he needed help.

Finally, she was finished with her exercises, and her master allowed her to rest. She found herself back sitting on her bed with her back to the wall. She discovered her master eyeing her appraisingly.

"What you felt for Alex was not real, Amelia." Kevin smiled, yet it didn't reach his eyes.

"I don't understand, Master. What do you mean?" Amelia didn't know what to think. She trusted her master, yet she remembered that time, even if it was dreamlike. She had loved Alex.

"Put your mind at rest, Amelia. It was Healer Bates that prompted your affection for Alex. We knew he needed help, but because of the healers at the palace, we couldn't assist him like we did with you. We thought we would be able to help guide him with you. Unfortunately, I think we were too late. We didn't get to Alex in time."

A series of images flitted through her mind, from when she was younger. The whispering mind voice that she recognised as Healer Bates instructing her, coaching her to go after Alex. It wasn't just once, there were many, many occasions, one of the last being when she had been attacked in the court. It was Healer Bates's voice that had told her that she loved Alex, over and over again during the night.

Amelia wilted in relief, no longer conflicted. As her master had shown her, she had never loved Alex. Her master had been using her to help Alex, but he'd fought and pushed her away, choosing to embrace darkness. Amelia smiled, determined to learn everything her master had to teach her. She would be reforged as her master's tool to fight the darkness.

46

THE ASSASSIN RETURNS

Kyle assessed his own internal state, a satisfied smile spreading on his lips as he realised that while he was a little nervous about heading out into the world again, he was essentially back in control. He hadn't felt this calm and stable in what seemed a lifetime. Primarily he felt relieved to be free, swearing to himself he would never be that stupid again.

Kyle felt his resolve strengthen. It was time to face down his own demons. He would never have been able to do that with Joanna or anyone else in the back of his head as a safeguard.

"Damn it!" Kyle looked at himself in the mirror, his lips thinning. "Joanna is not your friend. If it wasn't for William and Alex intervening, she never would have released you."

His narrowed brown eyes stared back at him in the mirror, yet he couldn't keep the hint of fear at bay. He hadn't been back to Joanna's estate due to William's order—the regular kind of order that he had to use his own strength of will to obey rather than an enforced compulsion. William had kept a close eye on him, with Marcus and James being tasked to watch over him when he hadn't been present. Of course, there was nothing that

Marcus or James could have done to stop him if he'd decided to disobey his orders.

It was hard for Kyle to admit that it had been harder than he'd ever dreamed possible to obey a simple order. In those first few days after recovering from Joanna's withdrawal from his mind, he'd struggled with panic attacks. He was ashamed to admit now that he'd wanted to run back to her. He'd had sessions with Aaron, where he'd talked about what he was feeling, about the battle within himself not to go back to her or find another to bind him. Somehow those sessions with the healer had helped.

A sardonic smile grinned back at him from the mirror and he impatiently pushed a lock of his black hair out of his eyes. He'd been trained well in his responses by both Alyssa and Joanna. He didn't even want to contemplate how quickly he'd gone from independent, strong and confident to being someone's willing slave. He closed his eyes, taking a breath. At least he knew what it was like to be genuinely ruled, subservient to another will. None of his contemporaries could ever know what that was like.

Alex and William had both been right. It was well past time he stood back up and took responsibility for his own life, rather than fall back into that insidious pattern of allowing someone else to do so. That wasn't who or what he wanted to be. It wasn't the kind of person he could respect.

He wanted to believe that Joanna hadn't kept him as her thrall well past the time she should have released him on purpose, especially if Alex's friend Isabella had been correct in saying that the process of binding another to your will was detrimental to both parties.

Kyle took a breath and looked around his rooms in the Fourth's wing. He'd appeared back in here, carefully checking that none of the staff was in his suite. Of course, it helped that the bulk of the royal court was still at the Summer Palace, meaning there was only a skeleton staff and guards left here at the Winter Palace. It was embarrassing how much time it had taken him to realise he could just move in here. He couldn't impinge on William any more even if the thought of moving back permanently still made him nervous, and even if he'd been assured he could keep to the Fourth's Complex at the Summer Palace until he was ready to face the royal court again. He'd dutifully informed William of what he was intending. To his surprise, William had accepted the arrangement without argument, merely ordering a unit of the Elite to head back to the Winter Palace to alert the household staff when they got there, if Kyle hadn't done so himself by then. The crown prince had smiled, and commented that that should give him time to settle in and get used to the idea.

Kyle felt whole again wearing his weapons and clothes. Although he'd been training daily with Edward as a sparring partner, while he had been under Joanna's care the weapons had always gone away at the end of the training session. Kyle had a new appreciation for how Alex had gained his skill with the blade. Edward's ability to combine his sword work with his powers astounded him, and he had the sneaking suspicion Alex had learned that skill, even if he likely wasn't aware he was doing it. Kyle knew that he was the better swordsman, but Alex was better at combining and using his power to complement his fighting skills. Then again, he realised he'd been doing much the same himself, just not consciously. Kat was good as well, but she had trained him differently, and at that particular skillset, she was better.

Realising that he was stalling, Kyle pulled himself into the veil with effortless ease. The world blurred past, his destination clear in his mind. While Edward, Kat and Cal had all assured him they intended to check out the Order's stronghold themselves, none of them had managed to get around to it. Kyle had realised with frustration that the longer-lived of his kind frequently lost track of the meaning of time.

He hadn't needed William's request that he check them out; that was something that had been on his list since they had discovered the involvement of the Order in the kidnapping attempt. While it was entirely true that it could have been an isolated disaffected group, he doubted it. The Order was up to something. They hadn't been trying to kill him. They'd been trying to take control of him through Alyssa. Not only had they wanted *him*, but they had been after Alex and Jess as well. The why part was escaping him right now. However, that niggling little question could wait until his exploration of their base.

IT DIDN'T TAKE Kyle long to locate the mountain refuge of the Killiam Order. While he'd never been here before, he'd certainly heard about the place. Just about everyone had, even if they mocked those who locked themselves away from the world within its walls. Of course, it couldn't really help with their goal. Any with real power could gain access to the stronghold quite quickly if they chose to. Telling them that probably wouldn't help any of them with their own particular psychosis.

Kyle observed the old sprawling castle perched on the side of the mountain from the veil. It was quite secure from regular attack, with only one steep switchback road zigzagging up the side of the mountain to it. That would make it quite a challenge to approach unseen and anyone getting up that far would likely be out of breath when they did. Of course, the incline of the road and the excellent view anyone inside of the castle would have of those approaching didn't hinder someone like him in the slightest.

Noticing row after row of mounds stretching out at the back of the castle, Kyle moved closer to have a better look. It wasn't a tilled section of ground for food; he'd seen plenty of farmland before to recognise it when he saw it. Yet the trenches of earth were too symmetrical to be anything other than human-made. He could see some of the ridges were old, already grown over, yet others seemed to be freshly dug.

Growing uneasy but not really knowing why, Kyle drew his blades as he stalked closer to the mounds of earth. As he walked between them, scanning the ground around him, something in one of the older overgrown sections drew his eye. Moving over for closer inspection, Kyle frowned, seeing a scrap of fabric sticking out from the ground, caught on a gnarled white stick jutting out from the ground. He took a hesitant step forward, and the wind picked up, gusting around, and the change in direction causing the broken piece of fabric to snap and wave in the wind.

Kyle froze, face going pale. He gagged as the smell of rotting flesh from some of the freshly dug mounds wafted over him. Turning around, he scanned the hills all around him. Bones. Not sticks, but bones. Human remains were sticking out from the ground, scraps of what had been clothes and shoes.

This was a graveyard, a mass graveyard stretching out from the back of the castle where bodies had been dumped in trenches, only to be systematically filled in and another dug when it became necessary. Kyle shuddered to realise that he had been walking over graves. Seeing the apparent evidence of a new trench that hadn't been filled in yet, Kyle closed his eyes and breathed out. He shook himself, licking his lips, then opened his eyes and walked, carefully trying to pick his way across the mass graveyard towards the new trench. The putrid smell on the breeze got stronger the closer he got to the ditch and he could hear the buzzing from the thick cloud of insects hovering over the area.

At its edge, Kyle looked down and was nearly sick. There was a decomposing hand sticking out from the ground that had obviously just been covered with a couple of shovels of earth. There was evidence that animals had been taking advantage of the exposed flesh. Only the cold had kept the smell of the slowly decomposing bodies under control, otherwise he doubted the inhabitants of the castle would have been able to stand the reek. Kyle turned his back on the ugly scene. He didn't want to think about how many bodies filled the trenches. He looked at the stronghold that now seemed foreboding and, wrapping the veil around himself, moved towards it, scanning it with his second sight as he approached.

Not detecting even a hint of power within the Killiam stronghold, Kyle shrugged and moved to the balcony along the side of the castle. He'd seen the occupant open the window earlier. Kyle thought that given the hour he was probably airing out the room and, as a result it was hopefully unoccupied, making gaining access to the inside of the building undetected easy. It had been the only sign of life that he'd detected by his normal senses and with his powers. Still, he showed caution. He didn't want to go blundering in and find out he was wrong. Kyle jumped, hands grasping the edge of the stonework as he climbed up the side of the building. Carefully keeping the folds of the veil around him, he flipped himself up and over the railing of the balcony. He paused and glanced into the room and, not seeing or hearing any sign of the occupant, he climbed through the window. He smiled. Breaking old habits was hard; with the increase in his power he could just as quickly have appeared in the room or anywhere in the castle. Still, there was more chance of him running into someone that way, or rather them running into him.

He took a moment to look around the rather basic room. It was cold and the window being open didn't help one bit. Unadorned stone walls and floors, not even a hint of drapes on the window. That alone made Kyle shudder. He couldn't imagine trying to get any sleep at all with nothing to block out the streaming light from outside. There was a simple small bed off to one side with furs piled up on top of it that didn't look all that comfortable. The room was sparsely furnished; if the small assortment of clothing hanging in the hole in the wall hadn't given away that someone lived in these rooms, he'd think it was unoccupied.

Kyle shrugged and walked over to the only door, carefully listening for any sign of movement before he finally opened the door. Keeping the thinnest layer of the veil between himself and the real world, he stepped confidently out into the hallway, closing the door quietly behind him. It would take someone sensitive in the veil to detect his presence. Before their run-in with the Killiam Order, Kyle would have assessed that the members knew very little about the powers of those like him that were 'cursed' with the Taint. Now that was in question since, to do what they had done, to have the toxin and use it, meant they knew more than anybody had guessed.

It was something that niggled at him. The Order had always come across as fearful of those outside their own walls, sending representatives to the king and lords to have those with power killed at birth for the safety of everyone. No one had really paid them much heed over the years, except for the ignorant—or so he'd thought. Yet slowly their fear had spread like an insidious infection. While they hadn't managed to influence the king's decision—not likely, since his own son bore the Taint—they had convinced a great many in the realm. Some even killed their own children if they showed any inkling of high power. Also, the use of the small powers that most possessed was used discreetly and not put on display at all, even though they were universally known to be safe from inducing a Sundering. A long-held belief by the population was that the power ran in families—if an individual displayed the substantial use of the little skills, it was more likely that any children they had would be powerful enough to be Tainted.

Kyle spent what seemed like hours checking out the sprawling, mostly empty castle. It was clear that the place had been occupied with more people than were currently in residence. Those people had obviously gone elsewhere, or most of them had. For all intents and purposes, the castle was empty except for a few members remaining as caretaker staff. Empty, yet it held signs that it had been occupied in the not-so-distant past. The dust hadn't settled on the benches, tables and windowsills, there was the odd discarded and forgotten item—clothes, shoes, a half-drunken cup of what had obviously been coffee. All of the small bits and pieces testified that there had been many more occupants inhabiting this place, and that they had fled somewhere, guided by the hand of another who suspected someone would be coming after them.

Of course, that was a safe assumption when some of your members are caught in an attempt to drug and kidnap the son of the king. That tended to be taken a little personally, and answers would be sought to establish whether a small group had been responsible, or whether it had been a goal of the Order as a whole. Given they had seemingly fled their stronghold, their home, Kyle was beginning to suspect that the latter had been the case. That made him wonder how long they had been at their endeavour and what it was they were really after. It had to be more than capturing a prince, lord and lady of the realm.

On the surface, that whole debacle had seemed poorly thought out, yet Kyle couldn't help but think there was much more going on. It just frustrated him that he couldn't see what it was they intended or wanted. For a group that supposedly wanted the Tainted killed off at birth or as soon as they were discovered, it seemed strange indeed that they had tried to take Alex. Kyle knew that if they had wanted to kill Alex or him, they'd had the perfect opportunity to do so—and yet they hadn't. Their captors had obviously had something else planned for them; he just didn't know what.

KYLE FOUND himself in the cool, dark room, with no outside light filtering in from the outside. That generally meant the food cellars or the dungeons where lords kept people who had displeased them. Muttering to himself, he threw up a ball of power that glowed merrily, in stark contrast to the room he was standing in. It certainly wasn't the food cellars.

Kyle walked down a dank stone corridor to his right, the light floating along in front of him. On either side of the hall there were small cell-like rooms with wooden benches, shackles attached to the walls, and bars across the entrance and for a door. Kyle froze, seeing an unmoving form chained to one of the benches in a cell, the only other thing in the cell a small brown bottle lying near the cot. He glanced around, although he knew before looking that he was alone. Swallowing, Kyle drew one of his blades and walked, placing one foot carefully in front of the other, not making a sound. He was reasonably sure the young boy lying on the bench was dead. It could be a little problematic with the Sundered or anyone with talent, but somehow he knew this one was never going to heal.

Kyle looked down on the boy through the veil; he didn't show any traces of power flowing through him. Satisfied, Kyle crouched down and lay the back of his hand on the man's forehead. He was cool to the touch, without a hint of warmth. Kyle frowned. The boy couldn't have been dead too long, since he didn't smell that bad, yet given how cold it was down in the cellars, he guessed that wasn't necessarily true. A quick assessment showed no signs of any knife wounds, yet his wrists and ankles were bruised, the skin broken, with blood trailing down to the cot, as if he'd struggled against his bonds. Kyle remembered the healers warning that he'd nearly died as a result of the toxin because he was highly susceptible to it. He wondered if the lad had been the same, yet unlike him, the child hadn't had a Master Healer to look after him or one of the Kin to finish off the healing after.

Kyle shuddered, remembering the mounds at the back of the castle, wondering how many men, women and children had been killed by the Order, how long they had been doing... whatever it was they intended with their experimentation.

He continued down the hallway past all the cells—grateful no more bodies were lying discarded in them—to the door at the end. He carefully opened the solid-looking door and stepped through, his light revealing a large open room with bookshelves lining the walls, a couple of work desks with a few discarded papers sitting on them, and a long bench against the far wall.

Kyle walked slowly forward farther into the room, scanning the chamber and settling on a bench off to one side. Bottles and vials lay scattered on it, discarded as if whoever had vacated the place was in a hurry when they left. A mortar and pestle lay broken on the stone floor, with a pile of dried green leaves near the bench at the foot of a large bronze still standing cold and forgotten, a dark stain under its tap as if something had been spilled and dried on the stone, leaving a sticky residue.

Noticing a discarded brown nondescript bottle lying on the bench, Kyle walked across and looked down at it. The stopper had partially come out and the contents had spilled on the top of the desk. He frowned and dipped one finger gingerly in the pooling liquid and touched it to his tongue.

Kyle felt his body stiffen in reaction, his mind shrieking in response as the toxin raced through his body and mind. A part of him craved more of the liquid, and a sweat broke out on his forehead. Trembling, he took a step back, trying to stop himself from submitting to the craving to have more. He found he couldn't drag his eyes away from that innocuous-looking liquid spilled on the bench, and the small amount left in the bottle.

Gritting his teeth, Kyle forced himself to turn away from the sight in a series of jerking movements. One careful, hesitant step after the other, Kyle forced himself to walk away over to one of the walls and leaned against it. The damp coolness of the rocks seeped into him, giving his trembling body something to think about other than the liquid on the counter that he craved. His hold on the power started to stutter, and the light above him flickered in response.

Still, even in the sudden confusion his mind had descended into, he assessed he'd found what he was looking for in part. He had been right. The Order had been planning something, clearly making the toxin and administering it somehow to those with power. He just didn't know how they were fully containing the Sundered, how they stopped them from in turn slaughtering them all.

Kyle felt his mind freeze in sudden understanding: they were trying to do to others what they had tried and nearly succeeded in doing with him. They had more members with rogue mind gifts like Alyssa. They were trying to control those born with true power through a combination of their toxin and someone with a powerful mind gift. Still, they couldn't possibly have many people with the power that Alyssa possessed.

As he worried at the problem, Kyle began to purge the toxin from his body, grateful it was a small amount. He realised that he would need to show caution given how he reacted to even a little taste of the toxic liquid.

Kyle jerked upright as he felt himself starting to sink into unconsciousness. He wished that like Alex he'd been immune to the effects of the deadly poison. Shivering, Kyle fought against the toxin and nearly wept with relief as he felt the veil fold around him, fleeing to safety.

~

KYLE BECAME AWARE AGAIN, staring up, confused for a moment, then realised he was in his own bed in the Winter Palace. He stiffened as the memory hit him of his encounter with the toxin. Turning inward, he assessed his own state. Finally, he started to relax, straightening from the ball he'd been curled up in. He'd successfully flushed the toxin from his system, even if it had been mostly subconsciously, and that caused him to let out his breath in relief. Rolling onto his side, he chuckled. It had only been a small taste of the toxin, and it had driven him into a state of panic. Still, he'd managed to overcome it, without running back to Joanna or someone else to fix.

Hearing the distinct clatter of hooves in the courtyard, Kyle moved cautiously out into the common area and looked out a window. He frowned at seeing the mounted guards with the crest of the Fourth and his eyes widened. If the Elite had made it all the way here as William had ordered, he'd been fighting against the effects of the toxin for much longer than a night.

A cool, analytical part of his brain broke down his own reaction to the toxin. At least he knew now that he was sensitive enough to the stuff that he would detect it instantly, even in minute quantities.

A cold smile spread on his lips and lit his eyes, and assurance washed over him. They wouldn't be able to drug him again without him detecting it, even gradually over time. He would just need to react sooner if he encountered the poison again. That was something that had terrified him—that the Order would somehow insinuate their mental hooks into him once more and he would do their bidding.

Kyle stiffened, his eyes widening.

The Order; the toxin; Alyssa; control.

The whispered words echoed in his own mind as he remembered his last train of thought before he'd fled the nearly deserted stronghold for the safety of his room. Kyle thought through his logic and came to the same conclusion now: the Order was somehow obtaining people with a keen mind gift and attempting to control those born with the power of the veil—before they transitioned and came to their full strength—with the aid of the toxin.

Dosed with the toxin, those with power would suddenly find their tenuous control slip entirely, madness taking hold on their minds, allowing someone with a strong mind gift to punch their way through faltering mind barriers and gain control.

Kyle sat up in the bed and then stood up, moving over to the rack where a fresh set of clothing sat on the dresser. His course of action was clear. He needed to go back to the Order's stronghold and take the caretaker they'd left behind. While it was tempting to kill the remaining member of the Order that he could get his hands on, he knew that wasn't the sensible thing to do. The one left behind must know something, even if his memory had been altered, and the person who'd be best to glean those potentially hidden memories from them was Aaron.

Kyle paused, realising that meant going back to the Summer Palace, and he'd have to deal with all the issues that brought up. He closed his eyes, thinking of how the courtiers were likely to respond to his return. There were always some who'd feared what he might do to them. Admittedly, that was with the more mundane method of using a sword. Now he'd given them all legitimate cause for concern.

47

WHO?

*J*ess considered herself well-versed with Vallantia. It still took a fair amount of searching and finally an enquiry to the palace scholar, who'd happily produced maps to locate the village of Barinth. It was apparently a village well off the trade routes that hardly anyone ever went to and other than Scholar Clements no one knew anyone that claimed to have come from the town.

This time Jess chose a set of her old unadorned green and brown hunting leathers. Oh, they were well made and would place her as someone with some wealth, but they did not bear the crest of the Fourth. She slipped her brown cloak over her shoulders.

With the little bits and pieces she'd learned about this village, this time she decided to leave the Elite behind. There were times they were beneficial, but there were other times where she would find out more without them looming over her. The difficulty was trying to find the balance between those two things.

Without waiting more, she pulled the veil around her and travelled to the nearest town that she knew. From there it went a little more slowly as she made her way bouncing from town to town that she remembered from the map. Jess crossed back from the veil to the real world after checking no one was around just out of town. She took her time and walked into the miserable-looking town.

It wasn't that it was really that bad, it just looked like it had seen better days, perhaps a boom era that had caused the place to be built, then whatever that was had dried up and the town, being in the middle of nowhere, started to die. The dirt road into town was in disrepair with potholes, some of which looked big enough for a horse to get stuck in. Jess shook her head and followed the obvious path in the grass that people used to walk around them.

There was only one street to the village, although Jess was struggling to give it that label in her mind. The houses were simple wooden affairs with their own gardens, looking like they grew all their own vegetables and herbs. Jess shrugged. That at least wasn't uncommon for villages, even for some in the dual capitals of Vallantia and Callenhain. Jess shook her head. Half of the premises she could see were in a state of disrepair, some clearly abandoned, roofs and walls collapsing, gardens untended and overgrown with weeds. She was struggling to conceive of a man with the supposed history of Scholar Clements being a product of this village.

Finally seeing an older woman and man out in their front garden, Jess approached. The man had an old rough-looking wooden bucket that he was using to pour water on the vegetables. The woman was on her knees pulling weeds. They both looked up at hearing her approach and Jess was shocked when they smiled. Given the size and state of the village, she'd been expecting distrust.

"Good morning, you must have taken a wrong turn. We don't get strangers often in these parts." The grey-haired woman in her simple homemade dress stood and wiped her hands on her apron.

The man took in Jess's attire and placed his bucket down at his feet and went to stand near the woman. Jess smiled and kept her hands away from her weapons. She knew she had a habit of resting her sword hand on the hilt of her sword when she was standing and talking to people. She had the funny feeling that it might panic the couple.

"No, I don't believe I'm lost. This is Barinth?" She kept the friendly smile on her face.

"Yes, this is Barinth. Can't say I've ever met someone from outside who'd intended to come here since I was a lad." The old man's tanned skin crinkled as he chuckled.

"It's just that I heard a famous scholar came from here, so I thought I'd come and see the place." Jess cocked her head to one side as the pair looked at each other and laughed.

"You must be mistaken, lass. There isn't even a scholar based in this town. If we'd managed to produce a scholar, I'm thinking we'd know, particularly if they turned into a famous one. Hasn't been one as far as I can remember or have heard of." The old lady looked at her kindly.

Jess glanced up and down the road. She could see either end of the village from where she stood. She was amazed anyone still lived here at all. She didn't imagine the village would be here for many more years unless something happened to drive new life into it.

"Have you heard of Scholar Clements?" Jess kept her tone casual.

"Who?" The old man shook his head.

"Scholar Clements. At one point, years ago, he was the scholar appointed to train members of the royal family. It's said his wife lived here and died tragically at the hands of one of the Sundered." Jess carefully watched their faces, which remained blank with no sign of recognition.

"I'm sorry, lass, I think you must have the wrong village. Hasn't been a Clements here, scholar or otherwise. Nor has anyone ever been killed by a Sundered." The man sounded decisive.

"I'm thinking that is an event we'd all remember in Barinth. Not much happens in a town like this." The woman shook her head.

Jess nodded. After taking one last look around the dying town, she thanked the couple, handing them a few coins. They tried to refuse her offer but eventually conceded with effusive thanks. Jess guessed they must have to go to the next village every now and then for supplies, a few little luxuries. She doubted they had much to trade for goods they couldn't produce themselves, so the handful of coins she gave them would be a windfall.

Jess walked back out of town considering the old couple's words. The few snippets of history she'd been told about Scholar Clements did not make sense and according to the old couple they had never heard of the man. In a town like this, if he'd lived here, if his wife had been slaughtered here, they would have known, unlike in Vallantia and Callenhain, where you could hide a death in the masses of people.

Not looking back, she walked around the bend in the road out of sight, then gradually pulled the veil around her as she walked and contemplated the problem. A scholar whose life story didn't track. A scholar who, it was looking like, hadn't seemed to exist before he showed up to train as a scholar and get himself appointed to the palace. At least not in the village he reportedly came from.

If anyone had been watching, it would have looked like she gradually faded from sight.

48

INVESTIGATION

William repressed a sigh and placed his morning coffee on the side table as the doors to his rooms burst open. Elite poured into his rooms. It was morning, at least, but surely disasters that needed his attention could wait until he'd at least finished his breakfast. He frowned as Marcus bowed with an uncharacteristic expression of relief as he looked at him.

"I'm sorry to interrupt, Your Highness, but we needed to check you were safe."

"Why wouldn't I be safe?"

"Lady Amelia has gone missing from her suite at the Complex of the Fourth, Your Highness. We are searching the palace and grounds." Marcus looked grim.

"How can she go missing from the Complex?" William held up his hand. "Never mind, if you knew that she probably wouldn't be missing. Lock down the Complex and all the household staff, including the ones who are off duty."

"Of course, Your Highness, the lockdown has already occurred. We were waiting until the palace and grounds have been cleared before we question the staff in detail. Unless you want to be involved?"

William frowned. "I'll stay put here, or the conference room if needed. Probably better if you aren't all running around trying to find me as well. Get me Joshua and Miranda."

Marcus glanced at one of his men and they went running.

"With your permission I'd like to stay, Your Highness, in case they know something?"

"Of course, it will save me having to yell for you. Set up in the conference room, I'll have Shaun send out word that the council sessions for today are cancelled." William glanced at Shaun, who was standing quietly.

His servant nodded and quietly departed to action his orders, although he had no doubt he would pass the request onto others and call in more household staff to stand by. He was experienced enough to know runners would be needed.

Even though it seemed to take an exceedingly long time for Alex's servants to appear in response to his summons, William knew in reality it hadn't been. Shaun was only just pouring him a fresh mug of coffee.

Both servants bowed and waited. William could tell they were both upset, as well they should be. The Consort Elect of the Fourth shouldn't be able to sneeze without everyone being aware of it. Granted, Alex, Jess and Kyle had always had a tendency to run off and became remarkably good at evading their keepers. This was not a pattern of behaviour Amelia was known for.

"Tell me what has happened."

Joshua and Miranda took turns and reported that they hadn't interacted with Amelia for the longest time. They said Amelia had existed within the Complex of the Fourth like a ghost, not even acknowledging any of them once she was safely within its confines. Miranda had noticed Amelia wasn't in her room when she went in to set up the breakfast bar and alerted the Elite on duty.

"When was she last seen?" William rubbed his temples, taking a sip of his coffee.

"Last night, Your Highness. She went for a walk before bed with the healer. Perhaps she knows more?" Joshua's voice was filled with remorse, as if he took it personally that Amelia had gone missing.

William froze, his back stiffening. He looked up at his brother's long-term servant.

"Healer? What healer?" William knew his gaze and tone had turned sharp as he noticed Joshua swallow convulsively.

Joshua opened his mouth, then closed it again, glancing across at Miranda before looking back at William.

"Healer Bates, Your Highness. Lady Amelia wouldn't see anyone except the healer. There were standing orders issued." Joshua's glance darted between them all; he was keenly aware that a mistake had been made, yet he knew there was little he could have done about it at the time.

William frowned and glanced up at Marcus who stood quietly by the door.

"Who is Healer Bates? I'm not aware of a new healer being approved to tend members of the royal family?" William was confused. There were very few healers who tended to the members of the royal family, and all of them had to be cleared and bound by Aaron.

As both servants shook their heads William turned to one of his servants who stood near the door. "Fetch Master Healer Aaron, now."

Miranda frowned. "I'm not certain, but I think someone said that Healer Bates was the family healer who tended Amelia back on the Strafford family estate before the palace became her permanent home."

William looked at them, tone exasperated. "Why didn't any of you think to report this Healer Bates sooner?"

Joshua wilted. "I'm sorry, Your Highness. We thought she must have been cleared."

Aaron arrived a little out of breath, inclining his head. "You requested my presence, Your Highness?"

William didn't wait on any pleasantries. "Who is Healer Bates and why was she tending to Amelia?"

Aaron took a startled step back at the anger in William's voice, yet recovered himself promptly. "There is no Healer Bates in my team, Your Highness. A new arrival would have been cleared." Aaron shifted his glance from William to the Elite. "This has something to do with Amelia's disappearance?"

William nodded shortly and swore, and the servants cringed at the rare display of anger, aware that they had failed somehow, although from the bewildered expressions on most faces they didn't understand how.

"Fetch Lord Strafford and enquire about Healer Bates. If the healer is there, her attendance is commanded. Bring them here." William issued his commands to the Elite at the door. He smiled reassuringly at Joshua and Mrianda. "Is there anyone else unusual besides the healer who has been tending to Lady Amelia before she disappeared?"

This time Miranda stepped forward wringing her hands. "I'm sorry, Your Highness, there was her old nursemaid, Kate. She always came at the same time as the healer. Lady Amelia left standing orders that they were to be given access and she wasn't to be disturbed while they were with her." The words almost ran out of Miranda's mouth; she looked like she was about to burst into tears.

William let his breath out slowly. "It's all right. If any of you think of anything else, alert the Elite and let them know."

With that William dismissed the servants, requesting they be escorted back to the Complex of the Fourth. He didn't have to order Marcus to send some of his men to find and fetch the maid, the retreating thump of boots testified they were already doing so.

~

LORD STRAFFORD ATTENDED with one woman that bore the intense scrutiny of all of them in the room. Lord Strafford looked worried; he'd obviously already been apprised his daughter had gone missing. The woman looked at him wide-eyed.

Lord Strafford inclined his head towards William. "I'm sorry for the delay in answering your summons, Your Highness. We can't find Healer Bates right now, but Kate was in her rooms. I've told my people to notify me as soon as Healer Bates shows up. You think Kate can help? I've spoken to her myself and she assured me she didn't know anything about Amelia's disappearance."

William shook his head and noted that Lord Strafford looked stressed and tired. That wasn't surprising since he now had the worry of another of his children.

"The household staff informed me that Amelia wouldn't allow anyone to attend her except Healer Bates and Kate. This came as a surprise since none of us, even Aaron, had any idea who they were."

William's gaze became sharp as he looked over towards the woman, who shrank back towards the door only to stop abruptly when she ran into the Elite standing behind them. William smiled faintly at her shock. While he hadn't given permission for the Elite to remain in the room, he knew that there was no way they were about to leave the woman in his presence unattended if she might have had anything to do with Amelia's disappearance.

"Kate would you care to explain yourself?" William's tone was hard.

"I'm sorry, Your Highness. I meant no harm. I was little Amelia's nanny since she was a child." The woman looked at Lord Strafford, obviously hoping he'd intercede for her.

William's expression did not soften as he nodded at Aaron. The Master Healer didn't need any more prompting. He stepped forward to the former nanny, his expression firm.

As Aaron stepped forward, the terrified maid started weeping. "Please no, we were only helping Amelia, she was sick." She kept babbling, her own words confirming her guilt as she struggled unsuccessfully in the iron grip of the Elite.

William found himself watching the unfolding drama just as avidly as the others in the room. The woman's sobs and babbling stopped as soon as Aaron gained control of her mind.

He waited patiently, looking at the frozen tableau in fascination. Thankfully for all of their sanity, it didn't take Aaron long before he sighed backing away from her, a look of disgust on his face.

"She doesn't know all the details, but enough to confirm her guilt. I'm sorry, Your Highness, my lord. They've been drugging Amelia since she was a small child." Aaron opened his mouth, then closed it again, rubbing his face with his hands.

William's eyes narrowed. "Take her to the cells and make sure a watch is placed on her. She will not be given the opportunity to take her own life."

As the guards started hauling her to the door, the woman started wailing again, begging for forgiveness and insisting they had only been helping Amelia. The doors closed and the wailing retreated down the hallway.

"I can't confirm without a sample, but I think it may have been the same one that was used on my Lord Kyle. It started when they noticed that Amelia was displaying signs of possessing the power of the veil." Aaron's voice was soft as he continued to explain what he'd learnt and that the maid had a compulsion on her mind not to tell anyone about the medication they were giving to Amelia. He assessed the compulsion had likely been put in place by Healer Bates. The woman hadn't known who the healer worked for. The thought had never occurred to her.

Lord Strafford looked stricken by the news and sank onto a nearby couch. "My poor little girl didn't stand a chance. Why didn't she come to me? She should have known I would never countenance anyone harming her."

Aaron looked pale. "If the healer has been drugging her in combination with the toxin since she was a child, just as her powers were emerging..." he shook his head. "She wouldn't have been able to. The healer would have had complete control over her mind."

Lord Strafford's face screwed up as he suddenly stood up, his eyes wild.

"You were meant to be protecting her! Why wasn't she guarded better?" He stepped towards William, clearly distraught.

"I'm sorry, Lord Strafford, we are doing our best. Amelia was guarded, she was in the Complex of the Fourth surrounded by guards. It should not have been possible for her to disappear like this." William kept his voice calm, hands raised, hoping Lord Strafford would calm down. The Elite were edgy enough as it was right now.

"Well, obviously there were holes in the security. Someone needs to pay for this." Lord Strafford spat the words at him and spun, heading for the doors.

William waved off the guards who looked ready to intercept Lord Strafford. With first his son going missing and now his daughter, he could understand how stress could overwhelm the man. He was better off out of this; the coordination for the search would go better without him.

As the doors closed, William looked up at Marcus. "I doubt the missing healer is still here in the palace. Send out the guard. Get that healer and bring her back here. Now."

William was barely aware as Marcus snapped to attention, bowed and turned smartly to issue the orders he'd been given. He closed his eyes and took a deep breath. It was going to be a very long day.

WILLIAM STRODE down the hallway towards the healer's wing, his guards following close on his heels, another up front showing him the way. These were not corridors of the palace he normally walked. His mind noted absently that they were far more utilitarian than the hallways he used. The stone walls were bare with no artwork adorning them. The windows were smaller, allowing for light to filter in but instead of looking out onto the grounds they tended to have a view of plain courtyards and featureless walls. He also didn't miss the fact that the Elite were stationed at strategic intersections in the hallways as he passed by. He pushed down his irritation; it was to be expected under the circumstances.

It had been an increasingly frustrating couple of weeks but he'd been notified the missing healer had been found. No one on his security detail would agree for the healer who'd been implicated in Amelia's disappearance to go anywhere near the royal wing. Equally so they didn't want him going to the cells, so the compromise was the healer's wing. He shouldn't be irritated, it made sense, but he was.

The Elite standing at a door halfway down the corridor gave away his destination. The door swept open before he arrived so it didn't hinder his arrival. It did not appease his mood.

He walked into the healer's room, his gaze immediately

drawn to the woman being held by two of the Elite. Her face and demeanour showed no emotion at all.

William glanced across at Aaron, who stood to one side.

"You may commence."

Aaron bowed then stepped in front of Healer Bates.

"You know full well, Healer Bates, that all healers who attend to the royal family must be bound by me. From the moment Amelia became Consort Elect of the Fourth, she was no longer yours to tend to." Aaron didn't pause, his hands reaching up to either side of the woman's head.

She tried to jerk back, only to be caught in the firm hands of the guard behind her. She gasped and tried to twist in a futile attempt to escape his grip. Aaron's lips compressed and he grabbed her head, firmly gazing into her eyes. His own expression closed down as he felt her trying to resist and throw up mental barriers between him and her. Not that she had much chance. He was not only a Master Healer, but the Master in charge of all the healers in the palace. Her resistance was all he needed to sharpen his own metal probe and brush her mental barriers aside. He hadn't done it gently, and the healer shrieked and slumped, held upright by the guard. The only reason for any healer to back away or resist was if they had something to hide.

All healers were bound with constraints placed on them in childhood as soon as they were discovered to have the gift so they couldn't knowingly use their powers to harm another and to ensure their loyalty to the Healers' Guild. The mental web of binding was reinforced just before their journeyman accreditation and administered by their Master Healer. In the case of the healers that worked in the palace, and particularly those who tended to the members of the royal family, there were additional constraints. Aaron himself ensured their primary loyalty was to the Crown first and foremost. What most outside the

Guild were not aware of was that he held equal rank to the head of the Healers' Guild.

Just as Aaron breached her mental barriers, he felt a binding trigger just in time to withdraw his own mind as the woman stiffened and slumped.

The guard swallowed and lowered her to the floor, looking up at the healer. "She's not breathing, Healer."

Aaron shook his head and glanced over at William, his face grey. "She was compromised. It should not have been possible. Breaching her barriers triggered a warding on her brain, linked to her own healing abilities. She sent a current through her own brain to kill herself."

William took a sharp breath. "Did you learn anything from her before she died?"

Aaron shook his head. "No, Your Highness, I'm afraid not. Even if I'd known the trigger was there, I could not have stopped it."

ALEX STOOD, the glow of power in his eyes fading as he took a breath. Shaking his head, he groaned and looked around, recognising what had become his permanent room at The Last Stop. He felt the tension drain from him and breathed a sigh of relief. He wondered how much time he'd lost and what he'd been up to. He'd been here so often now it was almost like home. A sanctuary. Which was silly since it was nothing, only a single bedroom with plain stone walls, and a small wash basin in the corner and a shuttered window looking down into the courtyard below and over to the forest beyond. Alex walked across the room and leaned against the wall, looking out the window. The thick forest was all but inaccessible, at least to the average human. Alex knew what they didn't.

There was power and madness in the deep forest, and it both attracted and repelled him. There were Sundered who habitually roamed within its depths, and unlike normal humans they were not constrained by the need for roads and hunting tracks. Yet they too were both attracted to and limited by the power that was beyond, a beyond that was walled off to them by a barrier in the veil. It was the same barrier that had constrained him, yet he supposed that he could breach it if he put his mind to it. Eventually. It was an intriguing mystery, yet it was one that he felt he knew the answer to. That power beyond called to the Sundered Ones; it was why they came here. Just as it appealed to him. It was the power he recognised, like his own. The Kin and the Elder had to be somewhere, and Alex guessed that at least some of them were hidden beyond that barrier, and that they were responsible for that barrier to keep others out. He just didn't know why that unknown power had decided to lock them out. He suspected that Jess was somewhere beyond that barrier as well. She was nothing if not resourceful. It was the only place that he figured she could be since he couldn't track her at all.

Pushing off the wall, Alex removed his cloak, placing it on the hook to the side of the chest containing his clothes. He removed one boot at a time, sighing as they came off.

With a groan he, sank onto the bed, stretching full length, his head barely touching the pillows and the rough blanket pulled across before he dropped into a deep sleep. Alex moaned softly as he dreamed of better times. He dreamed of Amelia.

No, I couldn't. I wouldn't. It was you in control.

Alex sat up bolt upright in bed, his eyes wide, his breathing ragged, as Amelia's voice rang in his head. The pain and fear in her mind voice had been unmistakable. He lurched out of bed and, calling power to himself, he absently threw it at the lamp by his bedside, and it flared to life, illuminating the room.

Alex wasted no time, hastily cleaning up and pulling on the

fresh set of clothes from his trunk. He shoved his worn clothes into the basket near the chest that he gathered had been left there for that reason. Pausing long enough to pull his cloak from the hook, he'd no sooner swung it over his shoulders than he drew the veil to him and disappeared within its folds.

He thought of nothing except getting to the palace and seeing what or who had threatened Amelia. She should have been safe within the confines of the Summer Palace. Of course, she was probably perfectly safe, but he knew he wouldn't rest until he checked. Alex felt a little guilty that he hadn't thought about Amelia much for the longest time after their misunderstanding. He may not love her, but he didn't want harm to come to her either. Then suddenly his dreams had been plagued with thoughts of her, and he just knew something was terribly wrong.

It didn't take Alex long to traverse the distance through the veil. It was usually quick, yet he absently realised that this time he had no sense of travelling from where he was to where he wanted to be at all. One moment he was in the room at the inn, the next he was standing in his brother's room. What he saw did not reassure him.

William didn't notice he'd appeared at first, deep in consultation with the guard and the hunters, and he was issuing orders for a search. It didn't help Alex's peace of mind that he couldn't sense Amelia's presence in the palace. He couldn't detect her anywhere, which meant she was either shielding herself, or someone else was. Given their last communication—that he'd been hoping desperately was a nightmare—he was tipping she was being shielded by someone else. Feeling himself shutting down, and his anger building, Alex closed his eyes, taking a long, deep breath. Finally calm, or as calm as he could be, he opened his eyes to the sudden silence in the room. A faint smile touched his lips despite his growing panic. They'd noticed his appearance and looked, one and all shocked. Except for William—he looked worried but not, Alex thought, due to his presence.

"Just tell me what's happened? Where's Amelia?" Even to his own ears, his voice sounded flat.

"We don't know, Alex. She disappeared a few weeks ago. I tried to call you, but you didn't answer." William closed the intervening space between them and drew him in for a hug.

"A few weeks?" Alex allowed the close contact, taking a moment to breathe through the panic that threatened to overwhelm him at his brother's terse briefing.

Feeling a surge in the veil he recognised as Kyle, he felt some of his tension drain.

Kyle appeared moments later, the veil dropping from him, his posture becoming concerned as he took in the room and the people in it.

What's wrong? Kyle Looked to Alex and William.

It's Amelia, she's missing.

Alex flashed the communication he'd had from her to Kyle, and he stiffened, eyes flaring as he heard her words. Alex sensed Kyle conduct the same scan of the palace and further afield that he'd conducted, only to come to the same conclusion that he had: Amelia was gone.

Alex took a moment, concentrating on a tightly focused communication, putting as much power as he could behind the message that was intended for one person alone.

Jess, there's trouble, I need you here!

Alex felt her startled reaction as she received his communication. He smiled as he felt her prompt unquestioning response that she would be there shortly. Soon after he felt the incoming surge. Alex drew her in and flashed the dream that he'd had and the knowledge that Amelia really was missing.

Jess crossed the short distance separating them and pulled both Kyle and Alex into a three-way hug.

The three of them stared at each other, the power around them swirling and rising, the room, the world seeming to still around them as it always had when they needed that moment in time. In that split moment, communication passed between them—an understanding of where they had been, what they had learned and experienced.

Alex shook his head, forcibly bringing himself back to the present.

"Call in your searchers, William. Amelia isn't anywhere nearby. We'd know if she was." Alex didn't need to look at both Kyle and Jess to know they nodded in agreement.

Jess walked to William and lightly placed one hand on his arm, a silent promise. William relaxed incrementally, trusting their judgement, and issued orders for the searchers to be recalled—although he didn't relax the order for the double guard on the palace itself. That wouldn't happen for some time to come.

Although if what he suspected was correct, Amelia was already lost to them.

49

CONFERENCE

*K*yle sat at the conference table, the drone of the various councillors a background noise. He was lost in guilt thinking about how he'd failed his little sister. It didn't help at all that the practical side of his brain informed him that when Amelia had been drugged by the Order, he'd been living here in the palace, childhood companion to Alex. Even if he hadn't been, he'd been a child himself and there was nothing he could have done. Still, he felt like he'd failed her.

William frowned and glanced at Kyle. "Did you manage to check out the Killiam Order's stronghold?"

Kyle stirred, tearing his eyes from the window, pulling his thoughts back to the present to find everyone looking at him.

"Yes, Your Highness. It's deserted. Seems they aren't foolish and knew we'd get around to checking on them after they were implicated in the kidnapping attempt."

William sighed. "Did you learn anything from the place?"

Kyle grimaced. "They definitely had the drug. I accidentally tasted some so I can confirm that it was the toxin. It's what put me out of action for some time."

Alex swung around looking at him, wide-eyed. "Are you all right?"

Kyle smiled grimly. "Yes, Alex. It was fortunate." Kyle held his hand up at their immediate protests. "It was the tiniest drop on my finger, and I reacted to it instantly and was able to clear it from my system. No one will be able to drug me with it again without me knowing about it."

Alex stopped his pacing and returned to his seat, gazing at Kyle, finally reassured.

William's gaze sharpened. "There's more."

Kyle licked his lips and shifted in his seat. "Out the back of the stronghold, burial mounds were taking up the full plateau. Some were overgrown, old, but obviously man-made, too symmetrical to be anything else." He looked down at the table, still shaken by the memory of what he'd discovered. It was only the disappearance of Amelia that had pushed the horror aside.

Alex swallowed, certain he was not going to like what Kyle had found.

"What was it, Kyle?"

"Mass graves of the dead. There must have been thousands of bodies buried in them over the years. Some of the bodies were still decomposing. Down in the cellars, where I found the toxin, there were cells with shackles. I found a dead boy, still shackled to his cot, a discarded bottle on the floor the same as the one that held the toxin." Kyle took a long, slow breath as the memory of that incident threatened to overwhelm him.

There was silence around the room as everyone looked at him, each processing the information he'd passed on in their own way. William was pale, obviously shaken, yet it didn't show in his voice.

"You think the Order has been experimenting on those who have the potential to become Kin?"

Kyle looked up to meet William's eyes and nodded. "Yes. I think that is exactly what they have been doing. What they tried with me, the drug and Alyssa's mind control." Kyle shrugged.

Jess looked around the table. "I've done some digging into Scholar Clements. His backstory doesn't check. Scholar Beacham, the head of the scholars, said he'd get the records and send them to me. I thought it might be useful given his involvement in the Order and the kidnap attempt."

William looked at her and nodded. "What doesn't check so far?"

Jess shrugged uncomfortably. "He was meant to be well-travelled, yet apparently joined the scholars as a young man with no one knowing how or when he'd travelled. He was meant to have trained in his youth at his village, Barinth, where his wife was allegedly tragically slaughtered." Jess looked up to see several of the councillors nod in agreement. It was a part of the backstory that people knew. It had been a scandal when it had been uncovered he'd joined the Killiam Order.

The king nodded. "Yes, that was his excuse for joining them."

"I went to Barinth. There is one road leading through it, standing in the middle you can see either end. I spoke to an old couple there, and they had never heard of Scholar Clements or his wife and her slaughter." Jess looked troubled and shrugged. "That is all I know at this point. I'm beginning to believe that Scholar Clements is not who he said he was."

Silence descended on the council meeting for a moment before Alex stirred, his gaze swinging from William to Kyle, then looked to Aaron.

"This is the second compromised healer we have proof of. How did your investigation of the Healers' Guild go?"

Kyle frowned. "Wait. The *second* compromised healer?"

Alex nodded. "I came across one of the Sundered who was under the control of another. I brought him back here. Aaron confirmed he was a healer."

Jess looked at him, shocked. "You didn't kill him?"

Alex snorted. "No. It was tempting, yet I recognised it was important." Alex flicked his gaze over to Aaron once more. "How did your investigation into the Healers' Guild go?"

AARON SAT, frozen in the council as he listened to the input from the assorted people who had been called to the closed session. As much as he wanted to deny the sinking conclusion that the Healers' Guild had a hand in the Sundered, in the Order, he knew he couldn't. He had to confess the healers' own role in the development of the medication—their heart-rending secret that they had kept for generations, fearing the wrath of the people should they learn it was them that had unleashed this plague on their own people.

Aaron became aware of the sudden silence around the table and looked up. Everyone was looking at him.

"I'm sorry, Your Highness. What was that?" He was a little embarrassed that he'd been caught not paying attention, but decided there was no point in trying to hide it.

William raised his eyebrow at him. "Alex was asking how your investigation of the Healers' Guild was going, particularly since we now have proof of at least two healers involved in this mess."

Aaron cleared his throat. "The Healers' Guild went into lockdown. They tell me they have cleared all healers currently at the Guild." Aaron looked troubled. "Yet in light of this, I think they need to check again."

William went to turn back to Alex, yet stopped when Aaron indicated there was more he needed to say. His was one of the final pieces of information they needed. As all eyes turned to look at him, he shifted in his seat, looking down at the table top. In a soft but clear voice, he began to tell them about the tragedy of the incredibly gifted Healer Katrina in the time before what became to be known as the Sundered War—her burning ambition, her desire to help the talented through the transition so they didn't suffer and die like her brother. He told of the research, how promising it had looked, based on an herbal remedy used in small villages, and of the excitement they all had that soon they would be able to do more than suggest that the gifted limited their use of the veil.

Aaron's hand shook as he picked up the glass on the table in front of him and sipped. Clearing his throat once more, he went on, aware that he had the full attention of everyone in the room. He told how things had started to go wrong, how their volunteers had started showing worse signs of madness, becoming uncontrollable, dying. How some had even escaped, killing those in their path, leaving Healer Katina's office and notes ransacked. They had shut down the program as a failure. It was years later that the stories of what people now called the Sundered started to surface, leading to the events of the Sundered War. Aaron looked up to see that Alex's face had gone pale. He swallowed and transferred his gaze back to William.

"The Guild in that time thought the trial participants who had escaped had somehow spread their madness like a contagion amongst those with the gift. Healer Katrina tried for years to find a cure, but most of her notes of the original trials were never recovered, and she failed and took her own life. The Grand Guild Master of the day ordered the files sealed, so that no one was ever to pass on the information of how it had occurred to any outside the Guild." Aaron looked up again, his features crumpling in grief, looking over to Alex, then settling on Kyle. "I'm sorry. When the medication started to resurface, I just thought that the old folk remedy had resurfaced. That is, after all, where Healer Katrina developed her medication from."

Of all those in the room, it was William's face that was most devoid of emotion. "The Grand Guild Master of the day should have confessed what they had done back at the time of the Sundered War."

"It was an error of judgement, Your Highness."

Jess shook her head. "All these years of our people suffering..."

Aaron shook his head. "I'm sorry. I agree, what the Grand Guild Master decided then was wrong." At the sudden scrape of a chair being pushed back, Aaron looked up to see Alex begin to pace once more. That, if anything, betrayed his agitation, no matter how calm he'd seemed. He forcibly drew his gaze back to William. "I sent one of my assistants for the locked medical and meeting files from that time as soon as Lord Kyle was stricken with it. It took time for my messages to get to the Guild and back. I needed to be sure."

"You could have asked me. I could have obtained them, or taken your messenger to fetch them. You would have received them in moments. Of all here, you knew best what we were capable of." Jess's voice shook with uncharacteristic anger.

Silence settled on the room. Aaron realised that everyone was waiting on Alex. He could sense the waves of anger emanating from the Fourth, although he maintained his control. That impressed Aaron no end. He could sense the power that Alex had access to, that all of them did. Even he did, although he, like his brethren, utilised the energy differently. He couldn't perform feats like Alex—no healer could. He could, however, use the power to heal.

"We can't change what was done in the time before the Sundered War. By the time you suspected something, when Kyle was poisoned, it was too late." Alex stood staring out of the window, his back to the room and his voice so calm Aaron didn't know if he should be relieved or scared. "How do you think the Order got their hands on the toxin?"

Aaron looked around the room and found every eye had turned from Alex back to him.

"The man who founded the Killiam Order was a junior healer named Gale Killiam." Aaron smiled as both William and Edward nodded; this was something they both knew. "The old locked records confirmed that Gale Killiam was one of Healer Katrina's assistants during the trial."

Alex's voice, still calm, soft, floated across the room, yet one glance told Aaron that the prince still hadn't turned from the window. "This didn't cause anyone in the Guild in that day any suspicion, what with the timing of the healer's trial and the rise of the Sundered?"

Aaron sipped some water from his almost forgotten water glass before answering. "No, Fourth. It didn't. Not at the time. They thought he disappeared in reaction to the failure of the trial. Some of the other healers that were killed by the trial volunteers were members of his family. They thought his anger, the formation of the Order, was out of guilt, shock and depression at how things had turned out."

The silence stretched for a time as every gaze swung back to Alex. "So now you think there is a connection?"

Aaron nodded decisively, forgetting at first that Alex couldn't see his affirmation. "Yes. The bottles of the toxin, I analysed them against samples of the traditional herbal. The toxin, while based on the old folk herbal, is not exactly the same as that traditional medication. The samples I have, while clearly more refined, are the same as that documented in the old records."

Finally, Alex turned, and it almost made Aaron smile to see that he wasn't the only one who let out his breath. Unaccountably, Alex was in control, seeming calm as he walked back to the table and took his place.

"If you'd told me all this when Kyle was first hurt, I suspect there would no longer be a Healers' Guild. None of us were thinking straight at the time, and while a mistake was made in the past, people would be worse off without the healers." Alex smiled briefly despite the gravity of the conversation, causing Aaron to relax a little more.

Aaron paused to gather his thoughts before looking at William. "Your Highness, the person that Alex brought in, controlling the Sundered. He didn't just have a small amount of undetected healer's gift. He was trained by the Guild, as was Healer Bates. Despite the all-clear, I fear there is a Master in the Guild who is compromising the healers' bindings."

William looked at Alex, then at Kyle and Jess. "Will you go to the Healers' Guild, under my authority, and check this out?" William's lips pressed firmly together. "We cannot allow this if the Healers' Guild has been compromised."

Alex nodded. "Of course, Your Highness, I agree. We will go as you request."

William's eyes widened slightly, his mouth opening then closing again abruptly. He was clearly rethinking what he was about to say before he settled on a nod. "Thank you, Fourth. Aaron, as the Head Guild Master, I'd like you to go with Alex. The Crown grants you the right to invoke royal privilege to overcome objections from your Grand Guild Master, if he does not willingly submit."

Aaron nodded acceptance. "I'd like to bring a couple of my assistants with me as well, Your Highness. I think it might be prudent to check the bindings on every healer in the Guild ourselves. I will leave Jocelyn here in my place in case something goes wrong and my return is delayed."

Alex smiled despite the circumstances. "Probably better if I don't break all the healers looking for the enemy within their ranks." The smile fell off Alex's face, and his expression went cold. "The one I brought in was young for a fully-fledged healer, unlike Healer Bates."

Aaron nodded, aware that his own features hardened. "Yes.

He was compromised as a junior trainee, that much I could get. Whoever it was covered their tracks well. He remembered being in the Healers' Guild. Then there was a gap in his memory, carefully erased, and then he was a member of the Order. There was a dramatic change in the thought processes between the young trainee and the person who went on to fanatically follow the Order. I could determine that much before he died."

Kyle stirred and finally turned his attention back to the conversation, having been seemingly lost in his own world.

"When we find whoever it is, Aaron, leave them to us. I don't think whoever it is really is a healer. Or at least they aren't *only* a healer." Kyle's eyes had narrowed, and his voice was firm.

Suddenly everyone's attention had switched to Kyle. It was William who spoke up first, asking what Aaron was sure they were all thinking.

"What makes you think that, Kyle? If not a healer, who could do this?"

"A healer can be a little more subtle about what they are doing. I don't think a gifted healer would just use the expedient of wiping out a section of someone's memory." Suddenly Kyle grinned at Aaron. "Healers have different methods of getting compliance from people. Don't think I didn't notice."

Aaron's face flushed red all the way up to his hairline, like a child caught out doing something wrong.

"You needed to rest. There really wasn't—" Aaron suddenly spluttered to a halt as Kyle laughed and held up his hand.

"I did not make a comment to criticise, Aaron. As Alex said, it is good you are coming, or there wouldn't be a Healers' Guild left." The amusement drained from Kyle's face, and he gazed at Aaron intently. "We can heal too. You know that."

Aaron knew the colour had drained from his face. It was William who asked what he was thinking and hoping the answer was no.

"You believe it's one of the Kin or Elder?" William's forehead wrinkled.

Kyle shook his head. "As Aaron has indicated, the healers are all bound when they first enter the Guild. If what we suspect really has been done, the only group with that kind of ability that hasn't been bound from childhood are those of us who will become Kin or Elder. All of us can heal to some degree."

Jess stirred in her seat, her face grim. "Kin. I'd say Kin, not Elder. The Elder, with the power they control, would just flat-out take over any region or people if that is what they wanted. They would have no need to play these games."

Alex glanced over to his uncle and his companions who had sat through the conference giving little input, noting that they all looked pale. Alex felt some sympathy for them. Undoubtedly they were wondering how things would have turned out in that devastating war if they'd only been apprised of what the Healers' Guild had done.

"Uncle, will you, Cal and Kat stay here while we are otherwise engaged? Under the circumstances I do not want to leave the palace with no defence. My ranks are severely depleted compared to your day." Alex walked over to his uncle, laying his hand on his shoulder.

Edward looked at his companions and nodded. "Of course, Alex. We will shoulder duty once more in your stead. If only they'd confessed to us." Edward's face looked bleak.

Alex nodded his thanks, and with his eyes glittering with a dangerous light he turned back to William.

"With your permission, brother?"

At William's nod, Alex walked from the room with both Kyle and Jess at his side. Aaron hesitated a moment, bowing to William before scurrying in the wake of the dangerously intent trio.

50

ARRIVAL

*a*aron hurried into the unfamiliar Elite training grounds, a handful of his trainees and a couple of journeymen following on his heels. He tried—quite in vain, he was sure—to exude confidence, yet this was the first time he'd actually been within the grounds of the Elite. The intense, charged atmosphere hit him, causing him to draw in a startled breath. He'd dealt with their injuries before, but he'd never been in the presence of the whole squad like this. Feeling the shock and a little fear from some of his journeymen, he shook himself. The junior journeymen had never dealt with the Elite at all, having been sheltered until now from those who bore the Taint. Aaron cursed internally; he knew he had to stop thinking of the veil as 'the Taint'.

"Steady. The Elite all wield the veil, that is what you are sensing. It's why they are the protection detail surrounding the Fourth and his Companions." Aaron threw a glance at his senior journeymen, both of whom nodded, positioning themselves subtly near the trainees and sending calming impulses at them. "It has always been one of the traditional functions of the Elite, to guard us all against those who wield power."

Aaron smiled wistfully, almost wishing he was the journeyman that was being soothed. Instead, he endeavoured to
calm himself. He'd tended to Alex since he'd been a small boy
grieving the loss of his mother, and had been shocked to sense
a level of power in him, even back then, that he'd never
encountered or thought possible.

To learn recently that the queen had been interred alive all
those years ago before he'd arrived to take up his station had
left him shaken, although it did give him a sense of validation.
He'd arrived to learn the queen had died, and at that time there
had been only a handful of very junior trainees in the palace.
They hadn't thought to check the queen properly—after all, no
normal person could ever have survived those injuries. Even
though he'd seen Alex's harrowing memories of that attack,
he'd always felt a sense of guilt thinking that if he'd somehow
arrived earlier, he could have saved the queen's life. He'd vowed
then, after that tragedy, that even if something happened to
him, there would be someone equally capable of stepping up.

As a result, he had several Master Healers under his
authority now as well as his own journeymen and junior
trainees. The junior trainees at the Guild all vied for the positions in the palace when they became available, particularly
since with the smaller ratio of instructor to trainee they tended
to progress at a faster rate through to Journeyman rank, then
onto Master if they possessed the ability, than those who were
based at the Healers' Guild. So at least the suffering the queen
had undergone waking up in her own tomb would never
happen again.

The queen's circumstances had made him realise that
something else needed to change in healer training.
Currently, it was only when a healer reached Master level that
he or she learned more about those born with the real power
of the veil running through their bodies—those destined to
be Kin and, more rarely, the Elder Born. Aaron looked over at

Alex and smiled. If he hadn't met Alex as a small boy all those years ago, he would have continued in his belief that the Elder Born were nothing but a myth. Yet now there were the three of them, and, to his shock, he'd come to realise that Alex's and Jess's new friends, Damien and Isabella, were both Elder as well. Then there was the addition of Edward, powerful enough to be considered Elder, yet he was told that the ability had grown over the years. Edward was Kin who'd become Elder. There was so much the Healers' Guild had to learn in regards to the Kin—or rather, so much that they had to *relearn*. Aaron had started here with his own healers: they now began to learn more about the Kin when they progressed to Journeyman. Even so, they only treated the Elite unsupervised if it was within their capability, and never Alex, Kyle or Jess.

The trio stood off to one side, the Elite surrounding them, their posture relaxed yet clearly ready for the possible conflict to come. Aaron saw when Jess noticed him weaving through the clustered guards. She leaned forward, whispering to Alex and Kyle, her head nodding in his direction. He nearly stumbled as he found he was suddenly the focus of the intense gaze not only of the three of them—that was bad enough; he could feel the rise in their power with their regard—but also the Elite closest to them. He knew them by name, they'd been a part of Alex's security detail since he'd been young. Marcus, James and Megan, and then the recent addition, Matthew. The power those four had access to paled compared to those they protected, yet they were focused and in control, unlike most outside this company he'd encountered elsewhere in the realm. It was amazing what difference training made. Aaron cursed himself. That was yet another failing on his part in a growing list. He should have seen what was in front of him all these years: the benefits of training for those with power and the potential to become Kin, as compared to those with the misfortune to be born outside of these rarefied circles, who received none.

RYAN CONCENTRATED ON HIS DRILLS, just as Matthew had shown him, determined to perfect them. He knew that he didn't stand a chance of measuring up to the standard of Marcus or the other Elite, starting as late as he had with the sword. Yet Marcus seemed impressed with his abilities with the veil.

He'd also discovered the Royal Library since Prince Alexander had brought him here. The scholars had even assured him that as long as he didn't neglect his other tasks, he was free to go to the library at any time. He'd loved getting classes from the scholars again. He was behind the others of his age in the palace, even the children of the palace staff, yet the scholars had been impressed that he already had a good grasp of his letters and counting, and that he could read. He loved visiting the library on the palace grounds and took every chance to do so. He'd never known that many books even existed in the world. His mother had had only five books. She'd taught him to read, and he'd read all of them many times over before she died.

It was in the library that he'd started to read about the Sundered War, about the last Fourth, the Companions and Elite. He'd realised that Prince Edward in his day had many Companions and the ranks of the Elite had been many times their current number. That was when he decided he'd practice every day. He would become good enough to stand as one of Prince Alex's Companions. He'd learned that Alex only had two companions, Lord Kyle and Lady Jessalan. If history repeated itself and events like the Sundered War occurred again, Alex would need as many trained people as he could get.

Ryan grunted with effort as he struck the bails with his

practice sword again, pushing with the veil as well, as he'd been taught. He was determined that he would be good enough. He would stand and be counted as a Companion of the Fourth. He owed Alex his life and was determined to repay it.

Hearing a commotion near the gates to the training grounds, Ryan looked up and backed up a little to see the Elite crowd into the training grounds, all of them fully kitted up for duty, not training. None of them paid him any heed at all; he was like a fixture these days. Ryan's breath caught as he saw in their midst stood Prince Alex with two others who could only be Lady Jessalan and Lord Kyle, all three of them dressed for trouble.

Ryan carefully made his way through the crowded Elite, standing to one side of Alex, careful to keep some of the Elite in position to screen him from view. He doubted Alex would sense his presence given how much energy was leaking from all of the guards. Picking up on the excitement and determination from the guards around him, Ryan grinned. Carefully he sheathed his blade and stood in their midst, quietly hoping he'd be overlooked.

Feeling the Elite stirring and making way, Ryan peered between several of the guards to spot the healers weaving their way through all of the guards to stand near Alex.

"All right, everyone stand ready! His Highness, Lord Kyle and Lady Jessalan will transport us through the veil to the Healers' Guild. Stay close and don't panic." Marcus paused, grinning at his men. "We're not expecting trouble when we first arrive, but be prepared anyway. Form up!"

Ryan held his breath as he felt the power swirl around him, almost gasping as he felt himself hauled into the veiled world with all the guards.

～

KEVIN TOOK a sudden sharp breath his head snapped up, his chair clattering to the floor as he stood up. He whirled around, his eyes searching the grounds visible from his window. The shockwaves from the veil swept over him, the incoming signature of not just one Kin but multiple, all arriving en masse. His lips curled up and he gave an inarticulate growl. Down in the gardens below, spreading out behind those in the lead, marched guards wearing a crest that was familiar to him—the crest of the Fourth. The guards could only be his Elite Guard, although they paled in significance compared to his own day and era of wearing that crest.

Kevin's eyes were drawn to the self-assured young man at the front. He seemed to be perfectly ordinary to his other sight, yet Kevin knew him; even though they had never met before.

Alexander Edward Rathadon, the current Fourth.

Kevin cursed, wishing once again that Simon had disposed of the prince when the opportunity had presented itself. He'd been told Alex had bristled with enough power even then to give his friend pause. Simon had told him how powerful the young Rathadon had become. But even though he'd seen the potential the boy possessed as a child, he hadn't quite believed it until now. He could understand now why Simon had shied off from a direct confrontation.

Perhaps the idea of befriending the young prince would prove to be the better strategy. Despite his recent transition he appeared calm and in control; without a doubt Prince Alexander was masking his actual ability. That in itself was an incredible display of power, and if he didn't know otherwise, he'd think the prince was only a human. Kevin snarled. He might have power, but it was new-come for the boy. There was no way he could have mastered his talents in the time between now and when he'd confronted Simon. Kevin cursed again, turning around and sweeping the contents off his desk with his arm.

"Damn the Rathadon princes!"

Kevin turned back to the window once more, indecisive. He wanted to fight, but he knew that he wasn't ready. Not yet. All the work he'd put into his plans would come crashing down if he was discovered now.

Standing at Alex's shoulder, wearing the crest of the Fourth's Companions, was another that he recognised. Kevin's hand balled into a fist at the sight of Lord Kyle Xavier Strafford, so far from the broken man he'd been. He cursed their luck as he had many times since their plans had started to unravel. If Joanna hadn't been paying Simon a visit, as she so often did to check on Alex, Kyle would have been his right now. Instead, there he stood at his prince's shoulder like the perfect foil that he was. His power shone from him with no attempt to conceal it. That power was enough to give Kevin pause. Not a single trace of his servant's handiwork remained; it was like all Alyssa's efforts had been blasted from him and he'd been forged anew. Kevin made the begrudging assessment that Kyle was more powerful than his sister. Then again, Amelia was younger and still coming into her potential.

To Alex's other side a woman stood, calm, confident, beautiful—yet deadly. Still, that assessment turned Kevin's snarl into a smile, his tongue darting out to lick his lips. He'd never met her, yet he had no doubt that she was the Lady Jessalan Elena Barraclough. Her reputation preceded her, even here into the Healers' Guild, but didn't do her justice. To possess her, own her mind, body and soul, would be a delight. To control her power and have her stand at his shoulder, the way she stood with Alex and Kyle, would be perfect. Kevin's smile turned to a snarl once more. She wore the crest, a Fourth's Companion just as Kyle was, and shone with as much power. How the Rathadon princes attracted such loyalty in those closest to them was beyond him. He had no doubt the pair were choosing to show any enemy who might possess power that they were there—the perfect Companions making targets of themselves to protect their prince.

A man stood to one side of the prince's core group that Kevin didn't know, a cluster of people around him. By the intricate knot on his shoulder it was Head Guild Master Healer Aaron. The sight of the royal family's Master Healer was enough to move him into action. As a Master in the Healers' Guild and on the Council, Aaron was privy to the knowledge that few possessed. He outranked all the other Guild Masters that sat on the Council. The man even had the power to overrule the Grand Guild Master should the king grant him privilege and order an investigation into the Guild, separate from the rest of the Guild, the failsafe against the corruption of the Healers' Guild. In that circumstance he didn't answer to anyone except the king. For him to be here rather than at the palace meant trouble. If he'd come to look for it, Master Healer Aaron would discover what he had painstakingly hidden from the first sweep checking the healers' bonds. It was time to leave while he could still salvage some of his plans that had taken so long to nurture.

ALEX SCANNED the grounds of the Healers' Guild, noting the number of healers that had frozen at the appearance of him and his people. It only took a moment before one of them turned and bolted at a dead run towards the healers' complex and disappeared into its depths. Alex traded amused glances with Kyle and Jess, yet all of them kept alert for potential trouble and checked their immediate surrounds for a mental signature that would tell them that one of their own kind, one of the Kin, was here masquerading as a healer instead of what they really were. Interestingly, or irritatingly, the presence, the energy of so many healers in one place made the process a little harder than it usually was. Of course, if they were right, whoever it was could be hiding their own presence; they could hardly have failed to notice their arrival. The shockwave of their arrival en masse would have rolled out and been felt by all here, including by the healers of Journeyman rank and above, perhaps even the talented juniors, although it was unlikely they would know what it was they had felt.

Alex looked over absently as Marcus issued orders to his men. The inclusion of a couple of units of the regular guard had surprised him, yet Marcus had assured him that they were experienced and reliable units, and that they had been training with the Elite, so they would not freeze in shock at what they saw, and they could back them up without getting in the way and getting someone killed. The regular guard units broke off under direction, one of the Elite going with each to cover the gates spaced around the complex.

As the ranks around them thinned, Alex looked over his shoulder as he heard some rather impressive swearing behind him coming from Matthew, who was hauling a young man forward. Alex's eyes widened as he recognised the boy that he'd taken to Aaron for healing and requested Marcus look after. He groaned and traded glances with Jess and Kyle, filling them in quickly about his run-in with the boy with a burst of images. Kyle snorted in amusement as he looked from Alex to the boy and then at Matthew, James and Marcus, who looked like they were about to explode.

Alex threw Kyle a filthy look and crossed his arms as Ryan was hauled unceremoniously in front of him. The boy squirmed and twitched his tunic back down after Matthew released him and looked up at Alex, grinning.

"It's good to see you again, Your Highness." Ryan's grin started to slip as Alex continued to stare at him. "Sorry, Your Highness, I was in the training ground practising when you all came charging in and then, well, you dragged me with you."

Alex tried to maintain his stern expression as he regarded the lad, yet found it impossible as the boy grinned up at him. Alex shook his head, his lips rebelliously twitching into a smile.

Alex shook his head. "I'm guessing it didn't occur to you to speak up before we crossed the curtain to travel from the palace to come here?"

"Sorry, Your Highness, I didn't want to distract you all." Ryan kept his grin firmly in place, looking up at Alex, trying his best to look innocent.

Kyle looked at the lad gravely. "Here, this is a little sharper than the training blade you are wearing. Try not to use it unless you have to." Kyle reached into his boot, withdrawing one of his blades and handing it to the lad.

Alex sighed. "You'll stay will us. This isn't a game, Ryan. You will do exactly as you are ordered. Do you understand?"

Ryan nodded. "Yes, Your Highness."

He doesn't look as young as I remember.

Alex saw Marcus twitch slightly before he returned in kind. *Ryan was scrawny and malnourished. Good regular food is addressing that. He isn't as young as he looks, Your Highness.*

Your men are strong enough to call for us should things go wrong?

Yes, Your Highness, they can and will. Marcus's mind voice was calm and self-assured. He was in control and totally in his element, although he still looked like he wanted to clout the lad over the back of the head.

Alex traded glances with Kyle and Jess again, noting Jess's raised eyebrow. They had both seen that Marcus was a lot stronger in his use of the veil than he'd been when they'd first brought their ability to use the veil in their fighting technique to their attention.

This is all new, cooperation between the regular guard and the Elite. You've been busy while we've been gone, Marcus. A ripple of amusement could be heard through Kyle's almost absent observation.

Marcus finished his instructions and closed the distance between them, taking his customary position near Alex as his people spread out at his gesture.

To be honest, it was the leadership of the Guard who reached out to us, my lord. I just took them up on the offer. Marcus's attention was drawn by sudden movement and he gestured with his head towards the double doors to the grand multi-storey building that housed the healers.

Alex noticed Kyle's eyes narrow at that comment and resolved to ask him after this was settled what had caused his reaction, but it could wait until they resolved this current issue. He turned his attention back to the doors to see a flurry of movement as a cluster of senior healers walked out the doors and down the stairs, and made their way across the grass towards them.

ALEX KEPT his expression bland as he sat on the windowsill of the large meeting room they had been directed to. He could tell the gathered healers were agitated by his presence by the nervous glances they kept throwing in his direction. The Grand Guild Master had tried to get him to sit with them, a gesture he had declined. Taking their cue from him, Kyle leaned against the wall near one of the other windows with one booted foot propped up against the wall, playing with one of his daggers, the smack of the hilt as it landed in his palm causing more than one person at the table to flinch, while Jess had found a large couch, shoving it into position so she could easily watch the door. She slumped in it with her booted feet up on a low wooden table in her usual display of irreverence. A couple of the gathered masters looked like they were going to hurt themselves as their necks swivelled around and they worked out, to their distress, that they couldn't keep all three of them in view.

Ryan was standing in the corner, just as he'd been ordered to, keeping out of the way, but was watching Kyle toss his dagger avidly. Alex nearly laughed; it seemed Kyle had just made a fan.

Aaron, flanked by his own people, had taken over and was in his own element. Not that he hadn't tried to defer to Alex, but the prince had merely grinned at the healer and politely declined. Right now, the equivalent of what he guessed was pleasant healer chat was taking place while they waited for all of the summoned masters to show up.

The sudden opening of the doors had their instant attention as a muttering half bald Master Healer shuffled his way into the room.

"Really, Grand Guild Master, there is a set protocol for meetings, I really must insist..." Catching sight of Kyle, the old man's slow progress stopped, his querulous voice halting mid-complaint. He blinked, then gazed at Alex, squinting at him with a frown, then glanced at Jess, clearly perplexed by the strange company in the room.

The Grand Guild Master's eyes darted off with a nod and an apologetic expression on his face before looking back at the elderly healer.

"Master Healer Darius, as you see, we have guests. You know I wouldn't call an out-of-session meeting unless necessary. Please come and take your seat." The Grand Guild Master cleared his throat and looked back towards Alex before transferring his gaze to Aaron. "There is only Master Healer Kevin to arrive, he shouldn't be long now."

51

TOXIN

AFTER THE ATTACK ON THE QUEEN

*K*evin had to curb his impatience as he followed the party back to the Killiam Sanctuary. He'd known this place existed, of course—it had been ceded to the Order back in his own day—but he'd certainly never been inclined to check it out. Why would he? A handful of disaffected, frightened humans removing themselves from the world to live apart. He doubted any of the others had bothered either. Still, it seemed that perhaps they should have paid attention to them a whole lot sooner.

Kevin thought back trying to remember which had risen first. The rumours of the increasing numbers of those with power going mad and breaking, killing all around them as they went through the transition, or the tales of the movement against those born with the ability, and the ensuing killing of children in remote villages for merely having power, for having the potential of growing up to be Kin—the rise of the Killiam Order.

He'd never been able to work out how Edward could stomach seeing humans kill their brethren yet still side with and protect humans. Yet nothing he'd said or hinted at had made any difference to Edward's thinking, and Edward was Elder, way too strong for him to take on and win. So he'd bided his time over the years, in a way secretly happy that humans were doing the job for him in weeding out the potential competition and those who might be able to challenge him. He had plans, grand plans, yet he'd never been able to work out the means to carry them out and win. The Elder, in particular; Edward had always been the one stumbling block. Until now.

Kevin explored the Sanctuary on foot, half in the veil, half not, drawing on the power to shadow and hide his path as he walked down the corridors and into the rooms. He was the shadow in the corner of the eye that made some frown and turn, perplexed at seeing nothing; the sudden chill of the veil that made another shudder. They were ill-informed in this era, not knowing what it meant anymore, their small superstitious minds coming up with simple explanations of the departed ones, the dead coming too close to the living world, of ghosts.

Unaccountably, these humans, despite their ignorant superstition, had come up with their 'medication'. At least, that is what they called it. They had come up with something that could control those with the potential to become Kin. Of sorts. They still hadn't managed to gain full control. Many of their subjects died, while only some did they control for a small space of time. The bulk went mad. Simon laughed at the thought. It was the Order, for all its lofty self-proclaimed goals to protect humans, that were behind the rise of what was now called the Sundered.

The element they were lacking was control. They had little ability to control those they medicated. A cruel smile spread on his face. The young prince, of all people, in fear of his life, had shown him what was possible. With this medication, who knew what he could achieve when he finally moved against Edward and his Companions?

Kevin took the time to pilfer a row of vials containing their medication and a copy of the notes from their laboratory.

It was time that he reinvented himself and went back to the Healers' Guild. It was time that an earnest healer was born, trained and through devastation enter the ranks of the Order, bringing with him the impressionable healers strong with the gift to control minds. Impressionable healers that he commanded.

52

DECEPTION

*A*melia slid her sword into its scabbard, then bent down to grasp the strap, and she hoisted the leather pack over one shoulder. Frowning slightly in effort, she gathered the Sundered from their cells. She didn't have to look, she knew they followed her docilely through the cold stone halls in the long-forgotten bowels of the Healers' Guild. She led them just as her master had ordered her.

A locked-away, hidden part of her mind wondered what had prompted the sudden fear in her master. Ordering the Sundered to stay put in the back room, she opened the door and ghosted her way through the corridors to her master's office, as she had done many times in the past. None of the junior healers even noticed her passing; it was one of the reasons her master had his office in this corner of the complex. They weren't strong enough to notice if he slipped and let his true nature show. She knew what no one here did. He was powerful and not a healer at all despite the false mask he held up to everyone here. He was of the fabled Kin, of that she was sure.

Amelia opened the door to the office and let herself in,

walking through the room paying no mind at all to her master's other slaves that turned to watch her as she entered. She was stronger than they were and not under their control. She only answered to her master. They controlled the lesser of her master's servants, like the ones she had left in the backroom. Not her. They weren't strong enough for that.

Amelia moved to the window at her master's side and looked down into the gardens below. Her eyes narrowed as she saw the Elite with the crest of the Fourth on their uniforms and King's Guard in place at the exits.

"Alex and his companions are here in the Healers' Guild, Master. They are here for you." Amelia's voice was cool, calm and assessing the situation, even while the other part of herself was clamouring and shrieking for Alex to hear her, to come and rescue her from what she had become.

"Yes, Amelia, he is here along with his companions. We must leave." Her master's words were even, although there was the underlying hint of anger.

Amelia assessed the grounds below and the placement of the guards with the Elite. She didn't open herself up to find where Alex was. She knew if she did that, he would also see that she was here. That was something her master clearly didn't really need right now. Still, they had some advantage.

"Send your enslaved journeymen with some of the Sundered to attack the Elite and healers in the courtyard. It will weaken the Fourth's strength and enable enough of a distraction for us to escape. He will go to defend them." Amelia was certain of this. She knew Alex, Kyle and Jess. They would rush to defend the guards and healers in the grounds outside.

Her master looked at her and smiled.

AMELIA SHRIEKED inside her own mind, trapped, yet unable to

change or alter the assessment that came from her own mouth, from that part of her that really wasn't her anymore.

Then again, perhaps *she* was the imposter.

That thought caused her to freeze in the tiny space in her mind. She retreated to the far corner of her mind, curled up in a small ball, her fists pressed up against her eyes, and screamed her despair.

ALEX STIFFENED as a surge in the veil was quickly followed by screaming, then with the clash of blades with the smaller waves in power consistent with the fighting style of the Elite.

Captain, we're under attack, there are so many of them.

Alex recognised Matthew's mind voice, knew he'd been left to help coordinate the guards outside. He leapt off the windowsill. One glance out the window onto the grounds below showed him that Sundered, under the control of healers, were attacking those left to guard the grounds. The healers around the table sprang up from their seats only to be halted by Kyle.

"Stay put. This is not your fight." Jess's voice was firm, and the healers sat back, wide-eyed, each of them feeling the power of her command.

Kyle looked at Marcus, who was standing near the door. "Leave a couple of your people here with the Master Healers." Then he silently continued.

Watch these Masters. The one spreading corruption could be any of them.

Marcus nodded and, with a silent communication, the guards entered, drawing their weapons and taking up positions to guard the doors and the Masters within. Kyle knew without having to look that there were a couple more defending outside in the hallway.

Alex shoved Ryan back with a thrust of his power. "No, stay here with the healers."

He paused long enough to receive Ryan's acknowledgement before he shifted through the veil, gathering Marcus without giving it a second thought, aware that Jess and Kyle had brought Megan and James with them. He arrived to find the once peaceful courtyard had erupted into a scene from nightmares. Sundered worked in packs—something he hadn't seen before—attacking in different areas of the extensive grounds. Healers lay scattered, bloodied and dead on the ground, some of their colleagues attempting to heal while others still ran screaming, trying to get to safety. Alex's eyes narrowed as he saw behind each pack of Sundered one wearing a journeyman healer's knot on their shoulders. Some of the guards were down, while others still fought, trying to defend the healers and give them a chance to escape.

Drawing Marcus and a couple of the other guards with him, as they'd trained, Alex drew his weapon and power at the same time, jumping them through the intervening space, his own blade sweeping up to block the weapon of one of the Sundered. The small huddled figure of a junior trainee, sobbed on the ground. Alex, aware he had Marcus on one shoulder, another Elite on the other, snarled and pushed forward, using his power to force the Sundered pack back, blow by blow. They weren't as strong as him, but they were greater in number. Hearing the wail of a youth, Alex cursed as he realised that his booted heal had come down on the girl's arm. He staggered slightly, readjusting his stance to a more firm footing, and shoving the trainee back from him with a small thrust of power. Alex gritted his teeth and dismissed the girl from his attention. While she was wailing and crying, it meant she was alive. At least they were in the right place to heal the injured once the threat was dealt with.

Alex drew in his power, blocking the efforts of the Sundered in front of him, calling more power to him. He surrounded the Sundered, reinforcing the barrier against their attempts to escape, blocking them from accessing the veil. That was a trick he'd learned from when he'd inadvertently done it to himself, and it had taken Isabella to break him free. Marcus barely hesitated before he struck out at the momentarily frozen Sundered in front of him, their attention diverted to trying to free themselves. These ones clearly had some experience with swords yet didn't have the discipline of experienced guardsmen. They had let their guard down in panic as Alex cut them off from the veil, allowing him, along with Marcus and his accompanying guard unit, to whittle down their numbers by half in moments.

While it wasn't quite as seamless as fighting with Kyle and Jess at his side, he'd trained with Marcus enough that it was almost as good. They moved in concert, protecting each other and taking out their assailants.

Alex tried to search for that signature of someone that was Kin. He cursed in frustration as all the surges in power from the Sundered, and the healers themselves, produced an effective barrier of noise, making it impossible for him to pinpoint who that person was or where they might be.

Gritting his teeth, he fought on, aware that Jess and Kyle did the same from different corners of the gardens.

ALEX TURNED, looking for a new target and finding none. He could hear the ragged breathing from Marcus and the other guards as they sucked in air, yet none of them relaxed their stance. The sudden silence in the gardens was startling. Then the groaning, whimpering and wailing started from those who had survived.

Marcus bellowed instructions to his own men, who went about the messy business of making sure that the Sundered

Ones were dead and would not be healing themselves to fight and kill again, and having to push aside some well-meaning healers who attempted to stop them. Others spread out, covering the approach points of the garden and courtyard and ensuring there was no hidden corner where a nasty surprise attack could hit them. Alex smiled grimly at the horrified expressions of some of the healers who rushed out to help the injured when they saw the guards dispatching the Sundered. There was a desperate need of education needed in the ranks of the Healers' Guild.

Alex turned his gaze back to the journeyman on the ground that he had bound, physically and mentally, with power. The healers may be different to the Kin, but the mental barrier containing them, cutting off the veil, held them just as handily. More so, even, since it seemed they didn't have much capacity to fight back. He stalked over to the quivering healer on the ground whose eyes got wider on his approach. The man started struggling against bonds he couldn't see. Alex squatted down in front of him.

"Cut it out, you'll only hurt yourself. I won't kill you unless you force me to." Alex had to admit that his words would probably have come across as more sincere if he didn't have to battle with himself about whether to kill the man.

Alex looked over to see both Jess and Kyle dragging their own captives with them, obviously both having had the same idea as him. Alex stood watching, amused, as Jess yanked at the metaphysical bonds that bound the journeyman, scowling at him and clearly irritated as he grappled mentally with her trying to break her own barriers. He felt the small surge of power that made the man stumble and shake his head. Alex laughed, and in a twist of the technique that they all used to place barriers around their own minds, he enveloped Jess's prisoner.

Kyle, who was increasingly losing his patience as the

woman he dragged after him sent one probe after the other trying to gain access to his mind, stopped in fascination, his eyes narrowing as he caught what had been done.

"Huh. You could have told me that little secret earlier!" Kyle's tone was exasperated as he then turned and flung his own barrier around his captive, sighing with relief as her incessant attacks on his mind shut down.

Jess laughed and followed suit, placing her own barrier around her own prisoner before nodding at Alex, who withdrew his own.

"Thanks. Don't know why I didn't think of that myself." She smiled at them, then frowned at a healer who'd puffed out his chest and started striding in their direction.

Alex looked at the healer, unconcerned. "I wouldn't, Healer. Interfere, and you commit treason. There is more going on than you know."

Marcus and James moved to position themselves between Alex and the approaching healer. He nearly laughed as the man paled at the mention of treason and looked around for support but found none. He halted, looking at them, bewildered, clearly not understanding what had occurred, although he did realise what the guards meant, particularly since they both still had their swords drawn. He swallowed and looked around as more of the Elite moved into a protective posture around Alex and his Companions. Raising his hands, he backed away without comment.

Alex stiffened as a ragged call screamed at him through the veil. He wasted no time; he hauled himself—with the guards and his prisoner with him—back to the boardroom where they'd left the Master Healers.

RYAN STOOD at the window looking down on the fight below,

chaffing under the restriction Alex had put on him, requiring him to stay with the Masters.

"Now, lad, Alex and the others will sort out the trouble." Aaron's tone belied his words, holding a hint of concern as he stood next to him looking down at the fight as well.

Ryan glanced at the Master Healer, then back down again. He'd spotted Alex easily enough, and avidly watched him fight with the Elite at his side. They were much better fighters, yet clearly outnumbered. He knew realistically he would be more of a hindrance to those below, but that didn't stop him from wanting to help. Feeling a sudden surge in the veil, the cold blast of power washing over him, Ryan spun around from the window to be confronted with four Sundered and a man in healer's robes behind them.

Without thinking, Ryan sped forward, shoving the Masters back behind him with the veil. As the Elite in the room raised their swords, Ryan pushed himself forward and, gritting his teeth, he threw out his own power. He formed a shield, just like he'd been taught, yet bigger, trying to keep the Sundered from the healers. The Sundered snarled and threw their own combined power at the barrier that he'd put up. One pounding blow followed another, and Ryan felt himself starting to tremble with the exertion of holding his shield, and then he felt the Elite, who'd looked at him with stunned expressions, join their own power to his.

At the sight of Ryan stumbling and sinking to his knees, the Sundered Ones grinned and continued their attack, raining their strikes on his shield. Pain stabbed through Ryan's head with each blow that hit home on the shield, yet Ryan desperately tried to hold it as more Elite charged through the door and, in combination with the two that had been in the room, started taking the fight to the Sundered.

Ryan flinched when he felt the surge in the veil that signalled more arrivals, then nearly cried with relief to see

Alex, Kyle, Jess and their guards join the fight. He wilted, dropping his own shield and collapsing onto the ground, where he lay trembling and clutching his head as it throbbed. Where moments before there had been screaming and the ring of blades clashing, silence settled as Alex's arrival turned the tide of the small battle, finishing the conflict quickly.

Ryan felt another's hands lightly touch his temples, and he recognised Aaron's voice as the healer compelled him to sleep.

You did well lad. Sleep now, and let your mind heal.

THE MASTERS HAD BEEN angry and distressed over the obvious compromising of members of their guild. All of them had submitted willingly to Aaron searching their minds for any sign of tampering.

It was the old Master Healer Darius who had shown signs that his memory had been compromised, although his healer's bonds were still in place. He became distressed when the Guild Master gently told him and had him taken to a secure medical room until some of their mind healers had the time to assess him properly. They also needed to make sure he'd suffered no long-term harm or was under any further compulsion.

Aaron shook his head as the old healer was led from the room under the watchful gaze of healers and the guard.

"Who cleared him on your initial sweep? More importantly, whom did he clear?" Aaron looked at the Guild Master without a hint of criticism.

"I cleared him. There was no sign of tampering with his mind then." The Guild Master frowned. "I can't remember whom he cleared—"

"I believe it was Master Healer Kevin." The soft-spoken healer nodded as every set of eyes turned to look at her.

"Where is he? He never did answer the summons." The

Guild Master paled and looked out the window. "Someone should check among the injured out there and his rooms. Do you object if I send some juniors to check?"

Aaron quickly shook his head. "Send a couple of the Masters. We have already checked with some of the guards. A Master Healer had his memories altered. I doubt whoever we are looking for would have an issue with a junior healer."

Alex nodded his agreement and glanced at Marcus, who quickly assigned some guards to accompany the healers going on the search to find one of their own.

"Who is this Master Healer Kevin?" Alex kept his voice neutral. Just because he hadn't shown up to the Guild Master's summons, it didn't mean he was the one they were looking for. He could very easily be among the dead and injured.

"He's the Master Healer in charge of the journeyman healers. Ideal for the position, he's talented and an all-rounder skillset-wise." The concern in the Guild Master's voice was evident as he turned to look at the three journeymen that had been bound and brought back. "I think we need to see if we can find out something from these three. We cannot allow them to go on as they are."

Aaron nodded and thanked the guard who hauled the now sobbing journeyman forward. Alex curbed his impatience and tried not to interfere in the process, aware that both of the older men had much more experience with this than he did. He turned from the sight and began to pace the length of the room. An uneasy silence settled while everyone waited for a result, either from the two Masters engaged with searching the mind of a healer whose bonds had clearly been compromised, or from those who had gone in search for the missing Master.

Time had seemed to drag by at an agonisingly slow pace. It was the Masters who'd gone in search for the missing Master Healer Kevin who returned before Aaron and the Guild Master were finished with their own interrogation. The guards reported promptly to Marcus that the absent Master was nowhere to be found. His office was empty, and even his personal assistants had disappeared with him.

Alex paused in his pacing, trying not to jump to conclusions, yet it was looking more and more like the missing Master Healer Kevin, who had the duty of looking after the journeymen, could be the one they were after. It made a sick kind of sense, since every healer they had found so far that had their bonds compromised were all young and either journeymen or not long accredited as healers.

Finally, Aaron and the Guild Master straightened and stepped away from the journeyman they had been interrogating. The prisoner slumped unconscious as they withdrew, the guards who'd been restraining him carefully lowering the man to the floor.

The Guild Master shook his head, his face pale. "I don't know how this happened, but it was Master Healer Kevin."

Aaron nodded in agreement, looking over towards Alex. "He covered his tracks well, but he was hasty at the end. Our appearance here was a surprise. He ordered the attack to cover his own retreat."

Alex felt a small surge of triumph. The man may have gotten away, but at least now they had a name.

"Show me what he looks like." Alex looked at both Kyle and Jess, both of whom nodded and stepped forward. He could feel their anger simmering, much like his own, but now it had a target.

Aaron held up his hand to the Guild Master and stepped forward. "Of course, Your Highness, I'll show you those last few memories that one had before the attack."

ALEX WAS familiar enough with Aaron that he relaxed as he felt the mental contact. If Aaron had meant him harm, he would be dead several times over by now. Jess and Kyle joined in seamlessly, just as relaxed as he was himself.

The Master Healers had explained that those found with the talent to be healers were bound not to do harm with their powers from a very young age. Those bindings were tightened if they developed the strength and ability to become healers when they entered the Guild as junior trainees. There was no choice for those with the gift to be healers; it was deemed too dangerous for them not to be trained, as they would be a danger to themselves and to everyone around them. There were a variety of paths they could progress along—that had shocked Alex—but regardless of that, they would learn control.

The next most dangerous point was when the junior trainee decided to truly follow the healer's path and progress to Journeyman Healer. Their hard-fought-for barriers were dropped, and extra bindings were placed on their minds, along with injunctions for them to obey their Journeyman Master—in the current day, the Master Healer Kevin.

Alex's attention was drawn to the emotions, words and images that Aaron had pulled from the journeyman healer's mind. At the face that loomed up in his mind's eye, Alex felt himself stiffen at finally seeing the face of the person they were looking for. Another mind voice intruded, a figure darkened from the backlit window. The journeyman's fear flashed through them as the figure stepped forward, giving instructions for the assault in the courtyard. She was his master's pet and had an extraordinary amount of free will, unlike the other monsters. As she stepped closer, his fear intensified at the cruel smile and blank eyes, as her face came into focus.

Alex wrenched his mind from the contact gasping in pain, reeling in shock, feeling like he'd been assaulted with a physical blow.

Amelia.

The dark, feared figure trusted by the master, who instilled fear on his other followers, was Amelia.

Alex was aware that Kyle's reaction wasn't much better than his own and that everyone in the room, including Jess, their guards and the gathered healers, were deeply concerned by the response of them both.

Did anyone recognise the man?

Alex shook his head and closed his eyes trying to blank out the images, though they had been burned into his mind. He opened his eyes knowing they reflected the shock he felt, more for what Amelia had become than the face of the enemy.

53

ENSLAVEMENT

*K*evin paused in the veil to look back on the fight taking place in the grounds of the Healers' Guild, watching healers go down under the onslaught, unable to defend themselves against even those few servants he had with him. He grimaced. It was too much to expect that the Rathadon prince and his companions would be hurt. Still, Amelia had been correct, the distraction had served its purpose and allowed him the time to leave.

He looked at Amelia standing calmly next to him, her eyes narrowed as she observed the battle below. She was definitely his prize acquisition. He waited a moment, ordering a few of his more valuable journeymen to withdraw and join him. Kevin's back straightened, and he nodded to himself. This had been a close call, but the few losses sustained here would not impact his long-term goals. Indeed, the battle, if you could call it that —perhaps *skirmish* was a better word—had been educational. Thankfully the vast majority of his journeymen had not been in the Guild complex. Satisfied, he turned to gather his journeymen to him.

Enough of this, come all of you. We will relocate to our new home.

Kevin started as he felt Amelia exert her own power, assisting by following his lead and drawing the handful of Sundered and journeymen to her, drawing them through the veil with her, and following him placidly. Kevin laughed in delight. Yes, this was going to work. Perhaps it was for the best that this attack had occurred when it had, even if only to shake him out of his rut.

AMELIA SHIVERED in the back corner of her mind, weeping at what she had become, what she was now compared to what she had been. Mustering up her courage, she cautiously moved forward enough that she could see out of eyes that had once been hers. She trembled, frozen. She was in the veil with her master, following along, dragging some of the Sundered and journeymen with her. Her other self wasn't being compelled at all by their master. She was willingly going with him, and it seemed he trusted her. Oh, she knew he was here in her mind, she could feel and see the baleful cage on her mind and body. Yet her other self now had some free will.

Amelia didn't know if that other her knew that she was present, that they shared their mind, if not the body. She had spent many futile hours, days, months—she was perplexed and had no idea how long it had been—fighting, trying to gain possession of her body again. She had managed to look out of her own eyes, and she could see what her body was seeing, sense what her powers sensed, yet that was the extent of her abilities. Feeling her master's attention drawn to her, Amelia withdrew, collapsing into as small a ball as she could, rocking as fear shook her.

I'll be good. I won't fight. Please, Master, don't hurt me!

~

Kevin shook himself as they arrived at the Order's camp. He had to play the fiction of Master Healer Kevin for a bit longer. It was tempting to throw off that mantle now that he was done with the Healers' Guild, but that would cause some confusion and perhaps some suspicion among some in the Order.

Kevin smiled as they transitioned to the real world, walking down the main street of their new home. It was handy having his pet at his heels. He could get away with much more flagrant displays of power now that she was with him. Other members of the Order would assume it was Amelia acting rather than him.

Their arrival caused a stir, as members stopped and stared at the new arrivals, their relief palpable as they recognised him at the head of the approaching group.

He saw one of his healers, Jenny Medcalf, talking with Scholar Clements. Sensing his arrival, she turned at his approach and smiled a welcome. She had come a long way from her journeyman days to graduate to Master level and was one of his top people.

"Jenny, it's a delight to see you again. I can't thank you enough for your work in refining the medication and treatment." Kevin allowed satisfaction to shine on his face. All those years in the royal court, even if they had been more years ago than he cared to count, came in very handy.

"Thank you, Master." Jenny looked down at the ground, blushing, her pleasure at the compliment evident.

"Ah, now you don't need to refer to me as Master, your journeyman days are over and you are a Master yourself now, Jenny." Kevin was aware of the other ears listening, and added that last for their benefit.

Scholar Clements stepped forward to greet him, concern

written on his face. "It is good to see you, Kevin. I wasn't expecting you, has something happened?"

Kevin felt his smile falter, and he glanced around. "Perhaps we could discuss this in private?"

Scholar Clements nodded. "Of course."

Kevin signalled for Amelia to come with him, then spoke to his remaining journeymen.

"Wait here with the Sundered, I'll find out where you can all be accommodated."

KEVIN SAT at the meeting table with Clements and Jenny, watching with interest as Duncan and Amelia stood near each other, obviously assessing each other. They were both among the first of their kind in the Sundered ranks. It was clear they both recognised a kinship with each other. Unlike other Sundered, though, neither Duncan nor Amelia attacked each other or showed any inclination to do so. Of course, they weren't showing any desire to talk with each other either, even though their masters were otherwise occupied.

Kevin turned his mind back to business. "The king's men came after us at the Healers' Guild. We staged a distraction, enabling me and the few of my people I had with me to escape."

"You weren't hurt?" Jenny's eyes scanned him, and he felt her power lightly touch him, assessing, before withdrawing satisfied.

"No, we managed to get out just after they arrived. Thank you for your concern." Kevin smiled and turned his attention to Clements, who stirred.

"How did they know about our connection to the Healers' Guild?" The old man's voice held a hint of panic.

Kevin grimaced. "I believe they stumbled upon some of our

journeymen. They shouldn't have been able to gain anything from them, they are all protected, but it probably made them suspicious."

Amelia stirred, drawing her attention away from Duncan.

"They would have discovered Healer Bates's involvement soon after my disappearance. She shouldn't have been near me, and Kate wasn't protected, Master." Amelia's voice was flat, without a hint of emotion.

Kevin swung in his chair to look at her. "Kate?"

"My old maid, Master. She helped Healer Bates with me since I was a child. She made sure I had my medication even when Healer Bates couldn't be present." Amelia settled back against the wall.

"Since it seems our adversaries are aware of us now, I propose we take action." Kevin smiled, his eyes glinting with anticipation.

FOURTH'S COUNCIL

*S*hifting into the training grounds of the Elite, Kyle traded glances with Jess, knowing they both had the same concern. Alex had shut down since he'd seen the images of Amelia from the corrupted healer's mind, seen that she was the one that they feared. Kyle knew that he'd have to deal with his own feelings about his little sister. He felt himself stumble over the label.

Little sister.

He realised that Amelia wasn't the person he'd thought he knew. She hadn't been since shortly after the palace had become his permanent home as a child. He had been safe here in the palace, treated by Aaron and his people, while his little sister had come under the influence of a healer under the sway of the Order.

The problem was he didn't think Alex realised the full implications about Amelia. He was still under the illusion that what he'd shared with her had been real. Alex may have come to the conclusion that those moments with Amelia was an infatuation, yet he had no doubt his friend wrongly assumed guilt, that he felt responsible for what happened to Amelia.

Kyle pushed down the darkness that welled up in his own mind. He knew from personal experience that it wasn't. Simon wanted Alex. He'd tried and nearly succeeded in capturing his friend through the shell that had once been his sister. The problem was, he knew that Alex still wasn't seeing any of this clearly.

He glanced at the men who carried Ryan on a stretcher.

"See he gets taken to the healer's wing and receives treatment from Jocelyn. We'll check in later when the king has been briefed."

Kyle fell into step with Alex and Jess as they continued across the grounds and out the doors, not waiting for acknowledgement from the guards.

ALEX WALKED into the Complex of the Fourth, into the private lounging area, and slumped into one of the chairs, his mind whirling with everything they'd learned. The sheer scope of the plot, the people killed and driven mad since before the Sundered War, was sickening.

And then there was Amelia. The images they'd been given of her, the fear the others had of her. It was something he couldn't come to terms with. His mind spun and turned the images over and over again.

Seeing a goblet enter into his vision, he took it, looking up at Kyle and nodding his thanks. He took a long swallow, barely tasting the liquid as it slid down his throat.

"Alex, you know it's not really Amelia. Not anymore." Jess's voice was soft.

Forcing his gaze up, Alex looked over at Jess, then at Kyle, feeling the pain welling up inside, clamouring to be recognised. He ruthlessly pushed it down; he didn't have the time to wallow in his own pain.

"I can't think about that right now. Only the threat the Order pose to us, all of us." Alex looked up as the door opened and Joshua entered.

"Joshua, I'm calling the Fourth's Council. If you could liaise with Carl for a time that is suitable for the king and William, and then the rest of the security council members will have to fall in with that time, no negotiations."

"Certainly, Fourth. I'll see to the arrangements immediately." Joshua bowed, then supervised the household staff as they placed an assortment of finger foods on the table for all of them before herding them out of the room.

"Edward, Cal and Kat should attend, they may have insight." Kyle sat in his customary fashion with his legs thrown over the side of the armrests, cradling his drink.

Alex nodded.

Edward, you are needed at the Fourth's Council. Kat and Cal as well. You need to hear what we've learnt.

Alex felt a slight hesitation before Edward responded.

We will come, Alex.

KYLE WALKED into the council room attached to the Fourth's Complex with Jess close on Alex's heels, nodding to the various lords present. They were followed closely by Edward, Kat and Cal. The banter between the lords ceased as they noticed the new arrivals. The king and William had been apprised already, they weren't about to shock either of them with the surprise additions. Alex nodded to his father and William, who were already present at the table.

"My apologies, Father, William. We decided it would be prudent to get cleaned up first."

As Alex took his seat at the head of the table, he and Jess took their places own places to either side of him. Alex gestured to the remaining chairs, and Edward, Kat and Cal took their seats without comment.

"You called this meeting, Alex, surely you could have waited," Lord Kastler grumped.

Kyle didn't miss it as Alex stiffened at Kastler's comment his friends eyes flicked up, staring at the lord.

"Our men were set upon by attackers, Lord Kastler. Battles are a messy business, and our appearance may have shocked the finer sensibilities of some at this table." Kyle's tone was cold.

Kyle smiled as the lord paled and stammered an apology, noting that most of those present except for the king, William and his father looked shocked at the information.

Kyle settled back as Alex started to bring the council up to speed, taking turns with Jess in interjecting information. They started with a brief explanation regarding the Kin, and the identity of Ed, Cal and Kat. Several of the lords looked like they'd been smacked on the back of the head, while others looked incredulous. Without waiting, they continued with their discovery of the toxin after the kidnapping, Amelia's disappearance, the investigation of the Order's stronghold, and the tie they had identified with the Healers' Guild.

Kyle paused, thanking the servant for topping up his drink before taking a sip. After a stunned silence, the clamour of raised voices from the lords replaced the shocked silence that had held for a split second after he'd stopped talking. Kyle held up his hand, and much to his astonishment got the silence he wanted.

"Please, my lords. Let us finish, there is more. The king tasked us with following up and investigating the Healers' Guild, which we did."

The three of them continued the briefing, starting with their arrival at the Healers' Guild. Aaron interjected with details of the subsequent clearing of the members of the Guild, with a couple of exceptions, advising every one of their findings. Alex took up the briefing again, finishing with the attack by the suborned healers controlling packs of Sundered.

Kyle, his face carefully blank, advised the council of Amelia's own corruption and involvement in orchestrating the attack on the Guild to hide their escape. He finished with a tally of the deceased and injured, both on the healers' side and their own.

Kyle noted the fleeting look on pain flicking across Alex's face as he closed his eyes. Numbers never really did justice for the dead.

Finally, they told of seeing the healers face who'd been responsible for corrupting the healers bonds and their belief that he was one of the people in charge of the sick plot that had spanned generations unchecked. Silence settled on the room as the three of them settled back in their chairs.

"Why weren't we apprised of the true nature of the attack on Lord Kyle when it occurred? Surely if we'd known more guards could have been placed on the Consort Elect of the Fourth to prevent this." Lord Castilian looked indignant.

"I guess you're happy now. Disposing of Amelia neatly, allowing you to bring in your mistress!" Lord Strafford's face was flushed and angry as he flung his accusation at Alex.

Kyle stood, placing himself between his father and Alex. Silence descended on the council meeting as those present shifted uncomfortably in their seats.

Kyle shook his head. "Amelia has been drugged by a compromised healer at the Strafford estate since she was a small child. That healer was brought here to the palace in my lady mother's party. That had nothing to do with Alex."

"You protect *him*, but you didn't protect your sister." His father nearly spat his response at him, looking for someone to blame, anyone.

"Enough, Father. Did it ever occur to you, given how long

they have had their hooks in her, that Amelia was set on Alex by the Order? Amelia was a child, she could not fight what they did to her. Nothing could have saved her. I know that from my own personal experience." Kyle left it unsaid that it was probably just as well Alex had been away, distracted by transition and his affair with Isabella.

All eyes turned to the king as he stood and placed his hand on the shoulder of his long-term friend and advisor.

"You are understandably upset, Nathan. Please sit, if you will hear the rest of the council about those who are really responsible. Or retire, if it is too much for you right now, and I will brief you privately." The king squeezed Lord Strafford's shoulder in sympathy.

"I'll take my leave, with your permission, Your Majesty." Lord Strafford's face had closed down and, receiving the king's permission, he turned and left the council room.

No one spoke as both Kyle and the king both took their seats again.

Lord Marshal's eyes darted around those at the table and he cleared his throat. Everyone looked relieved that someone else was going to speak first.

"What about all those dead bodies you found buried? Are you certain it wasn't just the burial grounds for the Order's members over the years?"

Kyle nodded. "I'm certain. They had a smaller burial ground that I believe was used for their own members."

He took turns with Alex and Jess at answering the rapid-fire questions from the lords, grappling with the world they found themselves in. The seemingly unending questions continued for hours, only breaking when the servants brought in fresh food and drink. Finally, they all settled, yet Alex was sure that there would be more questions when their minds managed to process what they'd learned.

"Can you show me the face of the healer? Given all of this

mess started back in my day, we might recognise who it is." Edward hadn't said anything during the exchange of information but it was clear he'd been tracking the conversation.

The three of them looked at each other before Alex nodded and drew Ed, Kat and Cal into his mind, showing them the same sequence of images that had been drawn from the compromised healer's mind at the Healers' Guild. Kyle knew the second the three stiffened in response to seeing the face of Master Healer Kevin that it was someone they knew. Alex withdrew and looked at Edward expectantly.

Edward looked at his two companions.

Kat swore explosively. "That vile little man." She looked murderous.

"Kevin is no healer, or wasn't. He was a member of the Companions Cohort." Edward's eyes glinted with anger.

"Did Kevin ever give any indication back then that he could commit these acts?"

Edward traded glances with Kat and Cal before shaking his head. "Not really. He was always a little prickly in nature, but I would have killed him myself back then if I'd known what he would do."

Kat stirred in her chair. "He did go through that period saying you would be better on the throne than your sister."

"I doubt he was involved in this back then. Although it does explain the recent change in the behaviour of the Sundered." Cal's voice was grave as he looked around the table.

"You need to build up the Cohort, Alex. You three cannot fight this alone. Although I'm not sure, we have time." William's voice held nothing but certainty.

Alex turned his gaze to his brother—William had an uncanny knack of assessing situations correctly—then looked at both Jess and Kyle. They all shared an unspoken moment where they were entirely in accord with each other.

"We'll do what we must, William." Alex glanced over to

Edward, seeing his uncle exchange glances with Cal and Kat before they all looked at him and nodded.

All of them knew that the three of them could not counteract an army of Sundered.

"We need to find out where the members of the Order have gone. They must be holed up somewhere."

Jess nodded. "We can start checking, starting with the places that report attacks by the Sundered."

Alex traded looks with his friends, then looked at the king. "At least one of us will remain here in the palace, Your Majesty."

"I agree. With this new capability, both of you would be a target." Kyle frowned and looked at Alex. "You should stay here, Alex, and leave the search to us. Between Jess and me, with help from Ed, Kat and Cal, we'll coordinate and get it done."

"They could be anywhere but it makes sense to start here and expand out." Jess shrugged.

"Are we sure of this interpretation of what happened at the Healers' Guild?" Lord Kastler's querulous voice interrupted the conversation, causing everyone to look at him.

William's eyes narrowed. "What makes you say that, Lord Kastler?"

Lord Kastler blanched at William's tone. "I'm sorry, Your Highness, I misspoke. I just know I'd panic if my home was invaded by armed guards."

The silence at the council was deafening as everyone looked at Lord Kastler, astonishment being the overwhelming response.

Alex shook his head and threw a disgusted look at Kastler. He took a calming breath and looked around at those present, clearly choosing to ignore Lord Kastler.

"You know the information we had to brief you on, my lords. Thank you for responding so promptly."

The king stirred as the various lords and ladies that made

up the council stood at the dismissal and made their way to the exit.

"I'd like a word with all of you in private before we all break up." The king pinned Alex with his gaze before raking it across the six of them, finally resting on William. He waved for the councillors who'd paused at the doorway to leave the room.

～

ALEX WAITED until the door closed before turning his regard back to his father.

"What is it, Father?"

"Tell me about Joanna." The king's voice was firm. "William briefed me that she is alive, one of the Kin, but not... well."

Alex settled back in his chair and looked at Edward.

Edward sighed. "When going through transition, some become what we used to refer to as the Broken. Some recover remarkably well, some do not. We've never been able to pinpoint why."

Kat looked sad. "Those who transition suddenly and unexpectedly tend to suffer more."

"The abrupt increase to power, as happened with Joanna when she was attacked, forcing her from human to Kin, is rare, but it happens. That, added to the shock of the circumstances surrounding the attack and waking up in her own tomb..." Edward looked sad. "Well, Your Majesty, she has her good days, many of them, but at other times she becomes unbalanced and irrational."

Cal looked earnestly at the king. "We try to minimise any harm she might do to herself or others during those times. She is Kin, though, and we sometimes lose track of her. That is how she managed to bind Kyle."

Kyle shuddered a little in memory. "When Joanna is unwell, she can be a little scary."

"As all the Broken can be." Edward looked at him gravely.

"Will she ever heal?" The king picked up his glass before noting it is empty and placing it back on the table. Alex absently reached for the pitcher and refilled his father's glass before topping up his own.

Edward shrugged. "I wish I could tell you with any certainty, Your Majesty."

William bowed his head, a pained expression on his face, and Alex was aware that his own expression wasn't much better. He still wasn't sure at all what he thought about his mother. As if playing dead for all these years wasn't bad enough, binding his best friend and then forcing Kyle to stab and try to kill him was a hard hurdle to get over. The reasonable part of his mind insisted on pointing out that when she spiralled down into a maze of madness, it wasn't really her fault. If he was honest, there were times he didn't think he was much better, although that was an observation that he kept to himself.

The king looked troubled. "Would she be better off here under the care of the healers?"

Alex swung around to stare at his father. "No, definitely not. The healers would not be able to contain her. She may have had very little power as a human, and was birthed into being Kin through trauma, but she is strong enough that I warrant she can burn through anything the healers might do."

Kyle had paled at the thought. "I agree, Your Majesty. I don't even want to think what Joanna would do on one of her bad days if she perceived the healers as being a threat."

"Perhaps an invitation to visit? She is settled in my estate and doesn't want for much." Edward grinned at Kyle's startled look.

"Past is past, no matter how painful some of it was. This has always been her home. I will have rooms made up and set aside for her in the Royal Wing, and for the three of you as well." The king stood, walking to the exit and pausing as it swept open for him. "Keep me apprised, please."

Alex buried his face in his hands for a moment before looking back at his friends and brother.

"Well, he's taken the news about Mother better than me." Alex still couldn't reconcile all those years of thinking she was dead.

William laughed. "You and me both, Alex." William stood and followed their father out of the room.

COMPANIONS COHORT REBORN

*A*lex grinned at Kyle and Jess, flipping his blade in salute as they separated, and then sliding his sword into its scabbard. The pair grinned at him and followed suit; they'd all hit the training grounds, relaxing back easily into familiar patterns. The three of them had taken turns in showing each other what they'd learned, specifically with regards to incorporating the veil into their fighting technique. It was a slow and methodical session refining their fighting styles and abilities.

Alex sighed, his mind returning to mulling over William's assertion that they need to build and reform the Companions Cohort. Then he grinned, glancing at Jess and Kyle.

"So, how do you propose to reform the Cohort?" Alex kept his tone bland as they both spluttered.

Jess looked mildly alarmed at the thought. "Us? Don't you mean *you*, Alex?"

"Well I thought so at first, but it is the Companions Cohort, so it traditionally comes under your command." Alex felt a small glow of pleasure at neatly sidestepping that particular problem William had saddled them all with.

Kyle swore. "How does your brother propose we do that? There are not exactly many candidates we can draw from today, unlike in Edward's day."

Alex shrugged. His brother knew very well the problems they would face but expected them to get it done anyway. Not that he could fault William's request.

"What about the lad? I don't think there is any doubt that he will go through transition after that display at the Healers' Guild." Jess went straight to practicalities, as always.

Alex turned his head and gestured to Marcus, who stepped forward.

"You've seen more of Ryan than I have, Marcus. What do you think of him?" Alex accepted a goblet of water from one of the junior guards, nodding his thanks.

Marcus shook his head. "His blade work is appalling, he's never had any training before he came here. With intense training, we might be able to get him to the point of not stabbing himself."

Alex snorted in amusement, then, seeing Kyle's eyebrow raised in an unspoken question, he related how he'd met Ryan and the responsibility he felt for the boy.

Jess shrugged. "Well, he won't have as much to unlearn then. I'd say no training is better than bad training."

Marcus laughed. "You are right there, my lady. He'll never be of Lord Kyle's skill, but very few are. He's earnest enough and definitely more powerful in his use of the veil than the regular members of the Elite already, despite his age."

Matthew, who'd been trailing them with James, cleared his throat, causing them all to turn to look at him.

"I'm told the scholars are happy with his progress. He's had some training in his letters before his mother died and his life fell apart." Matthew was clearly impressed with the boy. All of the Elite seemed to be, particularly after his efforts at the Healers' Guild.

Kyle shrugged. "Giving Ryan a chance won't hurt."

"Of course, if you three showed up while he was in lessons with the scholars, it might help his position here in the court a little better." Matthew's tone was carefully neutral.

Alex looked at the guard, frowning. "What do you mean?"

Matthew ducked his head, then looked back at Alex. "The court brats know he's an orphan and lived on the street before he came here to the palace."

Jess's lips thinned. "Ah, so they think they are better than the lad and let him know it?"

Matthew nodded. "Ryan hasn't responded to their taunts, not even a peep out of him that it's His Highness that is his sponsor here at court."

Alex traded glances with Kyle and Jess, his eyes narrowing.

"Well, let's go set things up. If he agrees, he won't have to deal with those group classes again and he'll outrank the brats. They'll probably be fighting for his favour after this." Alex nodded his thanks and turned, leading the way out of the training grounds.

ALEX PUSHED his own concerns aside. He couldn't solve the issue of his mother, Simon and the Order in a day, but this was one small problem he *could* deal with. He paused in the entrance of the training rooms, aware of the hush that settled on the room as the students all became aware of his presence. Scholar Joseph kept talking for a few minutes before he became aware of the unnatural silence of his students. He paused and frowned, looking around the room. Spotting Alex leaning against the doorway, he bowed.

"Your Highness. How can I assist you?" Scholar Joseph straightened and looked at him earnestly.

Alex smiled, his eyes tracking around the room before

settling on Ryan. "I require Ryan for a training session, Scholar Joseph."

Joseph turned and looked at Ryan, gesturing for him to gather his books.

"Of course, Your Highness. Ryan can make up today's lessons another time."

Alex noted that Ryan looked somewhat depressed at that notion even though he was trying to hide it.

"Please speak with Joshua or Miranda, we will need to coordinate. Ryan has other duties and training he must attend, and that timing is scheduled around my availability and that of the Elite. Private tuition will need to be organised." Alex saw the eyes widen around the room, all of them sons and daughters of the lords and ladies that spent the bulk of their time in court.

Alex felt his lips twitch as he ushered the lad out of the room. Perhaps knowledge of who Ryan's patron was here in the palace might cause those who'd been giving him a hard time to rethink their strategy.

Jess and Kyle looked up from the conversation they'd been having a short distance away and, with a smile at Ryan, they both fell into step as they all made their way down the hallway.

Alex saw Ryan glance up at him several times as they walked, obviously trying to pluck up the courage to ask something. He waited patiently; he was sure the lad would get around to whatever it was eventually. Alex led the way through the palace, but other than a few curious stares, no one hindered their progress. That in itself was unusual, but then again many inhabitants of the castle were still a little skittish around all three of them, treating them like they were made of spun glass and might break and splinter at any moment. Alex wondered idly how long the current hesitance would last.

"Where are we going, Your Highness? I know it's not the Elite training grounds." Ryan looked around the hallways they were walking through, obviously in territory that he was unfamiliar with.

Alex smiled and glanced at him. "To the Complex of the Fourth. We have a proposal to discuss with you."

Ryan looked stunned at the prospect, falling back into silence, clearly digesting the information, as little as it was. As the doors opened before them, Alex led the way, relaxing with a sigh as the doors closed on their own private sanctum. Walking into the small dining area, Alex gestured for Ryan to take a seat as he, Jess and Kyle took their usual places around the table. Ryan looked at the assortment of food on the table, his eyes round with astonishment.

Jess grinned. "Help yourself to some lunch while we talk, Ryan."

Ryan blushed and slid his eyes over to Alex, who nodded, not able to stop the chuckle that escaped.

Alex looked up at Jess, who was clearly amused by the lad's reaction.

"Don't worry, Ryan, Jess doesn't bite. Much." Kyle poured himself a cold drink from a pitcher on the table before helping himself to some small savoury pastries from one of the platters.

Alex waited until they all had food before looking up at Ryan and catching his attention.

"You are free to refuse this offer; neither I nor Kyle or Jess will be offended." Alex sipped his own drink, looking at Ryan intently over the rim of his glass.

Ryan swallowed his mouthful of food, mumbling, "Yes, Your Highness."

"In the time before the Sundered War, the last time there was a Fourth, there were three times the numbers of Elite than we currently have." Alex watched Ryan intently, noting that he didn't seem shocked. He'd been told the lad loved reading and had a particular liking for accounts of the time of the Sundered War, so this would likely not be new information to him.

"Prince Edward had two close Companions of the Fourth, Kat and Cal—positions held now by Jess and me," Kyle chimed in, grinning as Ryan swung his gaze from Alex to him and nodded.

"There were also those who filled the ranks of the Companions Cohort, all of them with varying ability in the blade, power, strategy and command. All of them were assigned to duty with the Fourth." Jess smiled as the lad blushed again and refrained from laughing at the poor boy. He looked almost relieved to swing his gaze back to Alex.

"After your display at the Healers' Guild, I know your power level is high enough that there is no doubt you will go through transition and become Kin. Jocelyn confirms that assessment." Alex absently picked up a piece of fruit and continued. "We'd like to offer you a position in the reformation of the Companions Cohort."

The piece of bread Ryan had been holding fell from his fingers as he looked at Alex, astonished.

"Me, Your Highness? A member of the Companions Cohort?" Ryan's voice nearly squeaked with excitement.

Alex leaned back in his chair. "Yes, you. You'd still have to do your lessons with the scholar and continue your blade work and use of the veil in fighting with the Elite. I warn you, it will not be easy. You'll have to pick up extra one-on-one sessions as well as the theory of battle and command."

Kyle smiled. "You'd answer to Alex, of course, but the traditional rank structure of the Companions Cohort means you technically come under the command of Jess and me."

"The bulk of your training will be covered with private tuition. You will not have much free time. The choice is yours if you would rather another profession, and we will do everything we can to help you. We'd suggest you keep up your lessons on the veil, though." Jess looked at him earnestly.

Silence settled in the room as all three of them looked at

Ryan, who swallowed, then suddenly grinned, his eyes lighting up.

"Yes, Your Highness, my lord, my lady! I will work hard, I won't let you down, I promise." Ryan was nearly bouncing in his seat with excitement, causing Alex to laugh. Ryan was in those awkward years caught between the boy and the man he would become one day.

"Good. I was hoping that would be your answer. My servants have moved your belongings. You now have a room in the Companions Cohort wing, Joshua and Miranda will see to your outfitting. Feel free to spend the rest of the day getting used to your new surroundings. You are free to have your meals here in the complex, of course, we have our own kitchen staff. Or when you are suitably attired, you can join the court for meals. It is entirely up to you, unless we are all being official."

"Thank you, Your Highness." Ryan's happiness was contagious, causing all of them to grin.

Joshua appeared in the room promptly when summoned, bowing to Alex.

"Joshua, if you and Miranda can see to Ryan as we discussed. He'll be joining our household." Alex stood and nodded to Ryan. "Take your time, Ryan. Joshua will show you to your rooms when you are ready. I'm sorry, but the three of us have a meeting we must attend."

Alex hummed to himself as he walked from the room, leaving the astonished boy behind to marvel at his change in fortune.

56

INFILTRATION

*L*ord Kastler paced in the parlour of his house in town, impatient to get this meeting over with. He'd been doing his best to navigate the dangerous waters of the royal court in the current environment. It had seemed increasingly hard of late, ever since Prince Daniel's untimely death.

He'd tried to insert some sense into the discussion but was at a loss and appalled that the prince's death was shrugged off by everyone, including the crown prince. He sighed. It was so hard to do his duty as a lord of the realm. As a member of one of the great families, he owed it to the people of Vallantia to protect them. As much as he hated to admit it, the Crown was not taking action to deal with the threat posed by those with power, all because the king's youngest son was one of them, one of the Tainted. He should have been put out of his misery at birth to avert the risk he posed to everyone.

Hearing the doors open, Lord Kastler turned to see his cousin, Eric Janson, enter the room. Well, the man wasn't really a cousin. His uncle had enjoyed bedding the servants and one of the maids hadn't taken her tea and got pregnant. Still, as pained as the family had been, Eric had turned out to be a good addition to the family, even if he wasn't an acknowledged one.

"Eric, it's good to see you. I'm glad you could make it." Lord Kastler smiled.

"My lord, I can't be away for long, I'll be missed, but I came as soon as I could." Eric bowed.

Lord Kastler smiled. Eric had won a position as Commander of the King's Guard. It was disappointing he didn't make it into the Elite, but the Kings Guard placed him well.

"So what progress do you have for me?" Lord Kastler knew that Eric must have had some success since he'd learned that the Kings Guard had accompanied the Elite on their raid of the Healers' Guild.

"The Elite accepted the proposal, my lord." A grin spread slowly on Eric's lips.

"You have people on their details?" Lord Kastler could hardly believe their luck.

"Not quite, my lord, but I'm working on it. I have some of our people on the security details with the Elite. We are monitoring their movements with greater ease now so I can feed you more regular and accurate reports." Eric's eyes shone with pride.

Lord Kastler laughed in delight. "Well done, Eric! The Elite have always been a secretive entity. They have rarely allowed outsiders to join their ranks before."

"I'll keep working on angles to insinuate us further into their ranks. I must go, my lord, but I'll keep you updated." Eric bowed and retreated from the room.

Lord Kastler smiled, a feeling of contentment and victory washing over him. Finally something had gone right. They now had eyes and ears within the Elite, within the Royal Wing and the Complex of the Fourth.

5 7

REFUSAL

*W*illiam entered the anteroom tugging at his formal blue vest. As soon as he realised he was fussing with the ornate garment that he hated so much he smiled and stopped. His father was already present in the room and sitting on one of the couches. The king glanced at him and gestured for him to sit; they had time before the court session. William shifted uncomfortably in his seat as he wrestled with himself about whether he should broach the subject of his future consort.

"What is it, William?" His father knew him well.

"I'd like your permission to take the Lady Jessalan as my consort." William looked down at the table, not wanting to look at his father's face and see the denial.

The silence lasted long enough that he was finally forced to look up. His father sighed.

"William, we've had this discussion. I thought you'd grown out of that fantasy. Have you even spoken to Jess about this?" His father looked at him, exasperated.

William squirmed uncomfortably. "No, I thought I'd seek approval first. There isn't any point in pursuing this if you won't give approval. I thought it was worth asking again, since I know there are no negotiations ongoing to arrange a consort."

"The discussions regarding the contracts with The Heights Protectorate over a union between your sister and the son of the High Speaker have been stalled because of this mess with the Order, but I expect they will be finalised shortly." His father looked at him intently.

William smiled bitterly; he knew his father was getting him to think about matters of state to divert him.

"I know, I've represented you on some of those negotiations. Elizabeth seems content about the arrangements, at least when we've discussed them." William ducked his head. Duty. It was always duty that bound them all.

"I've been in discussions with Sylanna. I have given approval for them to pay a state visit." His father paused, looking at him.

William looked up sharply. "Sylanna? Why are they coming?"

"I've been in communication with the Emperor, and he proposed I consider his daughter to be your consort. Negotiations between us have gone well."

William felt like the world had dropped from beneath him. He closed his eyes and breathed. The prospect of a consort being foisted onto him that he didn't know nor want nearly sent him into panic. William knew he was being childish. He could admit it, even if it was only to himself, even Jess would tell him he was being foolish.

"Is it so wrong of me to want something for myself?" William's voice was soft. He finally opened his eyes to look at his father. Instead of the condemnation he expected to see, he saw understanding.

"No, it isn't. You take the moments you have and hold them to you for as long as you can." His father sighed. "William, think. Jess has transitioned. She is not only Kin, but from the advice I have received, Elder."

William felt himself stiffen. "She is, but she isn't a risk, she's transitioned well, learning control..."

An irritated expression flashed across his father's face and he raised his hand. "That isn't what I meant. Edward was born in the time of the Sundered War. He still looks like the portrait of him hanging in the gallery."

William looked at his father and shook his head. He knew his father was making a point but couldn't understand what it was.

"Father what...?"

"Jess will potentially live a very long time. Do you really want to tie her to you? To force her to watch you grow old and die while she stays young, just as she is now?" His father sounded tired as he spoke.

"I didn't think of that. What it would be like for her." William felt the colour drain out of his face. "Is that why you didn't object to Alex's affair with Isabella?"

His father nodded, his gaze steady.

"I didn't think you'd thought this through. In the long term, Alex's connection to someone who is arguably one of the rulers of Ilarith is a potential benefit." He smiled sadly. "By all means, continue to indulge yourself if Jess is willing. Get this out of your system, you have some time."

"You knew." William's eyes narrowed.

"That you've recently reignited your liaison with Jess? That she has been spending nights on and off with you since she reappeared? Of course I know. Just as you knew your brother was having an affair before he admitted it, even though he, unlike you, wasn't here at the palace." His father's expression was bland, and his tone chiding, like he was lecturing a child.

William groaned. "Is it all over the court?"

He'd never really had much sympathy for Alex when his

indiscretions ended up the talk of the court. That didn't mean he wanted them all gossiping about him.

"Not yet. You've at least managed some discretion. When the delegation from Sylanna arrives, you will be the perfect host. All going well, the daughter of the Emperor will be your consort after negotiations are finalised."

"She'll be coming here with the negotiation team?" William swallowed, trying to push down his panic. That meant negotiations had been ongoing between his father and Sylanna's Emperor for some time without his knowledge. It meant plans had almost been finalised.

"Your future consort's name is Rosalind, she will be confirmed as your Consort Elect soon after arrival. We'll settle this issue with the Order, then finalise Elizabeth's arrangements first. You have some months to get used to the idea." There was a finality in his father's tone. Or rather the king's tone.

William felt a weight settle on him. He shouldn't be shocked. He'd known his whole life that his future consort would be the best political union his father could arrange. Yet as the years had passed, and his father had not engaged in formal negotiations to arrange a consort, he'd harboured a hope—a hope that in this one little area he could have something for himself. A naive hope, as it turned out. Politically he understood. There was no way his father would turn down the daughter of the Emperor of Sylanna. He could understand it, even if his heart and mind rebelled.

He heard the finality in his father's voice, his words sinking in, his tone indicating the discussion was over.

ALEX THANKED the servants who opened the door to the small waiting room off the courtroom, knowing his father and brother would be here at this hour. It was the time the king set aside to hear the petitions. Thankfully it was a duty that never fell to Alex; on the rare occasion that William couldn't assist their father, it was Elizabeth who would step up. The tedious matters of state bored him.

Alex paused; he could almost feel the tension between his father and William. That was a circumstance which was exceedingly rare. William and his father broke from whatever they had been discussing and turned to glance at him, both equally shocked to see him.

"No, I do not intend to put myself through that." Alex gestured towards the door that led to the courtroom and the petitioners beyond.

William smiled at him. "I'd feel compelled to call for Aaron if you'd said anything else."

"To what do we owe your sudden company, Alex?" His father grinned at him, clearly in a good mood.

Alex relaxed back into one of the chairs, shaking his head at the pair who found his appearance so amusing.

"I know the pair of you will be busy for the rest of the day and evening, so I thought I would give you a quick status update." Alex looked up and smiled his thanks at Carl, who handed him a drink unasked for. His father's man knew not only what the king would want and need, but after all these years he was adept at choosing correctly for all of them.

His father straightened in his chair. "Progress?"

Alex ducked his head. "Of sorts. The Companions Cohort has one new addition. It will take some time to fill up the ranks. Those with a potential to become Kin are few and far between these days."

William looked at him, his interest sparked. "Whom did you find? The young man you find yourself responsible for?"

Alex nodded. "Ryan. He's young, and it will be years yet before he goes through transition, but he has more power already than most of the Elite, or most that I've met outside Jess, Kyle and myself."

"Other than our not-so-departed ancestors as well, I take it?" The king's tone was bland.

Alex grinned. "Yes, outside of them too."

William's lips twitched. "He's old enough that he doesn't need a nanny, but there should be someone who can help with the lad. We'll find a couple of people for the Cohort staff, that duty shouldn't be foisted onto Joshua and Miranda."

Alex shrugged. "Well, the Cohort is only Ryan right now, and he'll be regarded as a man in the next year, but I'm sure my household staff would appreciate it."

His father nodded his approval and Alex was confident Carl would have people assigned by tomorrow.

His father's gaze sharpened. "How is the search for the Order's new headquarters going?"

Alex grimaced. "Slowly. Jess and Kyle tell me it's a little tedious. They could be anywhere. They are both out now. We're starting with the villages that sent in reports of the Sundered, and we'll expand from there."

"Your Majesty, the Petitioner's Session is ready," Carl interrupted them discreetly.

His father sighed, and he stood, William a moment behind him, and headed to the door. He turned to throw his last comment over his shoulder just as the door opened.

"We'll discuss this more after the court session. You can wait in my rooms if you like, it's more comfortable, or I'll send a servant for you when we are done." With that, his father was swept out into the courtroom with his brother at his heels.

As the door closed behind his father and William, Alex turned and started walking down the hallway that led to his father's rooms. If he was honest, he had to admit that he was relieved to have a moment of peace. While it hadn't been formally acknowledged that he was back at the palace, most, in particular the inner circle of advisors, knew full well that he was. He hadn't made any formal appearances in the court, and he hadn't attended the dinners or balls. Instead, he settled for a quiet meal with Kyle and Jess in the Complex of the Fourth. Thankfully neither his brother nor father had put any pressure on him to return to the social side of his duties that were so much a part of palace life. Which was just as well, since he knew just being back here at the palace and taking up the responsibilities he had was already causing him stress. He was fighting the urge to retreat to his inn at the little town on the edge of the realm. One of the few things that stopped him doing so other than a sense of responsibility was that Isabella joined him most nights. He had no doubt his father and brother knew. When your whole life was conducted under the eyes of servants and guards, it was hard to hide anything. Still, neither of them had commented or raised an objection.

He had been attending the tedious security council meetings, one after the other. He didn't know how his brother and father dealt with them. His presence seemed to unsettle some of the lords who had a presence at the various meetings. Although not, he'd noted, his father's closest advisors. Alex idly wondered if his father and William had briefed them separately. Nodding at the guards stationed at the end of the corridor as they opened the doors for him, Alex entered his father's domain. Barely pausing to consider options, Alex walked across the soft rugs on the floor and out into his father's private courtyard. Choosing one of the cushioned lounging chairs, Alex slumped back, hauling some more of the cushions behind him. He might as well make himself comfortable.

Taking a deep breath, Alex closed his eyes, relaxing, allowing the veil to flow through him. It was something he'd been able to do since he was a child, that he'd somehow lost the knack for when he'd entered transition. Or at least he hadn't been able to maintain it for long, until recently. Yet when

413

he could manage it, the simple flow of power was soothing. It always had been. He was not shaping it, setting his will on it or trying to control it. He was simply letting the power flow through and around him as it willed, releasing the stress of trying to hold it at bay.

58

SUNDERED ASSASSIN

*A*melia strode along the shadow paths, the Sundered that she'd been entrusted with trailing behind her at her bidding. She had a moment to feel sorry for them. Their introduction to the medication had come too late for them. Being treated, as she had, from early childhood, she was now the mistress of her own decisions. She could see clearly.

Before Kevin had taken her, treated her, she had lived a tormented life, filled with the fear of the Taint she bore. She had no doubt that if he hadn't come into her life, if she hadn't been treated with the medication, she would be like the Sundered. Or worse. She would be mad, entirely out of control and killing indiscriminately. Like Kyle.

Amelia's steady pace didn't falter as she considered her brother; her one regret was the death of one who had been treating him—a moment in time where he was wrenched from his salvation. If only he hadn't run from Alyssa. If only Alex hadn't killed her before she could finish her work, Kyle might have been saved. Still, if Amelia could find him and pry him away from those who held him, could medicate him again, she knew she could bring him around. Kyle would stabilise under her influence. She had been assured that he had shown excellent signs that the medication could indeed help stabilise his condition. Yet not Alex.

Amelia considered Alex. Only months ago, to think of him would have caused her longing and a sense of loss. She knew now that the feelings she thought she'd had for Alex were not real. She didn't blame her master; he had merely been trying to reach Alex, and she had been his only way to do so. Yet despite those efforts, Alex was lost. She had been told he could never be brought back—he was immune to the medication—yet she felt her resolve harden on that score. She was determined to try to bring him back. If anyone could breach his barriers, to help bring him under control, she knew it was her. Alex would trust her where he wouldn't trust others. Her master had advised her she should tread softly. The ties he'd helped her forge between her and Alex might bring him around eventually. Without the medication, though, if he realised the connection between them, he would sever the loving bonds she'd created.

Amelia's flitting thoughts turned to the last of the trio. Jess. A frown creased her forehead. Jessalan would be a problem. She had no strong attachment to the woman like she had with the other two. Jessalan had been reserved, never letting anyone close to her except Kyle and Alex. A smile slowly parted her lips, and a chuckle escaped. That was the key to Jess. Guide Kyle back onto the path of healing. Alex would come after Kyle, she knew it, yet he loved her, and she could use that to bring Alex under her control. With both of them contained, Jess would fall into line. She was sure of it.

As she thought her way through the issues that she faced and came up with a plan of action, she passed through the veil at a quicker pace, eager to get to her destination. She felt Kevin's fleeting mental touch on her mind. Amelia's smile softened, and a breathy chuckle escaped her.

I'm fine, Master, you needn't worry. I know what I need to do.

After a brief hesitation, she felt calm under her master's ministrations, and then, after an assessment that evidently satisfied him, Kevin withdrew. Not that he was ever really gone from her mind. He was always there, yet now he trusted her enough that he could retreat and allow her some self-determination. The fact that he was still there in the back of her mind did reassure her. The horrors of becoming mad weren't that far back that she could totally dismiss them. He was her failsafe, her master, whom she could trust to haul her back from madness. The master that Alex, Kyle and Jess had never had and still needed.

I'll save you, all of you, despite yourselves.

Although her mind wandered, Amelia kept a tight control of the Sundered that had been transferred to her care. They needed her guidance, her control. That wasn't their fault. Still, it took a portion of her concentration and power that she knew could be spent on other considerations. Reaching out to them, she compelled them to halt. Amelia winced, feeling several of the Sundered fight back. She would have done the same herself, not that long ago. Still, it didn't stop her from ruthlessly crushing their weak attempt at rebellion.

Amelia assessed the scene before her. She couldn't control a sharp intake of breath as she saw Alex was present at the palace, in the king's private courtyard. She wrapped her personal shield around her more tightly, breathing a sigh of relief as she noted that Alex was distracted so probably wouldn't notice her presence until it was too late. Amelia closed her eyes, she breathed in, held it for a moment, then breathed out in a conscious effort to calm herself, knowing any undue distress on her part would draw her master's attention. It was something she did not want right at this moment. Alex wouldn't understand what she needed to do; he would fight her, forcing her hand.

Amelia waited there in that world between worlds, waiting

to gain her composure. She knew what she needed to do, but that didn't mean that a part of her wasn't saddened at the coming conflict with Alex.

She closed her eyes and took another deep, steady breath, letting it out slowly. There she paused, before opening her eyes in time with her inhalation. Her mind was calm, her purpose clear. She knew she and her Sundered Ones would have to be quick when the opportunity presented itself. Alex being present was a complication that she didn't need right now. She wasn't ready to confront him just yet.

Taking out the king and William would ensure that the Tainted had no champions in this world. Killing them in the open court had been a tactical decision. The more people who observed the assassination of the king and crown prince, the faster word would fly around the realm. It would also be impossible for Elizabeth or Alex to try to hide what had happened, unlike if she'd murdered her victims in their sleep. As soon as she'd completed her task, word would run from the palace and the people would rise up against any they perceived as having even the slightest connection with the Taint. The king was respected and loved throughout Vallantia. William was adored by the people, aristocrats and commoners alike. With their influence gone, the Order could step up its campaign to control those born with the ability to control the Taint.

Finally, her nerves settled, Amelia moved herself to the courtroom. Her eyes narrowed, and she drew her blades as she did so, appearing on the dais not far from the king. Her men were charged with dealing with the king's Elite. Amelia paused as she realised that William was not standing in his customary position near the king. She glanced quickly around the court-room. Within moments the shocked silence was replaced with screams and the clash of blades as her men traded blows with the Elite. She spotted William down on the floor, surrounded by courtiers, trapped in the panic of those around him and nowhere near an exit.

Her gaze tracked back to her primary target and she saw the king, isolated, his guards being cut down by her own men. She laughed, cruel and harsh, as she saw he'd drawn a weapon. The old man didn't stand a chance.

Amelia pulled on the veil, throwing up a barrier as the king lunged at her with his sword, surprising her. Although she had to admit it was a pleasant surprise; she never would have believed that the old man had it in him. Amelia shook herself out of her introspection, knowing that she didn't have much time. Reaching out with the veil, she shaped the power into a hard ball and threw it at the king, causing him to gasp and double up in pain as his sword was wrenched from his hands by a second carefully aimed blow.

Amelia stalked across the dais, closing the distance between her and the king. Sensing her approach, he fumbled for a sword from one of his own fallen guards. Amelia kicked it away from his desperately clawing hands. Snarling, she grabbed him by the hair, hauling his head up to look at her. She drew her blade back as she saw the shock and recognition in his eyes and face.

"Amelia, please..." the king pleaded, but her blade sliced across his throat, and she felt the warm splatter across her face.

Uncurling her fingers from his hair, she let him slump to the ground, his hands ineffectually holding his throat as the light went out of his eyes. Amelia dismissed him from her mind. Looking across the court, she spotted William struggling with his own guards and the courtiers to try to get to the king.

Amelia ran, using the veil to assist her as she leapt over the struggling Elite, who unaccountably was still alive and fighting with her own men. Her eyes widened as she felt the small pulses of power coming not from her own men, but from some of the Elite. She'd known that some of the Elite had limited skill with the Taint. She just hadn't known that they trained in the use the Taint in combat. They must do, or they wouldn't still be fighting against her Sundered. She'd thought in the battle at the Healers' Guild that it had just been Alex, Kyle and Jess using power to resist. Now she realised the Elite—or some of them—had more power than she'd thought. Not allowing herself to become distracted, she stored the information for later.

Drawing in more of the Taint, Amelia used it to pass through the crowded, screaming courtiers, flicking in and out of the veil as she ran across the ballroom towards William. She paid no mind to the throng of people around her that had once been her peers. They desperately tried to escape as they pushed and shoved against each other, even walking over the top of their fallen contemporaries in their desperation to get out of harm's way.

As she ran, she lashed out with her blades, cutting down those in her way, their screams of pain blending in with the fear emanating from all around her as they fell under the assault of her blades like the grass falling before the farmer's scythe. Like the grass facing the farmer, they stood no chance against her power and blades.

Amelia grinned in triumph, cutting down the last courtier that stood between her and William. The fool had even tried to stand his ground between her and the prince. A predatory smile parted her lips—prince no longer, she realised. With the death of his father, William was now the king. That was to be short-lived despite the efforts of gallant fools who tried to stand between her and him.

Finally, she closed the final few steps between her and William. Relishing the significance, she looked into William's eyes, knowing these moments would be his last. Drawing in the Taint, she swung her blade towards William. But her eyes widened as she was hit by a blast of raw, uncontrolled power.

She staggered back, falling to one knee, her short blade clattering to the floor and spinning away out of reach as she put her hand down to stop falling further.

She looked at William, her mouth gaping. She stared at him as he sat looking at her. It gave her small comfort that he'd been thrown back himself and apparently had little idea of what he'd done. Amelia felt her lips pull back in something she was sure did not look like a smile as she stood, her eyes narrowing. Drawing a second blade, she lunged.

ALEX FELT the surge of power, and his eyes flashed open in shock and confusion. It took a moment for him to realise that the wave of energy was not of his doing but due to others. He pushed himself from his seat, and pulling the veil around him he sped to where he sensed the power. As he appeared back in the anteroom, he heard the clash of blades and screaming from the court beyond and felt the small surges of power. Without further thought, Alex ran for the door to the courtroom, not wanting to shift into what he had no doubt was a fight occurring in the chamber beyond.

He drew his weapon from its sheath and punched the solid wooden door open. He didn't even pause to consider as the door splintered, shards flying ahead of him as he burst through. Only an absent part of his mind noted the effect and realised he must have augmented his own strength, punching at the doors with the power of the veil. The unconscious use of force was something that he understood he needed to get under his control. On this occasion, he was lucky it was just a door that was shattered into fragments.

Alex reacted instinctively, lashing out with his blades and power as he came under attack by Sundered, who turned to face him as soon as he appeared. His sudden appearance rallied the nearby Elite who formed ranks to assist and it wasn't long before they dispatched the attackers on this side of the courtroom.

Alex froze, confronted by the sight of his father on the floor, a red pool of blood spreading out from where he lay, lifeless. Alex wasn't aware of using the power, yet the next thing he knew he was at his father's side, gathering him in his arms, his weapon forgotten on the ground next to him. Heedless of the blood, he bowed his head, knowing without trying that there was nothing he could do. His father was gone, and no amount of healing of the damage inflicted on his body would change that.

"I'm sorry. Rest from the burden of this life, Father." Alex gently lay his father back down, oblivious of the blood that had soaked into his clothes, onto his hands. He stood, taking up his sword once more.

Without thought he turned, drawing in power as easily as he breathed, assessing the fighting that was going on around him. Seeing the Elite battling with multiple Sundered, he felt their pulses of power as they repelled that of the Sundered with controlled bursts of their own. He reached out with the veil, lending his own ability to theirs when needed. Still he scanned the room, and feeling the intense pulses of power, he froze, his breath catching as he saw the dark cloaked figure running towards William—the figure that was using the veil to flicker between this world and the next, to wade their way through the crowded courtroom with the liberal use of expertly wielded blades to cut down others.

Alex called out desperately to Jess and Kyle, throwing the picture of the devastation being wrought in the court by the Sundered. He started running, taking two strides before leaping, somersaulting in the air above the struggling guard where they continued to fight with the Sundered. Without pausing he shifted through the crowded, struggling courtiers much as he'd seen the cloaked figure do; he didn't even think about how he knew to do it.

Alex nearly froze as he felt the raw surge of power, undirected, lashing out at everything around. Yet he kept moving despite his shock. The surge of the veil had come from William, yet there was no time for him to wonder how his brother had released such power, even in panic.

As expected, he saw, almost as if time was slowing down, William thrown back. Alex connected in his own mind that he usually braced himself, even if it was subconsciously, so he didn't get thrown back by the use of force. He could see and sympathise with his brother's own confusion even if he did swear mentally for William to get up and defend himself. Alex nearly laughed despite himself.

Get up William! Panic later!

Alex was rewarded with William's shocked expression as he looked around, trying to spot him, but to his relief, he was already starting to move. He spared the time to throw a mind block on William, to at least shield out the confusion that hearing others' mind voices must be causing him. Then his eyes moved to the cloaked figure, who had fallen to the ground, short blade spinning across the floor out of reach as it opened a hand to halt its fall. Alex could tell the attacker suffered the same shock that he had, yet after a frozen moment the figure pushed up from the floor. As it did so, the hood fell.

Alex froze, skidding to a halt, his breath catching.

No.

The anguished word breathed from him and went out into the void.

The cruel sneer and hard, flinty eyes could not hide who she was. Her face was branded on his soul despite the dramatic changes. The Amelia that he knew never would have looked like the doppelganger that stood before him.

Opening himself up, Alex felt William's turmoil. Worse,

from Amelia he heard anger, hatred, determination to finish the job she'd started. The desire to kill.

Unbelieving, he saw her snarl; he knew she hadn't even noticed his approach as she pushed herself up from the ground and started drawing her blade back. Alex forced himself to move, blocking out his emotion, knowing that it would cost him later on. It always did.

Alex used the veil to push himself forward, his blade extending to catch and block Amelia's.

Amelia, please fight them, don't do this.

Alex felt something break inside himself as he saw the cold nothingness—not even a hint of emotion—as she turned, recovering, and swung her blade towards his throat. His face hardened as he responded instinctively to her blow, raising his own sword to block her.

ALEX FELT the rushing surge in the veil that signalled the incoming approach of those with power—great power. He smiled as he recognised the unique signatures. Kyle and Jess were here. While they were still outnumbered, with the three of them, along with the ability of the Elite, even if it was limited, he was sure that they could win this battle.

Alex pulled his mind back to the task at hand of fending off Amelia. She was a swordsmaster, way too good for him not to pay attention. Too good for him even when he was, at least if this was a training ground and they were obeying the formal rules. Although, he noted absently, she was not quite at Kyle's level, she had improved. That made him wonder if it was the control the Order had on her, cutting her off from emotion and all the associated distractions it could cause. He had to admit that he fought better himself when he lost himself in battle, rather than overthinking every little move. Still, there was always the element of strategy and using everything around you to your advantage. That was something that was harder to do when you disengaged your brain from the process, as tempting as that was to do.

Alex parried a vicious thrust from Amelia; *he* may not want to kill *her*, but obviously right now she was under no such limitations. His own hesitation, his inability to deal with Amelia, could cost him his life—he recognised this, yet still struggled with himself. He had the brief warning of a cold smile and triumph flashing on her face before she retrieved another blade from her boot and launched herself at him. Alex found himself backing away from her onslaught, his every move defensive both with his blades and the veil. Even using his power in combination with his sword still didn't stop him from having to lunge desperately to one side, and a sharp pain running down his upper arm told him she had managed to score him. Her grin widened.

Give in, Alex, you're not good enough to beat me.

Alex barely recognised her mind voice, her tone dripping with malice. She lunged again, seeing his hesitation, but before he could react another blade interposed itself between him and Amelia.

Go, Alex, leave her to me. Get William out of this.

Alex felt relief wash through him as his friend once again interposed himself between him and harm. Taking a breath, he watched as Kyle took the fight to Amelia, his own whirling style similar to her own. Yet unlike Amelia, he was fully in control, lost in the blade work as he had been of old, yet with a deadly serious edge that Alex hadn't seen in his friend before. Kyle was merging in and out of the veil so rapidly it appeared as if he was flickering in and out of sight. The effect causing Amelia to stumble and back off.

Alex shifted to William's side, assisting his brother in warding off the attack of one of the Sundered Ones Amelia had brought with her that had made his way through the court to him. Alex snarled. He had no hesitation in killing this one, or any sympathy for his fate even though from everything they had learned he knew it wasn't the man's fault.

With a quick glance around the courtroom, he spotted Jess off to one side fighting with some of the Elite at her side against a cluster of Sundered. She hadn't seemed to have lost any of her fighting edges either; it was clear she'd kept up with her sword work and worked on integrating the power to assist her own fighting style.

Alex grimaced as he realised that it was Amelia that was likely to be the one controlling the Sundered. She had drawn him away from protecting William in the hope that one of the Sundered would get through to kill William while she kept him distracted. Alex pulled his attention back to the task at hand realising that he had to be a little more careful than he usually was here in the court. There were too many others around who might be hurt. His eyes narrowed as he considered his options. One of the benefits of the gaggle of lords surrounding William —all with their own blades drawn, he noticed—was that an attacker would have to take them out first before being able to get at William.

Alex chuckled as he remembered the dream he'd had about his uncle confronting one of the Sundered. He wasn't quite sure how to do what he wanted, but there was always a first time. Deflecting a blow from the Sundered One almost absently, Alex traded blows with him. This one had obviously had some sword training in his past. Concentrating, Alex pulled in more of the power, noticing that both Kyle and Jess glanced in his direction in surprise. That was his only indication that he was likely pulling in more power than they were used to. With some alarm he noticed the bands of power thickening and arcing in his direction, caused by his momentary inattention. No one in the palace needed to see the more destructive side of his power, which they would if he didn't rein it in. Alex gritted his teeth and dampened his demand and draw on the energy around him. He noticed that the veil didn't always react the way he expected. It was as if once he opened himself to it, the strands of energy eagerly sought him out. Still, this time, with others to be attracted to nearby, he saw some of the power that had been surging in his direction divert, heading to Jess, Kyle, and Amelia, and smaller strands to the Elite and others in the court. Alex willed the energy he'd drawn in out towards the Sundered. He grunted in effort as the man was lifted off the ground. Maintaining his control, Alex used even more power to prevent the Sundered from reaching the veil to free himself. Alex chuckled again as the lords closest hastily backed up, their eyes wide at the sight and turning unerringly towards him as they realised he must be the one behind it.

Alex dismissed the reaction of the various lords even if a part of him was secretly amused by their response. He stepped forward, using yet more power to propel his sword, which thrummed with power licking up its length as if it was a possessed thing. The Sundered One's howl was abruptly cut short as Alex's blade sliced through him, extinguishing his life. Even with the Taint to assist, no one could heal a body split in two, particularly when he had been cut off from access to the power in the critical moment when his blade had struck.

Alex relaxed his hold on what had once been a man and let the pieces fall to the ground. Turning with a pool of silence around him, he looked for another target.

He saw that Kyle and Amelia were still engaged in their deadly dance, but as Amelia saw one of her minions fall to the ground in two pieces, she stumbled back. Her moment of inattention gave Kyle the moment he needed, and he lunged. Amelia fell back, gasping as she drew in power and fled into the veil, dragging the remainder of her men with her.

AMELIA SHRIEKED DENIAL, her mind voice echoing in her own head as she watched her other self—that self that had taken her blade and, in a cool, calculated strike, had killed the king. *Her* king. Without a second thought or remorse. Yet it didn't matter how much she railed inside this little part of her mind, it made no difference to the outcome. She willingly did as her master bid. She was his devoted servant now and would go into battle at his command, his defence, even against those that she had once loved. She cried in frustration as her other self fled from the battle. If only her brother or Alex had managed to kill her, then this nightmare would be over.

ALEX WALKED from the Complex of the Fourth, a couple of the Elite on duty falling in behind. He didn't bother telling them not to follow; he knew they would ignore such an injunction. The corridors of the palace were quiet, or at least as quiet as they ever really got. Dawn was still hours away so Alex knew there would be a party somewhere, he was sure one of the guards or servants could tell him where it was located. Right now he wished to be alone with his thoughts, yet he needed to be here at the palace, so he wandered absently, steering away from the areas that were habitually busy regardless of the time of day or night.

He had some time before he needed to relieve Jess from watching over William. His older brother, now his king—or he would be, if he recovered and ascended the throne. After the fight had ended, the adrenalin that had been pushing William on faded and he'd collapsed. He'd been taken to his rooms and the healers had descended on him. Aaron and the other healers had William heavily sedated, keeping him in a deep sleep.

They couldn't use their own healer's gift on him yet until his mind healed. Until then Alex had been taking turns with Jess and Kyle to maintain a shield on William's mind. Left unsaid, they were also protectors in case Amelia decided to come back and finish her handiwork.

Elizabeth had buried her own grief over the sudden death of their father and fear for her twin, to stand up and act as regent, taking over the reins of ruling the realm until William was able to take the throne. The everyday monotony of governing the realm didn't stop because the king had died; uncaring, the world and life went on, refusing to pause even for a moment to allow them to mourn. Between watching over his brother and stepping up in his own role as Fourth to help Elizabeth as much as he could, Alex hadn't had time himself to mourn either. Of course, between the three of them they'd been pulling duty to protect Elizabeth as well, a fact that had not gone unnoticed, at least by Elizabeth.

Alex only realised that his absent wandering had a destination in mind when he found himself looking at the large double doors of the public hall. He knew his father lay in state on the funeral bier. His guards, guessing his intent, split up, one of them going on ahead to quickly check the room. Alex knew it was likely no one was there at this hour. The doors that gave access to the public were only unbarred a few hours during the day. Still, he kept his pace steady, giving his guard time to provide the room with a cursory check. It was just as well that he was right and no one from the palace were paying their respects. If they had been, they would have found themselves unceremoniously kicked out with his approach.

It wasn't possible for the honour guard outside the hall to stand straighter, and all of them, on an unseen signal, withdrew their swords, falling to one knee, hilt of their swords pressed to their foreheads in a display of mourning and an acknowledgement of their failure—the failure to protect their king in this life. As he passed them, he heard the thump of booted feet on the stone floor, the scrape of swords sliding back into the sheath. Alex moved through the doors, pausing just inside to stare at the figure laid out in the centre of the hall.

"Please." Alex's voice was soft, barely a whisper.

He didn't have to say any more; his own guards halted at the entrance and he heard them close the doors to at least give him the illusion of privacy. If anyone did come to pay their respects at this hour, the door being closed would signal that a member of the royal family was inside. It was the only time access was restricted during the period of mourning. Otherwise, the doors were always open either on the public side or the palace side, although not generally at the same time.

As he drew up to his father's side, Alex felt anguish wash over him, lodging in his soul. Looking down, he noted that the high collar of his father's state robes hid the ugly slash on his throat that had ended his life. Alex reached out, resting his hand on his father's chest.

He bowed his head. "I'm sorry I caused you pain, Father. I failed you."

Feeling a shimmering in the veil, Alex spun, his sword half drawn before he recognised the person who had arrived. She froze, clearly startled to see him.

"Alex." Her voice was low, filled with a pain he recognised as being an echo of his own.

Alex took a settling breath and closed the distance between them, standing close, looking down at her. Madness skirted the edges of her mind as her grief and guilt rolled over him. Alex shuddered as it hit him and he pulled her into his arms, embracing her lightly, willing calmness on her, trying to soothe her as he'd seen parents do with small children.